F
HEL

Heller, Jane.

Infernal affairs.

$21.95

DATE			

INFERNAL
AFFAIRS

INFERNAL AFFAIRS

JANE HELLER

Kensington Books

KENSINGTON BOOKS are published by

Kensington Publishing Corp.
850 Third Avenue
New York, NY 10022

Library of Congress Card Catalog Number: 95-081483
ISBN 1-57566-021-0

First Printing: April, 1996

Printed in the United States of America

ACKNOWLEDGMENTS

Many thanks to the following people for their contributions to the writing of this book *and* to my career: all the folks at Kensington, who have worked so hard on my behalf—Ann LaFarge and Lynn Brown, in particular; Ruth Harris, who put all this in motion; Jane Dystel, who's been there since the beginning; my sister, Susan Alexander, who keeps me in Tiffany pens and good spirits; my old friends up north, who've been the best cheerleaders anybody could ask for; Graham Kirk and Candace Harman-Kirk, who took me fishing on the *Silver Goose* and put up with all my questions, not to mention let me catch that ten-pound kingfish; and my other pals in Stuart, who've made me feel right at home.

Special thanks to my husband, Godie, whose critical eye is unerring and whose loving support is unwavering.

For my mother, Jocelyn Reznick,
who knows what a devil I can be
and doesn't mind a bit.

PART
ONE

C H A P T E R

1

On July 13, 1995, my life, once so uneventful, became the stuff of movies—horror movies.

Yes, on that Thursday night, a typically fetid summer night in South Florida, the devil showed up at my house and took control of my body. And you thought *you* had problems.

Why me? I asked myself. I was Miss Family Values, a nice Jewish girl who flossed her teeth and recycled her plastic containers and tipped the mailman every Christmas. I wasn't exactly the type to join a cult or engage in Satanic rituals. Even the thought of piercing my ears made me queasy. And yet, it happened. The devil made an appearance at my—

Wait. I shouldn't be throwing the devil at you this early in the story. You'll think I'm just another flake who wants to get on the Maury Povich show. You'll snicker and roll your eyes and say, "Yeah, sure." But I'm not a flake. I'm a real estate agent with a bizarre-but-true tale to tell, a tale of dark forces and evil doings and—

Sorry. I did it again. Before I lose you altogether, let me tell the story just the way it happened. Let me back up and begin again with Mitchell, my husband, who on that same Thursday night in July announced that he was leaving me for another woman after ten years of marriage. . . .

"Go to hell," I was dying to say when he told me. Instead, I glared at him and said nothing.

"What is this, Barbara? The silent treatment? Try to act like a grown-up, would you please?" said Mitchell, whose idea of being a grown-up was cheating on his wife.

I just shook my head and thought of how badly I wanted to tell him off. But in those days I was incapable of telling people off, a complete coward when it came to confrontations. I only got angry at people who couldn't get angry back—characters in books or dead relatives. I was the type who was desperate to be liked and, therefore, never raised my voice or made snippy remarks or said anything the least bit provocative. In other words, for much of my life I sucked up to people and sucked in my true feelings.

I left Mitchell in the living room, escaped into the kitchen, and stayed there. Hiding like a scared kid. I poured myself a glass of red wine and drank it. Then I poured another glass. And another. When I was sufficiently anesthetized, I returned to the living room, carrying my glass and what was left of the bottle, and sat down.

"Come on, Barbara. Say something," Mitchell demanded as he paced back and forth. "Yell at me. Hit me. Throw something at me. Don't just sit there with that pained, pathetic look on your face."

"What do you want me to say?" I asked, after taking a long sip of wine. "Apparently, you've made up your mind to leave me."

Mitchell heaved a big, impatient sigh, as if he couldn't believe he'd spent ten years with someone so hopelessly passive. And then he scowled and said, "You never gave a damn about me, did you?"

I remained silent for several seconds as I tried to think of the right answer. The truth was that I had stopped caring about Mitchell Chessner two or three years into the marriage when I realized, to my great disappointment, that he was dull. Profoundly dull. The sort of man you initially think is dynamic, charismatic, challenging, because he always volunteers his opinion and never says "I don't know" and gestures wildly with his hands when he speaks, not to mention doesn't sit still for more than ten seconds. But what Mitchell turned out to be was a bore. A bore with a fast metabolism. Of course, I never let on. I acted as if I found him enthralling instead of exhausting. I thought that by playing the part of the happy little wife, I'd be one, and then I would never have to get divorced, never have to start all over again with another man. The devil you know is better than the devil you don't, I figured, not knowing anything about the devil then.

"Mitchell, I don't think there's any point in—"

"You never wanted to have sex," he interrupted in an accusatory voice after I had finally managed two responses in a row. "Night after night I'd approach you, try to touch you. But no. You were always tired. Tired from what? Showing houses?"

I did not reply. How could I? I had resisted Mitchell's sexual advances, not because I was so spent from my job as a real estate agent, but because he bored me as a lover the way he bored me as a human being. Given how hyperactive he was, you would think he would have been hot stuff in bed, a regular Energizer Bunny. But he was also extremely selfish and so he'd just lie there without moving a muscle, waiting for me to minister to him.

"You rejected me time after time," he went on as I refilled my glass. Again. "And after I did my best to satisfy you."

Satisfy me? You acted like you were half dead when we had sex, Mitchell, I thought. When I used to run my hand along the side of your neck during foreplay, I wasn't trying to turn you on. I was trying to find a pulse.

"Why are you dredging up our past?" I asked. "You've just told me you're in love with another woman. With Chrissy Hemplewhite." I tried not to gag as I invoked the name of the weatherperson on the Six O'Clock News, the woman for whom I was being abandoned. I was no prize, but Chrissy Hemplewhite had the overbite of a squirrel, the hair of a blond troll doll, and the voice of a helium balloon.

"Very much in love," he said proudly. "We're looking forward to a wonderful future together."

Some wonderful future. Mitchell was forty-six; Chrissy was twenty-four. In no time, he'd be having gum surgery and prostate problems and maybe even a hip replacement, and she'd be so put off by his decrepitude that she'd dump him the way he was dumping me. With any luck.

"Chrissy and I have the world by the tail," Mitchell continued. "My business is going gangbusters and so is hers. Television meteorologists are in big demand right now."

Meteorologist, my ass. Chrissy couldn't even read her own dopey TV weather map. She once said it was raining in Milwaukee when the map right there in back of her showed that Milwaukee was basking in high pressure. She was so simple she probably thought a tropical depression was that melancholy feeling you get when you come home from a vacation in the Caribbean.

"In fact, one of the things that attracted me to Chrissy was her job," said Mitchell. "I find the television industry fascinating."

"What about my job?" I asked. "You used to find real estate fascinating."

"What job?" Mitchell scoffed. "I haven't noticed you selling any houses lately."

More wine. I had to drink more wine. I took several sips and willed my eyes not to cross.

"I've been in a slump, that's all," I said. "Every real estate agent goes through slumps. Even top producers. It's a cyclical business."

My tongue had trouble maneuvering around the word "cyclical." It came out "sillical."

"A slump?" said Mitchell, tossing his head back derisively. "Your last closing was almost a year ago."

I involuntarily made a fist as Mitchell began to rub it in about how dismal things had been for me at work; how, no matter what I did, I couldn't sell anything. Not a house, not a condo, not a God-damn doghouse. At first, I told myself it was the economy. But then why were all the other agents in the office selling property like crazy? Then, I told myself it was a run of bad luck. But then why wouldn't it pass? Why was it that every time I had a customer on the hook, something would happen and the deal would fall through? I was jinxed, and I didn't need Manic Mitchell to remind me. I was hard enough on myself, and my feelings of worthlessness had become so overwhelming that I had stopped going into the office every day. I had taken to drinking wine in the middle of the afternoon. I had stopped brushing my teeth. A very bad sign.

"I'd rather not discuss my career," I said.

"You were the one who brought it up," said Mitchell. He scratched his head, which, over the past several months, he had been dousing with Rogaine.

"I suppose the two of you intend to have children," I said, moving on to yet another aspect of life at which I was a failure.

"As soon as possible. Chrissy loves kids."

Sure, she loves kids, I thought. Intellectually, she has so much in common with them.

"Unlike some people I know, she actually likes the idea of being pregnant," he added, the implication being that I didn't. It wasn't that I didn't *want* to be pregnant. It was that I *couldn't* be pregnant, because of what the fertility specialist called "nonspecific sterility." Mitchell had pooh-poohed the diagnosis. It was his opinion that I was somehow faking my sterility; that I was just being perverse; that I was malingering. Of course, whenever I suggested that we adopt kids, he dismissed the idea. Mitchell was so out of touch with his own ordinariness that he thought the only children worth having were those that sprang from *his* loins.

"Personally, I'm hoping for a boy," he went on, as if responding to a question. I looked down at my hand, opened my fist, and saw that I had dug bloody holes in my palm with my nails. "It would be terrific if I had a son to take over the restaurants when I retire."

The restaurants, I thought contemptuously. When Mitchell and I were first married, he was an accountant whose only experience with restaurants was eating in them. Then, several years ago, he confided that he had always dreamed of owning a restaurant. An Italian restaurant. An Italian restaurant that would become a magnet for actress-models and sports personalities and people who regarded garlic as the next oat bran. A few weeks after that, he went into business with a former client named Stan, who owned a chain of frozen yogurt shops. He and Stan took over the space that had been occupied by a failed Chinese restaurant, hired an architect, a contractor and a chef, and gave their eatery a name: Risotto!. The place was an instant success.

Of course, the reason Risotto! was so popular (trust me, it wasn't the food) was that Banyan Beach, the town where we live, had recently been "discovered." A once-sleepy fishing village on South Florida's Treasure Coast, about an hour north of Palm Beach, Banyan Beach had become, seemingly overnight, a Happening Place. Suddenly, there was a Home Depot and a Blockbuster Video, a Ritz-Carlton and a Four Seasons, a Gap and a Loehmann's, not to mention an actual Bloomingdale's. Suddenly, there were golf communities and high-rise condominiums and glitzy "Boca-style" houses where funky old Florida crackers used to be. Suddenly, there was talk of a casino.

Just as suddenly, there were residents who were dying for a restaurant like Risotto! because, they said, it would make them feel less homesick for New York. Mitchell and Stan were so encouraged by this turn of events that they opened a second restaurant, a Manhattan-style steakhouse called Moo!.

It was at Moo!, Mitchell explained, where he met and fell in love with Chrissy, who went there to "wind down" every night after her demanding performance on the Six O'Clock News.

"Look, Barbara. Since you're not going to say anything, I might as well leave now," said Mitchell after checking the time on his Rolex. It was nearly seven o'clock and we'd been talking—or, should I say, *he* had—for nearly two hours. Clearly, he was itching to go. Risotto! and Moo! were probably jammed and he couldn't resist showing up and taking a head count. He once told me it gave him goose pimples to see people begging for a reservation at his restaurants. I said it was just his psoriasis acting up and that he should make an appointment with his dermatologist.

"If you want to go, go," I said.

He came toward me, looked me up and down, and sighed with disgust.

"When are you going to snap out of it?" he asked.

"Snap out of what?" I said, knowing exactly what he meant.

"Out of your fog," he said. He was pacing again. "You're always so . . . so unemotional. Always holding things in. Always accepting whatever happens to you." Another disgusted sigh. "You never ask for anything, reach for anything. You just sit there and take what life hands you. Don't you have any . . . any *needs?*"

What I needed was some more wine. Much more wine. I drained my glass and was about to finish off the bottle when Mitchell snatched it out of my hand.

"Look at you," he said. "You're drunk. Is that how you're dealing with your problems these days?"

He came toward me again, grabbed me by the shoulders, and marched me over to the mirror in the foyer.

"Take a good look, Barbara Chessner," he demanded. "Take a damn good look at what you've become."

I forced myself to look in the mirror. I was drunk, so drunk that when I saw my reflection I wasn't quite sure who it was. I felt like I was gazing into a fun house mirror because the image that came back at me was distorted, unreal, frightening. I gasped.

I looked like a slob. A big, fat slob. My T-shirt was stained with red wine. My face was puffy, splotchy, not my own. My eyes, which used to be a crystal clear aquamarine, were tiny slits above my cheeks, milky and dull, like a couple of swimming pools that hadn't been cleaned. And then there was the chin. The *other* chin. The one that had sprouted when I'd discovered that overeating was another way of swallowing my unhappiness. Once thin and fit, my body had thickened in the past year, widened, softened. I wasn't obese by any means, just doughier, less shapely. Of course, despite the extra pounds, I remained as flat-chested as ever, the only difference being that now my flat-chestedness was even more obvious, in comparison with my newly protruding stomach. As for my hair, well, it always looked wild. Nothing new there. It was long and kinky and, even though I was only thirty-eight, almost completely gray. I remember when Mitchell's mother, Helen, once asked him, "Does she do that on purpose? To achieve a certain 'look'?" Mitchell had replied that kinky, prematurely gray hair ran in my family and that he thought it gave me "character."

But the truth was, I didn't *have* character. I *was* a character. A flabby mass of conflicts and contradictions. On one hand, I thought I was better than everyone else. On the other hand, I thought I was nothing. On one hand, I despised the redneck mentality of the people I'd grown up with in Banyan Beach. On the other hand, I resented the developers and the tourists and the very people who were trying to bring "progress" to the town, the very people who were giving the real estate business a boost. On one hand, I wanted to be the wife of a successful man like Mitchell. On the other hand, I wanted to be the wife of a man whose success wasn't linked to the public's appetite for arugula. I didn't know where I belonged or with whom. I only knew that in the span of twelve months I had allowed myself to go from a size eight to a size twelve, with a depression to match. Who would want me now?

No one, that's who.

The realization struck me with devastating clarity. Never mind that Mitchell was in love with another woman. I hated Mitchell. He was a jerk. Good riddance. Now I had to face the fact that I would be alone. Single. A divorcée. Just what the world was waiting for: another needy female with two chins and no tits.

I continued to stare at my reflection. I was repulsed by the image in front of me, yet I couldn't look away. There was something eerily fascinating about my own deterioration. I had failed as a real estate agent and I had failed as a wife. I couldn't sell a house and I couldn't save my marriage and I couldn't close the zipper on my jeans. What good was I? What kind of man would want Barbara Chessner in her present state?

"Good-bye," said Mitchell, interrupting my latest orgy of self-loathing. "I'll call you in a few days and we'll discuss the logistics of this thing."

This thing. Nice.

I wheeled around to face him. I couldn't let him go without telling him off for the first time in all our years together. I wouldn't wimp out. Not anymore.

Mustering every ounce of courage I had, I looked him in the eye and parted my lips to speak.

"Yes?" he said in anticipation.

I froze. My mind was full of angry words but nothing came out of my mouth.

"What is it?" he said, tapping his foot on the Mexican tile floor.

I tried again, but his disapproving glare paralyzed me.

Fed up, he turned away.

"Go to bed, Barbara," he said as he opened the front door, then walked down the stone path to his car.

"Go to hell, Mitchell," I said finally, when I was sure he was too far away to hear me.

C H A P T E R

I cried for about an hour after Mitchell left. Not because I was sorry to see him go, but because I was out of red wine. There's nothing worse than running out of poison when you're trying to kill yourself.

I decided to switch to vodka and made myself a Bloody Mary. And then I wolfed down an entire Tupperware container full of cold, sauceless spaghetti and made myself another Bloody Mary. And then I cried some more when it became clear to me that food and booze were no help at all; that no matter how much I ate and drank, I still felt like a hopeless failure with little chance of ever finding happiness.

I carried my glass into the living room, collapsed onto the sofa, and listened to the storm that had blown up outside. It was raining very hard, I noticed. But then it always rained hard in Banyan Beach in July, the middle of South Florida's dreaded hurricane season, when the snowbirds had all gone north for the summer and only the locals were left to grumble about the heat, the humidity and the mosquitoes. Even when the storms weren't hurricane-strength, they were often torrential, with booming thunder and swirling, battering winds. In fact, it was a loud crack of thunder that sent me weaving to the sliding glass door to flick on the outside light. Ever since we had moved into our four-bedroom/three-and-a-half-bath Key West–style house on a prime piece of oceanfront property, I had enjoyed watching storms from the living room. They were so dramatic, so intense. Everything my life wasn't.

As the wind and rain pelted the door, I pressed my nose against the glass and saw that the ocean was swollen and churning. It seemed poised to rise up and swallow the house and me whole.

Would that really be so bad? I asked myself as I peered out at the stormy waters below. Would it really be so bad to be swallowed up by the ocean and carried off into a sea of darkness, to a place where my problems and failures could no longer eat away at me?

I took another sip of my Bloody Mary and felt my legs buckle slightly. I held on to the door handle to steady myself, then drank some more.

I was beyond drunk, but I didn't care. I didn't want to be in control of my thoughts or my actions. Not anymore. I was sick of being in control, sick of being straitjacketed by my feelings. I just wanted to run, to escape, to get away from Mitchell and Chrissy and everyone else in Banyan Beach who thought they knew Barbara Chessner, away from the fact that I had become a self-pitying middle-aged woman who had once had dreams.

And then, despite the thunder and lightning and ferocious wind, I began to act out my unspoken wish. Almost as if someone were calling to me, beckoning to me, I clutched my glass, opened the sliding door, and staggered out onto the deck.

Within seconds, my clothes were soaked and my hair was matted against my head. I was numb to it, numb to the elements, numb to the fact that, by standing outside in a lightning storm, I was doing a foolish, dangerous thing.

Go back in the house, a different voice whispered from somewhere inside me. Go back in the house before it's too late.

"Too late for what?" I said out loud, over the roar of the storm and the waves and my beating heart.

I was acting crazy, I knew. Overwrought. But I didn't care if lightning *did* strike me. I was asking for it. I just didn't know what "it" was. How could I know? There was no warning, no hint that I was about to become a "darksider," as they call people who turn their bodies over to the devil.

The devil? What on earth did I know about the devil? My parents, the late Ira and Estelle Greenberg, had raised me to believe that there *was* no devil, just Republicans. Their idea of "evil" was a daughter who was still unmarried by the age of thirty. They were greatly relieved when I married Mitchell the week after my twenty-eighth birthday. But, as it turned out, I hadn't escaped evil after all. Because there I was, standing outside in that storm, only seconds away from being taken over by the darkest evil of them all.

As the wind and rain lashed at my face, I gulped down what was left of my Bloody Mary, then hurled the empty glass onto the beach below and watched the ocean carry it away.

The gesture made me feel ridiculous, even sorrier for myself than I felt before, and I began to sob. Which only made me feel worse. There's nothing more depressing in its redundancy than crying in the rain, except, maybe, crying in the shower.

"Please help me!" I wailed between sobs as I looked up at the black, angry sky. "I'm so alone and so repressed and so . . . drunk." I began to wobble and grabbed on to the railing of the deck to keep myself from going down.

"My husband has just left me. My career has stalled, absolutely stalled." I hiccuped. "And I'm fat and ugly and can't express my feelings and no man will ever want me again."

I was dizzy suddenly, and I felt a strange tingling sensation in my hands and feet, but I kept talking. It felt good to talk, good to let it all out at last.

"Please, won't you help me?" I cried loud enough for them to hear me in Miami. *"Please?"*

I had no idea whom I was addressing, of course. I had assumed it was God. Who wouldn't? Most of us believe that when we're in big trouble and things look bleak, God is the one to call. How was I to know that somebody else was listening in?

"If you help me," I went on, wiping my tears on the back of my hand, "I'll do anything you ask. *Anything*. All you've got to do is break my real estate slump. Give me one sale—once decent sale—say, a house in the $500,000 to $750,000 range."

I held my ears while I waited for a giant clap of thunder to pass.

"And on a more personal note," I said, "I've waited my entire life to find true love. I realize that I'm not a blond glamorpuss like Chrissy Hemplewhite and that men are not exactly lining up to take Mitchell's place in my bed. Well . . . what I'm trying to say is . . ."

I stopped. My old paralysis took over. I was about to say something revealing and I froze.

A strong gust of wind nearly blew me off the deck and I had trouble catching my breath.

"Okay, okay," I gasped, sensing that if I didn't finish my speech soon, I never would. "I'll tell you what I want. I want to stop being a mouse. I'm sick of living the life of the woman in the proverbial 'before' ad, the woman who doesn't get noticed, doesn't get taken seriously, doesn't get the man of her dreams." There. I said it. "I want things to change. I want *me* to change. I want—"

There was another crash of thunder, this one shaking the deck of my house, throwing me completely off-balance and sending me to the ground with a thud. I lay there for several seconds, trembling, clinging for dear life to the railing, shielding my face from the bracing wind.

And then, suddenly, at the very moment when I wondered if I might actually die in the storm, it was the wind that died. Just like that. One minute the air was turbulent, the next it was perfectly still. What's more, the thunder and lightning virtually ceased and the ocean became as calm as a lake. It was as if someone had pulled a switch to the "off" position.

Stunned by the dramatic change in the atmosphere, I bolted up and gazed into the sky. It was no longer black but a brilliant, almost transparent blue, which, in itself, was pretty weird, considering that it was nearly ten o'clock at night. Even weirder was the fact that there were dozens of silvery little faces dotting the sky. No kidding. At first, I thought they were stars, but when I looked again, I saw that they had eyes and noses and mouths—*and one of them appeared to wink at me!*

I laughed for the first time in months and figured I was having one hell of an alcoholic hallucination.

Little did I know that I was not hallucinating; that what I saw represented the opening round in a tug of war for my soul; that what I was about to become was no laughing matter.

CHAPTER

3

The first thing that struck me when I woke up the next morning was that I didn't have a hangover. In fact, given the amount of alcohol I'd consumed, I felt remarkably clearheaded.

The second thing that was strange was that I didn't miss Mitchell's presence in the house—not in the slightest—even though we'd been together for nearly a decade.

And then there was my singing, which was miraculously on key. I had always been tone deaf—the kid in school who was asked to *mouth* the words to "The Star Spangled Banner." But on that particular morning, the Morning After, I turned on the radio before getting out of bed and found myself harmonizing with Gloria Estefan. I didn't know what to make of it, but I can tell you that I sounded pretty damn good.

At six-forty-five I got up, put on a robe, and padded to the kitchen, thoughts of poached eggs, English muffins, and crispy bacon dancing in my head. I was just about to open the refrigerator when the barking started.

It was loud and insistent and incredibly annoying, and, since I didn't own a dog and neither did my neighbors, I wondered where it was coming from.

"Aw, shut up," I growled as the barking went on. And on and on. Exasperated, I walked to the front door, opened it, and looked outside for the offending canine. I didn't have to look far: it was sitting on my doorstep, taking in the warm sun, its tail wagging back and forth like an out-of-control windshield wiper.

It was a big black dog with a short, shiny coat, floppy ears, and a small white patch on its chest.

"Shoo! Get away!" I shouted and waved my arms at it.

I hated dogs, never could see why people found them so cute and cuddly. As far as I could tell, all they did was bark and drool and sniff your crotch.

"Wuf! Wuf! Wuf!" the dog barked again, looking at me intently, its eyes a rather intriguing hazel.

It's one of those Labrador retrievers, I realized, remembering Jethro, the dog my brother, Benjamin, used to have. A refugee from the sixties, Benjamin named all his dogs after his favorite rock groups or their songs. Consequently, there was the Lab named Jethro, as in Tull; the Boxer named Floyd, as in Pink; and the Golden Retriever named Vida, as in In-a-Gadda-Da.

Not knowing this dog's name, I opted for the generic "Fido."

"Pipe down, Fido," I said.

To my amazement, it did pipe down. It cocked its head at me and made that pitiful, whining sound that dogs make when they want to be petted or fed or thrown a Frisbee.

"Look, are you lost or something?" I said, knowing the feeling. My husband had dumped me, I was a bust at my job, and on a scale of one to ten my self-esteem was a minus seven.

As the dog continued to whine, I bent down and looked to see if it was wearing any tags. There were two.

I reached out and tried to examine them, but Fido took the gesture as an invitation to stick its nose up my bathrobe.

"Hey. Cut it out," I snapped.

Fido pulled his snout away from my privates.

I grabbed hold of its collar and saw that one tag had its Animal Control license number and the date of its rabies shots. The other tag had its name, which, apparently, was Pete.

"Pete," I mused. "So you're a boy. Now let's see where you live."

I squinted in the sunlight and tried to read the address on the tag. Then I bolted up straight.

"But this can't be," I said out loud. According to the tag, Pete's address was *my* address!

Was this somebody's idea of a joke? I wondered. Had Mitchell gotten a dog and forgotten to tell me? Or was the address on the tag a mistake, a typo or clerical error made by the Animal Control office?

There was one way to find out. I made a mental note of Pete's license number, left him barking and whining, and went back inside the house to call Animal Control.

"Hello," I said pleasantly. "I'm calling to report a stray dog. A black Labrador retriever named Pete."

"Do you know who his owner is?" asked the man on the phone.

"No, but I know his license number." I gave it to him.

"Hang on a second," he said. "I'll look it up."

I waited.

"Okay. I've got the owner's name," he said. "We'll pick the dog up and issue the owner a warning. We have a leash law in Banyan Beach, you know."

"I do know," I said. "That's why I called."

"Not that a lot of people care," he went on. "Some of them let their pets run all over town."

"So I see," I said. "Oh, there's one more thing."

"Yes?"

"There's some sort of mistake on the dog's tag," I said.

"What sort of mistake?" he asked.

"It says his address is 666 Seacrest Way," I said.

"Right. That's what I've got in my records," he said.

"I beg your pardon?" I said politely.

"I said that's what I've got in my records," he said.

"But that's impossible," I said. *"My* address is 666 Seacrest Way and I don't own a dog."

"You sure?"

"I'm positive."

"What's your name, lady?"

"Barbara Chessner."

"Well, according to my records, you're Pete's owner, Mrs. Chessner."

Maybe I *am* hung over, I thought. Or maybe I have Alzheimer's. Maybe I do own a dog and don't remember.

But that was absurd. I had never had a pet in my entire life. Not a dog or a cat or even a parakeet. Well, that wasn't quite true. When I was six or seven, I did have a turtle named Willie, but Willie didn't count. He never moved a muscle, not even when I'd poke his shell with a pencil. For the longest time I thought he was dead, and then it turned out that he was.

"I'm sorry, but there must be a mix-up," I said to the Animal Control officer. "The dog that's barking outside my front door belongs to someone else."

"Look, lady," he said, "I don't know what your problem is, but I suggest you get a grip. If you're Barbara Chessner of 666 Seacrest Way, then Pete is all yours."

I was angry now. How dare *he* tell *me* to get a grip!

I swallowed hard and felt all my muscles tense. I didn't appreciate being patronized and I was dying to tell the guy off. But I couldn't, of course. Not me, the gutless wonder. God forbid, a perfect stranger should get mad at me.

I was about to hang up the phone and sit in a corner with my tail between my legs when all of a sudden I heard myself say to the Animal Control officer in a loud voice:

"What's your name?"

"My name?" he asked. "Ted Benson. Why?"

"Because I intend to tell your superior how rude and insensitive you've been," I said in an angry tone I simply didn't recognize. "I'm not an idiot and I won't be treated like one."

"Gosh, I'm sorry, Mrs. Chessner," he said, suddenly full of remorse. "I didn't mean any disrespect."

"The hell you didn't," I shouted, and slammed the phone down.

Shouted? Slammed down the phone? Me?

Oh my God, I thought, as I sat there, my whole body trembling. Did I really do that? Did I really get angry at someone? At a live person? What was going on?

I shook my head and went back into the kitchen and tried to figure out why I had suddenly been able to vent my frustration. It wasn't like me. It just wasn't. I had to admit, though, that it hadn't felt terrible to say what I thought for a change, to get it off my chest. It was liberating—and so easy! What's more, it was fun. Why had I waited so long to try it?

* * *

I made myself a huge breakfast, then took a hot shower, hoping I could scald the alcohol out of my system and begin to make sense of everything that was happening to me. But when I emerged from the bathroom, there was a brand-new set of puzzles to solve.

As I looked down at my naked body, I noticed that my breasts were bigger! Not Dolly Parton size, by any means, but not my usual flat-as-a-board either.

I hurried over to the mirror above my dresser and peered at them. Yes, they were definitely bigger—two or three cup sizes bigger! And fuller, higher, voluptuous even!

I turned sideways and examined them in profile. It was uncanny! They really stuck out!

When I turned to face the mirror and squeezed my breasts together, I couldn't believe my eyes: I had achieved real cleavage for the first time in my life! Who needed the WonderBra!

Don't get excited, I told myself. Money doesn't grow on trees and boobs don't grow on thirty-eight-year-old real estate agents. It's probably just a matter of fat redistribution. And speaking of fat, it appeared that I had lost weight. My second chin seemed to have disappeared, and my stomach didn't protrude the way it usually did.

What was going on here? My flat breasts had gotten fat and my fat stomach had gotten flat—and I had just put away two poached eggs, two English muffins, six strips of bacon, and a half a package of frozen hash browns. Not exactly Lean Cuisine. Had I been visited by a space alien who liposucked me while I slept *and* gave me breast implants? Or had all the booze I'd been drinking melted my fat cells as well as my brain cells?

As I continued to stare at myself in the mirror, my eyes drifted upward and I saw that my hair had undergone a dramatic makeover too! The color was no longer gray; it was blond—a golden, glittering blond! And the texture was smoother, straighter, more "relaxed." Could it be the new shampoo I'd been using? I'd seen several over-the-hill movie actresses endorsing the product on TV infomercials and figured that if it was good enough for them, it was good enough for me. But turn my prematurely gray hair blond?

I gave myself the once-over and whistled. I had to admit it: I looked better than I had in years. And after living through The Night

From Hell. But how was it possible that I had been transformed while I slept? That I had gone to bed a dumpy matron and woken up a bodacious babe?

Maybe it's because Mitchell left, I decided. Maybe my body is celebrating.

Whatever the reason for the change in me—of course, I didn't have a clue then—I embraced it and dressed for the office with absolute gusto, singing in perfect pitch with Bonnie Raitt, Elton John, and Boyz II Men. I chose a blue cotton dress that had been relegated to the back of my closet because it was too tight. It fit like a second skin now, hugging the contours of my body as if it were sprayed on.

When I walked outside to my car, Pete was not only still planted on my front steps, but he greeted me by depositing a puddle of drool on the hem of my dress.

"Shit. Now look what you've done," I said, wondering what I was going to do about the dog.

I marched back inside and quickly called my brother, who was between dogs at the moment.

"Ben, it's Barbara," I said when he answered the phone.

"Oh, Barbara. Hi . . . Uh, just a second, okay?"

His voice was muffled, as if he had a sheet over his head, and there seemed to be someone else in the room with him. Apparently I had interrupted something.

"Sorry," he said when he came back on the line. "It's a little early for me. I'm still in bed."

"I sensed that."

"So how are you?"

"Pretty good, except that Mitchell left me for a twenty-four-year-old."

"Mitchell took off?"

"Yup."

"You must be ecstatic. Mitchell is an asshole. I can't stand him. Never could."

Without waiting even a second to consider what I was about to say, I said, "Mitchell has his faults, but the reason *you* can't stand

him is because he's successful, Benjamin. You have an abiding re-
sentment for people who are successful."

My hand flew to my mouth and I gasped. Had I really said that
to my brother? My dear sweet brother to whom I had never uttered
a harsh or unkind word? What on earth was happening to me?

"Barbara? Did you get up on the wrong side of the bed or something?" he asked.

"No. I'm just saying what I think for a change: You can't stand
people who make a lot of money. You act as if you think capital-
ists are agents of the devil." Another outburst. I didn't even know
it was coming. I just opened my mouth and out it came—including the bit about the devil, which, looking back on it now, should
have told me something.

"That's not true, Barbara. It really isn't."

But it *was* true. My forty-four-year-old brother was a deadbeat.
A nice deadbeat, but a deadbeat nevertheless. Our parents had been
killed in a car accident seven years before and they had left Ben
and me a little money in their wills. I saw my inheritance as a cushion, money to be saved for a rainy day. Benjamin saw his as an
opportunity to loaf for the rest of his life. He bought fifty acres west
of I-95, built a log cabin reminiscent of the commune he had lived
and screwed in during the sixties, and spent his time listening to
rock 'n' roll and having sex with half the women in Florida, many
of whom he impregnated. In fact, every time I saw a kid with the
kinky, prematurely gray hair that runs in our family, I was sure he
or she was one of Ben's offspring.

When he wasn't spreading his seed around town, he grew
things. One year, it was tomatoes. The next, it was orchids. His latest venture was raising emus. When I had asked why, he'd replied,
"Why not?"

He had about as much ambition as I had interest in emus, but,
aside from some thoroughly uninteresting aunts, uncles, and
cousins, he was the only family I had. We loved each other. I hoped
to take advantage of that love by dumping Pete on his doorstep.

"Listen, Ben. Remember that black Lab you had?" I asked.

"You mean Jethro? Sure, I remember."

"Would you like another Lab?"

"Whose is he?"

"That's a long story. Suffice it to say, he's mine to give away. Would you take him? Please?"

"Sure, why not? I've been thinking about getting another dog. Janice wants one too."

"Janice?"

"Yeah. My new lady. She moved in last week. Right, honey?"

I heard someone giggling in the background, someone very young, and then I heard Benjamin kissing her—loud, wet smooches. It was nauseating. When he came back on the line, I asked, "What happened to Denise?"

"Nothing," said Benjamin. "She's still in my life. As a friend. Janice is her younger sister."

"What does Janice do?"

"Do?"

"Never mind. I keep forgetting that the word 'do,' as in 'do for a living,' goes right over your head."

"Man, you must be more upset about Mitchell's defection than you're letting on," said Benjamin. "You're really bitchy this morning."

"I'm sorry," I said. "Maybe I'm still in shock about the whole thing." Was I? Was that the reason for my inexplicable candor?

"Sure. I understand. Now, what do you want me to do about the dog?"

"Would you mind coming over to pick him up? Tonight? I'd bring him to you, but I really don't want to mess up my car. A messy car is a turn-off to my customers, you know?" I hadn't shown a house in months and had forgotten what it was like to have customers, but I was hopeful my luck would change, the way everything else about me was changing.

"I'd like to, Barbara, but Janice, Denise, and I are having a séance tonight."

"A what?"

"A séance. You remember. Where you sit in a dark room and communicate with spirits? Everybody was into them in the sixties."

"It's the nineties, Benjamin. When are you going to grow up and get a life?"

I wanted to take the remark back the instant I made it, but it was too late.

"Hey, Barbara. Why don't you take your dog and your attitude and have a nice day."

He was about to hang up on me when I stopped him.

"Wait! Ben! Don't go! I don't know what I'm saying."

"Oh, come on. Get mad at me if you want to, but don't give me the 'I don't know what I'm saying' routine. It's pretty lame."

"But it's true," I said. How could I explain? I didn't understand what was happening to me. How could I expect someone else to?

"Fine. Whatever. Anyhow, we're having this séance tonight at seven o'clock," Benjamin went on. "Janice and Denise want to get in touch with their grandmother, who died last year without telling anyone the ingredients in her meat loaf. They say Grandma Patrice made unbelievable meat loaf and that if we contact her spirit, maybe she'll share the recipe with us. It's worth a shot, don't you think?"

"You don't want to know what I think," I said, wondering what out-there fad Ben would embrace next, trying to imagine how a brother and sister could be so dissimilar. We came from the same rigidly conventional parents, people who would rather die than shock their neighbors, and yet we conducted ourselves in such vastly different ways. Ben coped with our parents' sanctimonious-ness by rebelling, by refusing to move in their narrow world, by pursuing the kind of lifestyle he knew they disdained. I went in the opposite direction; I did exactly what they wanted me to, feared displeasing them, turned myself into a mouse. Where Ben became his own person, I became a nonperson. "Just make sure that if you happen to talk to Mom and Dad while you're communicating with the spirits, you keep quiet about Mitchell and me," I added. "They'd be mortified if they found out that their daughter was dumped for a buck-toothed weatherperson. You know how they were."

"I'll just give them your best," said Ben.

"I'd appreciate that. Now, back to the dog. If you can't come and get him, I guess I'll have to keep him until tomorrow."

" 'Fraid so, unless I ask Jeremy to stop by your house and bring the dog here in his pickup. He's coming for the séance and your house is sort of on his way over."

Jeremy Cook was Ben's best friend and my least favorite person, aside from Mitchell. A charter fishing boat captain who also sang in a rock 'n' roll band, Jeremy was an unrepentant redneck—crude, rude, and incredibly infantile. He once took Ted Kennedy fishing and when Kennedy didn't tip him, Jeremy showed his displeasure by pulling down his pants and mooning the senator. He wasn't any more dignified with me. In fact, he loathed me as much as I loathed him. It all started when we were in high school. He had asked me to be his date for the prom and, terrified by the idea of spending even five minutes alone with such a wild man (he rode a motorcycle, wore a black leather jacket, and was rumored to have had sex with Miss Peterson, our biology teacher), I had faked sick and stayed home. He never forgave me. Whenever we had the misfortune to run into each other, he made sure I knew how he felt. No, he didn't moon me; he just treated me as if I were bait fish.

"Do you think Jeremy would mind picking up the dog?" I asked Ben.

"Naw, he loves dogs," he said.

"Yeah, but he hates me," I pointed out.

"He does not. He just thinks you need a good . . . Well, let's just say he thinks you should loosen up a little."

"Give me a break," I said. "When Jeremy Cook says a woman should 'loosen up a little,' he means she should climb onto a pool table and dance topless in front of twenty guys who have more tattoos than they do teeth."

"Barbara, what is it with you this morning?" said Ben.

"Nothing. See if he'll stop by around six." I sighed, resigned to the fact that it was either put up with Jeremy's bullshit or listen to Pete bark. Talk about having to choose between the lesser of two evils. But then I didn't know the first thing about evil. Not yet.

CHAPTER

4

It had been nine years since I first became a real estate agent. I had chosen to work at Home Sweet Home because, unlike the other small firms in Banyan Beach, it hadn't been swallowed up by national chains like Coldwell Banker and Century 21. It was the last remaining independent real estate company in town and that had appealed to me. I was a hometown girl, after all, and I liked the fact that Home Sweet Home was a hometown business, not beholden to some parent company in Omaha or Dallas whose primary interest was in acquiring "units" and then selling them off.

Housed in a candy pink Victorian building on Main Street, Home Sweet Home was owned by seventy-two-year-old Charlotte Reed, a faded southern belle who fancied herself the grande dame of Banyan Beach society, even though there *was* no Banyan Beach society. Not in the way there was a Palm Beach society. There was just a handful of old-moneyed WASPs who had their main residences in places like Locust Valley and Grosse Point but who, when they wanted to get away from it all, repaired to the family compound in "Banyan" and had gads of fun drinking and fishing and pretending they were locals.

A short, benign-looking woman with watery blue eyes and wispy white hair that was always coming loose from her bun, Charlotte Reed could fool you. She appeared to be a ditsy, spacey relic of another time, a woman who had absolutely no head for business, but she was still, after thirty years, *in* business. A profitable business. Which was no small accomplishment, given that many local businesses had gone under. In recent years, she had delegated the actual running of the office to Althea Dicks, one of Home Sweet Home's longtime agents, and worked from home, coming in only to conduct her once-a-week meetings, during which she served us tea in delicate little Limoges cups, doled out lumps of sugar with sterling silver tongs, and showed us grainy old photographs of Banyan Beach the way it used to be. An anachronism, that's what Charlotte Reed was. Completely out of touch with the way real estate brokers operate in the nineties. She was so out of touch that when I once suggested that we get a toll-free number so that Home Sweet Home could attract out-of-state buyers, she asked me what I meant.

"An 800 number," I explained. "Where the caller doesn't get charged."

She gave me a bewildered look and then said that she didn't care for telephones; she much preferred written correspondence.

"Then what about getting a fax machine for the office?" I asked.

Another bewildered look.

"Fax!" I repeated, louder this time, not knowing whether she didn't hear or didn't understand.

She scowled, then drew herself up to her full five feet two.

"I don't find that sort of language very becoming, dear," she replied, and walked away.

Ah, Charlotte. As I said, she could fool you. When George Bush's second cousin went house shopping in Banyon Beach, it was Charlotte who sold him a two-million-dollar estate, not some hotshot from Prudential.

I got to work at ten o'clock that July morning, and the first person I saw was Althea Dicks, who was not only Home Sweet Home's office manager, but also its resident sourpuss. We had driven into the parking lot at the same time and then walked into the building together.

"What have you done to yourself?" she asked, seeming appalled by my new hair and figure. Althea hated change about as much as everybody hated Althea.

I didn't know how to answer her question, so I winged it.

"I spent a few days at Canyon Ranch," I said casually, referring to the expensive health spa in Arizona. Althea was hardly a health spa aficionado and wouldn't know Canyon Ranch from the Grand Canyon, but she nodded disapprovingly, as she always did when she pictured someone having a good time.

"Were you out with customers early this morning?" I asked.

"What else?" she replied.

"How did it go?" I asked with a twinge of envy. For the past year, I'd had to watch her sell one house after another, even though she was about as engaging as Scrooge.

"The usual," she said. Her lips were pursed, as if she'd been sucking on lemons instead of showing houses. She was forty-seven, but her grumpiness made her look ten years older. She had short, reddish brown hair, narrow, wary eyes, a tall, thin frame, and terrible posture. If anyone was a candidate for osteoporosis, it was Althea. Brittle personality, brittle bones.

"Tough customers?" I asked.

"Oh, please. Customers today just don't have their priorities straight. Years ago, I'd show them a house and they'd ask, 'Is it close to the schools?' Now, I show them a house and they ask, 'Is it close to the mall?' This town isn't what it used to be and neither are the people who want to live here."

"I wouldn't be so quick to put down your customers, Althea," I said. "Without them, you'd probably be selling vacuum cleaners door to door."

Her eyes bulged and her cheeks flushed—with good reason. I had never spoken up to Althea Dicks. No one in the office had. At least, not to her face.

Too stunned to reply, she gave me a long, withering look before turning away and proceeding to her desk.

My inability to censor myself was putting a crimp in my ability to make chitchat. But, then, chatting with Althea Dicks was more depressing than reading the obituaries. I wondered how her husband put up with her black moods and long faces, and then I remembered that he was an undertaker.

Suzanne Munson was the only other agent in the office when I arrived. She had just made a fresh pot of coffee in the little kitchen off the conference room and I went in and poured myself a cup.

"Barbara! My God!" she said when she saw me. "You have cheekbones! And your figure! And—you've had work done without telling me. Which plastic surgeon did you see? Danford? Milenowski? Who?"

"Come on, Suzanne. You know I'd never go under the knife. I won't even let the manicurist cut my cuticles."

"Well then, how come you look like you do?"

"I . . . I went on one of those liquid diets," I sputtered. "And I started lifting weights to build up my breast muscles."

"What about the hair? You never mentioned anything about wanting to go blond."

"You know what they say," I chuckled. "Blondes have more fun. Since I haven't been having any fun at all lately, I thought it was time for a change."

"I guess you *have* been kind of in the dumps lately," she conceded, knitting her brow in that ultraconcerned way people have when they wonder if you have a drinking problem. The last time I'd seen Suzanne, she had stopped by my house at ten o'clock in the morning and found me finishing off a bottle of Merlot.

"I've been better," I said.

"You haven't come into the office in days," she said. "I tried calling you last night, but I kept getting your answering machine."

"I'm sorry," I said. "You should be glad you didn't reach me though. I wasn't myself last night."

"God, I know what you mean," she said. "I wasn't myself last night either. I think I had my first hot flash at about nine-fifteen."

I braced myself for yet another discussion of menopause and how it was to blame for virtually everything that went wrong in a woman's life. Suzanne was obsessed with menopause. She had read Gail Sheehy's book so many times that she knew every page by heart, and when she was in her car, she'd listen to the audiotape version, even when customers were in the car with her. Nevertheless, in spite of how well read she was on the subject, she remained undecided on the estrogen/progesterone question and fretted over it whenever there was nothing better to fret over. What made all this particularly silly was the fact that Suzanne was only thirty-five.

I once told her that she still had a few good years left before menopause set in, but my comment had only provoked a long discourse on *peri*menopause, which, she had explained, could strike at any time.

"Listen, Suzanne. I may as well tell you: Mitchell and I are splitting up," I said. Suzanne had her quirks, but she was my best friend in the office. I had to tell someone about Mitchell and Chrissy and she was the someone.

"I don't believe it," she said, her jaw dropping. "What happened?"

"Last night he told me he's in love with the person who does the weather on the Six O'Clock News."

Suzanne gasped. "I don't believe it," she said again, this time shaking her head vigorously. "I just don't believe it. Mitchell never struck me as being the least bit feminine."

"Feminine? What are you talking about?"

"Well, all right. So you can't always tell who's the feminine one and who plays the man's part."

"Suzanne, I'm not following you."

"You said Mitchell's gay."

"I did not. I said he's in love with someone else."

"Yeah, the person who does the weather on the Six O'Clock News: Ron Baines."

"Ron Baines is on Channel Eight. Mitchell is in love with the weatherperson on Channel Five: Chrissy Hemplewhite."

"Oh." She sighed and knitted her brow yet again and patted me on the shoulder. "I don't know what to say. How do you feel about it?"

"Conflicted. Mitchell and I weren't exactly the love match of the century. We should have split up years ago. But it's a little scary to think I'll be back on the market. Used goods and all that stuff."

"Tell me about it. I've been on the market so long, the USDA's gonna stamp an expiration date on my forehead."

I smiled, but I knew that behind Suzanne's quips was real desperation. She'd never been married and hadn't had a boyfriend since she'd moved to Banyan Beach from New Haven three years ago. She was dying to find a husband and had come to Florida for just that purpose after reading an article in *USA Today* that said there were three times as many single men in the Sunshine State as there were in Connecticut.

I couldn't understand why Suzanne hadn't found a husband. Except for her menopause obsession and the fact that she went a little heavy on the makeup, she had a lot going for her. She had a petite little figure, big green eyes, glossy dark hair, which she wore chin-length and stick-straight, and pearly white teeth. She was warm and friendly and didn't mind paying her own way on a date, yet she couldn't seem to connect with men.

Not that she didn't try. For a while, she spent Friday nights planted on a bar stool at Conched Out, a riverfront singles' hangout whose Happy Hour attracted women in too-tight T-shirts and men who thought being called a redneck was a compliment. Eventually, Suzanne tired of Conched Out and moved on to the newer, far trendier Banyan Beach Grille, which was said to have a more upscale clientele. On her first visit, she discovered that the men who frequented the Banyan Beach Grille were, indeed, doctors and lawyers and stock brokers, and she licked her lips in anticipation of finding a husband from among them. The trouble was, they already *were* husbands—two-timing, skirt-chasing married men who'd slip their wedding bands into their pockets and assume nobody would notice the tan line on their ring fingers!

"Is there anything I can do?" Suzanne asked.

"Just be my friend," I said. "I'm going to need one."

"You can count on me," she said. "Really."

I touched her arm. "Thanks, I appreciate that."

"You know, in a way I'm glad you and Mitchell broke up. Now I'll have someone to go man hunting with," she said.

I groaned. "I don't think I'm in any shape for that," I said.

"Wrong. You're in fabulous shape."

"I meant emotionally. I really need to sell a house, Suzanne. If this slump of mine goes on much longer, I'll have a breakdown. My stress level has been off the charts."

"It's your hormones," Suzanne said with authority. "When a woman is almost forty, the menopausal process begins to—"

"Would you shut up about menopause for once," I interrupted.

I was immediately horrified by what I'd said. Suzanne looked as if she were going to cry.

"Forgive me," I said. "I didn't mean that. Between Mitchell's announcement and my slump here at work, I'm feeling really out of control."

Her expression softened. "I understand," she said. "We can talk about your hormones some other time."

"I'd rather talk about houses," I said. "Have any hot new listings come into the office in the last week or so?"

"Nothing 'hot.' Just that dump on Pelican Circle. You know, the Nowak house? The one with the nude ladies in the front yard?"

I rolled my eyes. The Nowak house on 46 Pelican Circle was a long-running joke in town. It sat on a prime piece of waterfront property and the houses on either side of it were in the million-dollar range, but it was dated and cramped and incredibly tacky, not to mention way overpriced. Its owner, a contentious old bastard named Victor Nowak, had built the house in the 1950s and then made it a shrine to unspeakably bad taste. The floors were covered with avocado green shag carpet, the walls with gold vinyl paper. The rooms had low ceilings and tiny windows and were jam-packed with bad sculptures of nude women. Out on the lawn were more nude women—six statues in all. Several people in town tried to get the Zoning Board to coerce Mr. Nowak to remove his "art" in the name of common decency, but he argued that he was within his constitutional rights and could decorate his front lawn however he wished. When he finally put his house on the market, his neighbors celebrated. Unfortunately, there hadn't been a single offer on the place. Not in three years.

"Wasn't it listed with Century 21?" I asked Suzanne.

"Yeah. And before that, with Coldwell Banker. Nobody can sell that place. It's a turkey and Nowak wants $700,000 for it."

"Obviously, he's out of his mind," I said. "Whose listing is it?"

"Frances's," said Suzanne, referring to Frances Lutz, one of the other realtors in our office.

"Why would she take a listing like that?" I said.

"The house is a ranch. Frances never turns her back on a ranch, remember?"

I laughed. Frances Lutz weighed three hundred pounds and did-n't like to move if she could help it, which meant that climbing stairs was out of the question. As a result, she dubbed herself Home Sweet Home's "ranch specialist," hoping she'd never have to show a house with more than one story.

"Whoops," said Suzanne after checking the time on her watch. "I've got to get going. I have a closing in fifteen minutes."

"A 'closing,' " I sighed. "Now there's a word that's dropped out of my vocabulary."

"Come on," Suzanne urged. "You'll get back in the groove. You're too good an agent to be down for too much longer. And besides, you're a blonde now, with a body to die for. I don't know how you managed it in such a short time, but if you weren't my friend, I'd hate your guts. Luckily, you are my friend, and I hope you sell a house. *Today.*"

"From your mouth to God's ears," I said.

I spent most of the morning on the phone, trying to drum up busi-ness—with few results. At around noon, I was planning to run out and get a sandwich, when Deirdre Wyatt walked toward my desk.

Deirdre was a thirty-two-year-old former beauty queen who had represented our state in the Miss America Pageant but lost to Miss Minnesota. Still smarting after nearly a decade, she blamed her loss on the fact that a Southerner had won the crown the previous year. The rest of us blamed her loss on the fact that, for the talent portion of the pageant, she had chosen to twirl a baton.

I smiled as she approached my desk. A strawberry blonde who wore conservative little cotton dresses and pale pink lipstick, she appeared to be the very essence of virginal purity, except for her occasional truck driver language. She wasn't the swiftest real es-tate agent in town but she didn't have to be. She got her listings the old-fashioned way: she put out.

"Barbs, could you do me a teensy-weensy favor?" she said in her breathy, babyish, Marilyn Monroe voice. I always expected her to go "Boop-boop-eedoo" at the end of every sentence.

"What's the favor?" I asked, surprised that she hadn't commented on my dramatically altered appearance, then remembering that it

was Deirdre's appearance that interested Deirdre. Maybe she did-
n't like the idea that there was another blonde in the office.

"I'm supposed to be on floor duty until three," she said. "But
I've got to meet with a gentleman at twelve-thirty. He's thinking of
listing his house with me. Could you cover for me, Barbs? Just for
an itty-bitty couple of hours?"

You'll have to trust me. I am not the type to be called Barbs or
Babs or even Barb, but I allowed Deirdre her nickname. What she
called me was better than what she called Althea Dicks, which was
Dickface. Behind her back, of course.

"Sure, I'll cover for you," I said, knowing that Deirdre would do
the same for me. She was actually a very nice person once you got
past the baby talk. Besides, who was I to stand in the way of a listing? Or a tryst?

"Thanks, Barbs. You're a sweetie."

She patted me on the shoulder and was about to run off when
she did a double-take and came back to my desk.

"Hey, you look different," she said, giving me the once-over. "It's
your teeth, right? You had them capped or something?"

"No, Deirdre," I said, amazed at her lack of observation. "But
thanks for asking."

"No, thank *you*. For taking my floor duty. Now have fun, huh,
sweets?" she said, and hurried out of the office.

Fun. I wouldn't exactly call being on floor duty fun. Not anymore. When I first became a real estate agent, I looked forward to
being the "duty cutie," as Deirdre called it. When you're the one
who's answering the phones and manning the desk, you're the one
who gets all the call-ins and walk-ins and before you know it,
you've sold a house. But after I went into my slump, I began to
dread floor duty because I'd sit by the phone, hour after hour, and
the only calls I'd get would be wrong numbers.

I moved over to the desk by the front door of the office and no
sooner did I sit down when the phone rang.

"Home Sweet Home. This is Barbara Chessner," I said, trying to
sound perky.

"Good afternoon. I'm calling about one of your company's listings," said the man, who had a deep, resonant, radio announcer's
voice that was distinctive and familiar at the same time.

"Which listing?" I asked, grabbing the MLS book and flipping it open.

"It's a house on Pelican Circle. I was driving by it and saw the Home Sweet Home sign."

"You mean 46 Pelican Circle?" I asked. Could somebody really be calling about the Nowak house?

"I don't recall the street number," he said politely.

"Were there statues on the front lawn?" I asked.

"I'm afraid so," he said. "I'm interested in the house in spite of the statues, not because of them."

I could hear the smile in his voice and it made me smile. It was a smooth, velvety voice, warm and melodious and friendly.

"How much is the owner asking?" he said.

"Seven hundred thousand," I said and braced myself for a kiss off.

But the caller didn't kiss me off. "Seven hundred thousand sounds pretty reasonable, considering the location," he said.

"Pretty reasonable? What planet are you—" I stopped myself just in time. This honesty bit was getting old. It was one thing suddenly to be able to express my anger constructively. It was quite another to blurt out insulting and obnoxious remarks to potential customers. I would have to be careful from now on. Very careful.

"Did you say something?" he asked.

"I was about to say that the house *is* fairly priced," I said, trying not to choke on my words. "Waterfront property is very scarce these days."

"Exactly," he said. "I'd like to see the house. Naked ladies and all. Could you show it to me?"

"I'd be delighted, Mr. —"

"Bettinger. David Bettinger."

David Bettinger. It didn't ring a bell. Must be new in town, I guessed.

"When would be convenient for you?" I asked, barely able to suppress my amazement. I couldn't get over the fact that somebody—anybody—wanted to see the Nowak house! I couldn't wait to tell Suzanne.

"How about this afternoon," said David Bettinger. "Say, around three o'clock?"

"That sounds fine. Of course, I'll have to call the homeowner to make sure it's all right with him."

"I understand. Why don't you call him and call me back," he said, then gave me his telephone number.

I tried to reach Frances Lutz, the listing agent, but only reached her answering machine. I assumed she was home but not picking up the phone, as was often the case when one of her beloved game shows was on TV. The woman was as addicted to "Wheel of Fortune" as she was to Hostess Twinkies.

When I couldn't contact her, I called Mr. Nowak directly. He said that he wouldn't be home at three, but that it was fine to show the house as long as we were careful not to touch his nude women.

I dialed Mr. Bettinger's number with the good news.

"It's all arranged for three o'clock," I said. "Why don't we meet at my office and drive over to the house together?"

"Sounds perfect, Barbara."

I loved the way he said my name. Bah-bar-ah. It sort of rolled off his tongue, like very rich ice cream.

"I look forward to meeting you, Mr. Bettinger," I said, and meant it more than I can explain. There was something about his voice, about the way he spoke to me, that inspired visions of long, decadent dinners and walks along the beach in the moonlight and—

"David," he insisted. "Please call me David."

"Of course. *David.*"

"Until three then," he said in his deep baritone, which sent pleasurable little vibrations up and down my spine and made me reluctant to hang up the phone.

But I did hang up and, when I did, I looked down at the doodles I had scribbled on my pad while we'd been talking. I had, without realizing it, written "David Bettinger loves Barbara Chessner" inside a big, dopey heart!

Why on earth did I do that? I asked myself. I didn't even know the man, never mind that Mitchell had only been out of my life for a few hours. What was I doing fantasizing about a customer I'd never laid eyes on? Was I that hungry for affection? Or had I written David's and my names in that heart because I was compelled to do it? Because something *made* me do it?

I ripped up the sheet of paper and reminded myself that I was a professional real estate agent who had better start concentrating on business if she wanted to make this deal. Still, I couldn't help wondering if David Bettinger looked as good as he sounded and whether my luck was finally about to change.

CHAPTER 5

I had never met a man like David Bettinger, but then the men in Banyan Beach weren't exactly the cream of the crop.

The good old boys I'd grown up with tended to be rather limited; their idea of a big career was bagging groceries at their neighborhood Winn Dixie. And the men who'd only recently moved to Banyan Beach tended to be either retirees or golf addicts. Which explains why I'd ended up with Mitchell Chessner.

Mitchell was different, more ambitious than the other locals. He spoke in complete sentences. He read the *Wall Street Journal*. He had goals. Unfortunately, what he didn't have was a personality.

David Bettinger, on the other hand, was so charming that I wondered if I'd conjured him up—as comic relief. When I first saw him, I actually started laughing.

He was ridiculously handsome, like something out of a cartoon: lustrous golden hair that curled up the back of his collar; a strong, square jaw; an even, lightly tanned complexion; gleaming white teeth; and deeply set, mesmerizing brown eyes framed by long, dark lashes. He was fortyish, I guessed, and in terrific shape. He was tall—six feet or so—with broad shoulders, slim hips, and an absolutely flat stomach. There wasn't even a hint of a paunch beneath the white cotton polo shirt tucked inside his crisp khaki slacks.

And when he smiled . . . Well, picture Robert Redford doing his Hubbell Gardner act in *The Way We Were*. David Bettinger's smile was even more implausible. And then there was The Voice. Deep, baritone, velvety smooth.

"So you're Bah-bar-ah," he said, shaking my hand when he arrived at Home Sweet Home at five minutes of three. "It's nice to put the face with the voice."

"For me too," I said, trying not to fawn or gawk or appear awestruck. The trouble was that David *was* awe-inspiring. He gave off something—a presence, a power, a magnetism, something that made you reluctant to look away from him. He had an aura of absolute deliciousness, and standing next to him was like standing next to a six-foot-tall bar of imported white chocolate. It was hard to keep my tongue in my mouth. He was *that* rich and creamy and decadent. An indulgence.

"Please, make yourself comfortable," I said, gesturing for David to sit in the visitor's chair opposite my desk. "I'd like to jot down some information before we go and see the house."

"Fine," said David as he lowered himself into the chair, then crossed his legs. I could feel his eyes on me, assessing me, appraising me, appraising my voluptuous figure which, as recently as the day before, hadn't been so voluptuous. "What would you like to know?"

I pulled out a blank file card. "Well, let's see. I've got your name and phone number, but I'll need your address, in case I want to mail you a brochure on some of our listings."

"It's a temporary address," he said. "I'm renting a house on River Road. Sixty-three River Road."

River Road. Very upscale, I thought as I noted the address on the file card.

"Are you new in town?" I asked.

"Yes. I just moved up from Palm Beach," he explained as he ran his fingers through his hair, which seemed to emit little glints of light, as if it were a halo. "I'm renting until I find my dream house."

"Well, let's hope that 46 Pelican Circle turns out to be that dream house," I smiled, trying to picture David Bettinger living in the Nowak house. It was like trying to picture Prince Charming in a Winnebago.

"Let's hope," he said, returning my smile. "Depending on how God-awful the house is, I'll either renovate it or tear it down and build something else. It's the property I'm really interested in. Dream houses should be situated on beautiful property, don't you think?"

"Absolutely," I said, nodding my head enthusiastically. "Tell me, Mr. Bettinger—"

"David, remember?"

"David." I trembled as I said his first name aloud. "Are you a developer, by any chance?"

"No. I'm in the import/export business," he replied, uncrossing his legs and then crossing them again. His shoes were expensive, buttery brown leather Italian loafers.

"Does your wife work in the business with you?" I asked. He was not wearing a wedding ring. There was no tan line on his finger, either.

"I'm not married," he replied. "Not at the moment, anyway."

I smiled knowingly, as if I, too, were worldly and sophisticated and merely between spouses, instead of a small-town girl who had, not twenty-four hours before, been dumped by the only man she'd ever slept with.

"The truth is, over the past several years I've been spending a great deal of time abroad," he went on. "Too much time. But now that I've moved to Banyan Beach, all the traveling is going to stop. I'm planning to settle down and devote myself to one thing and one thing only."

"And what's that?" I asked.

"Enjoying life," he said without the slightest guilt.

"An excellent plan," I said, thinking about my life and wondering when I would start to enjoy it. I checked my watch and looked up at him. "It's nearly three o'clock. Why don't we go and see the house?"

"I'd love to," he said. "But first, I'd like to ask you something, Barbara."

"Please. Ask away."

"Are *you* married?"

I was surprised. I hadn't expected David Bettinger to ask such a personal question. Was he flirting with me? Because I was blond and curvy? Did my new look give him the impression that I was "available"? Or was he just a little compulsive, the type who feels the need to get to know his realtor before plunging into discussions of linen closets, air-conditioning ducts, and septic fields?

I glanced down at my left hand. I had taken off my wedding ring right after Mitchell left the house the night before. Come to think of it, I didn't have a clue where I'd put it.

"I'm separated," I said finally.

He smiled. "Forgive me for saying this, but I'm glad."

"You are? Why?"

"As I told you, I'm new in Banyan Beach. I don't know many people here, particularly women. I was hoping that you and I might . . . have dinner some night."

I was absolutely stunned that such a magnificent specimen was putting the moves on *me*—and after only two seconds in my company! I knew I looked pretty "hot"—for me—but that hot? Maybe David wasn't especially discriminating when it came to women. Look at his taste in houses, for God's sake.

The truth was, I didn't know how to respond to David's invitation. Some women get angry if a man tries to pick them up during a business meeting, this being the age of sexual harassment, but how could I be angry at David Bettinger? He was my customer. I needed him if I was going to end my slump. Plus, he seemed very nice, very respectful. Not the least bit sleazy.

Of course, my instinct was to act coy. To make him think I was booked solid with dinner dates. Instead, I blurted out, "How about tonight?"

The instant I said it I nearly died of embarrassment. My new forthrightness was really beginning to get on my nerves.

"Tonight would be wonderful," said David, his eyes holding mine.

I was about to ask, "What time?" when I remembered that Jeremy Cook was coming over to pick up Pete. I had asked Ben to tell him six o'clock, but Jeremy liked to do things his way. There was no telling what time he'd actually show up.

"I'm sorry, David," I said. "I just remembered there's something I have to do tonight."

"No problem. There's always tomorrow night," he said in a way that wasn't cocky, just confident, as if he *expected* us to go out together, as if it were automatic.

I nodded in agreement. Saturday night with David Bettinger sounded just fine to me.

"Well, I guess we'd better head over to the house," he reminded me.

"Right."

David rose from his chair and held out his hand to me.

"Shall we?" he said.

Normally, I don't feel it's very professional to hold hands with my male customers, but when I started to hesitate, he laughed and said, "It's all right, Bah-ba-rah. I don't bite."

He continued to hold out his hand to me and as I gazed into his piercing brown eyes I suddenly felt very dizzy, light-headed, faint, and my hands and feet began to tingle. I grabbed onto the desk for support.

"Barbara? Are you all right?" David asked with obvious concern.

I didn't know if I was all right or not. Creepy things had been happening to me all day and I was beginning to wonder if I had a delayed-reaction hangover, the kind that gives you the shakes the *afternoon* after, instead of the morning after. Either that or I was losing my mind.

I didn't want to alarm David. That was all I needed: to land a new customer and then scare him off before I even got to show him a house. But I couldn't answer his question. I didn't have a clue what was wrong with me. Not then.

"Why don't we get you some fresh air," he suggested. Without waiting for a response, he took hold of my hand and slipped it into his. He clasped his fingers around mine and squeezed them.

A little sigh escaped from my lips as our flesh made contact.

"That's better," he said. "Much better."

I showed David the Nowak house, nude ladies and all. And then I walked him around the property, an acre and a quarter of rolling lawns, mature plantings, and towering palms, with over two hundred feet of riverfront.

"You really could do a lot with this house," I said, trying to make the sale without being pushy about it. The place was even more ghastly than I remembered—musty and claustrophobic and totally unappealing. But I needed a sale desperately, and I felt that if I could point out the ways in which David could improve the house, maybe he'd buy it. Money didn't seem to be an issue, given that he didn't blanch at the $700,000 asking price. Neither did the fact that the house had been on the market for three years and nobody else had wanted to buy it. "Just by getting rid of the arches, opening up the living room, and taking down the wall between the kitchen and dining room, you could change the whole character of the place and turn it into that dream house you were telling me about."

"Done," David said as we stood outside the front door.

"What do you mean 'done'?" I asked.

"I'm going to buy the house," he said. "You talked me into it. You're a terrific real estate agent, Barbara."

"Bullshit."

"Excuse me?"

Not again. I would have to get myself a muzzle. "No, excuse *me,* David," I said. "I had no business using language like that. It's just that I don't recall talking you into anything. I barely opened my mouth."

"Nonsense. You underestimate your selling ability. You're obviously very good at what you do. You convinced me to buy the house, Barbara. You *sold* it to me."

"Did I?" Now I was confused. It had seemed to me that David Bettinger had made up his mind to buy the house before he'd even looked at it.

"Now, you said the owner wants $700,000. How does a $675,000 offer sound?" he smiled.

"It sounds like you're a chump," I blurted out, knowing that the property was beautiful but worth much less. David Bettinger either didn't have a clue about land values or was so rich he didn't care if he overpaid for them. But when I realized what I had said, I wanted to crawl into a hole and die. How could I have said that to him? Now, he would walk away from the deal and cancel our dinner date, I was sure.

But he didn't do either. Instead, he threw his head back and laughed.

"Oh, Barbara," he said between chuckles. "You're so amusing. I love that in a woman."

Amusing? "Listen, David. I was only kidding about your being a chump," I said in a frantic effort to make amends.

"Of course you were," he smiled. "And let me tell you: You're the first real estate agent I've ever met who has a sense of humor."

"I am?"

"Yes, and I find it very sexy."

Sexy? I had called the man a chump and he found it sexy? Oh, God. He must be one of those men who likes women to humiliate them every now and then. He did come from Palm Beach, and, according to everything I'd heard about Palm Beach, there was some pretty kinky stuff going on there.

Well, I was no dominatrix. I was a small-town gal from Banyan Beach. To me, "kinky" still meant hair that needed a little conditioner. I ignored his reference to my animal magnetism and changed the subject.

"So you're sure you want to buy the house?" I asked.

"Absolutely," he said.

"My, you really make quick decisions," I said. "I'm not complaining, believe me. It's just that most people don't jump at the first house they see."

"They do if it's love at first sight," he said, then winked at me.

I laughed self-consciously.

"You said it yourself," he went on. "The property's gorgeous. All I have to do is find a good architect to redo the house."

"I can help you with that. Home Sweet Home has a list of architects and builders that we recommend very highly. But first, I've got to submit your offer to the owner."

"Tell him I'll pay cash. No contingencies. And I'll close in thirty days," said David. "That ought to get his attention."

"Yes, it certainly ought to."

This can't be happening, I thought. David Bettinger is buying the Nowak house. With cash. After seeing it once. For ten minutes.

David and I went back to my office and, for the second time that day, I tried to reach Frances Lutz. It seems she had called in sick that morning, saying she'd pulled a stomach muscle the night before. "It must have happened when she was lifting Oreos," Althea

Dicks had snickered. "Or maybe when she was turning up the volume on '$100,000 Name That Tune.' "

I was hanging up the phone when in walked Frances herself.

"I thought you weren't feeling well," I said when she waddled over to my desk, a vision in her voluminous orange caftan and wide-brimmed straw hat. She was in her sixties, but had virtually no lines on her face, which was as smooth and chubby as a baby's. She had short, close-cropped ash blonde hair and deeply set brown eyes—a pretty woman if a tad on the androgynous side. But it was her girth, not her face, that got your attention. It seemed to have a life of its own, each layer of fat shimmying and shaking like Jell-O under the brightly colored fabrics she always wore. As usual, she was out of breath and sweating profusely, a heart attack waiting to happen. But that didn't keep her from stopping at McDonald's on her way over to the office.

"I was a little under the weather earlier, but I'm just fine now," she smiled, shoving a bag of french fries at David and me. "Anybody want one? They're fresh."

"No, thanks. Frances, this is David Bettinger," I said.

"Frances Lutz," she replied, extending her hand to David after licking off a blob of "special sauce" that had dripped from her Big Mac. David rose from his chair politely.

"A pleasure to meet you," he said as they shook hands.

"Well, Barbara. You've been to the beauty salon, haven't you," she said, right in front of David, which made me extremely uncomfortable. Why not let him think I'd always been a vixen? Besides, how would I even begin to explain my transformation to him, to Frances, to anyone? I had already given each person who'd asked about my appearance a different explanation and I was at the point where I couldn't remember what I'd said to whom. More to the point, I didn't understand the transformation myself. I hadn't been to the beauty salon or to a gym or to some diet guru. I'd gotten drunk, passed out, and woken up with a new bod and a new 'do. And that's all I knew.

So I ignored Frances's question and distracted her with a subject I was sure she'd find more interesting than my appearance.

"David would like to make an offer on the Nowak house," I told her.

"A wise man. That property is going to be worth millions some-day," she said, nodding at David and then, when he looked away, winking at me. She was a good liar—a "must" for a real estate bro-ker.

"I'm counting on that," David said.

I told Frances how much he was offering for the house and mar-veled at her ability to keep a straight face.

"I'll get in touch with Mr. Nowak this evening," she said. "As soon as I have an answer, I'll call you, Barbara."

"Great," I said.

"Yes," said David. "I'm very eager to hear his response."

She smiled and dragged herself over to her own desk, only a few feet away from mine. When she got there, she maneuvered herself onto her chair, reminding me of a trained seal climbing onto a rock.

"Well, David. I guess the ball is in Mr. Nowak's court now," I said.

"So it is," he said. "Will you call me the minute you hear any-thing?"

"Of course."

"And you won't forget our dinner date? Tomorrow night?"

"Forget? Are you serious? Dentist appointments I forget. Dinner dates with Greek gods I don't forget."

David laughed. "I love your directness, Barbara Chessner. I re-ally do."

He gave me a little wave, turned, and walked out the door of Home Sweet Home, leaving me to shake my head in astonishment that he had come into my life.

It had been so unexpected, so out of the blue. If Deirdre had-n't asked me to cover for her, *she* would have been the one to take his call. *She* would have been the one to show him the Nowak house. *She* would have been the one he asked out to dinner. In-stead, *I* was there, in the right place at the right time, for a change. Maybe I was finally getting a break after the awful year I'd had.

Still, I couldn't quite believe how effortlessly I had sold David the least appealing house in Banyan Beach. There was something terribly wrong, and I must have known it. Even then. I just didn't want to face it. Who would?

CHAPTER

6

When I pulled into my driveway, Pete was sitting by the front door, his head buried in his balls.

"Sorry to intrude," I said as I got out of the car and walked toward the house.

He looked up, made eye contact with me, and bounded over to me, apparently beside himself with ecstasy at seeing me again. Either that, or he was hungry.

"Look, for the hundredth time, I'm not your owner," I said as I removed his muddy paws from the skirt of my blue dress.

Pete cocked his head and peered at me with his soulful hazel eyes. Then he opened his mouth, stuck his tongue out, and panted like a lovesick schoolboy. His breath was pretty grim, but it was a lot better than mine, which, I noticed, smelled faintly of brussels sprouts. Yet another bizarre change in my body chemistry, particularly since I hadn't eaten brussels sprouts since I was a kid whose mother believed that brussels sprouts were so foul-tasting that they had to be good for you.

"It's been swell meeting you, Pete," I said, stepping past him, "but if you think *I'm* fun, wait until you meet my brother. You and he will get along famously."

The comment provoked five straight minutes of loud barking. I held my ears and went inside the house.

Why was Pete hanging around *me* of all people? I asked myself as I waited for Jeremy Cook to come and take the damn dog away.

I'd always thought animals had sixth senses or something and could tell when you were scared of them—or found them repugnant. But not good old Pete, obviously. No, sir. He seemed oblivious to the fact that I had about as much affection for him as I did for the man who was due at my house any minute.

Still, I couldn't very well sit there and let the dog bark his heart out, could I? I opened the refrigerator, found some leftover chicken salad, and brought it outside to Pete. He sniffed the Tupperware container, shook his head, and then shoved it away with the end of his nose.

"What's the matter? Are you a vegetarian? Or do you just prefer your chicken salad with a little less mayonnaise?" I asked.

Pete responded by licking the tip of my right shoe.

Jeremy and his Chevy pickup arrived at six-thirty. Talk about a mixed blessing. As I watched my brother's best friend saunter up the driveway, hitching his blue jeans up over his beer paunch and running his hands through his shoulder-length reddish brown hair, I wondered where on earth he got his cocky attitude. He was a hick. A nobody. A crazy Irishman whose claim to fame was that he once caught a fifty-pound African Pompano and threw it back. What a guy, huh?

So he sang in a local rock 'n' roll band a couple of nights a week. Big deal. The band didn't even sing original songs. They sang oldies, for God's sake. A nostalgia act.

Jeremy's "career," if you could call it that, was chartering his fishing boat, a forty-six-foot Hatteras called the *Devil-May-Care*. (Interesting name, don't you think, given what was going on in my life? But more on that later.) He spent his days taking tourists out in the boat, trolling the waters for a big fish for them to catch, and then letting them catch it. Sort of the way a pimp does business, you know?

"Hey, if it isn't Ms. BS" was the charming way he greeted me.

"BS" was Jeremy's term of endearment for me and had been since high school. It was his idea of a double entendre: it meant BS, as in *B*enjamin's *s*ister; and BS, as in he thought I was full of it. Jeremy was a laugh riot, as you can see.

"Hello," I said politely, trying to avoid looking at his T-shirt, which pictured Cindy Crawford dressed as a mermaid, along with the caption: "Hook a tasty one. Call Cook's Charters." His rugged, sunburned face bore a thick beard of the same reddish brown hair that covered his head. His eyes were a pale green, his nose was upturned at the tip but wide at the bridge, his lips were thick and meaty, like the rest of him. He was five-foot-ten or -eleven, I guessed, but his build was stocky, burly, muscular, his forearms especially so. He was as crude as David Bettinger was smooth, as unpolished and unkempt as David was well-groomed.

"So Mitchell split, huh?" he said, reaching down to pet Pete, who was busily digging a hole in my driveway and showering my beige pumps with gravel.

"Ben told you?" I asked, feeling somewhat humiliated that this man I disliked intensely knew the details of my personal life.

"Yeah, he told me, but now that I've seen you, I would have figured it out for myself." He paused, looked me up and down, and erupted into obnoxious belly laughs.

"What, may I ask, is so funny?" I said, feeling my face flame.

"You," he said between laughs. "You women are too much. Instead of takin' some time to think about why your marriage fell apart, you run out and have one of those makeovers, so you can hook another sucker."

"What are you talking about?" I demanded.

"Ah, come on, BS. I'm talking about the blond hair, the tit job, the whole bit."

God. How was I going to explain the change in my appearance? To a chauvinistic half-wit like Jeremy Cook? I didn't know what was happening to me. All I knew was that I went to sleep looking like Barbara Chessner and woke up looking like Heather Locklear.

"I needed a change," I said casually, trying to make light of the situation. "There's nothing wrong with wanting a new look, is there?"

"There was nothin' wrong with your old look," he said.

I took a step back and blinked. "Jeremy, are you aware that you just paid me a compliment?"

He smiled and said, "Yeah, now that you mention it. But not to worry. It'll never happen again."

"Good. I wouldn't want us to start being nice to each other after all these years."

Now it was his turn to step back. He looked me over again and shook his head.

"There's somethin' else about you that's different," he said, scratching his beard. "Besides the hair and the boobs, I mean. It's your personality. You're more . . . What?"

"I don't know. You tell me."

"I can't put my finger on it exactly. All I know is that you used to be all buttoned up whenever I'd come around. Now you're giving me shit. I kinda like it."

"Really?" I said. "I would have thought you liked women to be meek, compliant, passive."

"Darlin', you don't know the first thing about what I like in a woman," he said. "And, judgin' by the way Mitchell ran off with that weathergirl, I guess you didn't know what *he* liked in a woman either."

"My marriage is none of your business."

"What marriage? Yours was a joke."

"Oh really? And what makes you an expert on the subject? You've never been married."

"How could I have been married? You were already taken," he said, his voice dripping with sarcasm.

"Look, Jeremy. Could we just stick to the reason you came over? To pick up the dog and take him to Ben's?"

"Sure, why not? When did you get a dog anyway? You don't seem like the type to have a dog."

"And what 'type' is that?"

"The type that gets all sloppy and sentimental over a pet. You're way too uptight."

"Not too uptight to tell you to go fuck yourself."

Jeremy grinned. "You really are different from the last time I saw you," he said, regarding me, his eyebrow raised. "Real different, and yet the same. Sort of."

"Are *you're* so articulate," I said. "Now could you take Pete? Please?"

At the sound of his name, Pete lifted his head, gave me one of those soulful looks, and proceeded to howl.

Jeremy tried to calm him down by stroking him under his chin, but Pete wriggled out of his grasp and began to nuzzle my leg.

"He's a great-lookin' dog," Jeremy remarked. "And he seems to like you, lord knows why."

"He is rather sweet," I conceded, patting Pete's head and then pushing him away from me. "Now take him. Please. Ben is probably waiting for you. You wouldn't want to miss a minute of that séance, would you?"

"No, ma'am. I'm a big fan of meat loaf and Janice says her grandma's recipe was the best."

I rolled my eyes.

"Here we go, boy," said Jeremy as he tried to steer Pete toward the pickup—unsuccessfully. The dog preferred to curl himself around my leg like a pretzel.

"Let's go, boy," Jeremy said again, this time grabbing Pete by the collar and practically dragging him over to the truck.

"This dog doesn't want to go anywhere," Jeremy called out as he pushed a whining Pete onto the front seat of the pickup and closed the door behind him.

Pete immediately stuck his head out the open window, desperate to take one last look. He stared at me with such intensity, such a plaintive sense of longing, that I suddenly didn't know if I was doing the right thing by sending him away.

"What?" I said as I stood in the driveway, watching him watching me. "What do you want from me, dog?"

Pete opened his mouth, as if to speak, but only a few pitiful whines came out. I felt a stab of guilt, but shrugged it off. It wasn't as if I had any responsibility for him, right? We were strangers. He had only shown up at my doorstep that morning. It wasn't as if we'd been together for years. What's more, I didn't know the first thing about dogs, except that millions of people treated them better than they did their own relatives.

"Hey, BS?" Jeremy shouted from the driver's seat of his truck.

"What is it?" I said.

"How about a 'thanks'?" he said. "I'm doin' you a favor, remember?"

"Sorry. Thanks," I said. "Really."

"No problem," he said and turned the key in the ignition.

I took one last look at Pete and started back toward the house.

"Hey, BS?" Jeremy shouted again.

I turned around. "What is it now?"

"You're lookin' real hot, but you gotta do something about your breath, ya know?"

Before I could respond, he and Pete drove away.

At about nine o'clock, Frances Lutz called to say that Mr. Nowak had accepted David's offer on the house. I was stunned. For an entire year, I couldn't put a deal together to save my life. Now, all of a sudden I had the magic touch. Sure, I wondered what was going on. But when what's going on is making you feel better, why complain?

"Oh, Frances!" I said with great enthusiasm. "Do you know what this means?"

"A commission," she giggled. "On the biggest dump in town. And the office only got the listing a couple of days ago."

"Yes, but it also means that I'm finally over my slump," I said with relief.

"I'm happy for you," she said. "For me, too. This is my third sale this week."

Frances was incredible. She'd been on a hot streak for the past year, about as long as I'd been down on my luck. Yet she was hardly the most aggressive agent in town.

Maybe we should all stay home and watch "The Price Is Right," I'd thought in recent months. Maybe Frances knows something about these game shows that the rest of us don't.

"Listen, Frances. I'd love to chat but I'm dying to call Mr. Bettinger and tell him the good news," I said.

"I don't blame you for wanting to talk to him, Barbara. He's a very nice-looking man."

A nice-looking man. Now there was an understatement. But then Frances wasn't very effusive when it came to men. She had never been married, never even had a boyfriend as far as I knew. We all wondered about her sexual preference, if she even had one.

As soon as she and I said good-bye, I found David's phone number and called him.

"David Bettinger," he answered in his deep baritone. At the sound of his voice, I felt myself forget to breathe.

"Mr. Bettinger. David," I began. "It's Barbara Chessner. From Home Sweet Home."

"Bah-bar-ah," he purred, sounding glad to hear from me. "You've spoken to Ms. Lutz?"

I was impressed that he had remembered Frances's name, as they had only met briefly. "I sure have," I said. "It looks like congratulations are in order. You've just bought yourself a home in Banyan Beach!"

"Oh, that's great news," he said. "I'm delighted. So Mr. Nowak accepted my offer."

"That's right. I'll just need a deposit from you and then we can get the contract signed and move ahead to the closing."

"Why don't we do the paperwork tomorrow night? Over dinner? How's seven o'clock? I could pick you up at your place and then we could go on to a restaurant. How does that sound?"

"It sounds perfect. I live at 666 Seacrest Way. Do you know where that is?"

"I do and I'll be there at seven. Then the next time we get together, I'll cook you dinner at my place."

So he was rich, gorgeous, and knew his way around a kitchen. The man was too good to be true.

I realized that I knew very little about David Bettinger. Only that he was single, that he used to live in Palm Beach, and that he was in the import/export business, whatever that meant. "But I wouldn't want you to go to any trouble. Not on my account."

"Come on, Barbara. You sold me my dream house," he pointed out. "Making you dinner is the least I can do to repay you."

"You're already repaying me. I'm earning a commission on the sale—my first in nearly a year. I should be making *you* dinner."

David laughed. "Ah, Barbara. Barbara. I keep forgetting how refreshingly direct you are."

Direct, my ass. I had no control over my mouth. Not anymore.

"Now. As far as tomorrow night's dinner is concerned, I'll make a reservation somewhere. Do you have a favorite restaurant?" he asked.

"Not really. Wherever you like is fine with me."

"Good. I'll see you at seven. I'm looking forward to it, Barbara. Very much."

"So am I, although I was just wondering why a hunk like you is alone on a Saturday night."

Damn. Why did every thought have to leap out of my mouth?

He laughed and then answered slowly and with feeling, "I *won't* be alone. I'll be spending the evening with a beautiful, witty, intelligent woman."

"Oh? Is someone else joining us?" I asked.

He laughed again. "You're really something," he said.

"Oh, I'm 'something' all right," I said, wondering what, exactly, I was.

C H A P T E R
7

I was just leaving the house on Saturday morning when Mitchell called.

"We have to talk," he began.

"About what?" I said. I had almost forgotten about him, but now here he was, sounding breathless, as if he had a matter of great urgency on his mind. With Mitchell, everything was urgent, right now, this minute. I could picture him pacing as he spoke to me, winding the telephone cord around his long, wormlike fingers, working his jaw muscles, blinking, twitching.

"About our living arrangement," he said. "Once we're divorced."

"What's to talk about? I'll live here, you'll live with the human weather vane."

"No, Barbara. Chrissy's condo won't work for the two of us. It's much too small. We've discussed the situation and we've decided we want the house."

"What house?"

"Seacrest Way. Chrissy's always dreamed of being on the water."

"Then get her a rubber raft and tell her to go float in her pool." So the bitch wanted to live in my house. Fat chance.

"On the *ocean*, Barbara. She wants to live on the ocean."

"So buy her another house. My office has plenty of oceanfront listings."

He heaved a big sigh and was clearly exasperated with me. I was delighted. I had finally talked back to him. I had finally gotten over my fear of making him angry. My newfound bluntness may have been a source of embarrassment when it came to people I cared about, but it was a real plus when it came to Mitchell.

"We want Seacrest Way, Barbara," he said. "Chrissy's seen the house and thinks it would be—"

"When did she see the house?" I interrupted.

"When?"

"Yeah, *when?*"

"I don't remember."

"Try."

Silence. Then another big sigh. "You don't sound like yourself this morning, Barbara. Have you been drinking?"

"No, Mitchell."

"Then what's with you? Your attitude has changed. You sound . . . I don't know . . . different."

You should only know *how* different, I thought as I glanced over at the mirror on the bedroom wall. Each time I caught a glimpse of myself, I was even more stunned by the changes in my appearance. Oh, I was still me. Same nose, mouth, eyes, ears. Same crooked right front tooth. Same birthmark on my left buttock. And yet, ever since the morning after Mitchell left, I looked as if an army of makeover artists had descended on me—makeover artists whose idea of perfection was Ivana Trump. Had the new shampoo I'd been using really turned my hair blond? Of course not. Had all the worrying I'd been doing really caused me to lose weight? No way. And even if it had, how could I explain my newly perky breasts? There was no rational, logical explanation for any of it. None. Was it time to consider irrational, illogical explanations? Was witchcraft, magic, or an ancient spell behind the change in me? Or was demonic possession the reason for the fact that I now looked like a Barbie doll?

"Let's get back to my question," I said. "When did Chrissy see the house?"

"I brought her over once."

"Be specific. When?"

"You really are a glutton for punishment. I brought her over when you were away at that realtors' convention."

I let his words sink in, and, as they did, my heart began to pound. I was so angry I could hardly breathe.

"I was gone for an entire weekend," I managed. "Did she sleep here the whole time?"

"Yes."

"In my bed?"

"Yes."

"You two made love in the house? My house?" Inhale, exhale. Inhale, exhale. I was trying not to hyperventilate.

"Barbara, you seem to have forgotten that Seacrest Way is in my name. *I* bought the house, remember? It's mine. Now, as far as your moving out after the divorce, I'm perfectly willing to play fair when it comes to a nice settlement for you. You'll want to buy a new place. Something small, less grand. When we get to that point, I'll—"

"Mitchell," I cut him off. "There's something I've always wanted to tell you but never had the nerve."

"What is it?"

"Remember when you made that speech in front of five hundred members of the Banyan Beach Business Association?"

"Yeah."

"Your fly was open."

"What?"

"You heard me. Good-bye."

My friend, Suzanne, was in the office when I got there at about ten-thirty.

"Don't tell me you didn't have liposuction and breast augmentation," she said, and wagged her finger at me.

"I already told you, Suzanne. I didn't have any kind of plastic surgery. Honest."

"Deny deny deny. I don't know why you're in such denial. Why not just admit that you've had a little work done? There's no shame in it. And as far as getting rid of the gray hair, a lot of women approaching menopause feel the need to—"

"Suzanne, I know this is going to sound crazy, but the change in my appearance happened overnight. I went to sleep looking like my old ratty self and woke up looking like this."

"Oh, I get it. You're the first person ever to lose twenty pounds because you got a decent night's sleep. Think what this will do for mattress sales."

"Look. I don't expect you to believe it. *I* don't believe it."

"Really, Barbara. I thought we were friends."

"We are friends, Suzanne."

"Then take my advice: find a good shrink. I'm no expert, but it sounds to me like part of you wants to be blond and sexy and glamorous and the other part feels guilty about it."

"No. Part of me wants to be blond and sexy and glamorous and the other part wants to change the subject. Have you heard the good news?"

"You mean about the Nowak house?"

I smiled. "I sold it, Suzanne. I actually sold that sucker."

"I'm happy for you," she said, warming up a little. "It's weird though. The way you and I were just talking about the house and then a few hours later you ended up selling it."

"That's what I've been trying to tell you," I said. "Everything that's happened to me in the last couple of days has been weird. And here's something else: David Bettinger, the guy who's buying the house, is single, adorable and rich—and he seems to like me. He's taking me to dinner tonight."

"It should only happen to me," Suzanne sighed.

"Hey, maybe he's got a brother," I suggested.

"They always have a brother and the brother is always bald."

I laughed. "I'll ask him when I see him," I said as I started to move toward my desk.

"Barbara, wait," said Suzanne.

"Yes?"

"I hope you don't mind me saying this, but if I were you I'd buy some breath mints before I went out tonight."

I winced. "Is my breath really that bad?" I asked, remembering Jeremy Cook's wisecrack about it.

"Not if you're a fan of brussels sprouts," she said. "Unfortunately, not many people are."

I nodded. "I'll take care of it. Thanks."

It was amazing. I'd only been in the office for twenty minutes when a customer I'd sold a house to four years before called to say he wanted to sell that house and buy another one—a larger, more expensive one. Before the day was over, I had not only listed his house (for $499,999) but showed him three others, one of which he fell madly in love with and offered to buy (for $750,000). I was hot, red-hot, and I'd be lying if I said I wasn't happy about it. I was feeling so good about myself that I went straight to Bloomingdale's after work and bought a new dress—a very short dress in a size eight that showed off my snappy new figure. As I modeled it in the mirror in one of Bloomie's dressing rooms and saw how sensational I looked, I started to fantasize about my date with David. And then a thought struck me: how would I know if David liked me for *me,* now that I was such a knockout? I mean, would he have asked the old, dumpy me out to dinner? Probably not. Would he have found the old, dumpy me so amusing? Definitely not. Would he have let the old, dumpy me sell him the ugliest house in town? Not a chance.

By the same token, would I be jumping for joy at David's dinner invitation if *he* weren't so gorgeous?

Yes, I told myself. Yes. I was not a superficial person. I did not judge people on the basis of their looks. I was attracted to more than David's handsome features and expensive clothes. It was his manner that intrigued me. His velvet voice. His smoothness. His . . . what? His hypnotic quality. Just speaking to him on the phone put me in a kind of trance. It was eerie and wonderful at the same time.

I paid for the dress and left the store. As I drove home, I considered Suzanne's advice. Maybe I *should* see a shrink, I mused. What if I did have plastic surgery and was so conflicted about it that I blocked it out? Maybe I did feel guilty about being blonder, thinner, sexier. Maybe I was as uptight and repressed as Mitchell always accused me of being. But if I'd had plastic surgery, where did I get the money? Where were the doctor bills? Where were my scars?

David showed up at five minutes of seven. He was a vision in his crisp white cotton slacks and navy blue polo shirt, the arms of his white crewneck sweater draped casually over his broad shoulders. Blond bangs fell across his forehead and his brown eyes sparkled as he smiled at me. I found him utterly irresistible in the true sense of the word; it was hard to look away from him even for a second. I invited him in for a drink, but he declined, saying he was hungry and preferred to go straight to the restaurant.

"Where are we going?" I asked as we pulled away from the house in his gleaming black Mercedes.

"There's a restaurant I've been hearing a lot about since I moved to town," he said. "I thought I'd like to try it."

"Which one?"

"Risotto!, the Italian place on Island Road."

Well, what was I supposed to do, refuse? Jump out of the car? Make a big deal out of it? Not on my first date with David. Not when he had been nice enough to invite me out.

"Is something wrong?" he asked, looking over at me.

"Not really. It's just that my husband—my soon-to-be ex-husband—owns Risotto! and spends a lot of time there," I said.

"Oh. Forgive me. We should go somewhere else. I wouldn't want you to feel uncomfortable if you ran into him."

"I won't feel uncomfortable. As a matter of fact, I'm looking forward to going there and seeing Mitchell. He doesn't scare me anymore."

David raised an eyebrow. "He scared you? In what way?"

"He intimidated me. He has this disapproving glare that used to paralyze me. I could barely talk when I was around him."

He smiled. "I find that very hard to believe, Barbara. You seem so . . . so self-possessed."

Oh, I was possessed, all right. I just didn't know it at the time.

"I've gone through some changes lately," I explained. "I'm not the person I was."

He smiled again, a bit wistfully, I noticed. "Neither am I," he said. "Neither am I."

I was about to ask what he meant when he turned on the radio to the local classical station and filled the car with music.

"Ah, Mozart's Piano Sonata Number 14 in C Minor," he said.

I nodded, knowing nothing about classical music. Rock 'n' roll was more my speed.

David began to hum along with the music, his voice a rich, deep baritone.

"You have a beautiful voice," I remarked. "Did you ever sing professionally?"

"No," he said with regret. "It was only recently that I realized I even had a voice."

"That's funny. It was only recently that *I* realized I had a voice," I said.

"Well, then," he said, "that's another thing we have in common."

"What was the first thing?" I asked.

"Don't you know?" he asked, his brown eyes full of mystery.

I shook my head.

"I'll let you guess," he said, and pulled the Mercedes into Risotto!'s parking lot.

I didn't see Mitchell when we entered the restaurant, but then the place was in absolute chaos. The blue-hairs in walkers who had shown up at five-thirty for the Early Bird Special were taking their time getting out the door, while the pumped-up, coked-out gel/mousse crowd were elbowing each other to get in. And then there was the frenetic activity on the part of the waiters and waitresses, who were dressed in black to match the furniture, which, in turn, matched the floor. The walls and ceilings were white, and the black and whiteness of the place gave it a cold, sterile, totally alienating feel. "We're trying to achieve a look that says, 'This restaurant cops an attitude,' " Mitchell told me when Risotto! was still in the planning stage. "Why would anyone spend money to eat in a restaurant with an attitude?" I asked at the time. Mitchell shook his head as if I were the most hopelessly dense person on the planet. "Because if people wanted a *homey* atmosphere, they'd stay *home,*" he said.

As I looked around the restaurant, it struck me that I didn't recognize a single person. Banyan Beach had once been such a small town that you couldn't go anywhere without running into someone you knew. But there I was, gazing out over a sea of strangers—people who moved to Florida so they wouldn't have to pay income taxes, people who couldn't pronounce "conch" but didn't have any trouble with "tiramisu," people who didn't go anywhere without their cellphones. It was odd, really, the way the change had come about almost overnight, almost without my realizing it, almost without my caring about it. I had been so focused on my own life, so caught up in my relentless unhappiness, that I hadn't been paying attention to anything else.

"I believe you have a seven o'clock reservation for Bettinger?" David said to the maître d' when we had finally made our way to the head of the line.

The twenty-something maître d', who sported the obligatory earring and ponytail, looked up at David and nodded. "Mr. Bettinger," he said without smiling, holding fast to the restaurant's no-smile rule. "Your table isn't ready. Why don't you have a drink at the bar and we'll call you when—"

"I reserved a table for seven o'clock," David interrupted, politely but firmly. "It's just after seven. I expect to be seated. Now."

I looked at David with admiration. So did the maître d', who studied his reservation book yet again and this time came up with a table.

He led us through the maze of diners toward the rear of the restaurant, to one of six banquettes that lined the back wall.

"Your waitress will be with you shortly," he said when we were seated. Then he hurried off, leaving us in a cloud of Polo Sport.

"Mr. Personality," I said, gesturing toward him. "He must be new. I don't remember seeing him before."

"He reminds me of Palm Beach," said David. "I think the maître d's there must go to a special school where they're taught to make people feel insignificant."

"Maybe so, but you showed this one who was boss," I said. "I've always had trouble being direct like that. Until recently, that is."

"I know what you mean," said David. "I wasn't always so sure of myself."

"You weren't? I can't believe that."

"It's true. You're not the only one who's done some changing, Barbara. My move to Banyan Beach is just part of my transformation."

I regarded him. "What were you like before this 'transformation'?" I asked.

He grinned. "I'll tell you after we've gotten to know each other a little better."

I was about to respond when a young woman with very short,

spiky red hair appeared, introduced herself as Nikki, and tossed some menus onto the table.

"Do you want to hear the specials or not?" she asked with the warmth of granite.

"Not if you'd rather not share them with us," David replied, winking at me.

"Whatever," she shrugged.

"Why don't you take our drink order first," he suggested.

"Okay," she said. "Whaddyawant?"

David ordered a Dewars on the rocks, I asked for a club soda with lime. Ever since my run-in with the thunderstorm two nights before, I'd been laying off the booze. I had enough going on inside my body. I didn't need a hangover to complicate matters.

"Tell me," David asked. "Do you see your husband anywhere?"

"Not yet," I said. "But the night's still young."

"And you're sure you're all right about seeing him?"

"I'm sure. Really."

We had our drinks, discussed David's purchase of the Nowak house, and went through the fine points of the contract, which he signed. Then we moved on to more personal subjects. We talked about our families, our childhoods, our work. David's business, he explained, took him to Europe, the Orient, and South America. He related fascinating anecdotes about the cities he'd been to, the hotels he'd stayed in, the people he'd met. As I had never been out of the state of Florida, except to New Jersey, where I had relatives, and to St. Barts, where Mitchell had taken me on our honeymoon because a CPA friend of his had told him it was chic, I felt incredibly provincial. David was obviously a sophisticated world traveler, a man who had been there, seen it, done it, while I was a small-town nobody, a woman whose idea of adventure was trying a new brand of paper towel. I wondered what he could possibly see in me. He was wonderful company—interesting, intelligent, confident, yet with a surprising, self-deprecating humor. And then, of course, there was his face, which was so handsome I couldn't help studying it. There were moments when he seemed *too* perfect—unreal, fabricated. And then there were moments when he was so real I wanted to leap across the table and wrap my legs around him.

Fortunately, I didn't act on my desire. I sublimated it by stuffing myself. Bread sticks, penne puttanesca appetizer, Caesar salad. Never mind my brussels sprout breath, which David didn't seem to notice. By the time the main course arrived, I was expelling enough garlic to offend everyone in the place.

Nikki delivered our entrees with the lack of enthusiasm we had come to expect from her. David had ordered one of the specials, which was risotto with several types of mushrooms I'd never heard of. I had opted for the oak-grilled tuna, in spite of the fact that it made me think of Jeremy, who had gotten his picture in the paper the week before for winning some dumb tuna fishing tournament.

We were sampling our food when I spotted Mitchell. He was making his rounds, just like a doctor, only without the stethoscope; what was hanging from Mitchell's neck was a cross. A large, gold cross. Mitchell was Jewish, but he had seen the owner of several very successful Manhattan restaurants wear a cross and figured there must be something to it.

There he was, going from table to table, bowing and scraping and saying things like "Is everything all right?" and "You absolutely must try the calamari." I did not see Chrissy and guessed she was at the condo, leafing through back issues of various home decorating magazines in anticipation of taking possession of my house and putting her own personal stamp on the place.

"There's my husband," I whispered to David, then pointed at Mitchell.

David turned around to look. "I think he's walking this way," he warned.

My heart began to beat faster as Mitchell moved in the direction of our table. He looked as intense as always—dark, thin, wiry, hyper, a mass of nervous energy. I had no idea how he'd react to seeing me with David—or to seeing the new me, for that matter.

As he came closer, I held my breath and braced myself for a confrontation. Then, suddenly, a blonde woman intercepted him, slid her arm around his skinny waist, and began to pull him in the opposite direction.

"Chrissy," I muttered, recognizing her from the Evening News. She was even more dreadful-looking in person. Big, poofy platinum hair, buck teeth, tacky outfit, the works.

"Someone you know?" David asked, watching me watch Chrissy.

"You must not be a fan of Channel Five," I said. "That's Chrissy Hemplewhite. She does the weather on the Six O'Clock News. She's also my husband's new love."

I hated Mitchell and didn't want him back under any circumstances, but the words stung nevertheless. So did seeing Chrissy with her arms draped all over Mitchell. I stared at the two of them as they flaunted their adulterous behavior in front of everyone in the place, totally unaware that I was sitting a few feet away from them. Not that they'd care. I was the old shoe, the ball and chain, the one who got dumped, discarded.

"Let's leave," David said after my face must have revealed my feelings. "We'll have dessert somewhere else."

"No," I said. "I'm not going to let them chase us out of here. No way."

I narrowed my eyes and continued to watch Mitchell and Chrissy as they strolled from table to table, shmoozing, joking, showing off. It was nauseating.

"I hope the two of them burn in hell," I said suddenly, then flushed with embarrassment.

I was about to apologize for harboring such an unkind thought against my husband and his mistress when Nikki, our warm and fuzzy waitress, whizzed by Mitchell and Chrissy carrying a tray of six cappuccinos. In what seemed like a scene shot in slow motion, she appeared to lose her balance—and her control of the tray— and before you could say "burn in hell," the boiling hot contents of all six glasses rained down upon the lovebirds! Chrissy screamed as the coffee tore into the skin on her back. (She was wearing a skimpy little halter top, poor thing, which goes to prove that when you dress like a slut, you take your chances.) Mitchell, who had been in the midst of an obsequious bow when catastrophe struck, was hit with the hot stuff on the back of the head—right smack on his bald spot. So much for the Rogaine.

There was a big commotion, of course, as everyone hovered around Mitchell and Chrissy, offering their opinion about how you should treat a burn.

"Put butter on it!" a man shouted.

"No, ice!" another man volunteered.

At one point, Mitchell actually yelled, "Is there a doctor in the house?"

The whole thing reminded me of the pandemonium that breaks out when somebody starts to choke and the people he's with don't know how to do the Heimlich maneuver.

Eventually, Mitchell took Chrissy out of the restaurant, to the hospital, I assume. The rest of us went back to our meal.

"Are you all right?" David asked when the tumult had died down.

I didn't know how to answer. I was all right, except that I was convinced that *I* had caused Mitchell and Chrissy's accident. I had said that I wanted them to burn, and then they did. I'd expressed the wish—out loud—and then it had come true.

For the first time, it dawned on me that I might have some sort of weird new power. Over myself. Over others. Over events.

And yet, in other ways, I felt utterly powerless. I seemed to be able to lose weight without dieting, turn my gray hair blond without coloring it, speak my mind instead of holding back, but I couldn't really control any of it, couldn't make it stop. I seemed to be able to cause our waitress to drop a tray of hot coffee on my miserable husband and his girlfriend, but I had no idea how I did it or how not to do it again.

"Maybe I should have a drink after all," I said as my hands began to tremble. "A real drink. I'm feeling a little shaky."

"Yes, after-dinner drinks," David said. "But not here."

"No, not here," I agreed. "I don't want anything else to spoil our evening."

David nodded and signaled for the check. When it arrived, he paid quickly and guided me out of the restaurant. As we waited for the valet parking attendant to bring the Mercedes around, he took my hand and squeezed it.

I suddenly felt light-headed, dizzy, tingly, the same odd sensation I'd experienced the last time David had touched me. That time, I'd chalked the feeling up to a hangover. This time, I attributed it to the overwhelming attraction I felt for him. Even the slightest physical contact sent electrical currents through my body. Sure, it had been a long time since I'd been with a man, but I was drawn to David in a way I'd never been drawn to Mitchell. Mitchell held about as much mystery and passion for me as doing the laundry. David inspired thoughts of *taking off* my clothes, not *washing* them.

He wrapped his arm around my waist and steadied me, then drew his face very close to mine.

"Now," he whispered. "We have a decision to make."

"A decision?" I said, feeling myself flush from his nearness. As he spoke, his lips were practically brushing my cheek.

"Yes," he murmured. "Your place or mine?"

I swallowed hard. The question was provocative, or so it seemed to me in my feverish state. I had only spent a couple of hours with David, hardly knew the man. He could have been a serial killer on the prowl for his latest victim—the type that went after real estate agents instead of prostitutes or strippers. And yet I was ridiculously trusting of him, enthralled by him, captivated by the penetrating look in his brown eyes, and didn't even think about the fact that we were complete strangers. Normally so cautious, so timid, so up-tight when it came to giving in to my feelings, I was, at that moment, willing to go anywhere with David Bettinger.

"Should we have that after-dinner drink at your house or mine?" he repeated.

"Mine," I heard myself say. "Mine."

He smiled and placed his hand on the small of my back.

"I'm looking forward to being alone with you, Barbara," he said. "All alone."

C H A P T E R

When we pulled into my driveway, David and I discovered that we would not be alone after all. Pete was back.

The minute we got out of the car, he came bounding over to us, barking and jumping and wagging his tail. He was not a pleasant surprise, let me tell you.

"What are you doing here?" I said as he slobbered all over my nice new dress. "You're supposed to be at Benjamin's."

"Is he yours?" David asked warily. He seemed even less enthusiastic about dogs than I was.

"No. Yes. Well, what I mean is, he used to be mine, briefly, but I gave him to my brother," I said.

"Do you think he ran away?" David asked, reaching out to pet Pete. In response, Pete turned nasty, baring his teeth and growling at David.

"Hey! Cut that out!" I yelled at Pete.

"He doesn't seem to like me," said David.

"It's probably your cologne," I suggested. "They always say that dogs either like your scent or they don't."

"Clearly, he doesn't like mine," said David as Pete continued to growl at him.

I grabbed the dog by the collar and pulled him away from David.

"I can't figure out what he's doing here," I said. "My brother lives a good fifteen minutes away. Pete couldn't have found his way back. He just couldn't have." I paused. "Maybe Ben changed his mind about taking him and dumped him on my doorstep."

"Would your brother do that without telling you?" David asked.

"Probably not," I said. "Unless there was a good reason."

"Look, why don't we leave the dog here and go inside and have that after-dinner drink," said David. "You can decide what to do about him tomorrow."

David attempted to reach for my hand but Pete growled at him so ferociously that it took both of us by surprise. David quickly retreated.

"Why don't you go first," I said, handing David the key to my front door. "I'll hold on to him until you're inside. Then I'll follow you in. The bar's to the right, just before the dining room. Pour yourself a drink, make yourself comfortable, and I'll be there in a flash."

"You're sure? It's not very chivalrous of me to duck inside while you're out here."

"I'll forgive you. I can see that you're not a dog person. Now go ahead," I urged.

He nodded, opened the door to the house, and let himself in. When he was safely inside, I bent down, took Pete's face in my hand, and looked him straight in the eye.

"You're a nuisance, do you know that?" I said. "And your timing stinks."

He replied by licking my nose.

I reached inside my purse for a tissue and wiped the saliva off. "I have a very special evening planned," I went on. "A quiet, romantic evening with David. Just the two of us. No dogs allowed. Get it?"

Pete began to whine.

"Okay. I'll put it another way," I said to him. "The day before yesterday my husband tells me he's leaving me. Then, out of the blue, I meet this incredible guy and he seems to like me. Now he's waiting for me to come inside so we can get to know each other better. Let me have a little fun, huh? Be a good doggie and go on home, wherever that is."

The request provoked more whining.

"Fine. Be that way," I snapped, then let go of Pete and turned to go into the house.

I was about to open the front door when a car tore into the driveway and came to a screeching halt, sending gravel flying in all directions. It was Jeremy in his battered old pickup truck. Gregg Allman's "I'm No Angel" was blaring on the radio and Jeremy was wailing right along with the music, sounding like a cat in heat. So much for my quiet, romantic evening.

"You could have called first," I said when he finally climbed out of the truck. He was wearing his usual blue jeans and T-shirt and carrying an opened can of Bud Lite. He took a long swallow of beer, some of which leaked out the side of his mouth and dribbled down his neck, and then he belched. Every woman's fantasy, right?

"I did call, BS, but you weren't home," he said as he walked over to David's Mercedes and ran his hand over the shiny black hood. Then he peered into the car and checked out its creamy "palomino" leather interior. Pete, who had ceased barking the minute Jeremy appeared, wriggled out of my grasp and trotted over to him. Jeremy bent down to pet Pete and the two of them had a little love fest. I found it odd that the dog preferred a beer-guzzling slug like Jeremy to a suave and sophisticated hunk like David, but then what did I know about dogs' tastes?

"I'm home now," I said with my hands on my hips.

Jeremy looked up at me and grinned. "So I see," he said and moved his eyes up and down my body, not unlike the way he had inspected the Mercedes. I felt naked in front of him, the way you feel with someone you've known since childhood, someone who remembers you when you weren't blond and thin and glamorous, someone who suspects that you're a fraud.

Neither of us spoke for several seconds. Jeremy stared at me, while I stared at the ground. Then he took another sip of beer and belched again. He did not ask to be excused.

"Nice wheels," he said, returning his attention to the Mercedes. "Yours?"

"Hardly."

"No? I thought maybe they went with the new hair and boobs."

"Then you thought wrong. They belong to a friend."

"A male friend?"

"Yes."

"Anyone I know?"

"I doubt it."

"What's his name?"

"Trust me, you don't know him, Jeremy. He's new in town. I met him through business."

"Oh, so you're his realtor?"

"You guessed it."

He digested the information, then said, "If you're his realtor, what's he doin' at your house at ten o'clock on a Saturday night?"

"What are *you* doing at my house at ten o'clock on a Saturday night?"

"I came lookin' for the dog. No other reason. I figured that since I was the one who took him to Ben's yesterday, I ought to be the one to bring him back there."

"So he ran away?"

"Yup. He took off late this afternoon when Ben let him out to piss."

"But how did he get here? And why did he come here? Ben and I don't exactly live around the corner from each other."

"Pete's a boy dog, BS. Maybe he's got a thing for you and couldn't stay away."

"Sure, just like *you* can't stay away. Come to think of it, isn't Saturday night your big night? With your band, I mean?" Jeremy's band, The Fire Ants, usually played at one of the local clubs on Saturday nights.

"We kind of take it easy in the summer. Only one or two gigs a month."

"Your fans must be bereft."

He smiled. "I think I liked you better when you weren't such a wiseass."

"I thought you didn't like me—period."

"Let's get back to Pete. Do you want me to take him over to Ben's or not?"

I considered the question. On one hand, I wanted Jeremy to take Pete back to Ben's in the worst way. The very thought of Pete drooling and shedding and hurling hair balls all over my nice clean house made me sick. On the other hand, I had this uneasy feeling that Pete was a canine version of a boomerang; that no matter how I tried to get rid of him, he'd keep coming back; that I should just let him stay with me, where I could keep an eye on him and figure out what the hell was going on.

"Yes? No?" Jeremy prompted.

I shrugged. "I don't know what to do," I confessed. "The thing is, Pete isn't really my dog."

"I thought you said—-"

"His tag says he's my dog, but he isn't. There's been some kind of mistake. A clerical error or whatever."

"Then why did he run twenty miles to come back here?" asked Jeremy.

"I have no idea," I said. "All I know is that he keeps showing up at my door, like a Jehovah's Witness."

Jeremy laughed. "Sounds like you're stuck with him. For now, anyway."

"But I don't know the first thing about taking care of a dog. I can't even take care of my plants. They all have spider mites."

"Ask your new boyfriend to help you."

"He's not my—"

I stopped in mid-sentence when I saw that David had emerged from the house.

"I thought you'd forgotten about me," he said, nodding at Jeremy and keeping his distance from Pete, who started growling the minute he saw David.

"Not at all," I said. "I just had an unexpected visitor. David, this is Jeremy Cook, a friend of my brother's."

"Pleasure to meet you," said David.

"Same," said Jeremy.

They shook hands in that overly enthusiastic way men have when they want to appear as if they're not sizing each other up, as if they don't view the other guy as competition.

"Jeremy says the dog ran away from my brother's," I explained to David. "He came over to see if Pete had turned up here by any chance."

"So he did run away," David said. "What are you going to do now?"

72 / Jane Heller

"I guess I'll keep him for tonight," I said. "I'll figure out what to do with him in the morning."

"Sounds sensible," said David, who turned to Jeremy and said, "It was very thoughtful of you to try to help Barbara."

"Oh, I'm a very thoughtful kind of guy, right, BS?" he smirked.

"Very. But I wouldn't want to take up any more of your time, Jeremy," I said. "You're probably expected somewhere, aren't you?"

I was dying for him to leave so that David and I could resume our date. I had visions of us sitting close together on the sofa, sipping our nightcaps, exchanging endearing little anecdotes about our pasts, sharing confidences. Then David would draw his face next to mine and murmur something flattering, and I would smile and say something flattering back. He would be so powerless to resist his attraction to me that he would lower his mouth onto mine and kiss me, tenderly at first, then with greater urgency. He would prove to be an exquisitely gifted lover, igniting my long-dormant capacity for real passion. I would become a tigress, inspiring him to new heights of ecstasy. We would—

"No, I'm not expected anywhere," Jeremy said casually, interrupting my descent into pornography. "I'm free as the wind tonight."

Speaking of wind, Pete picked that very moment to pass some. Talk about timing. There was an uncomfortable silence as the three of us stood there looking at the sky.

"David and I were about to have an after-dinner drink," I finally explained to Jeremy.

"Sounds good to me," said Jeremy, clearly enjoying his irritating little game. "Got any of that Randy Martin stuff around the house, BS?"

I couldn't believe it. The man refused to take the hint.

"If you mean *Remy* Martin, no, I don't have any," I said angrily.

"Then I'll settle for another Bud Lite," Jeremy said, draining the can he'd been holding and then belching once again. Louder this time.

"I don't have any Bud Lite either," I said. "Actually, Jeremy, David and I have a lot to talk about. He's just bought a house on Pelican Circle and he wants to—"

"Pelican Circle? No shit," said Jeremy. "One of the guys I fish with lives on that street."

"Really? What's his name?" David asked with genuine interest.

"Sam Akins. He lives at 44 Pelican Circle," said Jeremy. "He's a pistol. Salt of the earth. You'll like him."

"Good. He'll be my next-door neighbor," said David. "I'm buying number 46."

"Hey, that's great. I'll have to get you guys together," said Jeremy.

He brushed by me and moved next to David, who seemed not to mind his presence nearly as much as I did.

"I'm looking forward to meeting people in Banyan Beach," David said. "I don't have many friends here yet."

"No problem. I've lived here all my life. Know just about everybody in town. Right, BS?"

I nodded dully and watched the two men bond with each other. It was maddening.

"I can introduce you to plenty of people," Jeremy said to my date, as they began to chat like long-lost fraternity brothers.

Before I knew it they had gone inside the house—my house—without me. I stood there with Pete, feeling like *I* was the uninvited guest. Some romantic evening. And all because of Jeremy, who deliberately set out to ruin my good time. Why, I couldn't fathom.

"I hope he gets a flat tire," I muttered as I glanced over at his pickup and stuck my tongue out.

No sooner did the words pass my lips than the left rear tire on the pickup suddenly deflated—right in front of my eyes! One minute, it was full of air. The next minute, it was totally flat!

My God, I thought. *I* did it! I wanted the tire to go flat and then it did! Just like I had wanted Mitchell and Chrissy to burn and they had! I had caused both events, I was sure of it. I had had negative thoughts and seconds later they had come true.

I felt an ice-cold shiver pass through my body. Pete seemed to sense my terror, judging by the almost-compassionate look in his hazel eyes.

"What is going on with me?" I said out loud.

I'd read about the power of positive thinking, but not about the power of *negative* thinking—except in Stephen King's books. Was that it? Had I turned into some ghoulish character from a horror novel?

Of course not, I told myself. No matter how dramatically my physical appearance had changed since the morning after Mitchell left, I was still Barbara Chessner, your average, garden-variety person. I was probably suffering from some rare disease that had yet to be written up in the *New England Journal of Medicine*—a disease where the patient *thinks* he's causing events to happen but doesn't. Either that or I was having a good old-fashioned nervous breakdown.

I began to tremble as I stared at Jeremy's flat tire, wondering if whatever was wrong with me was fatal. Something was going on inside me, all right. Something very wrong. Something I couldn't control. Something that, whether I liked it or not, could put me and everyone around me at risk.

"I don't know, Pete," I said, as I shivered again. "If I were you, I'd get the hell out of here."

C H A P T E R

9

I spent most of Sunday trying to learn how to take care of a dog, seeing as pets don't come with an operating manual.

First, there was the matter of getting to know Pete's palate. Silly me, I had assumed that all dog food was created equal; that you simply stuck a bowl of mystery meat in front of an animal and he'd eat it. So I went to the supermarket and bought several cans of Alpo. Pete, it turned out, didn't like Alpo. I went back to the supermarket and bought a bag of Gravy Train. Pete didn't care for Gravy Train either. I went back to the supermarket a third time and bought some Kibbles and Bits. Pete wouldn't touch the stuff. Utterly frustrated, I opened the freezer, nuked a Lean Cuisine and said, "Here. Try this."

Pete ate every morsel of the frozen dinner. I was relieved that I had finally found something that pleased him.

The second thing I learned about Pete was that he was a klutz. I mean, the dog was incapable of watching where he was going, particularly when it came to his tail. After a mere twenty minutes in the house, he had knocked over knicknacks, toppled lamps, sent plants to the ground, you name it. He also had a habit of running into me. I'd be standing in the kitchen, minding my own business, when he'd come barreling into me, like a football player making a tackle. I sensed that he didn't mean me any harm; he was just exuberant in a way that I had always longed to be.

Most bizarre was his clingyness. He seemed hopelessly attached to me, as if I'd been his master for years instead of thirty-six hours, and would follow me from room to room, sniffing and scratching and begging to be played with. If I went to the bathroom, he'd sit there guarding the door, and when I'd come out, he'd rush at me, curling himself around my legs and nuzzling me. It was oddly flattering. I had never inspired that sort of devotion in anyone and wondered what I had done to deserve Pete's.

On Monday morning I made a doctor's appointment. No, not for Pete, for me. I was hoping against all hope that my "condition" (what else could I call it?) was physical, not metaphysical. So I called the office of Dr. Henry Messersmith, my internist, and asked if I could see him right away.

"What seems to be the problem?" asked his nurse.

"I might have a brain tumor," I said.

Well, what was I supposed to say? I'd heard that people with brain tumors go through personality changes. Maybe they also take on strange powers, I thought. Like being able to make a tire go flat just by wishing it.

The brain tumor thing got the nurse's attention because she didn't even put me on hold the way she always did; she said I could come and see the normally booked-solid Dr. Messersmith that very afternoon.

But first I had to sit through Charlotte Reed's ritual Monday morning meeting at Home Sweet Home. Yes, once a week, from nine until ten, Charlotte held us all hostage in her corner office, which was decorated in early shabby gentility and reeked of her scent: stale Nina Ricci. I know. Nobody wore Nina Ricci anymore. But, as I already told you, Charlotte was an anachronism. If something was over, she was just discovering it. She still called suitcases "valises" and stereos "victrolas" and thought a microwave was a type of home permanent.

On that particular Monday morning, we were all gathered in her office, sipping tea and filling each other in on new listings, sales, or closings. In addition to Charlotte, there was Althea Dicks, the sourpuss; Deirdre Wyatt, the beauty queen; Frances Lutz, the ranch specialist; and my best friend, Suzanne Munson, the menopause expert. There was also June Bellsey, a part-time agent at Home

Sweet Home. June's husband, Lloyd, was a famous defense attorney who regularly and with obvious zeal represented celebrities—movie stars, sports legends, business tycoons, etc.—accused of heinous crimes, usually murder. What's more, Lloyd Bellsey often appeared on network news broadcasts as a "legal analyst," and had even written a best-seller in which he recounted his most celebrated cases. Needless to say, June didn't *have* to work, as she never ceased to remind us. She could have stayed home eating bonbons all day long. But no. June wanted to be independent, have her own career, earn her own money. I don't think she sold a single house in the nine years that I'd worked at Home Sweet Home, but she never missed one of Charlotte's Monday morning meetings. They were her chance to drop the name of some celebrity she'd just met through her husband. I always pretended to be impressed. And why not? The only celebrity *my* husband knew was Chrissy Hemplewhite.

Before the meeting began, everybody was asking me about the dramatic change in my appearance—what I'd done to my hair, how I'd managed to lose weight so quickly, whether I was taking diet pills. Only Charlotte didn't seem to notice that I looked different. When she saw me she smiled and told me to give her regards to my parents. My parents had been dead for seven years.

"Now, ladies," she said, calling the meeting to order. "Who has something she'd like to discuss?"

June raised her hand.

"Yes, June?" said Charlotte.

"Lloyd told me that Sylvester Stallone is thinking of selling his place in Miami and buying here in Banyan," June announced.

"Sylvia who, dear?" Charlotte asked.

"No, not Sylvia. *Sylvester,*" June said impatiently. "Sylvester Stallone. You know. *Rocky.*"

Charlotte shook her head. "I believe that the fellow you're talking about passed away some time ago," she said. "Pity, too. After all those lovely movies he made with Doris Day."

"No, that was Rock *Hudson,*" June corrected Charlotte. "The actor I'm talking about played Rocky, the boxer who . . . Oh, never mind."

"My God, if Stallone moves here, it'll be the end of life as we know it," Althea scowled.

"Come on," said Deirdre. "I think he's adorable. A real cutie-pie."

"He's also rich," added June. "Think of the house he'll buy. And before you know it, his friends will want to buy in Banyan, too. Home Sweet Home will become the realtor to the stars."

"Just what Banyan Beach needs," Althea snapped. "Stars. Doesn't anybody realize that if Stallone moves in, Madonna will be next? And then where will we be?"

"Selling a lot more real estate," Suzanne replied. "Luxury real estate. Nothing wrong with that, is there?"

"Not a thing," Frances chimed in. "I, for one, would be happy to sell Madonna a house."

"Barbs would probably be the one to sell her the house," Deirdre said with a touch of sour grapes. "She's on a hot streak all of a sudden. She covered for me on Friday afternoon and ended up with the $700,000 customer *I* should have gotten."

"I was due for a little good luck," I pointed out. "Besides, Deirdre, I was doing you a favor by taking floor duty, remember?"

"Ladies, ladies," Charlotte interrupted. "Let's try to stick to our agenda, shall we? June was telling us about the movie actor. What was his name, dear?"

"Sylvester Stallone," June answered.

"Does he play golf?" asked Suzanne.

"Probably," said June. "Why?"

"Because there's a $4 million house coming on the market in Cotswold Cove, that new golf community on the Intracoastal. It's glitzy enough for a movie star."

"Cotswold Cove? Give me a break," I groaned. Like many of the so-called "country club communities" that had sprouted up across South Florida, Cotswold Cove took its name from merry old England in an effort to appeal to people who admired all things old and staid and yet lived, wore, and drove all things new and flashy. The place was a joke, especially the houses. You would think that, for $4 million, you'd get a house of true distinction, a property that afforded complete and total privacy. Well, not at Cotswold Cove. The residents there didn't want privacy or distinction. What they wanted—and got—was a Levittown for exhibitionists. Every single house looked exactly like the one next door. What's more, the houses were so close together you could hear the messages on your neighbor's answering machine.

"Let's wait and see if Sylvester Stallone actually shows up in Banyan Beach," Frances suggested. "He could decide to stay in Miami after all."

"Miami," Althea sniffed. "That's what Banyan Beach is becoming. Another Miami. The crime, the traffic, the pollution, the—"

"This is still a beautiful town," Frances protested. "I don't know why you're always so down on everything, Althea."

"Beautiful town? Don't be naive," Althea said, looking first at Frances, then at the rest of us. "Haven't you all seen what's happened? Haven't you?"

"No, what's happened?" Charlotte asked, totally bewildered by Althea's ravings. To her, Banyan Beach would always remain an unspoiled, picture-perfect paradise. In a way, I envied her ability to distance herself from reality.

"I'll tell you what's happened," said Althea, growing more and more angry. "Banyan Beach is going to hell. Little by little. Inch by inch. I don't know exactly when it began or why. But I do know that while we weren't paying attention, while our backs were turned, the devil came to town and decided to make it his own."

Suzanne and I looked at each other and started to giggle. Obviously, Althea was more than just grumpy; she was certifiable. A lunatic. She reminded me of those holy rollers who rant and rave about the devil on Sunday morning television. And then I remembered that her father *was* an evangelist who claimed he could heal people if they paid him $150. In cash. In advance.

"Go ahead and laugh," Althea sneered at us. "There will come a time when you'll see that I'm right. You'll think about the fact that the murder rate has gone up and the beaches have eroded and the river has become polluted and you'll say, 'Althea Dicks knew what she was talking about.' "

"Have some more tea," Charlotte said to Althea. "It will calm your nerves, dear."

"My nerves don't need calming," said Althea. "I'm just trying to make a point."

"What point? That the devil is behind all of Banyan Beach's problems? That he's living right here in our little town?" Suzanne said, trying to keep a straight face.

Althea nodded.

"I bet he lives in Cotswold Cove," I said between snickers. Charlotte's Monday morning meetings were always a little bizarre, but not this bizarre. "I bet he's the one who's putting his four-million-dollar house on the market. He wants something bigger. He's dying for a trade-up."

"Either that, or he's unhappy with the golf course there," Suzanne suggested. "It does get crowded on weekends."

"Maybe he lives in your building, Suzanne," I said. "Didn't you tell me that one of your neighbors never leaves home without his pitchfork?"

"Fine, Barbara. Make jokes if you want to," said Althea. "But don't say I didn't warn you."

"I won't," I said, stifling a laugh.

I leaned over and whispered to Suzanne, "There are times when I'd like to put a muzzle on that woman."

Suzanne giggled and was about to respond when Althea began to speak—but all that came out of her mouth was a croak.

She cleared her throat and tried again, but her voice was so hoarse we couldn't hear her. Only seconds before, she'd been going on and on about the devil. Now, all of a sudden she couldn't talk at all.

"Sounds like you've developed a case of laryngitis, dear," Charlotte said, patting Althea on the shoulder.

Suzanne looked at me and raised her eyebrow.

"Didn't you just say you wanted to put a muzzle on Althea?" she whispered to me.

I gulped. "I did, didn't I?"

Suzanne nodded and then smiled weakly. I couldn't help noticing that she moved ever so slightly away from me.

Dr. Messersmith had been our family doctor for years, so it was only natural that I would seek his advice about my curious condition. He was a highly respected physician in town and projected a real air of authority and competence. The only problem with him was that his office was as busy as a golf course on Saturday morning. There were always zillions of people in the waiting room and no matter how early you got there the good magazines—not to mention the chairs—were all taken. So you ended up spending an hour trying to find something reasonably entertaining about *Popular Mechanics,* and then the nurse would finally call your name and lead you into an examining room. You'd take off your clothes, anticipating Dr. Messermith's imminent arrival, and wind up staring at his diplomas for another hour. Then he'd march in, clutching your chart in his scrubbed and gloved hands, and before you could get out a single syllable, he'd take a phone call. You'd sit there on the examining table, feeling insignificant, shivering in your skimpy little hospital gown, the backs of your legs sticking to that God-awful wax paper, while he'd be gabbing with some other doctor about Mrs. So-and-So's gall bladder.

"Hello, Barbara," he said when he entered the examining room smelling faintly of rubbing alcohol. He was a rather imposing figure—tall, terrific posture, gray-haired, bushy eyebrows. "What can we do for you today?"

"I haven't been feeling well," I said.

"Really? You look awfully well," he said. "You've taken off a few pounds, I can see. And the hair's different, isn't it?"

"Yes, yes, but I don't *feel* well," I said.

"In what way?" he asked.

"Well, it's sort of hard to—"

The phone on the wall buzzed. Dr. Messersmith picked it up and, after instructing his nurse to put the call through, began to discuss the gastroenterological side effects of erythromycin.

"Now then, Barbara. You were saying?" he said after hanging up the phone.

"I was saying that I'm not myself. I think you should give me a blood test, take X-rays, do a CAT scan, the works."

Dr. Messersmith eyed me. "Is there trouble at home?" he asked, his tone becoming paternal.

"Yes, Mitchell and I are splitting up. But my marriage has nothing to do with this. I really am sick."

"Tell me your symptoms."

I took a deep breath. "My short-term memory is gone," I said, thinking there was a possibility that I *had* colored my hair, taken diet pills, undergone cosmetic surgery, and bought a dog, but didn't remember. "And I've been having—"

The phone buzzed again. This time, Dr. Messersmith was lured into a conversation about carpal tunnel syndrome.

"You've been having what?" he asked when the call was over.

"I've been having thoughts . . . What I mean is, I seem to . . . Well, let's just say I believe that I can make things happen."

"Excellent," said Dr. Messersmith with a big smile. "That's just what I like to hear. It's very important for people to feel a sense of empowerment, especially in this modern age where we have so little control over our lives. Bravo, Barbara. Bravo."

"No, Doctor. This has nothing to do with empowerment. I feel totally impotent about my own life. Yet at the same time, I'm under some sort of delusion that I can cause things to happen to other people. Bad things."

Dr. Messersmith stepped back to look at me. "And so you think you have a brain tumor? Isn't that what you told my nurse?"

"Yes. Is there any way you could check it out?"

"Are you having headaches?"

"No."

"Blurred vision?"

"No."

"Seizures?"

"No."

"Dizziness?"

"Yes. Occasionally." Whenever David Bettinger touches me, I thought but didn't say.

The doctor buzzed for his nurse. She took my temperature and blood pressure and asked me to give her a urine sample. Then he examined me. He listened to my heart, palpated my abdomen, felt my neck for lumps, shined a little light in my eyes, and inserted a tongue depresser into my mouth.

"Say 'Aaaaah,' " he commanded me.

"Aaaaah."

Dr. Messersmith pulled away from me, a look of dread on his face.

"You saw something?" I asked with alarm.

"No, I smelled something," he said. "Did you by any chance have brussels sprouts for lunch today, Barbara?"

"No. I didn't have lunch at all," I said.

He made notes on my chart and continued with his examination. When he was finished, he told me to get dressed and meet him in his office.

"What's your diagnosis, Doctor?" I asked as I sat facing him across his desk. I prepared myself for the worst.

Dr. Messersmith didn't answer me. Instead, he scribbled something on the top sheet of his prescription pad and handed it to me.

It read, "Dr. Louise Schaffran," along with a local phone number.

"You want me to see a specialist?" I asked.

He nodded, his expression somber.

"Is this Dr. Schaffran a neurologist?" I asked, still clinging to my brain tumor theory.

He shook his head.

"A throat specialist?" I asked, thinking of the reaction people were having to my breath.

He shook his head again. I was becoming a little exasperated.

"Look, Dr. Messersmith. I'd rather not play twenty questions. Why don't you just tell me what Dr. Schaffran's specialty is."

"She's a Freudian psychiatrist," he replied. "A very fine one."

I sank back into the chair.

"So I'm having a nervous breakdown, is that it?" I said.

"Well, I didn't find anything physically wrong with you during my preliminary examination," he said.

"Yes, but you didn't—"

"You mentioned that you and your husband have broken up. You were married for several years, weren't you?"

"Yes, but I don't think that has anything—"

"And the last time you were here you told me that there were problems at work, that you were concerned about your ability to earn a living as a real estate agent."

"Right, but what's happening to me now isn't—"

"Call Dr. Schaffran, Barbara," he cut me off. "She'll be able to help you."

Sure, doc, I thought sourly. Keep me waiting for two fucking hours and then pass the buck.

Dr. Messersmith reached for the phone on his desk and dialed. Obviously, my audience with him was over.

"I hope your damn phone goes dead," I muttered under my breath as I left his office.

I was halfway down the hall when I heard Dr. Messersmith shout, "What the hell's the matter with this phone?"

Nervous breakdown my ass.

CHAPTER

10

"Will you have dinner with me on Saturday night, Bah-ba-rah?" David asked.

I had gotten home from my appointment with Dr. Messersmith, curled up in the fetal position on the living room sofa, and fallen asleep, with Pete standing guard at my feet. The ringing of the phone had jolted me awake.

"I'd love to," I said.

Sure, I could have played hard to get and pretended I was busy on Saturday night. But I was delighted that David was still interested in me and I couldn't hide it. After the way our last date had ended—with the two of us having to rouse Jeremy out of a drunken slumber, drag him to the pickup truck, and help him fix his flat tire—I wasn't sure he wanted to see me again.

"Wonderful. This time we'll have dinner at my house. Just the two of us," he said. "No interruptions."

"No interruptions? And I thought you *liked* Jeremy," I teased.

"That's funny. I thought *you* liked Jeremy," said David. "I was just being polite to your friend."

"My *brother's* friend," I corrected him.

"Are you sure?" he asked. "I had the feeling that you and Jeremy were . . . well, close."

I laughed. "Yeah, close to strangling each other."

"Sorry. I must have misread the situation. In any case, I'm looking forward to seeing you on Saturday night. I intend to cook you a dinner you'll never forget. How's seven-thirty?"

"Sounds fine."

We chatted for ten minutes or so, and, after we hung up, I closed my eyes and anticipated having dinner at David's house. It was nice to have something to look forward to for a change, I thought, remembering how bleak my future had seemed when I was married to Mitchell, how the weekends were just as empty as the weekdays, how one day melted into another. Now, in addition to my renewed excitement about Home Sweet Home, where I was becoming the hottest agent in the office, I had a man to be excited about, to daydream about. Suddenly, life was filled with possibilities.

Even so, there was still the matter of my supposed nervous breakdown. I called Dr. Schaffran's office and made an appointment for Wednesday.

Dr. Schaffran turned out to be my age. She had long black hair, pulled back into a braid, and she was dressed in what I would describe as the Southwestern look: mid-calf–length blue jeans skirt, white cotton shirt, cowboy boots, lots of silver-and-turquoise jewelry, you get the picture. She was pleasant-looking, had a nice smile and told me to call her Louise.

"I've never been in therapy before, Louise," I admitted as the session got underway.

"How . . . does . . . that . . . make . . . you . . . feel?" said Louise, who spoke very slowly, elongating every word, in a way that was probably meant to be comforting but sounded ridiculous.

I replied that I felt a little strange, being asked to unburden myself to a complete stranger, but that Dr. Messersmith had suggested I come after I had told him I had the power to cause bad things to happen to people. "He seems to think my problems are related to the breakup of my marriage," I said, then went on to explain that Mitchell had left me for a younger woman.

"How . . . did . . . that . . . make . . . you . . . feel?" Louise asked, looking pleased that we were getting right to the meat of things.

"Angry," I said.

"Tell . . . me . . . about . . . the . . . anger."

So I did. I told her how I'd been angry and resentful toward Mitchell for most of our marriage but had never expressed it. I told her that he had always been critical of me, judgmental, unwilling to accept me as I was. I told her that I hadn't really loved him but had stayed with him because I was afraid to displease him and, in the end, had displeased him so much he left me for another woman.

"Tell . . . me . . . about . . . your . . . parents," said Louise, seemingly out of the blue. Then I remembered that she was a shrink and shrinks always traced your problems back to your parents.

I told her about Ira and Estelle Greenberg. All about them. How my father's allergy to ragweed and my mother's allergy to snow had motivated them to move to Florida from New Jersey when my brother and I were babies. How my father, a stock broker, had gone to work at the newly opened Banyan Beach office of Merrill Lynch. How my mother, a social climber, had gotten herself on committees to renovate historic buildings, support local artists, beautify the public parks, etc. How their lives had been defined by their relentless pursuit of acceptance, their overriding need to fit in. Whether it was because they were new in town and desperate to make friends, whether it was because they were Jewish and felt they already had two strikes against them, or whether it was because they were just hopelessly insecure, they were always following the crowd, always fearing ostracism, always obsessing over the ubiquitous "they." My mother, especially. *"They* aren't wearing brown this year," she would announce. Or: *"They* say those people aren't worth getting to know." Or: *"They* wouldn't be caught dead in a place like that." My brother and I used to joke that it wasn't our parents who raised us; it was *"they"* who dictated what we ate, wore, read, watched on television.

"So . . . you . . . married . . . your . . . parents," Louise said.

"Excuse me?" I said.

"You chose to marry a man who made you feel as weak and insignificant as your parents did."

"I suppose so," I conceded.

Louise asked me about my parents' deaths, which I rarely discussed with anyone.

"They were killed in a car accident," I said.

"How . . . did . . . that . . . make . . . you . . . feel?" she asked.

God, that question again. The woman was a broken record.

"How do you think it made me feel?" I said, becoming uncomfortable. I hated the subject of my parents' accident. It was too painful, too complicated.

"Tell . . . me . . . about . . . the . . . accident," said Louise.

After some false starts, I told her how my parents were on their way to Palm Beach to have lunch with a man my father hoped to snare as a client. They were traveling south on I-95 when a mattress came loose from the roof of some guy's van and landed smack in the center lane, where my parents were cruising along in their silver Cadillac Seville at fifty-five miles per hour. My father swerved to get out of the way of the flying mattress, shot into the right lane and collided with a tractor trailer that was on its way into the center lane. My brother got the call from the police and came over to the house to tell me that our parents were dead.

"How . . . did . . . you . . . feel . . . when . . . he . . . told . . . you?" said Louise.

I didn't answer right away. I couldn't. The little lump that had formed in my throat when she first started asking about the accident had grown to the size of a grapefruit.

"Guilty," I said finally.

"Guilty? Why? You weren't driving your parents' car, were you?"

"No."

"You weren't driving the tractor trailer, were you?"

"No."

"And you weren't driving the van with the mattress on it, were you?"

"No."

"Then why did you feel guilty? You didn't cause your parents' accident."

"Yes, I did." My throat closed again, and this time I began to cry—big, heavy, wrenching sobs. Louise leaned over to hand me a box of tissues.

"How?" she asked.

"I . . . They . . . called me from their car phone a few minutes before the accident," I managed between sobs.

"What about?"

"It was a silly thing. Really. A silly, nothing thing that turned into—" I started to cry again.

"Take your time," said Louise.

"I'm okay," I said, trying to pull myself together. Dr. Schaffran's fifty-minute sessions didn't come cheap. I wanted to be sure I got my money's worth.

"Tell . . . me . . . what . . . happened," Louise urged.

I took a deep breath. "My parents called me from the car to say they were having a dinner party that Saturday night and expected Mitchell and me to come. I said I wasn't sure if we could make it. I mean, I had no desire to sit around with my parents' friends and perform like a circus act, just because I was *expected* to. I had a life of my own—or at least I tried to. But my parents insisted that Mitchell and I show up. Insisted! I was a grown woman, yet they were still ordering me to do things I didn't want to do—and I let them do it. I couldn't stand up for myself. Not to them. Not to anyone."

"But the day of the accident you did stand up for yourself?" asked Louise.

I shook my head. "I said, 'Of course Mitchell and I will come to your party.' In the end, I always caved in. And I always hated myself for it. I loved my parents, I really did, but I resented them for making me feel so helpless, so impotent."

Louise didn't say anything. I guess she was waiting for me to continue, so I did.

"I hung up the phone and worked myself up into a rage, not about the dinner party, but about the power my parents had over me. Mitchell wasn't home at the time so I just let my emotions rip. I took a photograph of them off the fireplace mantel and shouted at it. At one point I said, 'I wish you both were dead!' But I was just angry and frustrated, the way a kid gets during a tantrum. I was being childish. Irrational. I didn't mean it. I really didn't mean it."

I hung my head and started to cry again.

"Of course you didn't mean it," she said, her voice soothing.

"But I said it," I countered. "I wished they were dead and then the accident happened. Probably at the very second I said the words. My parents' deaths were my fault, don't you see? I had wanted to cause them harm and it came true, just like it was my fault that Mitchell and Chrissy got burned by the cappuccino, that Jeremy's tire went flat and all the rest."

I couldn't go on. I was worn-out.

Louise nodded and wrote things down and waited for me to blow my nose before resuming our conversation.

"Barbara," she said with compassion, "stop punishing yourself. You didn't kill your parents and you didn't cause all the other things to happen. You've set up this scenario as a fantasy."

"Some fantasy."

"What I'm saying is, by imagining that you bring about these calamities, that *you're* the one who causes them, you give yourself power—power you never believed you had. But you didn't cause any of it, Barbara. You didn't."

"I didn't?"

"No. You're suffering from the *delusion* that you caused these people harm. There's something in it for you to do that. In psychotherapeutic terms, there's a 'secondary gain' for you to believe you're harming others."

I shrugged. It was all psychobabble to me.

"There are healthier ways to feel powerful," she said. "And once we've done more work together, you'll begin to see that."

"More work together?" I said.

"Yes," said Louise. "Your problems are serious, Barbara. I'll want to see you three or four times a week."

"But I can't afford to come three or four times a week," I protested.

"You can't afford not to," she said gravely.

I didn't go home after my session with Dr. Schaffran. I didn't want to be alone. Not after she insinuated that I was a lunatic. Who knows what I might do if left to my own devices? So I drove to the pier that overlooked the St. Lucie River, parked the car, and sat there, staring out over the water until the sun went down. I had hoped the tranquil scene would ease my anxiety, but it hadn't. The session with Dr. Schaffran had stirred up too many memories, too many feelings I had tried hard to bury.

Once it got dark, I decided to drive over to Ben's cabin. I wanted to confide in him, to tell him what I'd been going through, to lean on him. He was family. He had lived under the same roof with my parents. He would understand.

When I pulled up to the cabin I noticed that there were cars in the driveway, including Ben's beat-up old Volkswagen Beetle, but no lights on inside the house. Could they all be asleep? I wondered. It was only eight o'clock.

I walked up to the front door and knocked. No answer. I knocked again. Still no answer. I peered inside a window and saw a flickering of light but couldn't tell where it was coming from. I went back to the front door and knocked again. No one responded. Then I heard something: There was music coming from inside the house. Obviously, somebody was home.

God, they're probably having an orgy, I thought suddenly. They're all piled on top of each other, committing lewd and illegal acts. With Ben, anything was possible.

Still, I did want to talk to him, so I tried the door and discovered that it was open. Tentatively, I stepped inside and attempted to get my bearings. It was dark in the small living room where I stood, and yet even in the daylight it was hard to figure the place out. Ben had built the cabin himself and it looked it. It had absolutely no "architectural integrity," as we say in the real estate trade. No curb appeal whatsoever. It was just a series of unmemorable rooms that meandered one into the other with no color scheme or decor or flow. Ben wanted it to be primitive and it was. In other words, if you're picturing one of those charmingly rustic cabins in the Adirondacks, forget it. Ben's place was more trailer park than Relais et Châteaux.

"Hello?" I called out. "Anybody home?"

All I could hear were the sounds of a musical instrument which, after a few seconds, I recognized as a sitar. I laughed. Ben was probably listening to his Ravi Shankar records again.

"Ben? It's Barbara," I called out as I walked toward the back of the cabin, in the direction of the music.

There was no answer so I kept going. When I got to the screened porch, I found Ben and his friends and discovered why they had been too preoccupied to come to the door: they were in the middle of another séance. A half dozen people were sitting around a table on which there were several candles, flickering in the light breeze, complementing the moonlight. Everyone appeared to be in a state of deep concentration; their eyes were closed and they were perfectly still. Of course, there was always the possibility that they were asleep. Too much Ravi Shankar music could do that to a person.

"I'm sorry to interrupt," I said.

They all opened their eyes and stared at me.

"Barbara. I didn't hear you come in," Ben smiled. "Pull up a chair and join us."

Without asking me why I had arrived at his house uninvited or showing even a hint of surprise that I was there, he held open his arms. I went over to him and gave him a hug. I had almost forgotten how warmhearted and kind he was, how loving, no matter how long it was since we had seen each other. He really did buy into the peace, love, and happiness thing. It wasn't an act with him and never had been.

I had also forgotten how much we looked alike—at least, before my transformation. He had gray hair and blue eyes and strong features and was on the pudgy side, like I used to be. He reminded me of a mad scientist, the way his hair stuck out in all directions. An Einstein in a tie-dyed shirt and love beads.

"Is it the candlelight or do you look amazing?" he said as he held me at arm's length. "Jeremy said you'd had some kind of makeover, but I didn't believe him."

"Oh, I just lost a few pounds and colored my hair," I said nonchalantly. I wasn't about to unburden myself to Ben in front of a bunch of strangers.

"Well, whatever you did, you're a knockout," he said. "Everybody, meet my knockout of a sister."

Ben introduced me to his new girlfriend, Janice, and her older sister, Denise, and to two other women, whose names were Wendy and Gail. By way of describing them, I'll simply say that, like Ben, they were wearing tie-dyed shirts and love beads. I felt as if I'd stepped into a dinner theater production of *Hair*.

"And this is Constance," he said proudly, pointing to the woman at the head of the table. "She's a medium."

"How nice," I said. Constance was in her seventies, I guessed.

She had white hair down to her shoulders and wore a black dress and black hat. All that was missing was her broomstick.

I sat down in the empty chair next to Ben. "Please go on with whatever you were doing," I told everybody. I could talk to Ben some other time, I figured. What I really needed was a distraction. Something to take my mind off my own problems. I assumed the seance would do just that.

"We're trying to contact Janice and Denise's grandmother," Ben explained.

"Again? I thought you already did that," I said.

"We didn't have any luck the other night," he said. "That's why we called Constance and asked her to help us this time. She communicates with the spirit world on a regular basis."

I glanced over at Constance, who had closed her eyes once again and appeared to be in a trance.

"Just focus your energies on Grandma Patrice," Ben whispered to me.

"I never knew Grandma Patrice," I reminded him.

"Shhhh," Janice hissed. "Constance can't work if there are negative vibrations in the room."

"Sorry," I said.

I closed my eyes and tried to picture a grandmotherly sort of woman who made great meat loaf. The mental image that came to me was a cross between Julia Child and Aunt Jemima.

"Oh!" cried Constance, breaking her silence. "Oh, my!"

"Is it Grandma Patrice?" asked Denise. "Have you contacted her spirit?"

"Oh! Oh! The spirits are telling me to be careful," Constance shouted. "Very careful."

"Of what?" asked Janice. "Grandma Patrice was a sweetheart."

Constance shook her head vehemently. "They're not giving me . . . I can't read their . . . Oh! Oh! . . . I'm not sure I can go on . . . not sure I can stay here . . ."

Here we go, I thought, wondering how much Ben and the others were paying Constance for this performance.

"What is it, Constance?" asked Gail. "Please tell us."

"The spirits are saying I . . . we . . . are in terrible danger," she said, turning the drama up a notch.

"What kind of danger?" Ben asked. We had all opened our eyes by this time and were hanging on Constance's every word.

She clutched her hands to her bosom, furrowed her brow and said very theatrically, "They have warned me that there's a powerful negative entity in this room. A force of great darkness."

"In this room?" said Ben.

Constance nodded.

I tried not to laugh or even smirk, but it seemed to me that Constance had a great racket going, getting paid to show up at people's houses and scare them to death. I was about to ask her if her spirits could be more specific about the "powerful negative entity" when the candles on the table blew out.

"Hey. What was that?" said Ben.

"Must have been a gust of wind," I said.

"I didn't feel any gust of wind," said Gail.

"Neither did I," said Wendy.

"The negative entity is showing itself," Constance said with authority.

"Wow," said Ben. "I've never—"

He was interrupted by an abrupt halt in the music. For no apparent reason, the Ravi Shankar record ceased to play.

Ben got up and checked the stereo system to see if there had been a power failure.

"The juice is still there, but the music stopped," he said, looking mystified. "I mean, the turntable is still moving, but there's no sound coming out."

"Maybe you need a new needle," I suggested.

"Maybe," he said, sitting back down next to me.

"It's not the needle," said Constance resolutely. "It's the force of darkness."

Nobody said anything for several seconds. Then Janice started making sniffing noises.

"What's wrong?" Ben asked her.

"I smell something. Something really gross," she said, holding her nose.

"Oh, God. I smell it too," said Denise. "It's foul."

I sniffed but didn't smell anything.

"It's putrid," Wendy chimed in.

"It's . . . It's . . ." Gail was groping for her own description of the odor that seemed to be offending everyone but me. "It's like—"

"BRUSSELS SPROUTS!" the four women shouted in unison. "IT SMELLS LIKE BRUSSELS SPROUTS!"

I felt a chill pass through me as I recalled that Jeremy and Suzanne had commented on my breath, on the fact that it, too, smelled like brussels sprouts.

"The force of darkness often reveals himself through his foul odor," Constance explained.

The force of darkness? A negative entity? What did all this New Age mumbo jumbo have to do with me and my brussels sprouts breath?

"Do you smell it, Ben?" I asked him with bewilderment.

"No, but my septum's really deviated. I can't smell anything."

Suddenly, there was a blinding flash of lightning, followed by a loud clap of thunder.

"Looks like we're about to have some rain," Ben said.

But no rain came. The moon disappeared behind a dark cloud, plunging us into almost-total darkness, and the thunder and lightning grew fierce and unrelenting. Yet the threatening weather did not produce a single drop of moisture.

"This is the work of the entity," Constance announced. "He is revealing himself to us tonight. To show us his power."

At the mention of the word "power," I thought back to my session with Dr. Schaffran, during which "power" had certainly been a theme. Was there a connection somehow? Something that linked my apparent psychological problems with Constance's ravings? Was there a single thread that tied together all the things that had happened to me recently? Was there a reason why my life had suddenly taken such a bizarre turn? A reason that involved dark forces and negative entities?

Of course not, I told myself. Get a grip.

I rose from the table, walked over to the screen and looked up at the sky. I shielded my eyes momentarily as a bolt of lightning flashed before me. When I refocused my gaze, I saw something truly astonishing and, at the same time, vaguely familiar. Tucked between the storm clouds, dotting little slivers of sky, were silvery starlike faces. Yes, they had eyes and noses and mouths, and they were sitting up in that sky as surely as I was standing on Ben's screened porch.

And then one of the little faces winked at me!

I saw it! I swear I saw it! It looked right down at me, gave me a sly half smile and winked!

I was completely flabbergasted and yet I'd been winked at before by a starlike face in the sky. I knew I had. Once before. On another stormy night. But which night? Where? Under what circumstances?

I couldn't remember. I wanted to remember, but I couldn't. Something wouldn't let me.

"Barbara? What are you looking at?" Ben asked.

I turned around to face him but I was unable to answer his question.

"Barbara?" he tried again. "Did you see any negative entities lurking out there?"

His tone was lighthearted, playful. He didn't understand what was happening. How could he?

"Barbara?" he said once more.

Involuntarily, I glanced at Constance, who held my eyes for several seconds.

And then she crossed herself.

CHAPTER

11

I spent the rest of the week shuttling back and forth between Home Sweet Home, Dr. Schaffran's office, and the supermarket, where I was forever scouring the aisles for something Pete would eat. To say he was finicky about his food was an understatement. Forget Purina Dog Chow. Forget Ken L Ration. Forget Gaines Burgers. Even Milkbone Dog Biscuits, the canine equivalent of Saltines in their innocuousness, got the cold shoulder from my Pete.

The odd thing was that no matter how little he ate, he never seemed hungry. He never stuck his nose in my plate, lusting after the meals I made for myself. He never whined when I opened the refrigerator to browse. He never barked when the Domino's Pizza guy delivered my large pepperoni with extra cheese. It occurred to me that he might be finding sustenance from the great outdoors, that perhaps his taste in food ran toward small rodents. As I said, it was odd. But then what wasn't these days?

Saturday night was my dinner date with David. I had been looking forward to it, obviously, and talked about my feelings with Dr. Schaffran. Louise.

"I can't imagine what he sees in me," I confided to her during our Friday afternoon session. "He's everything I'm not—movie-star attractive, wealthy, well traveled. I'm sure that the only reason he's asking me out is because he's new in town and doesn't know any other women."

"Isn't . . . it . . . possible . . . that . . . he . . . likes . . . you?" asked Louise.

I shrugged.

"How . . . do . . . you . . . feel . . . about . . . him?" she asked.

"I'm mesmerized by him," I said. "Literally. When he looks at me with those big brown eyes and talks to me in that low, velvety voice, I'm powerless."

"Powerless?"

"Yeah."

Louise nodded and made notes and nodded again.

"Oh, I get it," I said. "You think I'm attracted to David because he reminds me of Mitchell; that they both make me feel powerless; that it's some kind of neurosis that draws me to men who intimidate me. Well, let me tell you: David Bettinger is nothing like Mitchell Chessner. Nothing. David is kind and considerate and respectful of my feelings. He finds me amusing, clever, intelligent. Oh, and he's very romantic, unlike Mitchell, whose idea of a romantic evening is taking you to one of his restaurants, where the only things he kisses are his customers' asses."

"You . . . seem . . . angry," Louise commented.

"I'm not angry," I said. "I'm just glad I'm having dinner with David on Saturday night and not Mitchell."

"Are . . . you . . . sexually . . . attracted . . . to . . . David?" asked Louise.

I blushed. "Yes. Very much so. But I'm so sheltered, so inexperienced. Mitchell was the first and only man I ever slept with. I don't know how to act with men. Sexually, I mean."

"How . . . do . . . you . . . want . . . to . . . act?" asked Louise.

"I . . . Well . . . Gosh. I don't know. Come to think of it, if David tried to initiate sex, I'd probably freak out."

"Why?"

"Because I wasn't raised to have sex on a second date. I was raised to have sex after the man produced the engagement ring. My mother always said, 'Why should he pay for something he can get for free?' "

"Do you agree with your mother, Barbara?"

I considered the question, then said, "Yes and no. I would love to have sex with David, but I don't want him to think I'm . . . a slut."

"Why don't you just wait and see how you feel about David when you're with him," Louise suggested. "Your mother won't be along on the date. *You'll* be in charge of your own destiny, Barbara. It'll be *your* decision whether or not to have sex with this man. *Your* choice."

My choice. The idea was terrifying.

The house that David was renting was Bahamian in style. It was painted pastel pink, had a white tile roof and overlooked the St. Lucie River. With its spacious bedroom suites, ceiling fans, pickled hardwood floors, and lushly landscaped swimming pool and spa, the house was one of Banyan Beach's prime rental properties. If memory served, its owner, a businessman from Singapore, had paid over $3 million for it.

When I arrived at seven-thirty, David greeted me at the door with a smile and a quick kiss on the cheek. I inhaled his scent, an expensive cologne, and felt light-headed, dizzy, off-balance, the way I always felt when I was close to him.

"It's good to see you again," I said, taking him in. God, he got more gorgeous every time I saw him. Strands of his golden hair fell casually across his lightly tanned forehead. His brown eyes were penetrating, impossible to look away from. He was wearing a bright red polo shirt that went well with his coloring and showed off his broad shoulders and hard, muscular chest. It was tucked into a pair of worn blue jeans—extremely tight blue jeans that hugged his thin hips and long legs and fit extra snugly around his crotch. How did I know that? I looked, that's how. I couldn't help it. My eyes just gravitated there, and when they did, I thought, Boy, this David Bettinger is well-hung. As I had told Dr. Schaffran the day before, I was a novice when it came to sex. I was even more of a novice when it came to a man's sex organ (except, of course, for Mitchell's, which wasn't worth talking about). But even a novice couldn't miss the bulge in David's pants. The question was: would I know what to do with it when and if the opportunity presented itself?

"Welcome to my temporary quarters," he said as he took my elbow and guided me into the house.

"They may be temporary quarters, but they're pretty sensational," I said, thinking that I wouldn't mind renting a place like David's. Now that Mitchell and Chrissy intended to kick me out of the house on Seacrest Way, it wouldn't be long before I'd be looking for a new home. Unless, of course, David fell madly in love with me and begged me to move in with him.

"It's very comfortable here," he agreed. He asked me if I wanted a tour of the house and, as I hadn't seen it since it had been put up for sale by the previous owner, I said yes.

The house was stylishly appointed and tastefully furnished with a mix of antique and rattan pieces, upholstered in light fabrics with tropical motifs. Each room had a breathtaking view of the water and nothing was the slightest bit askew or out of order. In fact, everything looked eerily tidy, more appropriate for a photographic shoot than a bachelor pad. Either David was incredibly neat or he had a terrific housekeeper.

"This is the master bedroom," he said when we'd reached the west wing of the house.

I sighed as I stood in the doorway. The room was straight out of an ad for a romantic Caribbean hideaway—brass bed, vaulted V-grooved ceiling, paddle fan, potted palms. I had seen a lot of nice bedrooms in the nine years I'd been a real estate agent, but David's was especially seductive. Or was it David himself?

"Come," he said, offering me his hand. "Let's get you a drink and something to nibble on."

Nibble on, I thought, as I admired his left earlobe and took his hand. I experienced another wave of dizziness when I felt his fingers curl around mine. My heart beat faster and my face flushed.

"Aren't you going to show me the kitchen?" I asked as we walked back toward the living room. The minute I'd entered the house I'd been aware of the intoxicating aromas that were emanating from the kitchen. I was dying to see what David was making for dinner.

He shook his head. "You're my guest. *I* slave in the kitchen, while *you* relax out here and enjoy the view."

He motioned for me to sit on the sofa that faced the pool and, beyond, the river. Then he disappeared into the kitchen. A few minutes later he returned, carrying an ice bucket containing a bottle of Dom Perignon and two fluted glasses.

"My, my," I said appreciatively. "When you invite someone for dinner, you don't mess around."

"No, I don't," he smiled. He poured us each a glass of champagne and handed me one. "To my first dinner guest since I moved to Banyan Beach," he toasted.

"I'm your first? Really?"

He nodded. "Why? Does that surprise you?"

"Yes. I can't imagine you sitting here by yourself night after night, watching TV and eating SpagettiOs out of the can."

He laughed. "You have the impression that I'm a real ladies' man, is that it?"

"Well, aren't you?"

He shook his head. "Hardly."

I considered his response and thought it strange. I mean, the guy was rich and gorgeous and nice. Any woman would find him irresistible.

"You told me you were divorced," I said. "Have you been single long?"

"About six months," he replied. "And it's been a lonely six months, let me tell you."

"Come on," I scoffed.

"It's true," he said. "Believe me."

"Where is the former Mrs. Bettinger?" I asked, hoping she wasn't a possessive ex-wife. That type could snap under the strain of a divorce and turn into a stalker.

"In Palm Beach," he said.

"Was the divorce bitter? Or was it a mutual thing?" I asked.

"It was bitter," said David, offering no further details. His expression had darkened and it was clear that it was time to change the subject.

"Will you excuse me for just a minute?" he said. "I've forgotten to bring out that nibble I mentioned."

"By all means," I said, perfectly content to sip my champagne, admire the view, and be catered to.

David emerged from the kitchen five minutes later with an exquisitely garnished platter of hors d'oeuvres: smoked salmon on black bread, Beluga caviar, assorted cheeses. Quite a spread for his real estate agent, I thought, wondering if he went all out like this when he entertained his accountant, his insurance agent, and his periodontist.

"This is lovely, but you shouldn't have," I protested, as I reached for some smoked salmon.

"Why not? We deserve the best, you and I," he said. "After what we've been through."

"After what we've been through?" I repeated, a bit mystified by his remark.

"Well, our marital breakups, for one thing," he explained.

I nodded as I polished off the salmon and went for the caviar. David refilled my champagne glass.

"What else have you been through? From the look of things, your life has gone pretty well," I said, indicating his plush surroundings.

He smiled ruefully. "Ah, Bah-ba-rah. There's that directness I find so refreshing." He sipped his champagne. "Let's just say that, while I may appear to have everything a person could want, my life hasn't gone as smoothly as I would have liked. There's a lot you don't know about me, you see. So much you don't know."

"Like what?" I said, then drank more champagne.

He shook his head. "Not now," he said. "Not yet. Just know that I've been as unhappy as you've been. And you *have* been unhappy, haven't you?"

I nodded. "Very. Until recently."

"Yes, I know. Same here. Now I don't mean to sound sorry for myself," he went on. "I just want to suggest that we have more in common than you might think, Bah-ba-rah."

"You said that once before. About us having a lot in common," I recalled, going for another hors d'oeuvre. A slice of Camembert this time.

"It's true," he said. "And I have a strong sense that by the time this evening is over, you'll understand why I said it."

With that, he poured more champagne into my glass and offered me a smoked salmon canapé. I washed down the Camembert with the champagne and took the hors d'oeuvre from him. I noticed that

I was outdrinking and outeating David by at least three to one, but decided not to worry about it.

At some point, David left me alone in the living room and went to the kitchen to finish making dinner. I offered to help but he told me to relax and enjoy myself. So I did. I polished off the rest of the hors d'oeuvres, had a few more glasses of D.P., and wandered around the room, admiring the decor. It struck me that there were no personal effects whatsoever. No magazines indicating David's interests or hobbies. No souvenirs from any of his business trips. And no photographs. Not of David or anyone else. I reminded myself that he was only renting the house and that his knicknacks were probably in storage somewhere. Still, the lack of personal memorabilia gave the place a rather cold and sterile feeling, almost as if David Bettinger had no past at all.

We sat down to dinner at about eight-thirty. I wasn't exactly drunk by then, but I was at that stage in the inebriation process where words get harder and harder to pronounce. For example, when David led me into the dining room and I saw how beautiful the table looked, I said, "Oh, David. I can't tell you how much I 'appreeshit' this." I made a mental note to try to avoid words with more than one syllable.

The meal was truly amazing and David was obviously an accomplished chef. He had prepared a roast tenderloin of lamb with wine sauce, garlicky mashed potatoes, sautéed spinach, and a Caesar salad—all of which was accompanied by crusty French bread and a very dry Merlot, my favorite.

I don't remember the precise moment when I knew that he wanted to sleep with me, but by the time I had finished eating (the food was so good I'd had to restrain myself, not only from licking the plate but from asking for seconds), I knew. I just knew. There was something in his brown eyes, something about the way they narrowed when they looked at me, something about the way his hand kept brushing mine, something about the way he kept refilling my wineglass in spite of the fact that I'd told him I'd had enough.

And I'd had enough all right. I could tell because I could no longer see David's handsome features clearly. His face had become a blur and the room was starting to circle my head like a wagon train.

Still, I refuse to sound like one of those women who has sex with a man she hardly knows and then claims it was because he got her drunk. No way. I knew what I was doing. I wanted David to seduce me. I wanted him to find me so desirable he couldn't control his ardor. I wanted him to let me see the *real* him—and that included that big bulge in his jeans. Most of all, I wanted us to be intimate, not just physically, but emotionally. I wanted David to confide in me, to share the source of his unhappiness, to allow me to know him. Really know him. I wanted, for the first time in my life, to *bond* with a man.

And so when he told me he was as skilled at giving neck rubs as he was at roasting a lamb, I said, "Prove it."

He put his hands on my shoulders and then began to massage the muscles in my upper back and neck. I'm telling you, the guy was gifted. I purred like a cat as he kneaded me, rubbed me, stroked me.

"Bah-ba-rah," he murmured at some point in the massage, then parted the hair on the back of my neck and pressed his lips to my skin.

Every molecule in my body exploded with sensation.

The next thing I knew he was holding out his hands and pulling me up out of my chair. He stood facing me, our bodies so close I could feel his breath on my lips. And then he kissed me on the mouth. It was some kiss, let me tell you. It got me so hot I thought I was melting. Sure, it's a cliché, but melting is what it felt like. A slow, hot, liquid surrender.

Part of me—maybe, five percent—had misgivings about the way things were headed. As I had told Dr. Schaffran, I wasn't raised to sleep with a man after only a couple of dinners. What's more, Mitchell had only been gone a week. I was still, technically, a married woman. But the other ninety-five percent of me was powerless—yes, powerless—to resist. From the moment I'd first heard David's deep voice on the telephone, from that fateful Friday afternoon when Deirdre had asked me to cover for her and he had called Home Sweet Home about the Nowak house, I had been drawn to him, mesmerized by him, under his spell.

David led me to the master bedroom, stopping only once. To kiss me.

When we got there, he did not turn on any lights. Instead, he reached into his jeans pocket for a book of matches and lit the pair of candles on the dresser opposite the bed.

He's done this before, I thought nervously, as I noticed the smoothness, the ease with which he prepared the room for love-making. I guessed that he was an experienced lover, a man who knew just what to do to give a woman pleasure. I hoped I would-n't disappoint *him*.

"Bah-ba-rah," he murmured as he stroked my hair, then kissed me. On my temples, my eyes, my nose, my chin. Mitchell had never kissed me anywhere but on my mouth, and even then the kisses were tight, dry, passionless.

Sensing that there was virtually no resistance on my part, David raised my arms and gently lifted my sweater over my head.

"They're so beautiful," he whispered after removing my bra and fondling my breasts.

"You should have seen them a couple of weeks ago," I blurted out, remembering that, before my miraculous transformation, my boobs had been the size of mosquito bites.

"What did you say?" he asked.

"Never mind. Just go on with whatever you were doing," I said.

He smiled and began to unzip my slacks. I stepped out of them and let them drop to the floor along with the rest of my clothes. All that remained were my panties.

"I'm so glad this is happening," he said softly as he pulled them off me. "So glad I can be myself, don't have to hide anymore."

"Hide? What do you mean?" I asked as his fingers caressed my body. It was difficult to think, impossible to concentrate on any-thing but his touch.

"And now it's my turn," he said, ignoring my question.

He placed my hands on his chest as a cue for me to remove his red polo shirt.

I took a deep breath as I helped him lift the shirt over his head. Then I ran my fingers over his broad, hard, hairy chest. I was al-most sorry that it was dark in the room, despite the candles. It would have been nice to see David in the light, all of him.

In the morning, I told myself. You can see him tomorrow morning. When you wake up together.

He reached down to remove his jeans and underwear. I moaned at the mere thought of his nakedness against my own.

At last he pressed himself to me, clasping my body to his, and kissed me on the mouth. It was a soul-stirring kiss, and I felt my legs buckle from the force of it.

I placed my hands on his upper back, stroking it, rubbing it, tickling it lightly with my fingernails. Then I worked my way downward, along the curve of his spine, to the small of his back.

"Ummmm," he murmured, as I massaged him. "That feels so good."

And then I moved my hands downward still, to his buttocks. I was about to massage them, too, when I felt something whip across my wrists.

"Ouch!" I said. "What was that?"

David didn't say anything. His eyes remained closed and he continued to hold me tightly around the waist.

I shrugged and picked up where I left off, placing my hands back on his rear.

Then whatever had whipped across my wrists the first time did it again. But this time, thinking the whole thing must be yet another of my neurotic delusions, I kept my hands where they were.

Seconds later, something swatted at me again.

"Hey! That hurts!" I said, pulling my hands away from David's butt.

"Sorry," he whispered. "It goes with the territory, I'm afraid."

"What does?" I asked.

"Touch it," he said. "I'd like you to touch it."

It wasn't exactly an answer to my question but I just assumed David was in the throes of passion and was, therefore, too aroused to respond appropriately.

"I think you should touch it," he said again.

I gulped as I guessed he wanted me to touch his "throbbing manhood," as they say in romance novels. I closed my eyes and reached down to grab hold of it. It turned out to be smaller than I'd expected, but then it was only the second one I'd ever touched, so I didn't have much to go by.

"No, Bah-ba-rah. Not there," David said.

He removed my hand.

Obviously, my inexperience was showing. I had done the wrong thing, touched the wrong place the wrong way.

"Tell me how you like—"

I was about to ask for David's guidance when he said, "No. I meant, touch *this*. So you'll be more comfortable with it. So it won't frighten you."

Frighten me? So *what* won't frighten me?

Before I could speak, David had taken my hand and put it around his back, near his buttocks again, on his tail.

On his TAIL?

The man had a TAIL?

"OH MY GOD!" I screamed when I felt the long, thin appendage that whipped back and forth, just the way Pete's did. "What the hell is going on?"

I wrenched myself out of David's grip, hurried over to the lamp beside the bed, and turned it on.

In the harsh reality of that seventy-five-watt bulb, I saw what I had touched, saw who David Bettinger really was, and then I fainted. Dead away. Just keeled right over. According to him, I was out for ten whole minutes and when I came to and took another look at that tail, I passed out again.

Well, what do you expect? It isn't every day that a woman is about to have sex with a man who is "anatomically correct" only by Satanic standards.

David was filled with remorse for scaring me. Totally apologetic. He had his tail between his legs—literally.

"I thought you knew" was his explanation.

"Knew what?" I demanded. "That you're the devil?"

So Althea Dicks was right, I thought suddenly, remembering her ravings at Charlotte's last Monday morning meeting. She had insisted that the devil was alive and well and living in Banyan Beach, that he had moved to town to bring damnation on us all. But Althea was such a grouch, a grouch who was always grumbling that this one was the devil and that one was the devil. Nobody took her seriously. Until now. Now, I took her very seriously. Now, the devil himself was right there in front of me, a blond god in jeans and a red polo shirt. Not only was he living in our quaint little town, in one of our finest rental properties—he was one of my customers! A person to whom I'd just sold a house! A man who made incredible roast loin of lamb!

Oh, why did it have to be David? I thought as I began to cry. I'd had such high hopes for us.

"I just can't believe you're the devil," I said, shaking my head at David.

He shook his head back at me. "I'm not the devil," he said. "Any more than you are."

"Any more than *I* am? What are you crazy?" I had put on my clothes by this time and was standing by the front door, ready to bolt.

"Sit down, Bah-ba-rah. Please." He reached out to touch my shoulder but I wouldn't let him.

"You keep away from me," I warned, then grabbed an umbrella from the brass stand near the door and waved it at him. "You keep far away."

He raised his arms in a gesture of surrender. "Fine. I'll keep away," he said. "Only please sit down and let me talk to you. Just *talk* to you. We have so much to say to each other, have so much in common."

"So much in common? You're out of your mind," I shouted. "Look at me. I don't have a Goddamn tail, do I?"

"No," David conceded. "But females don't get the tail. Not usually. They get the brussels sprouts breath but not the tail."

"The brussels sprouts breath?"

I gasped and felt all the color drain out of my face.

He nodded.

"Sit down, Bah-ba-rah," said David Bettinger, as he motioned toward the living room sofa. "I'll make us some coffee, and then I'll tell you everything."

PART
TWO

C H A P T E R

12

"I'm not hungry," I said when David offered me a slice of the key lime pie he had made for our dessert. It looked smooth, velvety, perfect. Nauseatingly perfect, just like David. As he set it down on the coffee table, next to the two mugs of decaf, I felt sick to my stomach, sick with the image of him and his . . . tail.

"Oh, please try it," he urged, as if nothing out of the ordinary had happened between us. "I used real key limes."

"I'll alert the media," I said.

He shrugged. "Maybe you'll change your mind in a little while. When you're feeling less hostile."

"Hostile? I'm not hostile. I'm . . . I don't know what I am," I said. "I'm in shock, I guess. Why else would I be talking to you? A normal person would have gotten the hell out of here."

"But that's the point, Barbara," said David. "You and I aren't 'normal' people. Not anymore. We're darksiders now."

"Darksiders? Aren't they a brand of boating shoe?"

"No, those are Docksiders."

"Oh."

"Darksiders are people who have gone to the side of darkness, to the side of the *force* of darkness."

"Please. Give me a break, would you? Just cut the woo-woo stuff and tell me what you mean."

"All right, I'll put it another way. Darksiders are people who come to a point in their lives when they're desperate—so desperate they're willing to do anything for a little happiness, even sell their souls."

"Sell their souls? To the highest bidder or what?"

"To the *devil,* Barbara. Darksiders are people who've sold their souls to the devil."

"You can't be suggesting that *I* would ever sell *my* soul."

He nodded.

"But that's absolutely ridiculous," I said.

"Why?" said David.

"Because I'm not the type, that's why. I admit I've never been a particularly religious person. I don't belong to temple and I haven't celebrated Passover since my parents died and I'm guilty of using the lord's name in vain now and then. But I'm hardly what you'd call a devil worshiper. I don't even eat deviled eggs."

David smiled. "Eggs aside, you were unhappy, weren't you? Desperate even? Willing to do anything for some improvements in your career, your social life, your appearance? Before your transformation, that is?"

"My transformation?"

"Yes. You know, before you became blond and trim and projected a sexier image. Some people ask the devil to give them more intelligence. Others wish for a happier family life. Still others, like you and me, ask to be made more attractive, among other things."

"But how did you know that I used to be . . . I mean, I never told you anything about a transformation."

He smiled again. "There's no point in playing coy, Barbara. I've undergone a similar transformation." He paused to hand me a mug of coffee, which I declined. "You didn't really think I came out of the womb looking like this, did you?"

"You didn't?"

He shook his head. "Nobody's *born* this handsome. Now, I'm so handsome it embarrasses me at times."

I stared at David. "You're saying you didn't always look like you do now?" I asked. "The hair? The face? The body?"

He laughed ruefully. "Six months ago, I was short and fat and bald and you wouldn't have paid the slightest bit of attention to me. Unless, of course, you needed braces on your teeth."

"What? I don't understand."

"Before my transformation I was an orthodontist, Barbara. In West Palm Beach."

"An orthodontist? But you said you were in the import/export business."

"I thought the import/export business sounded more glamorous than orthodontia," he admitted. "More in keeping with my new persona."

I continued to stare at David and tried to picture this golden boy, this blond Adonis, this sophisticated world traveler, as a short, fat, bald man who regularly stuck his hands into the mouths of middle-class teenagers in an attempt to correct their overbites.

"Was *anything* you told me about yourself true?" I asked, recalling our previous conversations.

"Well, I did go through a bitter divorce," said David. "My wife left me for the dentist I shared the office with." His expression darkened. He seemed to grow angry at the mere mention of his ex and he paused to collect himself. "Her name is Priscilla," he said finally, his tone full of vitriol.

"How long were you and Priscilla married?" I asked.

"No, no. Priscilla is the dentist I shared the office with. My ex-wife's name is Valerie."

"Oh. Sorry."

And I was. It's devastating enough to have your spouse leave you, but to have your spouse leave you for your business partner, who happens to be the same sex as your spouse, puts an additional sting on cuckoldom.

"I was in terrible shape after I found out about the two of them," David went on. "I couldn't sleep, couldn't eat, couldn't work. I let my practice slide, my friends slip away. Before I knew it, I was broke and alone."

"Broke? This house doesn't exactly rent for peanuts," I pointed out. "And you seem to have enough money to buy the Nowak house. With cash."

"I'm not broke anymore," said David. "Just like I'm no longer short and fat and bald. Thanks to the devil, I won the Florida lottery." He smiled. "The jackpot was nineteen million, remember?"

"Yeah, about four months ago," I said. "Some guy down in Palm Beach won the whole—" I stopped. "That was you?"

"Yup. I wanted to be handsome. The devil made me handsome. I wanted to be rich. The devil made me rich. Very rich."

I didn't respond. I was too busy recalling how I had wanted to be blond and thin and now I was; how I had wanted to sell a house and break my slump and then I did; how everything I had wished for had come true. Well, not quite everything. I was possessed by the devil. The *devil,* for God's sake.

"As I was saying, I was broke and miserable and so lonely," David said, picking up the tale of his transformation. "I didn't want to live."

"You contemplated suicide?"

"I contemplated contemplating suicide, if you know what I mean."

"Oh, I know what you mean all right." Only a couple of weeks before, I had considered whether or not to consider suicide as a solution to my problems.

"I told you we had a lot in common," said David, reaching out to pat my hand.

I yanked it away from him before he could make contact. I wasn't ready to embrace him as a soul mate. Not with the image of that tail still burning a hole in my memory.

"So go on with your story," I said. "Get to the part where you became a . . . a 'dark horse' or whatever you called it."

" 'Darksider,' " he corrected me. "Well, what happened was that I had gone into a major depression. My career was down the drain, my marriage was over and my self-esteem was nil."

I can relate to that, I thought. David's story was beginning to sound eerily familiar.

"One night, after a few stiff drinks, I took a walk in a thunderstorm," he went on. "It wasn't the smartest thing I could have done, what with all the lightning, but I really didn't care. I wound up on Flagler Drive and sat down on a bench overlooking the Intracoastal. I stared out at the water, numb to the heavy wind and rain, numb to the fact that I was soaking wet, numb to the fact that I was behaving bizarrely."

"Go on," I said with growing dread. It was as if *I* were the one telling the story, as if David's foray into the thunderstorm were my own.

"I looked up in the sky and began to cry," he said. "I felt sorrier for myself at that moment than ever in my life. I railed against my situation, sobbed with the unfairness of it all. I don't remember exactly what I said but I do remember that at one point I asked for help."

"The devil's?"

"Of course not. I assumed I was talking to God, even though I didn't mention Him by name. How was I to know that someone else—some*thing* else—was eavesdropping?"

I nodded. How was any of us to know?

"So I blithely went along and asked—no, begged—for help," David continued. "I said something like: 'Please transform me from the unhappy, unlovable man I've become into the kind of man women drool over—rich, handsome, self-confident.'" He chuckled. "I even asked for *this.*" He sang a few bars of "I Left My Heart in San Francisco." He wasn't Tony Bennett, but he had quite a voice. "Before my transformation, I couldn't sing worth a damn."

I was amazed. "I didn't ask for the voice but I got it anyway," I said suddenly, thinking of the morning I'd discovered I could sing on key after years of tone deafness.

"As I understand it, all darksiders get the voice, whether they ask for it or not," said David. "Apparently the devil has an ear for music and sees to it that his agents can carry a tune."

"His agents," I muttered, shaking my head in disbelief. "This is crazy. Absolutely crazy."

"I know."

"What happened next, after you asked for help?"

"I said the magic words."

"Which were?"

"I said, 'I'll do anything if you help me.' I didn't know it then, but by offering myself for service, I had made an inexorable bargain with Satan."

I'll do anything if you'll help me. The words reverberated in my mind. It was all coming back to me now. The booze. The thunderstorm. The ocean. My own plea for help. My own promise to do anything in return for a favor. *I'll do anything if you'll help me,* I had said, just as David had. I remembered it. All of it.

"There was a loud clap of thunder that literally knocked me off the bench, onto the wet ground," he said. "And then the strangest thing happened. The wind died, the rain stopped, and the night air became completely still. I looked up into the sky and I saw—"

"Don't tell me, let me guess," I cut him off. "You saw silvery objects that looked like stars but weren't."

"Yes."

"They had eyes and noses and mouths."

"Yes."

"And one of them winked at you."

"That's right."

I sank into the sofa and sighed. So I hadn't been seeing things that night on the deck, hadn't been having alcoholic hallucinations. David had seen what I had seen and now we were both darksiders.

"What are those silvery faces anyway?" I asked him. "Or, should I say, *whose* faces are they?"

"They belong to some of the devil's pals from hell," said David. "Whenever he takes a new darksider, he summons them up here to greet the person. I guess you could call them Satan's version of the Welcome Wagon."

I laughed. What else could I do? The situation was worse than I thought. Much worse.

"I don't get this at all," I said. "We hit a bad patch in our lives and all of a sudden we're devil bait?"

"I take it that I was right? That you had a similar experience?" said David.

"Not similar. Identical," I said. "My husband had just left me, my career was down the toilet, I was drinking too much, the whole enchilada. I went out in a thunder-and-lightning storm, yelled and screamed about wanting to sell a house, meet a man, and be happy, and boom! When I woke up in the morning I had blond hair and big boobs, and later that day you not only bought the tackiest house in town from me but asked me to have dinner with you."

"I'm afraid that was Satan playing Cupid," said David, almost sheepishly. "You see, it's all part of his plan, part of what he wants in return for granting us our wishes."

"Plan? What plan?"

"He wants us to act on the attraction he created between us. He expects us to make love and have children. *His* children. That's how we hold up our end of the bargain."

I shot up from the sofa. "You're out of your mind," I shouted. *"He's* out of his mind."

"Sit down, Barbara. Please."

"Not until you explain, until you tell me how you know all this."

"I'll explain if you sit."

I sat.

"Now. Explain," I demanded. "How do you know all this?"

"I know about the devil's plan for us because before I left Palm Beach, I met another darksider," he said. "A very helpful man who'd been through what we're going through now. He told me everything he knew about the situation."

"And now *you're* going to tell me everything *you* know about the situation, starting from the beginning."

"All right," said David, sitting back, getting comfortable. "According to this darksider, the devil came to South Florida about ten years ago."

"I suppose it was the weather that appealed to him?"

"Yes—and the fact that there aren't any earthquakes here. He'd been living in Southern California—in Brentwood—but couldn't handle the aftershocks. So he decided to move cross-country. To Miami."

"If only he'd stayed in Miami," I said. "Why did he have to come to Banyan Beach?"

"He was redundant in Miami," said David. "Superfluous. Nobody noticed him, what with all the crime there. Bringing evil and malevolence to Miami was like carrying the proverbial coals to Newcastle."

He smiled. I did not smile back.

"Anyhow," he continued, "according to the darksider I spoke to and to another one I met later, the devil left Miami and spent the next few years moving up the coast: Ft. Lauderdale, Boca, Palm Beach."

"Palm Beach. That's where he pressed you into service."

"Yes. Then he went on to Jupiter and kept moving up the line until he finally settled in Banyan Beach. He probably took one look at the place and decided it was as ripe for decadence and debauchery as it was for development."

I nodded sadly, remembering how quaintly "Floridian" Banyan Beach had seemed before Boston Chicken and Big Apple Pizza and Morton's of Chicago had turned the town into Anyplace U.S.A. I remembered, too, how free of pollution Banyan Beach used to be—and how safe. Yes, safe! We never had to worry about crime when I was a kid. The only one I knew who ever got into trouble with the law was Jeremy Cook, and while he wasn't a model citizen, he wasn't exactly Death Row material. But all you had to do was read the local paper to see that Banyan had become a haven for murderers, drug dealers, and con men, not to mention gun fanatics. Even children had guns now. When I was in grade school we brought stuffed animals to Show and Tell. Now, they bring Uzis. Oh, why did the devil have to come here and destroy the town's very soul, I thought, tears filling my eyes. Why did he have to come here and destroy *my* very soul?

"As far as you and I are concerned," said David, returning my focus to Satan's little plan for us, "it turns out that the devil always fixes it so his male agents pair off with his female agents and have children. His goal is to populate the entire world with darksiders."

So that's what this is all about, I thought, seeing the Big Picture at last. In exchange for making us beautiful, rich, or successful, the devil expects us to make babies! Darksider babies! Babies who will grow up and produce more darksider babies!

I began to tremble uncontrollably.

"Barbara? Are you all right?" David asked, his tone concerned, tender.

"Of course I'm not all right," I said, wiping away my tears. "But I'll tell you one thing: Satan can forget about me spreading his seed around. I'm not having his children or anyone else's. I'm infertile."

"Maybe you were before your transformation, but you're not now," said David. "The devil wants what he wants and doesn't stop until he gets it."

"Yeah, well, not this time. No baby of mine is gonna have a tail, see?"

I started to get up again.

"Wait, Barbara. You haven't heard all of it."

"I've heard enough to know I want out. OUT. I don't want to be a darksider, a docksider, or even an insider. I just want to be my old self again. My graying, flabby, infertile self."

"It's too late to go back," said David wistfully. "We're his now. Let's make the best of the situation and be a comfort to each other. I find you very attractive and I know you're attracted to me."

"*Was* attracted to you," I corrected him.

"Barbara, trust me, there's no point in resisting. We *need* each other. It's lonely out there for darksiders. We're different from everyone else. We don't fit in anymore."

"Speak for yourself. *I* don't have a tail. *I* can take off my clothes in those public dressing rooms at Loehmann's and nobody will point at me."

"What about your power? Doesn't it give you away?"

"My power?"

"Yes. I was with you the night your husband and his girlfriend were burned by that hot coffee. You made it happen, Barbara. And you've made other things happen, haven't you?"

So David knew about that.

"Yes," I admitted. "A few things. Nothing terrible but nothing I'm proud of either. My therapist said I was only deluding myself, that I imagined I caused people harm so I'd feel more powerful, that I was having a nervous breakdown."

"You're not having a nervous breakdown. Your power is real and it's only going to get stronger. Believe me, I know. Before long, we'll be causing more and more 'accidents' to happen. It's the devil in us. We can't help ourselves. That's why we need each other. To confide in. To lean on."

I was speechless. Only hours before, I had been hoping that David would become my . . . my lover. Now all I wanted was to get out of his house and out of the deal I appeared to have made with the devil. But how? I couldn't very well hire a lawyer and sue for breach of contract. Still, there had to be a way to extricate myself from the mess I was in. There just had to.

"David," I said, standing up from the sofa yet again, "I hope you won't take this personally. I'm sure you were a very nice man before your transformation—actually, you're a very nice man now and I'll bet there are plenty of women who'd be willing to overlook the business with the tail. But I'm not going to sit back and let the devil destroy me. No way. I've spent my entire life letting people walk all over me and I'm all through with that. I'm going to save myself *and* my town. I'm going to fight this, David. I really am."

My impassioned little speech surprised me. I had never been much of an activist, obviously, what with my fear of displeasing anyone. But for the first time in my life, I had something to fight for—or, more accurately, fight against.

"We're going to get ourselves out of this situation," I told David with conviction. "We're going to get our old lives back, miserable as they may be from time to time."

He shook his head. "Not me," he said. "Aside from the loneliness inherent in being a darksider in a population of normal people, things are going pretty well for me now. I don't think I want my old life back. I don't miss orthodontia at all."

"Then do something else. It's not an either/or situation. You don't have to be an orthodontist *or* an agent of the devil. You could be an agent at Home Sweet Home, for example. Real estate's a lot of fun when you're not in a slump."

"I don't know."

"Well, I do. I'm getting myself out of this nightmare even if it kills me." I sat down again. I was exhausted.

"Oh, Barbara. Please don't say that. I wouldn't want anything to happen to you. You're the only woman who knows the truth about me. I care about you. Very much."

"If you care about me, then help me."

"How?"

"Tell me where to find the devil."

"The devil? You want to speak to him personally?"

"That's right. When you quit a job, you should tell the boss to his face."

"But I don't know where he is."

"Oh, come on, David. You've been a darksider longer than I have. You've talked to other darksiders. You're up on all this stuff. For all I know there's a twelve-step program for darksiders and you're a member. You seem very knowledgeable about the . . . the . . . 'problem,' for lack of a better word."

"Yes, but that doesn't mean I know where the devil actually keeps himself."

"Doesn't it?" I regarded David for a moment. He hadn't been truthful with me in the past. Why should he be truthful with me now? He had his own agenda, after all. I couldn't trust him completely, and yet he was the only one who could give me any information.

"I don't know where he is, Barbara."

"I don't believe you, David."

He heaved a big, agonized sigh and then got up from the sofa and began to pace, back and forth across the living room. He grimaced and grunted and worked his jaw muscles and seemed to be debating with himself whether or not to help me. He was probably thinking that if he helped me and told me where the devil was, he'd win my undying gratitude and get me into bed. Of course, the flip side of that argument was that once I confronted the devil and got myself out of the bargain, David would lose me forever. Poor guy.

"So? Are you going to tell me where he is?" I said.

He sighed again and sat back down next to me. Then he said wearily, "I'll tell you what I can."

"So you *do* know where the devil is?"

"Yes."

I gasped. "You've actually seen him? Here in Banyan Beach?"

"Yes."

"My God. Where is he?"

"He's . . . in the body of . . . of someone," he said, almost in a whisper.

"In the body of someone?"

"Yes, someone here in town."

"You're joking." I had pictured the devil as a sort of Darth Vader with horns, a cartoonish character who lived under a rock and only ventured out at night. Something dark and slippery and reptilian.

"No, this is nothing to joke about, Barbara." David looked pained.

"Fine. Just tell me what you mean when you say he's in the body of someone."

"When he comes to a place, he selects a body to . . . to inhabit, so to speak."

"Inhabit?"

"He enters the person's body and takes up residence there, for the duration of his stay."

I couldn't get over this. "Does the person know what's going on?"

He shook his head. "Essentially, the person ceases to exist while the devil is present. He or she shuts down, remembering nothing of the experience."

"God, that sounds even worse than what he's done to you and me. We may have gone through a transformation, but at least we're still us."

"That's what I've been trying to tell you. It's not so bad being a darksider, once you get used to it."

"Yeah, well I'll never get used to it. Now tell me more about the devil and his game of hide-and-seek. You say he comes to town, slips into someone's body and takes on that person's characteristics?"

"Yes. That's what makes it so hard to spot him."

"But surely that person takes on some of the devil's characteristics, too. I mean, doesn't the lucky man or woman start acting differently all of a sudden? Strangely? More evil? And wouldn't other people notice?"

"Possibly, but don't forget: the devil's specialty is deception. He can make us believe whatever he wants us to believe."

"Then how am I supposed to figure out whose body he's hiding in?"

David didn't answer right away. Again, he seemed to be in conflict, troubled.

"You're not," he said finally. "That's the point."

"David, please. You can keep on being a darksider if you want to. But help me get out of this. Help me save my soul. Help me save Banyan Beach. Once I'm myself again, we can get together for dinner now and then. I'll stick by you. Honestly I will."

He smiled. "I do care for you," he said.

I felt sorry for him suddenly. He was just a poor schlemiel in the same mess I was in. If he told me everything, the devil would probably punish him somehow—maybe even kill him, or, at the very least, send him away from Banyan Beach. And if that happened, I'd lose my only source of information, not to mention the only person who would be idiotic enough to pay $675,000 for the Nowak house.

"Tell me how to find the devil," I urged. "If you can't tell me the name of the person whose body he's hiding in, then give me a couple of hints."

"This isn't a game, Barbara."

"I know, but let's try it. Be a sport. I'll ask questions and you answer them if you can. Okay?"

He shrugged.

"Does the person the devil is hiding in have brussels sprouts breath, like we do?"

"No. Only darksiders have The Breath."

"Oh. Does the person the devil's hiding in have a tail, like you do?"

"No. The devil is in disguise, remember? He doesn't change the appearance of the person."

"Right. Well does the person the devil is hiding in have a good voice? You said he's got a real ear for music and can't stand it when someone sings off-key."

"That's true, but there are plenty of people the devil *isn't* hiding in who have good voices. I don't think that's much of a clue."

"Then give me a better clue. Something I can use." I thought for a minute. "For example, Banyan Beach is a small town. I've lived here for most of my life. Do I *know* the person whose body the devil is hiding in?"

David did not reply this time. Instead, he abruptly got up from the sofa and walked toward the front door, motioning for me to follow him, which I did. Without speaking, he opened the door and held it open for me. Apparently, I had hit pay dirt and he wanted to call it a night.

But I wanted an answer to my question. Facing him, I made one final attempt to pull information out of him.

"Do I know the person whose body the devil is hiding in?" I repeated.

Our eyes met. David waited several seconds before responding.

"Yes," he conceded. "You certainly do."

And then, before I could say another word or even register my shock and horror, he ushered me gently out of the house and closed the door behind me.

CHAPTER
13

Pete was especially clingy on Monday morning. As if I didn't have enough on my mind, what with learning that I was a darksider and trying to figure out who among the people I knew was the devil and rushing to get to Charlotte's weekly meeting on time, Pete decided to have an attack of separation anxiety. No matter what I did or said, he wouldn't stop whining and nuzzling and curling himself around my legs, making it impossible for me to walk out the door.

"What's the matter?" I asked as I bent down to scratch the white patch on his chest. Massaging that spot, I had discovered, usually calmed him down—temporarily. But not this time.

I regarded him with genuine concern. Yes, concern. While I wasn't wild about him in that nonsensical way some people are about their dogs, I had become . . . well, let's just say I had developed a tolerance for Pete. For one thing, having a pet eased the loneliness brought on by Mitchell's defection. For another, Pete was better company than Mitchell—i.e. he didn't yammer on about the restaurant business while I was trying to watch "Seinfeld." For a third thing, he seemed attached to me in a way no one else ever had been. Of course, after my chat with David on Saturday night, I no longer trusted the way anyone felt about me. I had thought David was attracted to me when it turned out that the attraction was merely part of the devil's "plan."

And speaking of the devil, I was now exhibiting yet another

manifestation of his evil influence. The previous evening, I'd been sitting at the kitchen counter, reading the newspaper, when I heard myself growl! I mean, *really* growl, like some kind of savage animal! I thought it was Pete until I remembered that he was outside on the deck, barking at seagulls. Just when I decided the sound couldn't possibly have come from inside me, I heard it again. There was no getting around it: *I* had growled!

I ran to the phone and called David.

"Do you growl?" I asked, as one darksider to another.

"No," he said. "Do you?"

"I do now," I said. "I was sitting in my kitchen, minding my own business, when this bestial noise came out of me. It was bizarre."

"My guess is that the devil is sending you a message," David said. "He's probably warning you not to tangle with him."

"Oh, so you think the growling is his idea of a threat?" I asked. "A macho thing to show me who's boss?"

"It wouldn't surprise me," said David. "If you don't like the growling, Barbara, you should change your mind and accept your fate. We weren't so bad together, were we?"

"Oh, David," I sighed. "David David David. You're a nice guy, really you are. But I told you last night and I'll tell you again. I'm a real estate agent, not an agent of the devil. I will not have the devil's babies in exchange for the body of a *Sports Illustrated* swimsuit model. I'll get my old life back if it kills me."

I hoped it wouldn't kill me but I wasn't about to be scared off. I had spent my whole life being scared off. By my parents, by my husband, by grumpy supermarket checkout ladies. Anyone and everyone. But not anymore.

"Look, Pete. I really have to go to this meeting," I told the dog that Monday morning. "I may be under the influence of the dark forces, but I've got to at least project the appearance of normalcy, you know?"

Pete nodded. I swear he did. If I could growl, he could nod, right?

I arrived at the office at nine-fifteen, popped a couple of BreathAssure capsules into my mouth so I wouldn't offend anyone with my darksider halitosis, and hurried into the meeting, which was already in progress. June Bellsey was reporting that she and her husband, Lloyd, had run into Donald and Marla Trump at a charity function in Palm Beach and that The Donald had mentioned he was looking for land in Banyan.

"To build on?" asked Deirdre with her customary obtuseness.

"No, to sit on," said Althea with her customary sourness.

"Althea, please," Charlotte scolded. "There's no need to snap at Deirdre. We're all ladies here."

Well, not quite all, I thought. I was no longer sure what category of person I was.

"Sorry," said Althea from between pursed lips. "But it's fairly obvious that if Trump is looking at land here, it's because he wants to put something on it. Something with his name on it." She snorted derisively. "I can see it now. A big, grotesque Trump Tower where our beautiful nature conservancy used to be."

"Oh, there you go again, Althea," said June as she rolled her eyes. "Always the voice of doom and gloom. You're not going to start that business of how the town has gone to the devil, are you?"

The devil.

I recalled David's words as I regarded Althea. *The devil is hiding in the body of someone you know.* Well, I knew Althea. For over ten years. She was always grousing about the devil, about the way Banyan Beach had gone to hell. And when she wasn't grousing about that, she was grousing about something else. She was the most negative human being I'd ever met. The perfect person for the devil to call home. Was he living inside *her* body? I wondered as a chill went through my own. Was he sitting right there in that room with me? Watching me? Studying me? I narrowed my eyes to examine her closely. Was *Althea Dicks,* the office manager at Home Sweet Home, Satan's cover in Banyan Beach?

I glanced over at June as she continued to drone on about Donald and Marla. Maybe she was the one who was harboring the devil. The woman was a relentless social climber, the sort of person who wanted everyone to view her as a big shot even though it was her husband who was the big shot while she was just a big mouth. She was a phony and so was the devil. Didn't David say that Satan had a talent for deceiving people? What's more, she and Lloyd spent a lot of time in Miami and Palm Beach, the devil's previous pit stops.

Maybe *June Bellsey* was the one whose body he chose to hide in while he was in Banyan Beach. Maybe she, not Althea, held my fate in her hands.

"Did you tell Trump you'd show him property?" Suzanne asked June. "We've got that twenty-five-acre listing on McGregor Avenue. The owner's pretty motivated."

June shook her head. "It was a social evening," she pointed out. "I wasn't about to shove my business card in his face, although I did slip one inside Marla's purse when we went to the ladies' room together."

"Atta girl," Frances cheered, clapping her hands together. The gesture made the layers of flesh around her middle jiggle. "I think that shows real creativity."

June stood up and took a self-congratulatory bow, and as she bent over, the button holding her skirt around her waist popped open.

Frances, in a burst of comic spontaneity, erupted into a lively rendition of the old show tune, "June Is Busting Out All Over."

Hey, she's got a good voice, I thought, as Frances sang with the gusto of Ethel Merman. Had I never heard her sing before? Or had I never noticed that she could? Or was her musical talent something brand-new? Could it be that the devil was hiding in *Frances Lutz*'s body, not Althea's or June's? At over three hundred pounds, Frances could certainly be carrying more than herself around, couldn't she? Who knew what lurked beneath that voluminous caftan? What's more, it was Frances who'd been the listing agent on the Nowak house, the house that had brought David and me together. Maybe Frances had engineered the whole thing under Satan's influence.

I spent the rest of the meeting observing the other women, one by one.

I focused my attention on Deirdre, the ex–beauty queen. She was so wholesome-looking with her blond, blue-eyed coloring and clean, clear skin. The fact that she had sex with strangers in order to get their listings didn't automatically qualify her for a bodily takeover by the devil, did it? On the other hand, if I were the devil and I had my pick of bodies to enter, I'd certainly take Deirdre's over, say, Frances's.

I turned to Suzanne Munson, my best friend in the office. There was no way the devil could be hiding inside her. None. I knew her better than I knew the others. I'd be able to tell if there were anything different about her. We were attuned to each other's moods and temperaments. We commiserated with each other about our problems. Of course, *I* had become a darksider and hadn't commiserated with her about that. Was it possible she was keeping her relationship with the devil a secret from me? No, I decided. It wasn't possible. If the devil were hiding inside Suzanne's body, he'd have to listen to her talk about menopause all day long and why would he want to put up with that, given the choice?

And then there was Charlotte. As she congratulated me for being "Agent of the Week" (I had signed up the most listings of any other agent the week before and, therefore, merited a Whitman's Sampler), I wondered if she could possibly be the one the devil had chosen as his cover. She was the least likely. So proper. So ladylike. So genteel. Then again, maybe that's what the devil did: he picked the person nobody would ever suspect, someone whose behavior had always been beyond reproach, someone who never drank or cursed or drove through exact change toll booths without paying.

"Now, who would like more tea?" Charlotte asked us as she poured herself another cup.

I was about to say "I would" when a ferocious growl emanated from somewhere deep inside me—the same savage animal sound I'd made the night before. Everyone turned to look at me. I was mortified.

"If you'd prefer a beverage other than tea, you only need to say so, Barbara dear," said Charlotte.

"No, tea would be fine," I said, feeling my cheeks burn with embarrassment.

And then I growled again, this time even more viciously.

My God, maybe David is right, I thought with a shudder. Maybe the devil is making me growl in order to send me a message: that I'd better do his bidding or else. Or else what? I didn't want to know.

"Barbara?" said Suzanne, arching an eyebrow, a look of bewilderment on her face. "Was that you?"

I laughed, trying to feign nonchalance. "I'm afraid so," I said. "I was in such a hurry this morning that I forgot to eat breakfast. I guess my stomach isn't happy."

Suzanne nodded tentatively.

"It's true. Really," I said. "Whenever I skip breakfast, I growl something fierce."

She relaxed a little and then shook a finger at me. "You look terrific after taking off all that weight, but you really shouldn't skip breakfast," she advised. "As you approach menopause, you need all the nutrients you can get. We all do."

"Right you are," I said, wanting desperately to flee the room. Instead, I sat there, sipping tea and listening to the conversation move back and forth between menopause and real estate, as if the subjects were related somehow.

As the meeting broke up, Suzanne followed me over to my desk and plunked herself down in the visitor's chair.

"I didn't want to ask in front of the others," she said, "but I'm dying to know how your date was on Saturday night. With David Bettinger."

If only I hadn't told Suzanne about David, I thought. If only I had never mentioned his name. Now what would I say? That he turned out to be a devil's agent? That he had entered into a bargain with the force of darkness? That he had a *tail?*

"It was okay," I told Suzanne as I shuffled papers on my desk and tried not to meet her gaze.

"Just okay? A couple of days ago you couldn't wait to go out with the guy," said Suzanne, surprised by my air of indifference.

"I know, but David wasn't . . ."

"Wasn't what?"

"Wasn't what I thought he was."

"In what way? You said he was the most perfect man you'd ever laid eyes on. You were going to ask him if he had a brother for me, remember?"

"I remember. But truthfully, Suzanne, he's not what he seems. He . . . he has a dark side."

Suzanne's eyes opened wide. "A dark side? You mean he's changeable?"

"He's changeable, yes."

"Changeable, as in moody? Or changeable, as in indecisive?"

"Neither."

"Well then how? Does he have a temper? The type that goes berserk? Ballistic? Into a tailspin?"

"A tailspin," I nodded. "That's it exactly."

David's tail hadn't actually spun, of course; it had snapped, back and forth against my wrists, which still smarted.

"Gee, that's too bad," said Suzanne. "I was hoping you'd have a great time with him. You deserve a break after what happened with Mitchell. Does David want to see you again?"

"Yes, but I told him there was no possibility of a romantic relationship," I said. "I'm sure we'll continue to see each other though. He's my customer, and we close on the Nowak house in three weeks."

"Hey, that's something, isn't it? After that awful slump you went through?"

I nodded.

"Tell you what," said Suzanne, getting up from the chair. "You and I are going man hunting tonight."

"Man hunting?"

"That's right. There's this place that's opening up on Route 1, next door to Sam Goody."

"Thanks anyway, but I'm not the singles bar type, Suzanne."

"It's not a singles bar from what I hear. It's just a really cool restaurant and bar where they have live music. It's called The Hellhole."

The Hellhole. Oh, swell. I couldn't escape the devil if I tried.

I shook my head. "I don't think so," I said. "I'm not up for that kind of thing. I've got a lot on my mind these days."

"Oh, come on, Barbara. One bad date and you're ready to hang it up? I've had hundreds of bad dates and I haven't given up, have I?"

I looked at Suzanne and wondered how why she hadn't given up. She'd been out with everything under the sun—deadbeat dads, men who couldn't commit, Peter Pan Syndrome sufferers, the whole gamut of self-help book characters. Still, she kept at it, night after night, forever in search of that special someone.

"What do you say, Barbara?" she urged. "You didn't lighten your hair and lose twenty pounds so you could sit in your house by your-self, did you?"

"No, I guess not," I said, not knowing what else I could say.

"You improved your appearance and now it's time to show it off," she said.

"At The Hellhole?" I said, making a face. "It sounds like a dive."

"I don't think so," she said. "It didn't look too bad from the photo on the flyer they sent out. Tonight's the opening. There's going to be a rock 'n' roll band, free welcome rum punch, and a lobster din-ner for $10.99. What do you say? It could be fun."

Fun. I had forgotten what the word meant. Maybe a night out with Suzanne was just what I needed. A way to forget my predica-ment, if only for a few hours. And I did love lobster . . .

"Okay," I said. "I'll go."

"Terrific. Who knows? You just might meet your Mr. Right the minute you walk in the door."

CHAPTER
14

There was no point in continuing my therapy with Dr. Schaffran, I decided, given that I was in the throes, not of a nervous breakdown, but of a demonic possession. Besides, I didn't have time to sit around whining about my childhood; I had to figure out which of my acquaintances had been taken over by the devil. I had become obsessed with the subject, racking my brains for something, anything, that would lead me to the person who was harboring the Evil One. What would make him choose one type of man or woman over another? I asked myself. Was it a random thing? Did he simply hop inside the first body he saw when he came to town? Or did he give it a lot of thought? Did he watch people and study them and make his decision on the basis of their personality? Their looks? Their religious affiliation? What?

I was tempted to call Louise and break the news over the phone that I was canceling our sessions, but I felt I owed it to her to show up for my Monday afternoon appointment, to tell her in person that I would not be coming again. This was the new me, after all. The new and bolder me.

The session began with her question about Saturday night.

"How . . . was . . . your . . . date . . . with . . . David?" she asked. "You were a little apprehensive about it, as I recall."

I wasn't sure if I should tell Louise the truth about David. First of all, she probably wouldn't believe me. And if she did, she might blab the story to someone—her pal, Dr. Messersmith, for instance.

Pretty soon, everyone in town would know that I was an agent of the devil and I could kiss my career in real estate good-bye. On the other hand, Louise was a shrink. *My* shrink. We had a doctor-patient relationship and she was duty bound to keep her mouth shut about me. Besides, if this was to be my final session with her, there was no point in wasting my time or my money by lying to her. And it would be a relief to tell someone what really happened, I decided. An unburdening.

I cleared my throat. "It started off okay," I began. "David was a very gracious host. He served champagne and hors d'oeuvres and gave me a tour of the house he's renting. And then he made this fabulous dinner for me."

"How . . . did . . . that . . . make . . . you . . . feel?" Louise asked.

"Pampered. Cared for. Special. It was a nice feeling."

"Go on."

"We were sitting at the table, sipping our wine, when David got up to massage my neck and shoulders. I was incredibly aroused by him—and a little drunk, to tell you the truth—and I just let myself enjoy his touch. Before I knew it, we were kissing. Passionately. I don't think I ever wanted a man so badly and I didn't try to hide it."

Louise nodded. I guessed she was pleased that I had been able to throw off my inhibitions.

"David took me to his bedroom," I went on. "He lit candles. Then we stood in the middle of the room, embracing. He undressed me. I undressed him. It was thrilling."

"Then why doesn't your expression reflect that?" asked Louise. "Didn't the lovemaking go well?"

"There *was* no lovemaking," I said. "Once David was out of his clothes, I discovered that he had a tail, just like the devil. Obviously, I was no longer interested in him—sexually or any other way."

Louise didn't say anything for several seconds. First, she just stared at me. Then, she reached for a notepad and began to write. Finally, she looked up at me and said, in that self-parodying manner of hers, "Are . . . you . . . trying . . . to . . . punish . . . yourself?"

"Punish myself?"

"For your parents' accident."

"What do my parents have to do with my date with David?"

"Barbara," Louise sighed, as if I were the village idiot. "Haven't we talked about your guilt over the way your parents were killed? How you felt you caused the accident by standing up for yourself, by stating your own needs? Haven't we?"

"Yes, but I don't—"

"And haven't we talked about your recent delusion that you cause other people's accidents, merely by willing them to happen?"

"Well sure, but—"

"And haven't we talked about your subconscious desire for power? How you tell yourself you make things go awry in order to control these situations?"

"Yes, but all that has nothing to do with my date with David. I wasn't trying to control anything on Saturday night. I was standing stark naked in the middle of the man's bedroom when I felt this thing sticking out from his backside. This tail! I didn't will it to be there. It just was!"

Louise laughed. Laughed! And then she said, "Barbara, I've got to hand it to you. You're one of the most creative patients I've ever had. You come up with such innovative ways to sabotage your happiness."

I hadn't expected her to believe me, but I would have preferred a little more sympathy, a little more mothering, a little more respect!

"You think I invented David's tail so I'd have a reason to ruin our evening?" I said.

She laughed again. "Do you remember the Paul Simon song '50 Ways to Leave Your Lover'?" she asked.

"Sure. Why?"

"Because you've just invented Number 51: My lover has a tail."

"But I didn't invent the tail. It was real," I said. "I swear it was."

She nodded dismissively and made more notes on her pad. And then she looked up and said, "I wonder if I might ask you something, Barbara."

"What?"

"I'm writing a book," she said. "It's a study of the ways in which people deny themselves pleasure."

It didn't sound like a big seller to me, but I tried to look impressed.

"I'd like your permission to use your devil's tail anecdote in my book—without giving your name, of course. It's not only ingenious. It's very entertaining. I'm trying to reach a mass audience with the book and your anecdote—along with the stories of how you imagine you caused a tire to go flat and a telephone to go dead and hot coffee to burn your husband and his girlfriend—will certainly get people's attention. You see, once the book is published, I'm hoping to get on 'Oprah.' "

So Louise was just another shameless self-promoter! I was horrified! To think I'd trusted her, unburdened myself to her, told her things I hadn't shared with anyone. And now she wanted to use the very stories I'd told her—in confidence—to entertain people! She wanted to exploit my traumas for some bullshit book!

I gave her a dirty look as she scribbled some more in her notepad. And then a thought came to me: could the devil be hiding in Louise Schaffran's body? *Dr.* Louise Schaffran's body? Was *that* why she had laughed when I'd told her about David having a tail? Was *that* why she hadn't taken it seriously? Or was I becoming ridiculously paranoid, suspecting virtually everyone I knew of harboring Satan?

Yes, I decided. I *was* being overly suspicious and I had to stop it, had to get a grip. I couldn't go around pointing a finger at everybody. I'd drive myself crazy wondering if it was the mechanic who serviced my car who was hiding the devil or the woman who worked behind the counter at the dry cleaner or the kid who was always trying to sell me Girl Scout cookies. No. I had to cut it out. But could I? Could I just sit back and wait for the devil to reveal himself to me, knowing that his grip on me, on my body, on my town, was getting stronger by the day? By the minute?

"I'm leaving," I said suddenly as I rose from my chair.

Louise glanced at the clock on the wall and then went back to her writing. "Your fifty minutes aren't over," she said as she scribbled.

"My therapy with *you* is over," I said, making my way toward the door. "I won't be coming here again."

"You're angry at me," said Louise, looking up.

"Yes."

"Tell . . . me . . . about . . . the . . . anger."

I shook my head. "I don't want to tell you," I said. "I'd . . . rather . . . show . . . you."

"Show me?" she said.

"Yup. You know how you think I only *imagine* that I cause things to happen to people? So I can feel *powerful?*"

"Yes, Barbara. That's what I've been—"

"Well, now I'm going to show you that you're wrong," I cut her off. I paused, crossed my arms over my chest and gave her a long, appraising look. And then I said, "I've decided to cause you to grow a mustache."

"What did you say?" asked an incredulous Louise.

"I said I've decided to cause you to grow a mustache."

Within seconds, Dr. Louise Schaffran, Banyan Beach's answer to Sigmund Freud, sprouted not only a mustache, but a matching goatee.

"What on earth?" she sputtered as her hand flew to her chin.

"A going away present," I said. "Bye-bye."

The Hellhole turned out to be the black one-story building on Route 1 that used to house a strip joint called Titters, a dive whose parking lot was always jammed, even though no one in town ever admitted to going there.

"The flyer said the new owners have completely changed the atmosphere of the place," Suzanne explained when she saw my look of disdain as we were about to enter the restaurant.

Actually, The Hellhole's interior wasn't that bad, particularly if you weren't expecting much, which I wasn't. The lighting was dim, the tables and chairs were your basic diner furniture, and the walls were decorated with generic devil paraphernalia—pitchforks, horns, tails, etc. I felt right at home.

The place was packed and we were lucky that Suzanne had reserved a table for us right beside the dance floor, near the stage. As we were being seated, I reached into my purse surreptitiously, opened the bottle of BreathAssure I'd been carrying around, and swallowed a couple of capsules. I'd gotten so paranoid about people smelling my brussels sprouts breath that I didn't go anywhere without my BreathAssure anymore. God, I was probably becoming a drug addict on top of everything else.

"I wonder which band is playing tonight," I said, glancing up at the stage.

Suzanne didn't answer. She was too busy surveying the room for men. And there were many—mostly young, badly dressed, and drunk. I doubted very much if either of us would find our Mr. Right from among them.

We ordered drinks and talked and perused the menu, which featured such themed entrées as Satanic Shrimp, Devilish Dolphin, and Hellish Hamburger with Fiendish French Fries. I had an urge to find the owners, grab them by the throats, and yell, "Okay! We *get* it!" Talk about beating people over the head with a gimmick.

"What are you having?" Suzanne asked.

"I'm going with the Tail," I said. "I mean, the lobster tail. At $10.99 it sounds like a bargain." This coming from someone who had recently become an expert on tails *and* bargains.

"I'm having that too," she said.

Several minutes later, the waitress, who was dressed in a red devil's costume, took our orders.

"Who's playing here tonight?" Suzanne asked her.

"The Fire Ants," said the waitress. "They're an oldies group."

I groaned.

"What's the matter?" Suzanne asked when the waitress was gone.

"That's Jeremy Cook's band," I said. "He's their lead singer."

"Who's Jeremy Cook?"

I had forgotten that Suzanne was relatively new in town. She'd never had the pleasure of meeting Banyan Beach's very own rebel without a cause.

"A friend of my brother's," I said. "He's a charter boat captain by day and a really bad lounge act by night."

"How do you know he's really bad? Have you ever heard him sing?"

"Yes, when we were in high school. He used to sit next to me in math and the minute the teacher would leave the room, he'd lean over and sing that dopey oldies song: 'Ba-ba-ba. Ba-ba-bra-ann.' God, it was so annoying."

"Maybe that was the point: he was *trying* to annoy you. Back in high school, boys always tried to annoy you—especially if they really liked you."

"Please. Jeremy Cook didn't like me then any more than he likes me now. We only tolerate each other because we both love my brother."

"Is this Jeremy Cook single?"

"Yeah, but trust me, Suzanne. He's not for you. He's immature, irresponsible, and insensitive. Not husband material at all."

"He's never been married?"

"No, and he's almost forty. Doesn't that tell you something?"

"Yeah. It tells me he hasn't found the right woman. I'm almost forty, and I don't think I'm immature, irresponsible, or insensitive. In fact, the older I get and the closer to menopause I come, I—"

"Forget it, Suzanne. There's no comparison between you and Jeremy Cook. You're ready to make a lifetime commitment to a man. He treats women the same way he treats fish: He catches them and then throws them back. To him, the chase is everything. For years, my brother has been regaling me with stories of Jeremy's conquests, not that Benjamin's record with women is anything to write home about."

"Men," Suzanne sighed. "What is it with them anyway?"

"I'm the wrong person to ask," I said. "I thought Mitchell was husband material and look how he turned out."

Suzanne nodded and patted my hand. I wished I could tell her what was really going on in my life. I was sure she'd be more compassionate than Dr. Schaffran had been.

We were on our third round of The Hellhole's "Diabolical Daiquiris" when one of the restaurant's owners, a fifty-something with a bad hairpiece, walked onstage and spoke into the microphone.

"Ladies and gentlemen, welcome to The Hellhole!" he intoned. "To celebrate the opening of Banyan Beach's hottest new club, we thought it only right that we book the area's hottest oldies band! I hope you'll join me in giving a big round of applause to . . . THE FIRE ANTS!"

The revelers at nearby tables virtually leapt to their feet at the mere mention of Jeremy's band, then applauded wildly as the band members walked onstage. I shook my head in disbelief.

"What's the matter with these people?" I muttered. "You'd think they were at a Grateful Dead concert."

"Maybe they know something we don't," said Suzanne. "Maybe Jeremy Cook's a better singer than you remember. Which one is he anyway?"

I pointed at the stage. "You can't miss him," I said. "He's the one who looks like an escapee from a Bud Lite commercial."

"Come on. They all do. Which one's Jeremy?"

I regarded him more closely. He obviously hadn't dressed for the occasion. He was wearing his usual blue jeans, T-shirt, and sneakers, and his hair was as straggly and unkempt as ever. Still, he did have a certain authority as he strutted around on that stage.

"He's the redhead," I told Suzanne. "The one with the scruffy beard."

She nodded. "I see him now," she said. "He's kind of cute, in a lowbrow sort of way."

"Cute? You'd better ease up on the daiquiris, Suzanne. The guy's—"

Before I had a chance to trash Jeremy further, he strode up to the microphone, gave his band a cue and launched into "Devil with a Blue Dress," the old Mitch Ryder hit.

"The owners must have requested this song," I said, rolling my eyes.

"What?" Suzanne yelled over the loud music.

"I said the owners of this place must have asked for the song. It goes with their Goddamn theme."

Suzanne didn't answer. She kept her eyes glued to the stage and was tapping her fingers on the table and bobbing her head to the beat.

I glanced around the room and noticed that Suzanne wasn't the only one who seemed entranced by Jeremy's performance. Everybody in the place was singing and clapping and having a rousing good time, and several couples had taken to the dance floor.

Maybe I'm missing something, I thought, and started paying attention to what was happening up on stage.

What I heard and saw surprised me. For starters, Jeremy could sing. I mean, really sing. He had a rugged, raspy Rod Stewart–type voice that was both hard-edged and soulful. And then there was his body language . . . the way he moved his hips to every beat of the song . . . the way he shook his shaggy red hair to punctuate the lyrics . . . the way he held the microphone to his mouth, nearly caressing it. He had the crowd in the palm of his hand. Screeching young women waved their arms in the air, calling his name and blowing kisses. I had to keep reminding myself this was Jeremy who was causing such a scene—my brother's crazy friend Jeremy Cook—and then it dawned on me: maybe *he* was harboring the devil!

Well, why not? It could just as easily be Jeremy as anybody else in town. My mother always said he had the devil in him. Maybe she knew what she was talking about. Maybe the devil picked Jeremy's body to hide in because Jeremy always acted like such a hell-raiser. Maybe Satan figured he'd be less conspicuous that way. Maybe he knew a soul mate when he saw one.

"He's sensational," Suzanne exclaimed when the song was over. "Let's invite him to join us for a drink when he finishes this set."

"Who?" I said distractedly, thinking only of whether Jeremy could be the one who was taken over by the devil.

"Jeremy," said Suzanne. "You said you knew him."

"Maybe not as well as I thought," I said.

"What do you mean?" she asked.

"Nothing."

Was Jeremy really the person I was hoping to find? The one I *needed* to find if I was ever going to extricate myself from the supposed "deal" I made with the devil? Was he the key to helping me get my old life back? My mind raced as I watched him onstage, prancing, strutting, playing the rock star. The more I thought about it, the more obvious it seemed: Jeremy was the logical choice for Satan's cover in town. He had the morals of an alley cat, didn't go to church, didn't care what anybody thought of him. And let's not forget the name he'd christened his precious boat: the *Devil-May-Care.*

After he and The Fire Ants had performed a half a dozen more songs, they took a break. As they were stepping down from the stage en route to the bar, Suzanne called out to Jeremy.

"Over here!" she waved, then pointed at me. "Barbara wants you to stop by and say hello."

"Why did you do that? I have no desire to talk to him yet."

"Yet?"

I had hoped to gather my thoughts before confronting Jeremy, to figure out how I was going to deal with my suspicions. But it was too late. He saw me and headed right for our table.

"Now this *is* a surprise," he smirked as he pulled up a chair and sat down. "You couldn't resist coming here to catch my act, huh, BS?"

"Hardly," I said. "I had no idea you were performing here, Jeremy. I came for the lobster."

"Sure you did," he grinned, wiping the sweat off his face with my napkin. Then he turned to Suzanne. "Who's this?"

The man had impeccable manners. "*This* is my friend, Suzanne Munson," I said. "We work together at Home Sweet Home."

"How're you doin', Suzanne," he said, and winked at her.

"Great. I'm really enjoying your music," she said, gazing at him approvingly. Why, I couldn't fathom. I suppose he did have a certain macho charm. Well, not *charm* exactly. It was more of an attitude, the sort of tough-guy pose that some women found irresistible but I found asinine.

"Well, that's the point, right? You're here to enjoy yourself," he said to Suzanne. As the waitress passed by our table, he reached out and grabbed the woman around the waist and pulled her toward him. "How 'bout a cold Bud, huh, sweetheart?"

"You bet," she said, kissing him on the cheek before hurrying off. Two minutes later she was back with his beer and kissed him again. It was sickening—but not nearly as sickening as what happened next. A very young woman, a redhead in tight blue jeans and an even tighter tank top, barged right over to our table, nearly knocking me onto the floor, and draped her arms around Jeremy's neck, then sat on his lap. She couldn't have been more than nineteen.

"Gee, Jeremy, I didn't know you had a daughter," I couldn't resist saying.

He laughed. "Melanie's an old friend," he said, patting her on her ass. "Aren't you, honey?"

Melanie wasn't much of a talker, it turned out. Nodding and giggling and whispering in Jeremy's ear was about the extent of her communication skills.

The two of them played kissy-face for several minutes, completely ignoring Suzanne and me. They were getting on my nerves. Big time. When I couldn't take it anymore, I muttered to myself, "I wish Melanie would slap his face and tell him to fuck off."

A scant two seconds after I'd uttered the words, Jeremy's little playmate hauled off and smacked him hard across the face, picked herself up off his lap and said, "Go fuck yourself, you old letch." And then she left the table without so much as a good-bye. Just like that.

Maybe David was right, I thought, squelching a smile as Jeremy massaged his aching cheek. Being a darksider did have its advantages.

"How do ya like that," said Jeremy, looking more amused than angry. "The young babes are real spontaneous, huh? You never know what they're gonna do."

"If you say so," I said. "I'm not the connoisseur of jail bait that you are."

He laughed as he got up from his chair. "I'd love to stay and listen to you insult me, but my break's over," he said.

"Oh? So soon?" I said with unmistakable sarcasm.

"Yeah, and I'm heartbroken," he said. "How 'bout you, BS?"

"Heartbroken," I said.

He nodded. "Well, it was nice meetin' you, Suzanne," he said, shaking her hand. "Glad one of you is enjoyin' the show."

As he strode off to join his buddies onstage, I kept my eyes on him, assessing him, studying him, trying to catch even a hint of the devil's presence in him. I had a strong feeling that he *was* Satan's cover in Banyan Beach, but then I'd had the same feeling about a dozen other people. I needed a sign. Something concrete. Something that would provide me with evidence that Jeremy was the one I was looking for.

When I got home from The Hellhole, I called David.

"Barbara. What a nice surprise," he said.

"I haven't changed my mind, if that's what you're thinking," I said. "I'm not going to sleep with you and conceive the devil's baby."

"Maybe not now," he said.

"Not ever."

"All right, but why can't we at least keep each other company? I'm lonely."

"Then find another woman to keep you company. As I said on Saturday night, my guess is that there are plenty of women desperate enough to overlook the little matter of your tail."

"The devil wants *us* to be together, Barbara, and we owe it to him. It's part of the deal we made. If you don't hold up your end of the bargain, I won't be able to hold up mine, and who knows what will happen then? For all I know, the devil will turn me back into the nebbish I was before my transformation."

"Would that really be so bad?"

"Yes."

"I'm sorry you feel that way, David. Because I don't. I want out of the deal, which is why I called. Remember when you said Satan was hiding in the body of someone I know?"

"I can't answer any more questions. I already told you that."

"Oh, come on, David. Just one more."

"No."

"You said you cared about me."

"I do. You're my only friend now."

"Then prove it. Answer this one question. Please."

Silence.

"Please."

More silence. I was getting to him. I could tell.

"Pleeeeze."

"All right," he said. "One more. But only to prove how much I value our friendship."

"Great. Now, here's my question: Is Jeremy Cook the devil's cover in Banyan Beach? Is he, David?"

"Jeremy Cook? The fellow who came over to your house that night and made a nuisance of himself?"

"That's right."

"What makes you think he's the one you're looking for?"

"You said the devil was hiding in the body of someone I know."

"Yes, but you're a real estate agent. You know lots of people."

"Not as 'devilish' as Jeremy. When we graduated from high school, he wasn't voted the Most Likely to Succeed; Mitchell was.

Jeremy was voted the Most Likely to Appear on a 'Wanted' Poster. He was always getting into trouble."

"So?"

"So isn't he the sort of person the devil would choose to hide in?"

"Possibly."

"Oh, come on, David. Just tell me the truth: is it Jeremy?"

"I can't confirm or deny that."

"It *is* Jeremy, isn't it?"

"You don't give up, do you?"

"Not when my soul is at stake. No."

David didn't say anything for several seconds.

"Are you there?" I asked.

"I'm here," he said.

"Are you going to answer my question? Is Jeremy Cook the one?"

"If I said yes, would that make you believe that I'm willing to sacrifice my own safety to help you? That even though I'm a dark-sider, I'm a good guy?"

"The answer's yes," I said breathlessly, sensing David was caving in.

He hesitated. "Then mine is, too."

CHAPTER
15

Now what? I asked myself after hanging up the phone and sinking into the living room sofa. Now that I knew that the devil had taken up residence in the body of Jeremy Cook, what was I supposed to do about it? Drive a stake through Jeremy's heart? Throw crosses at him? Or Jewish stars? Tie him to a chair and force him to listen to that CD of Benedictine monks performing Gregorian chants? What?

Before I could ponder the subject any further, Pete decided to have one of his periodic bouts of barking. It was odd. Every time I really needed a little peace and quiet to deal with this devil business, the dog had an absolute fit. For no reason. He didn't appear to want food or water. He didn't appear to want to be let outside to relieve himself. He didn't appear to have fleas. He just barked at me. Woof! Woof! Woof! Woof! Nonstop.

"Hey," I said, reaching out to scratch the white patch on his chest. "I'm trying to think."

"Woof! Woof! Woof!"

"Look, Pete. I'm not a mind reader," I said. "Are you lonely for your real owner? Is that it?"

The question only provoked more barking. I was about to put him outside, whether he liked it or not, when he trotted over to the corner of the room. In my rush to call David after coming home from The Hellhole, I had dumped my purse and briefcase onto the floor and left them there in a heap. Now, Pete had his face in the briefcase and appeared to be going through my things. Then he did something truly bizarre: he gripped my MLS book between his teeth, dragged it out of the briefcase, and brought it over to me, like a cat with a mouse in its mouth. He dropped the book on the floor and started poking through the pages with his nose.

"Oh, I get it. You're in the market for a new house," I laughed as he rifled through the Multiple Listing Service reference, the realtors' bible that featured all the properties currently being offered for sale in the county.

I stopped laughing when I saw that Pete had opened the book to a specific page and placed his right front paw on top of it, as if he were marking it. And then he began to bark again. He seemed to be trying to tell me something, trying to *show* me something.

I got up from the sofa and knelt down beside him. To my amazement, he had opened the book to the exact page where the Nowak house was pictured—the house that had brought David Bettinger into my life!

What in the world was going on? Was it a coincidence that Pete had brought that page to my attention? It had to be. He was probably just playing around, the way dogs often did, and happened to paw that page by accident. Still, it was a pretty funny bit.

"Hey, Pete," I said. "Maybe you should audition for David Letterman's Stupid Pet Tricks."

He stared at me with his soulful hazel eyes, barked a few more times, and then lay down at my feet, licking my shoes.

At least he's quiet now, I noticed, as I sat back down on the couch and let the events of the evening replay in my mind. It was late by this time—midnight or so—and I was exhausted.

Tomorrow, I decided as my thoughts grew muddled and my lids heavy. Tomorrow I'll figure out how to confront the devil, Jeremy and all the rest. Now I'm going to sleep.

And, with my trusty canine by my side, I did.

The growling returned on Tuesday morning. Not Pete's. *Mine.* I growled during the "Today" show. I growled as I ate breakfast. I growled while I got dressed for work. If David was right, and the growling was the devil's way of telling me to stop fighting my fate, I was getting the message loud and clear. The problem was, I couldn't stop fighting my fate. I wasn't about to be a darksider for the rest of my life. I yearned to be Barbara Chessner again, double chin and all.

As I drove to the office, I decided that if I really wanted to get the devil out of Banyan Beach and out of my life, I'd have to communicate with him somehow. And the only way to do that, I now knew, was through Jeremy Cook. Which meant that I'd have to spend time with Jeremy, a man I loathed, a man who, according to David, didn't even realize that the devil had taken over his body. I'd have to follow him around, observe him, get to know him, in order to figure out the best way to confront Satan. I couldn't just walk up to him and say, "Come out, come out, wherever you are!" This wasn't a game, as David had reminded me. This was serious business, a battle between Good and Evil. I had to handle the situation with care, with tact, with subtlety. I'd have to work up to a confrontation, take things slowly, wait for the devil to reveal himself.

I spent the morning showing houses. When I got back to the office, I called my brother and asked him for Jeremy's phone number.

"Let me get this straight. You want Jeremy's number?" he asked, stunned by my request. "Jeremy, the guy you can't stand?"

"Yes," I said. "I want to ask him something."

"What did you want to ask him?"

Think of a good one, Barbara. "I had a customer this morning who wanted to know about the fishing in Banyan Beach," I said. "I told him I'd find out what I could. Since Jeremy's so knowledgeable about the subject, I thought I'd ask him."

"I'm sure he'll be surprised and flattered to hear from you," said Ben, who gave me Jeremy's home number as well as the number of the marina where his charter boat was docked. "Come to think of it, Jeremy's kind of hard to reach by phone. Why don't you just go down to the marina and talk to him?" he suggested. "He's usually back there by four o'clock."

"Maybe I will, thanks," I said.

Eddie's Marina was not frequented by the country club set. It was a hangout for men whose arms were disproportionately larger than the rest of their body and virtually covered with tattoos. (Think Pop-eye.) These men didn't own sleek and sophisticated sailboats; they owned "stinkpots"—big, macho power boats with tuna towers and 750-horsepower engines and serious fishing gear. And speaking of fishing, the place reeked of fish—dead fish *and* male body odor. Where was potpourri when you needed it?

"Could you please tell me where I can find Jeremy Cook, the captain of Cook's Charters?" I asked the first man who didn't leer at me.

"Sure. He's at 'C' dock, slip 14," he said, pointing to the maze of docks to my left. "But I don't think he's come in yet. You wanna talk to his father?"

"His father?"

"Yeah, the old captain. Mike Cook was the original 'Cook' in Cook's Charters," the man explained. "He fished with Hemingway, ya know."

"Is that right?" I said, trying not to look blasé. Unfortunately, every old guy in Florida claims to have fished with Hemingway, the same way that every young girl in Florida claims to have slept with a Kennedy. These men claim to have fished with Hemingway in Key West, in Islamorada, in Bimini, you name it. If all the people who say they fished with Hemingway really did, the man would never have had time to write novels.

"Yup. He can tell some amazin' stories, old Mike. All ya gotta do is ask him."

I nodded politely. I didn't want to sit and listen to fish stories. I wanted to see Jeremy and convince the devil living inside him to leave town.

"Go on," the man urged. "He's sittin' right over there."

He motioned in the direction of a thin, white-haired man sitting in the folding chair at the foot of the "C" dock, reading the newspaper and smoking a cigarette.

"Thanks a lot," I said, then popped a couple of BreathAssures before walking toward Jeremy's father. I hoped he could tell me when his son was due back at the marina, as I didn't plan to camp out there all night.

"Excuse me, Mr. Cook?" I asked when I reached Mike Cook. He was wiry and weathered—seventy-something, I guessed.

"That's me," he said, looking up at me with lively green eyes and drawing on his cigarette. "What can I do for you, darlin'?"

"I'm looking for your son," I said.

"For Jeremy? Now why would a pretty thing like you be lookin' for an ugly son of a gun like him?" He laughed a congested smoker's laugh, but it wasn't at all derisive. It was proud, paternal, full of admiration. It was clear that "ugly son of a gun" was a term of endearment, that he adored Jeremy. The love was there on his face from the moment he mentioned his son's name. I felt a stab of envy, having never seen that look on the faces of my own parents.

"I wanted to speak to him," I told Mike Cook.

"Not about a charter, I bet," he chuckled. "You don't strike me as a lady who's done much fishin'." He was appraising my outfit— a tasteful black sleeveless linen dress, a single strand of pearls, and black patent leather sandals, the tiny heels of which kept getting caught between the wood planks of the dock.

"I've never done any fishing," I admitted. "I've played a little tennis, but no fishing."

"You oughta try it sometime," he suggested. "Jeremy'll take you out in the Hatteras."

"Thanks anyway, Mr. Cook, but I'm really not a fish person."

"A fish person? Is that what they call it now?" He threw back his head and laughed.

His laughter was contagious and I began to laugh right along with him. I liked the easiness of this man, the lilting Southern accent, the laconic manner, the warmth. I felt comfortable with him, more so in thirty seconds than I'd felt during a lifetime with my own father.

"You must know my brother," I said suddenly.

"Your brother? And who might he be?"

"Benjamin Greenberg. I'm Barbara Greenberg Chessner. I was in Jeremy's class in high school."

Another grin broke out across Mike Cook's leathery face. "You're Benny's sister?" he said, his voice teasing yet kind.

I nodded.

"Well then, shake my hand, darlin', and be quick about it."

He extended his gnarled, arthritic right hand and I shook it enthusiastically. It was odd that we'd never met, I thought, given how close Ben and Jeremy were. On the other hand, my parents would never have socialized with people as low-rent as the Cooks. And they certainly would never have encouraged me to.

"So you're the one Jeremy fell for back then," said Mike Cook, running his eyes over me as he took a drag of his cigarette.

"Oh, no," I protested. "Not me. You must be thinking of one of the other girls we went to school with. Jeremy and I sort of moved in different crowds." To put it mildly.

Mike shook his head. "Nope. You were the one. My wife remembered."

"Then you might want to tell her she's wrong," I said.

"Can't," said Mike. "She's been dead for over a year."

"Oh. I'm sorry. I didn't know."

" 'Course you didn't. Only Jeremy knew."

"What do you mean, Mr. Cook?"

"Patty never told a soul she was sick. Only Jeremy knew she had cancer without her sayin' anything. Jeremy's got a sixth sense about stuff like that."

Sure he does, I wanted to scream. He's got the devil living inside him. He can see death coming a mile away.

"Anyhow, Patty used to hear him talk about Barbara this and Barbara that. You damn near broke his heart, huh?"

I stared at Jeremy Cook's father and wondered if he was senile. Why else would he say that Jeremy had genuinely cared for me and I had broken his heart?

It wasn't possible. For starters, Jeremy didn't have a heart to break, not in high school and not now. As I'd said to Suzanne only the night before, he viewed women the same way he viewed fish— as objects of conquest. Once he caught one, he'd throw her back.

For another thing, I had never been anyone's idea of a heartbreaker in high school, much less Jeremy's. Back then, I was an uptight princess with unfortunate hair and an even more unfortunate body. I compensated for the boys' lack of interest in me by telling myself I didn't have any interest in them either. Not me. *I* was holding out for Prince Charming or Paul McCartney or whoever came first. As for Jeremy, his taste seemed to run toward sluts—girls with names like Ricki and Tawny and Candy, girls who rebelled against their parents and did whatever they wanted, girls who weren't holding out for anybody.

Of course, Jeremy *had* asked me to be his date for the senior prom, but that was only because of my brother, who had felt sorry that I was such a wallflower and pleaded with Jeremy to take me. I had accepted and then pretended to be sick and Jeremy had never forgiven me. That was the way it *really* was.

No, Mike Cook was mistaken. The "Barbara" Jeremy mentioned to his mother must have been Barbara Delafield. *Bobbi* Delafield. The girl who graduated from high school and went immediately into a career on the stage—at Titters, the strip joint that was now home to The Hellhole.

While we waited for Jeremy to come in off the *Devil-May-Care,* Mike Cook talked about fishing. I braced myself for the fabled Hemingway stories, but, mercifully, I was spared. Instead, he told me how he and his wife had started Cook's Charters in the fifties.

"I loved to fish and was pretty damn good at it," he recalled without modesty. "So Patty and I decided to make a business of it. We went to the big hotels south of here—Banyan Beach only had the Driftwood Motel in those days—and got a couple of charter concessions. I took the hotel guests out for the day and Patty kept the books. 'Course, the minute Jeremy was old enough to sit up, I taught him to fish like his daddy, startin' him out in the river and then graduatin' him to the deep sea stuff. One weekend—I think it was in '59 when he was two—I took him fishing on the St. Lucie and before the day was over we'd caught over five hundred snook."

I smiled and nodded, even though I didn't know a snook from a schnook.

" 'Course you couldn't do that today," he went on. "Not around here."

"Why not?" I asked.

He laughed. "You sure aren't a 'fish person' if you don't know what's goin' on," he said, his tone not accusatory, just surprised. "Well, let me educate you: the reason you couldn't catch five hundred snook in one day is 'cause there aren't as many snook in the water as there used to be."

I was confused. "But doesn't Jeremy take people fishing every day?"

"He sure does."

"Well, if there aren't as many fish in the water, how does he stay in business?"

He laughed again. "You're mixin' up two kinds of fishing. Jeremy takes people deep-sea fishing in the Hatteras. In the *ocean*. He catches tuna and snapper and fish like that. If you're lookin' for snook, you gotta go in shallow waters in a shallow draft boat. But you're not gonna find 'em like before. We used to get out there on the river and be able to see clear to the bottom. There'd be massive schools of snook and mullet feedin' on the sea grass. Now there's no sea grass and no fish. Only mud."

"Mud?" I showed houses along the river practically every day and I hadn't seen any mud. Of course, I'd never actually *looked* at the water, really looked at it. It was just there—the "water" in waterfront property. It provided wealthy homeowners with a nice view, was an "amenity" that could be hyped to customers. That was about as much as I knew about it or cared.

"Darlin', we got ooze where the sea grass used to be and algae where the fish used to be. You gotta go south of here if you're lookin' for snook."

"What killed the fish?" I asked, realizing I sounded like an environmentally challenged person.

"Real estate," he said matter-of-factly. "The developers started buildin' houses along the river and the real estate agents were only too happy to sell 'em. Before we knew it, we had pesticides and herbicides, fertilizer and sewage running off into the water. And that's only part of the problem. Once the houses started going up west of here, along Lake Okeechobee, everybody started worryin' about floods after heavy rains. So the Army Corps of Engineers got this brilliant idea to dump the runoff into our rivers. If I had a couple of minutes alone with one of those guys I'd—" He laughed.

"You'd what?" I asked.

"Oh nothin'. I'm a talker, not a doer," he conceded. "Jeremy's the doer in the family. 'Course, sometimes he goes overboard. Gets himself into trouble. 'Specially lately."

"Lately?" I asked with interest. "Has he been acting differently? Getting himself into more trouble than usual?" Now that he's been taken over by the devil?

"Well, let's just say he's been involved in things he won't tell me about."

"Really?"

"Yeah, and I'm worried about him. Patty's not here to worry, so it's up to me now."

Mike Cook sounded like a man who loved his wife and missed her now that she was gone. I wondered how his son got to be such a womanizer, flitting from one tramp to another, never being able to commit.

"Hey, there's Jeremy now," said Mike, shielding his eyes from the late afternoon sun.

I turned to look and could see the *Devil-May-Care* pulling into the slip. Jeremy was standing at the steering wheel, barking orders at the two teenage boys who were lowering the fender boards and readying the dock lines.

"Do you and Jeremy still fish together?" I asked Mike Cook as Jeremy gave his crew instructions.

"Once in a while," he said. "When he's got a free day. I retired in '86 and handed the charter business over to him. I help him keep track of the bookings but he's the captain now and he's done a good job of it. Got a couple more hotels on board, done some promotion. 'Course the fact that he sings in that rock 'n' roll band doesn't hurt. He gets up on stage wearing the Cook's Charters T-shirts. It brings people in, ya know?"

"I'm sure it does. Tell me, did he always sing as well as he does now? I mean, is that something new?" Something brought about by the devil?

Mike regarded me as he lit up another cigarette. "You here to interview Jeremy or somethin'? For the local paper? You never did say what you came to see him about."

"No, I guess I didn't." I paused to think. "It's about Benjamin," I said.

"Benny?" he asked with concern.

I nodded. "He's—"

"Hey, that can't be BS, can it?" Jeremy yelled when he stepped off the boat and saw me talking to his father.

He had a big smile on his face as he strutted along the dock, his cheeks and nose rosy with sunburn. He looked awfully cheerful for a person who had the devil living inside him.

The devil, I thought, my heart beating wildly. This wasn't Jeremy Cook walking toward me, I reminded myself. This was Satan. The Force of Darkness. The Evil One. The guy that made me a darksider and expected me to produce more darksiders. The guy that was responsible for plague and pestilence and, whether Mike Cook knew it or not, the pollution of his beloved river. After days of wondering how it would feel to be face-to-face with him, to actually speak to him, it was finally going to happen. The adrenaline was pumping, let me tell you.

"Would'ya look at this. BS has gone slumming two days in a row," said Jeremy when he reached us. He patted his father on the back and then focused on me. "First, The Hellhole. Now, Eddie's Marina. What's the world coming to?"

"If it were up to you, the world would be teeming with darksiders," I said, speaking louder than normal, so the devil would be sure to hear me in there.

"Teeming with what?" said Jeremy, looking perplexed. God, the devil was such a phony, pretending not to understand.

"You know exactly what I'm talking about," I said.

I couldn't get over it. The person standing next to me looked like Jeremy, talked like Jeremy, even smelled of beer like Jeremy. And yet . . . he wasn't Jeremy. Not really. As David explained it, the person whose body the devil chose to hide in no longer existed. Which meant that *Jeremy* no longer existed. I was speaking directly to Satan, even though he was playing dumb, perhaps because we were not alone.

"So what are you doin' here, BS?" he said, ignoring my odd behavior. "I see you've met my dad."

His dad. I bit my lip. It was sad, really. Mike Cook seemed like such a nice man. He'd already had his wife taken away from him, and now his only son had been taken away, too. At least, for the time being.

"Sure, Barbara and I are old friends now," Mike volunteered. "But it was you she came to see. About her brother, she said."

"Is Ben sick or somethin'?" Jeremy asked.

No, it's you who's sick, I thought with revulsion as I tried to look *through* Jeremy, into the eyes of the evil one.

"What's the matter with Ben?" Jeremy asked again when I didn't answer.

"I don't want to bother your father with my family problems," I said. "It's something I should discuss with you alone, if possible."

Jeremy licked his lips lasciviously. "Sounds like she *wants* me, Dad. I think all this stuff about Ben is a cover."

"You ought to know about covers," I said, hoping the devil would realize that I was not a person to be toyed with, not a person to let him parade around in the body of my brother's best friend.

"What's that supposed to mean?" said Jeremy.

"As if you didn't know," I said.

He shrugged. "Obviously, I'm not followin' you, sweetheart, but I can see that somethin's got you all upset. Why don't we go back to my place and you can tell me all about it?"

He threw his sweaty arm around my shoulder but I moved away.

"Fine. Don't," he said, then proceeded to talk to his father about the day's adventures on the high seas.

As the two of them engaged in a lively debate on the issue of whether it was better to fish after a storm than during one, I tried to figure out what to do next. The thought of being alone with Jeremy at his house, wherever that was, was frightening. Who knew what the devil might do to me when there was no one else around? On the other hand, going home with Jeremy would give me just the opportunity I was looking for—a chance to sit down with Satan and speak my piece, maybe even convince him to leave my town and me alone.

"Jeremy," I interrupted just as they were moving on to a discussion of rods or rigs or some such thing, "I *would* like to talk to you. At your house, if I wouldn't be imposing."

"Sure," he said, looking utterly confused, as if he didn't know what was going on. The devil was such a snake. "Dad? You gonna go on home now?"

"Pretty soon," said Mike Cook. "I like to wait for all the guys to come in. Tell 'em good night. The way I always do."

Jeremy nodded. "Then I'll see you in the morning. We got that group from Hutchinson Island tomorrow, right?"

Mike regarded the clipboard on his lap. "Yup, four of 'em. At eight o'clock."

Jeremy nodded. "Have a good one," he said, patting his father on the back once again and motioning for me to follow him down the dock to the parking lot.

16

Jeremy got into his pickup truck, bellowed for me to follow him in my car, and then drove off in a cloud of dust.

When we reached the first traffic light, I leaned out the window of my Lexus and yelled, "How far are we going?" I knew he lived somewhere near me but had no idea where.

"How far do you wanna go, sweetheart?" he yelled back. "There won't be anyone around to chaperone us."

"That wasn't what I meant," I muttered, wondering exactly what *would* happen once I was alone with Jeremy.

We drove toward the beach, toward "Millionaires' Row," as we realtors call the rarefied strip of oceanfront property on which palatial, multimillion-dollar houses and condominiums had been erected on once-deserted sand. Seacrest Way, where I lived, occupied a more modest section of beachfront—a cul-de-sac for wanna-bes. That's what Mitchell Chessner was: a wanna-be. Actually, to be more precise, he was a look-at-me. While I was pathologically obsessed with people liking me, with their thinking I was a nice person, Mitchell was pathologically obsessed with people envying him, with their thinking he was a *rich* person. When I had showed him the house at 666 Seacrest Way, he'd insisted that we make an offer on it, not because it was on the ocean—Mitchell never set foot in the water, claiming he had too much salt in his diet as it was. No, his explanation for wanting to buy the house was: "It makes a statement."

Ah, Mitchell, I sighed as I recalled our life together. What could I have been thinking when I hitched my wagon to yours? Was I so hell-bent on pleasing my parents that I'd sell myself out by marrying a fool like you?

Sell myself out, I thought as I drove. Wasn't that what I had done the night Mitchell left me? Hadn't I stepped outside in that thunderstorm and cried that I would do anything for a five-hundred-thousand-dollar customer, a better body, a man to love? Hadn't I sold myself out yet again, this time to the devil? Was I thoroughly incapable of figuring out what *I* really wanted out of life and then getting it for myself? Was I so passive that I had to depend, first on Mitchell, then on some supernatural force, to fulfill my dreams for me? Was I?

No, I decided. This time it's different. That's why I'm risking everything and going after the devil. This time I'm not taking the easy way out.

We passed my street and continued along Ocean Avenue until we came to a series of narrow side roads, each named for a tropical flower and each leading down to the water. Jeremy's blinker indicated that we would be turning left onto one of these roads, Hibiscus Street.

So that's where he lives, I mused, remembering a house I had listed there several years before. It was an area of older homes—beach shacks, really, with spectacular views and unspectacular everything else. Many of the houses were rental properties that had been abused by college kids and surfers and people who were more interested in having a good time than in getting written up in *Architectural Digest*. Some of the houses belonged to old-timers who didn't have the money or the inclination to fix them up. Nearly all the houses were without air-conditioning and cable TV and three-car garages, the sort of amenities that were absolute necessities everywhere else. (Actually, three-and-a-half-car garages were all the rage with the moneyed set, the "half" representing the space reserved especially for their golf cart.) Leave it to Jeremy Cook to live in one of these shanties, I thought, as we drove by Number 3, Number 4, Number 5, and so on.

When we got to the end of the street, to Number 8, Jeremy signaled that we'd be turning into the driveway, which was unpaved and ungraveled—a dirt path with a line of grass growing up the middle.

I braced myself for a hopeless dump, given the neighborhood—and the fact that Jeremy had never exhibited even the slightest interest in his own appearance, nor had he struck me as the type who would be home enough to care about his living quarters.

I was, therefore, shocked when the driveway meandered down to a small but strikingly charming house—a weathered shingled cottage surrounded by a profusion of hibiscus plants, as well as bushes of brilliantly colored bougainvillea. Aside from the tropical flowers, it had the romantic, beachy feel of a house in Cape Cod, not in South Florida. Moreover, it looked neat and tidy, so unlike Jeremy.

But then what did I really know about Jeremy anyway? I realized as I sat in my car and watched him walk up to his front door. I mean, I knew him, had known him, since I was a kid. He'd been in my life for as long as I could remember. Not in an important way, of course. Just tangentially. In the background. A vague but chronic irritant. My image of him was shaped by my childhood memories of him, by his friendship with my brother, by the stories I'd heard about him. And yet, it had been years since I'd actually spent any real time with him. He and Mitchell had despised each other ever since high school, so I wasn't about to invite him to dinner. And then there was the thoroughly obnoxious manner in which he always treated me. So crude, so cocky, so determined to shock me or piss me off. In the past, I'd never had any reason for getting to know the man behind the image. But now, I did. Now, I needed to know as much as I could about Jeremy. Now, my life depended on it.

"What's the matter?" he asked as he waited for me to get out of my car.

"I . . . well I didn't expect this," I said, walking over to him. "Is this place really yours?"

"No, it's the devil's," he said sarcastically.

I stared at him, stared into his eyes. So Satan has decided to show himself to me, I thought with a mixture of fear and excitement. He realizes that we're finally alone and he's going to let me see him.

"*Now* what is it?" asked Jeremy as he looked at me quizzically.

"There's no need to play games," I said, keeping my voice steady and my eyes glued to his face. "Not anymore."

"Games? What are you talkin' about, BS? You've gotta start makin' sense or it's gonna be a long night. Now come inside."

Fine, I thought. If the devil wants to show himself to me one minute and run for cover the next, I'll just play along. I'll act as if I'm simply having a casual visit with Jeremy, as if he's an old friend I haven't seen in a while. I'll bide my time. See what happens.

He went into the house and I followed him, continuing to observe him but at the same time stealing glances at my surroundings. The entire house couldn't have been more than a thousand square feet, I saw, and consisted of only two rooms: the room in which we stood—an open, airy living room/dining room/kitchen with beamed ceiling, hardwood flooring, stone fireplace, and breathtaking ocean view—and a small bedroom around the corner. It wasn't fancy, by any means, but spare, simple, cozy, livable, the only "artwork" being the grainy, black-and-white photographs of men in fishing boats that hung on the walls.

"Want a beer?" Jeremy asked, still looking at me with curiosity. He was standing in the small, jalousie-windowed kitchen, a dated but nevertheless spotless area.

"No," I said. Then on second thought, figuring that beer was probably all Jeremy had in the way of alcoholic beverages and feeling the need for some fortification, I changed my mind. "Yes, I'll have one."

He shook his head at me, then reached into the refrigerator and got us each a can of Bud Lite.

"Have you lived here long?" I asked him, trying to be chatty.

"Fifteen years," he said, opening his can of beer and taking a swig.

Hmmm, I thought. According to David, the devil had only been in Florida for ten years.

"It's really nice. Did you have to fix it up or did you buy it like this?" I asked.

"The place belonged to my aunt. When she went to live with her sister in Ocala, I bought it from her, then did the floors, replaced the windows, painted, stuff like that."

He walked over to the stereo system on the other side of the living room, where there were scores of CDs and tapes, plus a cabinet full of albums. He searched the cabinet and eventually removed one of the albums from its sleeve.

"You like the Stones?" he asked, holding up an old vinyl record.

"Sure. Whatever," I said.

He placed the record on the turntable, and seconds later, the sounds of the Rolling Stones filled the large space. But was it just *any* Rolling Stones song that Jeremy played? Nooooo. It was "Sympathy for the Devil." From the *Beggar's Banquet* album. Obviously, Satan was intent on having a little fun with me. First, he'd have Jeremy act as if nothing out of the ordinary was going on; then, he'd play "Peekaboo!" with me, showing himself to me through song lyrics. It was maddening.

"You don't deserve anybody's sympathy," I snapped when Jeremy rejoined me in the kitchen.

"What are you talking about now?" he said.

"Never mind." Snapping at Satan wasn't going to get me anywhere. I had to stick to my strategy. Pretend that Jeremy was still Jeremy instead of the empty shell he'd become. "Why don't we sit down?" I suggested.

Jeremy scratched his beard in frustration and led me to the chairs facing the water. They were framed in pine and upholstered in a heavy white canvas. Like the rest of the house, they were simple and comfortable.

"So," I said as we sat. "You were saying that you fixed the house up yourself."

"And *you* were sayin' that you wanted to talk to me about Ben," he said. "Is somethin' wrong with him, BS?"

"No, he's fine as far as I know," I said. "I only told your father it was about Ben because I didn't want to tell him the real reason I needed to speak to you."

"And that reason is?"

"Real estate."

"Give me a break."

"No, really. I didn't want to say anything to your father because he seems to have a low opinion of real estate agents." I was winging this, obviously. "Here's the thing. I have this customer who's ninety-nine percent sure he's going to buy a place in Banyan Beach, but he wants to know about the fishing here. He's a fishing nut, I guess." And I'm not a bad liar, I thought.

"If he's such a fishing nut, how come he doesn't already know about the fishing here?"

"Because he's only fished up north. He doesn't know about the fishing in Florida. I'm not knowledgeable enough to answer his questions, so I thought maybe you could tell me a few—"

"That's it? That's the reason you came over here?" Jeremy cut me off.

I nodded.

He looked disappointed.

"Have the guy call me," he said abruptly.

"That's nice of you, but I'd rather you talked to *me* about the fishing and then I'll talk to him. That way I can seem like the authority. The object is to convince him to buy property from *me*, Jeremy."

"Anything to sell a house, huh?"

"It's not a house he wants to buy. It's a condo. In a very exclusive new building," I said, keeping my little charade going.

"You're not talkin' about the River Princess, that fancy high-rise they're puttin' up on the river?"

"As a matter of fact I am," I lied. Well, actually, that part wasn't a lie. I did have a customer who was ninety-nine percent sure he was going to buy a condo in the River Princess, but the man wasn't the least bit interested in fishing. Polo was his sport.

"Then you oughta be ashamed of yourself," said Jeremy. "The River Princess is the worst thing to happen to this town in years."

"Why do you say that?" I asked. The twenty-eight-story River Princess was the latest real estate venture of a group of very successful developers from Miami. It was being promoted as Banyan Beach's most luxurious waterfront condominium, complete with twenty-four-hour security, heated pool and spa, marina, tennis, riverside clubhouse, and apartments that were dripping in marble. Preconstruction prices had started at $750,000 for a one-bedroom unit, and went as high as $2,500,000, for a three-bedroom apartment. Occupancy was scheduled for August 15, with the gala opening celebration only a week away. I was very familiar with the building because Home Sweet Home was the listing agent on the property—or, more specifically, Frances Lutz was. Suzanne had remarked that Frances, the self-proclaimed "ranch specialist," was an unlikely listing agent for a building with twenty-eight floors, but I reminded her that the River Princess had two banks of elevators. Frances wouldn't even have to *look* at a flight of stairs.

"Why do I say that? Because it's monstrosities like the River Princess that are pollutin' our rivers and promotin' crime in our town," said Jeremy.

"I think you're exaggerating."

"And I think you've got your head in the sand, or should I say *ooze*. The runoff from the River Princess—I'm talkin' about the oil and the pesticides and the sewage—is killin' the fish, sweetheart."

"You sound like your father."

"He knows what he's talkin' about, 'specially when it comes to the slimy, backroom stuff that went on between the zoning guys and the developers of that building. It would make your hair stand on end."

Maybe that's next, I thought wryly. First, the devil makes my hair blond. Now, he's going to make it stand on end.

"I'm tellin' you, BS. The River Princess is bad news for this town," Jeremy went on. "Bad news."

I arched an eyebrow at him. Why on earth would the devil mind if the town went to hell? I wondered. Why would he care if it was overrun by pollution and crime? Wasn't that the point? Wasn't that why Satan had come to Banyan Beach in the first place? To ruin the town? To re-create it in his own diabolical image? And yet, here was Jeremy acting as if he were opposed to the very evils that were Satan's calling card. Was there a chance that David was mistaken about Jeremy being the devil's cover? Or were Jeremy's words just a decoy?

"You'd better make your money on those condos while you can," he warned. "In a few days, they won't be worth a damn."

"Why?" I said, thinking of the huge commissions Home Sweet Home would earn once all the units in the building were sold.

"Just forget it, BS. Forget I said anything."

"How can I forget you said anything?"

"Just do it, okay?"

He was being awfully mysterious, but then consider the source. The devil wasn't reputed to be the quintessence of openness and forthrightness.

"Fine. I'll forget it." I pondered what to do next, how to keep the conversation going without making the devil angry. "Let's get back to fishing," I suggested. "For instance, tell me about the people you took out in the *Devil-May-Care* today."

He swallowed some beer. "You wanna know about today's charter?"

"Yes."

He was about to begin speaking when he stopped and grinned awkwardly. "I gotta tell you, this whole thing is a little weird."

"What is?"

"The fact that you and I are sittin' here talkin'. Like we do this every day. Like we haven't spent the last twenty years avoidin' each other."

"Nonsense. I certainly haven't been avoiding—"

"Sure you have," he interrupted. "Except for the night you wanted me to pick up your dog and take him to Ben's. I was doin' you a favor so you tolerated me. But basically, you think I'm pond scum. So what are you really doin' here, huh, BS?"

I didn't answer.

"First, you show up at my gig last night. Then, you show up at the marina," he continued. "And now, you sit here askin' me about fishing. What's the deal?"

"The *deal* is exactly why I'm here," I said, figuring that since the devil brought up the issue of our "bargain," it was okay to talk about it.

"Run that by me again?"

"I want *out* of the deal," I said.

"Look, I don't have a clue what's eatin' you. All I'm sayin' is that I don't buy the fishing bullshit. There's gotta be another reason you're here."

"There is. The deal is the reason I'm here."

"What deal are we talkin' about?"

"You know. The deal. The bargain. Whatever you want to call it."

Jeremy laughed again. "You real estate agents. All you talk about is The Deal." He took a long sip of beer. "If you came here to try and get me to put my house on the market, forget it."

"No, that's not why I—"

"But if you wanna talk about something else, I'm all for it. It's nice havin' you here."

So he's stalling me, I thought. Putting me off. Fine. I'll wait. He'll have to confront me at some point.

"Okay, no talk about deals," I agreed. "At least, not right now. Why don't you talk to me about your singing. Tell me what it's like to be a rock 'n' roll star."

"I'm not exactly a star, BS."

"Oh, come on. No false modesty. It must be fun to have groupies throw themselves at you."

"There are worse things."

"And the money must be nice."

"I don't take any money for the gigs."

"What do you mean you don't take any money?"

"Just what I said."

"You're telling me you sing for free?"

"Yeah. The other guys in the band keep their money, but I give mine away. To the Save the River Initiative. When you really believe in something, you gotta put your money where your mouth is, ya know?"

I was stunned. Was it possible that Jeremy Cook had principles? That the man I'd written off as a lowlife had values? That David had the wrong person? That Jeremy wasn't hiding the devil after all?

No, it's Satan talking, I reminded myself yet again. He's trying to delude me and he's doing a good job. That's part of what makes him so evil.

"But I don't sing for the money anyway," Jeremy was saying. "I sing because I love to sing. Next to fishin' and fuckin', it's the best."

"What a quaint way of putting it," I said.

" 'Course, I don't know how I'd feel about it if I had to stand up there and sing all by myself," he added. "Havin' the guys in the band up there with me makes it easier, less intimidatin'. And then there's the fact that we don't do original songs. If I had to stand up there and sing my own lyrics, I'd feel naked."

I actually blinked to make sure I wasn't imagining things. Was this really Jeremy Cook talking? Expressing himself? Exploring his feelings? Where was the usual bravado? The cockiness? The boorishness? Or was the devil specifically trying to make me view Jeremy in a whole different light? Trying to recast Mr. Retro as a shy, sensitive nineties man? So I'd feel closer to him? Relate to him? Think I'd been wrong about him, wrong about his being Satan's cover in Banyan Beach?

Yes, it has to be a trick, I decided. According to David, there *was* no more Jeremy because Jeremy Cook had been taken over by the devil. What came out of his mouth now were the words of Satan—words to be distrusted at all costs.

"Haven't you ever written any original songs?" I asked, hoping to keep him talking.

"Tried to. I've got a trunk full of 'em, but I've never been able to finish one. Scared to, probably. Creatin' something that comes deep from the heart is a scary, scary prospect."

I regarded him once again. It was inconceivable that the Jeremy I'd always known would talk to me about being scared of anything. Where was the bluster? The insufferable boasting? The I'm-too-cool-for-words attitude?

No, it was the devil who was playing up to me, up to my sympathies. And it wasn't going to work.

"Let's get back to the fishing," I said. "You were going to tell me about today's charter."

He stroked his red beard and smiled at me.

"You really must be desperate if you came *here* for conversation," he said. "I'm not exactly a raconteur."

Never mind that he bungled the pronunciation so badly that the word came out "reckanter." I had never seen Jeremy so self-deprecating.

"Sure I came here for conversation. You lead such an interesting life," I said, heavy on the sarcasm.

"Now I *know* you're bullshitting me," he laughed.

"No, really. Tell me about your charter."

He shrugged. "I took out three guys from Ohio. They're down here for that big drugstore convention," he began. "Their company makes hand lotion or some damn thing and the whole group of 'em are stayin' at the Ritz-Carlton."

"I didn't realize you had the concession at the Ritz," I said. I was impressed that Cook's Charters was doing so well. "Did these men catch any fish?"

"The CEO did. We were trolling ballyhoo in two hundred feet north of the St. Lucie Inlet."

"Ymmmm. Ballyhoo's delicious. I adore it deep fried, although it's perfectly good grilled, with a little pesto sauce on the side."

Jeremy threw back his head and laughed at me, just the way his father had hours before. I could see the family resemblance now. The Cook men weren't bad-looking when they laughed.

"What's so funny?" I asked.

"You are, BS."

"Why?"

"Because ballyhoo is bait fish. You don't eat it. You catch other fish with it. You're probably thinking of wahoo."

I shrugged. Ballyhoo. Wahoo. What did I know?

"The CEO caught a dolphin, BS. You've heard of dolphins?"

"Of course I have."

"Well, the one Mr. Hand Lotion caught was about twenty pounds."

"He must have been pleased."

"I couldn't tell. These corporate guys are hard to figure. They come on the boat with their cell phones and their tight sphincters and they don't know how to have any fun. I guess I'm lucky that way. I practically grew up with a fishing rod in my hand, so it's second nature to me."

"Your father told me how he taught you to fish when you were two," I said.

"He did. On the river. He was a good teacher, let me tell you. He took me down to the Keys, to the Bahamas, every place. I loved spendin' time with him. Still do."

I felt a stab of envy, just as I had when Mike Cook's face had radiated love for his son. I'd never spent much time with my own father and when I did, it was a kind of punishment. Ira Greenberg wasn't anything like the Cook men. He was stern, self-absorbed, humorless. Just like Mitchell.

"Did your father and mother have a happy marriage? He seems to miss her," I said.

Jeremy nodded. "He misses her a lot. When you love a woman the way my father loved her, it's gotta kill you when you can't be together."

I blinked again. Was this really Jeremy Cook who was waxing poetic about true love? The guy who'd never committed himself to any woman? The guy who pawed waitresses and nuzzled nineteen-year-olds and acted as if he'd rather die than say, "I do?"

No, it was the devil, I reminded myself for the hundredth time. It was Satan who was talking to me, confusing me, making me feel an attraction to Jeremy I'd never dreamed I'd feel.

An attraction? To Jeremy Cook? Where did that come from? I wondered. My face flushed as I had to admit that, for a split second, as he'd spoken about his father loving his mother, I had felt something for him. A pull. A tug. A sense of actually *liking* him.

I thought of David, of how fiercely attracted to him I'd been in the beginning, before I found out who and what he was, and I figured the devil was up to his old tricks, creating a chemistry between Jeremy and me to suit his own purposes.

Yes, of course, I decided. That has to be it.

"My father's such a good guy," Jeremy was saying. "Never complains even though his body's frail and he's got too much time on his hands. He's bored and lonely, which is why he likes to hang around the marina all the time. Not much else for him to do."

I didn't say anything. The realization that I was suddenly finding Jeremy anything other than irritating was scaring me.

"If you're the product of such a blissfully happy marriage, why haven't *you* ever been married?" I asked.

"You proposin'?" he smirked as he ran his eyes over my body. So much for the sensitive, vulnerable act. The macho crap was back.

"No, I'm not proposing. I was just wondering why you've never fallen in love."

"Who says I've never fallen in love?" he said. "You can't write love songs unless you've been in love, right?"

"Yes, but you've never finished a song. Isn't that what you told me?"

"What is this, an interrogation, BS? Am I on trial or somethin'?"

he asked, then checked his watch. He took a last sip of beer and said, "Hey, I gotta get goin'. Time to make some mischief."

Mischief? I thought, remembering Mike Cook's words. *Jeremy's involved in things he's not tellin' me about,* he'd said. *Things that could get him in trouble. Things that worry me.* Did Jeremy have to hurry off to do the devil's work? To bring death and destruction down on my town? To bring yet another darksider into the fold? What?

I panicked as he started to get up from his chair. I hadn't accomplished anything yet, hadn't been able to communicate with Satan at all, hadn't been able to talk to him about releasing me from his service. I couldn't let him go like this. Not yet.

"Jeremy, cancel your plans. Let's have dinner together," I said impulsively.

He looked surprised. "What's goin' on, huh? Until today, you never wanted any part of me."

"I was wrong," I blurted out before I could stop myself. "You're not so bad after all."

"Gee, thanks," he laughed. "But I'm busy tonight."

"With what?"

"None of your business, sweetheart."

"Is it a secret?"

"Yeah, it's a big secret, but if you promise not to tell, I'll confide in you."

"I promise."

He leaned over and brought his mouth close to my ear. I could smell him then. The beer, the sweat, the heat of his body. I felt myself tremble as I tried to anticipate what he might say. Or do.

"The secret is: I'm goin' out to destroy the town," he whispered, then laughed.

My eyes widened and I bolted up in my chair. He had tried to make it sound like a joke, of course, but I knew the remark was no joke. The devil was finally showing himself to me for the evil force he was. Now was my chance to talk to him, to plead with him not to destroy Banyan Beach, to beg him to leave town right away. I couldn't let him walk out the door. I had to stop him, had to make him release me from our bargain. It was now or never.

I jumped up, grabbed Jeremy by the shoulders and started to shake him.

"Please," I shouted. "Please let me go."

"*Me* let *you* go?" he said, stunned by my assault. "You're the one who's grabbin' onto me!"

"No, I mean, *really* let me go. Release me from your service," I pleaded, ignoring his bewildered expression.

"My service?"

"Yes, but this isn't just about me. It's about Banyan Beach. I beg you not to destroy the town."

"Beg me not to *what?*"

"You heard me."

"Hey, I was only kiddin' about that. It was just a crack. A joke. I was bustin' your chops, ya know? Tryin' to get you to lighten up."

"I don't need lightening up."

"Honey, you need it worse than I thought."

"No. I need you to leave town. I know all about your evil plan for Banyan Beach. David Bettinger told me everything."

"David Bettinger? That guy who was at your house the other night?"

"Yes, and I want your solemn promise that you won't hurt him. He's an innocent in all of this. Just another darksider."

"He's a dorksider, all right. As dorky as they come."

"No, not *dork*sider. *Dark*sider. As if you didn't know."

Jeremy shook his head. "You been doin' drugs, BS? Is that what's makin' you act so nuts?"

"Yeah, I'm a BreathAssure addict. Thanks to you."

"Thanks to me?"

"Look, let's cut the I-don't-know-what-you're-talking-about bit. I know you're in there, *okay?*"

"In where?"

"In Jeremy Cook's body, that's where."

"Jesus. You need help, sweetheart. Bad."

"That's right. I do need help. *Yours.* I want you to leave Banyan Beach. Just pick yourself up and go somewhere else. I hear Bora Bora is nice this time of year."

Jeremy wriggled out of my grip and started to walk toward the phone.

"I'm gonna call Ben," he said. "You've lost it."

I ran over to him and grabbed the phone out of his hand.

"Listen to me. I'm begging you," I said. "Give me back my old life. I don't want the blond hair and the big boobs and the flat stomach. Not if it means I have to have your baby in return."

"Have my *baby?*" That got his attention. "Hey, look," he said, "If you and I had ever . . . I mean, I've never been so drunk that I couldn't remember . . . What I'm tryin' to say is that, no matter what you might have been told by this David Bettinger or anyone else, you're *not* havin' my baby. You got that?"

"Oh, I've got it all right. Go ahead and pretend that you don't have a grand plan for this town—to turn it into your own personal chamber of horrors, to populate it with your followers. Well, here's one person who isn't following." I paused to take a couple of deep breaths. "Now, I don't claim to be a paragon of virtue," I went on. "I've never helped a blind person across the street. I've never worked in a soup kitchen. And I've never given one red cent to the American Heart Association or the Fresh Air Fund or even the Banyan Beach Volunteer Firemen. But I'm not an evil person. I'm on the side of Goodness, of Decency, of Love! Amen!"

"Oh, brother. So *that's* what this is about. You've turned into one of those Born Agains," said Jeremy.

"You don't want to talk to me about the baby you want me to have? Fine. Talk to me about my blond hair," I challenged. "I want my gray hair back and you're going to make it happen."

"*I'm* going to make it happen? Just go to the fuckin' beauty parlor and tell *them* to dye it back."

"Oh, really? And what am I supposed to do about the boobs? Drop them in the recycling bin like a couple of old telephone books?"

"You're totally flipped out," said Jeremy as he grabbed me by the arm and walked me briskly toward the front door.

"Oh, I see," I said as he opened the door. "You've heard enough. Is that it? I'll bet you're not used to having your darksiders rise up and demand their freedom. Well, you'd better get used to it because I'm not giving up until you leave Banyan Beach."

"I'm not goin' anywhere, sweetheart," said Jeremy, literally picking me up and depositing me outside his house. "It's you who's goin' bye-bye."

He closed the door and left me standing there, hyperventilating. With shaking hands, I fished in my purse for the BreathAssure bottle and popped a couple of capsules into my mouth. Well, why not? If Avon's Skin So Soft could kill mosquitoes, why couldn't BreathAssure capsules soothe raw nerves?

I had just swallowed the capsules when I involuntarily let forth one of those awful, fiendish, bestial growls. I sounded like a wild animal, for God's sake, and I nearly scared myself to death. Another little warning from Satan, I assumed.

"Okay, okay," I said, hurrying into my car before Jeremy's neighbors either called Animal Control or came after me with their shotguns. "I'm going, but I'll be back. You can count on it."

As I pulled out of the driveway, a blinding bolt of lightning suddenly lit up the sky, nearly sending the car into a tree.

Must be another warning from the devil, I figured, given that there wasn't a single cloud in sight.

C H A P T E R

17

The phone rang at seven-thirty on Wednesday morning. It was Ben.

"Are you all right, Barbara?" he asked, his tone concerned, brotherly.

All right? I thought ruefully as I wound a strand of my hair—my long, straight, blond hair—around my finger. There was nothing all *right* about me. I was all *wrong*—from my bogus Barbie doll looks to my supposed "hot streak" at work. The whole thing was fake. *I* was fake. A fraud. An impostor. A creation of the devil.

"I'm fine," I told Ben, wishing I could tell him the truth. "Why?"

"Because I got a call from Jeremy last night. He said you went over to his house and acted like a complete nutcase."

"That was sweet of him."

"He said you were going on and on about some real estate deal and when he tried to shut you up, you started making these wild accusations."

"They weren't wild, believe me."

"What do you mean? Did Jeremy try anything?"

"Try anything?"

"Yeah. Did he come on to you?"

"No," I said.

"That doesn't sound like Jeremy. I've never known him to be alone with a woman and *not* come on to her."

I wasn't sure if I should be flattered or insulted.

"Since you know him so well, Benjamin, why don't you tell me about him," I said, wanting to be talked out of believing that Jeremy was Satan's cover in Banyan Beach. Despite David's confirmation that Jeremy *was* fronting for the devil and despite the rather incriminating remarks Jeremy himself had made to me, I had my doubts. For starters, there was Jeremy's oh-so-politically correct stance on the environment. Would the devil, who had probably never met a river he didn't want to pollute, actually allow his cover to speak out against pollution? Then there were the corrupt, backroom deals that Jeremy had insisted went into the development of the River Princess. Would the devil, who was as corrupt as it gets, really let his cover go around town exposing corruption? And what about the business of Jeremy's donating the money he made from The Fire Ants concerts to the Save the River Initiative? Would the devil, the very antithesis of faith, hope, and charity, permit his cover to behave in such a charitable manner?

"Why ask me about Jeremy?" said Ben. "You've known him as long as I have."

"I know him but I don't really *know* him," I said. "What sort of person is he? Behind the macho image, I mean."

"He's the most decent guy there is," said Ben. "He's always fighting for the underdog and standing up for what he believes in. His methods may piss people off, but his heart is in the right place. I really admire him."

"But he acts like such a jerk sometimes," I pointed out.

"Who doesn't?" Ben countered. "So what if he isn't the type of guy that Mom and Dad approved of. He didn't go to Harvard and he never shed the redneck accent and he doesn't care if he's on somebody's Best Dressed List. He's just Jeremy. What you see is what you get."

"Maybe. Maybe not."

"No maybes about it. Take the time he spends with those kids."

"What kids?"

"Those poor kids that live over on Trent Avenue." Trent Avenue was Banyan Beach's very own slum, a section of town that was never mentioned in travel brochures.

"What does Jeremy do with those kids?" I asked.

"One Saturday a month, he takes a different group of them fishing on the Hatteras," said Ben. "He spends the whole day with

176 / Jane Heller

them, teaching them how to fish, showing them how to operate a boat, feeding them lunch, the whole thing. He doesn't brag about it. He just does it, even though it means giving up a Saturday's worth of charter business. That's the kind of person Jeremy Cook is."

Now I was more confused than ever. Could David have been wrong about Jeremy? Was it possible that the devil had fooled him, too? Or was Satan *causing* my doubts, deliberately keeping me off-balance so I'd have to remain a darksider, carry out his mission, have his babies. . . .

I stopped myself. The thought was too gruesome to contemplate.

"Barbara? Why the sudden interest in Jeremy?" asked Ben. "You told me you wanted his phone number so you could talk to him about fishing. But that wasn't really why you went to see him, was it?"

"No," I admitted.

Ben was silent for a moment. "You're hot for him, is that it?"

"Oh, please."

"Well, then why the interest?"

"Mom always said Jeremy had the devil in him. I just want to find out if it's true."

After I finished talking to Ben, Pete launched into one of his barking routines. He had been sitting quietly on the floor, right beside my bed, throughout my conversation with my brother, but the minute I hung up the phone, he started up, as if it were *his* turn to talk to me.

"What is it this time?" I asked as I leaned over to scratch the furry white patch on his chest.

He became calm for a second or two, but when I lay back down in bed, the barking began again.

"Woof! Woof! Woof!" he said, standing now. He stared at me, his hazel eyes blazing with intensity, and I couldn't look away. I sat up, threw the covers off, and continued to be held by his gaze. Suddenly, he stopped barking and, with tongue hanging and tail wagging, bounded out of the bedroom.

I leapt out of bed and followed him into the bathroom, where I watched in amazement as he crouched in front of the vanity underneath the sink, gripped its door between his teeth, and pulled it open.

"What are you doing now?" I asked, recalling the episode with the MLS book.

His tail wagging furiously, Pete barked once in response, then turned away from me and began to burrow inside the vanity.

"Hey, don't go in there. You'll knock everything over," I wailed as I watched Pete's nose topple a bottle of Scope, a jar of Vaseline, and a container of Band-Aids.

I attempted to shoo him away from the vanity, but he wasn't budging. He actually seemed to be searching for something, although I couldn't imagine what, given that there weren't any doggie treats stashed in there, just your basic Walgreen's merchandise. He continued to rummage around, his body practically stuffed inside the narrow but deep storage area, until he finally found an object that interested him: my scale. It was a typical bathroom scale, a rather sterile-looking white model, the kind you stand on and watch the little needle waver between the black numbers until it settles on your actual weight. The morning after my transformation, when I'd awakened and found that I had miraculously shed twenty pounds, I'd stuck the scale in the back of the vanity, figuring I no longer needed to weigh myself. Now here was Pete, wrapping his teeth around the side of the scale and dragging it out of the vanity!

He set it down on the bathroom floor and then stepped onto it, like a fat person at a Weight Watchers weigh-in. The scale was too small to accommodate all four of his paws, of course, so first the back two, then the front two, kept slipping off. But there was no question about his intention. He was trying to stand on that scale and weigh himself, as if he understood the scale's function! Or so it seemed to me.

"What's going on?" I asked, thoroughly puzzled by the latest of Pete's Stupid Pet Tricks. As I had never owned a dog before, I could only assume that he was behaving in a bizarre (for a dog) manner. For all I knew, every dog was obsessive about his weight. On the other hand, Pete wasn't much of an eater and only picked at his food when he did eat. Maybe there's such a thing as an anorexic dog, I thought, and Pete *is* one. Why else would he care how much he weighed?

Or was I missing something? Was Pete attempting to communicate with me in some strange way? And if so, what in the world was he trying to say?

Pete barked several more times as he stood on the scale, then hopped off of it and trotted back into the bedroom, as if what had just occurred were merely part of his morning ablutions.

I remained in the bathroom, struggling to make sense of what I had witnessed, until I realized that if I didn't hurry up and get dressed, I'd be late for work.

Charlotte usually held her weekly meeting on Monday mornings, but she had assembled all of us on a Wednesday so we could discuss the forthcoming open house for the River Princess, which was set for the following Tuesday night. As Home Sweet Home was the listing agency on the condominium, we would be hosting the gala celebration on the building's spectacular waterfront patio, along with the developers. Invitations to the gala had been mailed two weeks before to all the movers and shakers in town, as well as to Home Sweet Home's customers, many of whom *were* movers and shakers. We hoped to ply our wealthy guests with liquor, wow them with the building's numerous amenities, and sell them a condo. We also hoped to draw the media to the event so that those who couldn't make the party would be sure to hear about it.

"How about going over the assignments?" Frances suggested, after we had all gathered in Charlotte's office. Since Frances was the Home Sweet Home agent who had worked with the developers in the past, she was the actual listing agent on the property and had the most to gain if the party was a success.

"I'm right on target with *my* assignment," said June Bellsey, who had volunteered to handle the media coverage for the party. "Generally, the TV stations won't commit to sending a crew until the day of the event, but Lloyd knows the news directors at Channel Five, Channel Eight, and Channel Ten, and he guarantees they'll come."

"Not if there's a murder that day," Althea said sourly. "The way the murder rate in this town has been skyrocketing lately, there's a good chance we won't see a single TV camera videotaping our guests. Not when they can be videotaping corpses."

"Aren't we being a little morbid, Althea dear?" asked Charlotte. "Perhaps if you had some more tea . . ."

"I don't think Althea's being morbid at all," Deirdre announced. "I'd never say this to a customer, naturally, but this town is beginning to scare the pants off me. Did everybody hear about that poor old woman who was set on fire yesterday?"

"Oh, God. That was horrible," said Suzanne. "Imagine someone doing a thing like that to an innocent woman. She was in her eighties, wasn't she?"

"Eighty-two," Deirdre volunteered.

"With sixteen grandchildren," June added.

"A widow," Althea chimed in.

While the others traded bits of information about the case, I sat there, frozen in my seat. According to news reports, the murderer had doused his unsuspecting victim with gasoline just as she was leaving the First Presbyterian Church on Franklin Avenue. And then he lit a match, threw it at her, and fled, while she burned to death. There had been a similar killing ten days earlier. That victim, too, had been torched to death. Now the residents of Banyan Beach were afraid. And I was afraid for them. Because I knew that the murders weren't the work of your average, garden-variety pyromaniac. It was the devil who was making the residents of Banyan Beach burn. I knew it as surely as if I had committed the crimes myself. And if I remained a darksider and gave birth to a darksider baby, I would be just as guilty as Satan himself.

No, I thought, feeling the perspiration form above my top lip. I refuse to carry out my end of the bargain. I can't do it. I won't do it. I'm going to make the devil leave town if it's the last thing I do.

But first, I reminded myself, I had to find him.

"Barbara? How are you coming along with *your* assignment for the gala opening?" said Frances, jarring me out of my thoughts.

"My assignment," I said, trying to make myself care about a dopey party while the devil was out there toasting people like marshmallows at a campfire. I had been given the task of writing the copy for the promotional brochure we were having printed up. It was to extol the virtues of the River Princess—from the fabulous water views virtually every unit enjoyed to the building's state-of-the-art recreational facilities. I was to make special mention of the three large fountains that adorned the patio; of the fact that in the center of each fountain there was a marble sculpture of a mermaid, the creation of DeWitt Charney, some mucky-muck artist from Palm Beach; of the fact that each mermaid's mouth formed a spout out of which water trickled. The fountains and their accompanying mermaids were either works of art or symbols of wretched excess, depending on whom you asked. They were being covered by heavy tarpaulins until the night of the gala opening, at which time they were to be unveiled as part of the festivities.

"The copy's all written," I reported to Frances, who had put herself in charge of the hors d'oeuvres. I only hoped that, given her gargantuan appetite, she would leave some of them for the guests. "It's ready for the printer."

"Wonderful," she beamed, her fleshy cheeks bulging. "I knew I could count on you, Barbara. Now, what about the music, Deirdre? Has that been taken care of?"

"Oh, sure, Lutzie," said Deirdre. "I found a harpist."

"Oh, please. Not a harpist," Althea groaned. "Talk about pretentious."

"What's pretentious about it?" Deirdre asked.

"Let me put it this way. When was the last time you sat around listening to harp music?" Althea challenged.

"Never," Deirdre admitted. "But that's the point. The party is a special occasion, and special occasions call for special music."

"Yeah, but harp music?" Althea said, rolling her eyes.

"Why not?" Charlotte asked innocently. "Harp music is the music of the angels."

"The people we're trying to sell condos to aren't angels, believe me," Althea said.

"Yes, but angels are very 'in' right now," said June, who considered herself an authority on popular culture.

Althea was about to respond when I let out one of those awful growls. Everyone in the room turned to look at me. It was humiliating, but I was getting used to it.

"Sorry," I shrugged. "It's my stomach acting up again. I've got an appointment with a gastroenterologist."

Obviously, there was nothing wrong with my stomach. My guess was that the devil didn't like all this talk of angels and was making his feelings known. Through me.

"I agree with Althea on this one," said Frances, moving the meeting along. "Harps are a little much." She turned to Deirdre. "How about finding us someone else? An accordionist maybe?"

Deirdre sighed and made a few notes.

"That leaves the guest list," said Frances. "Suzanne, how are the RSVPs coming in?"

Suzanne pulled a folder out of her briefcase. "So far, about fifty people have accepted," she reported. "I have a feeling we'll be close to a hundred by next week. Since we're having the party out of season, we don't have much competition for partygoers. There's nothing else going on next Tuesday night."

"And let's not forget about the hundred invitations we distributed to local businesses for their customers," Frances said. "I bet we'll get over two hundred people at this party." She was practically licking her lips in anticipation of selling condos. Lots of condos. We all were. At least, I thought I was. After hearing Jeremy and his father talk about the way waterfront development was killing the fish and destroying the river, I had to admit that I wasn't quite as pumped up about the River Princess as I used to be.

"Oh, this is all so exciting," June cooed. "I love a good party."

"Even if no celebrities show up?" Althea sneered.

"Oh, but celebrities *will* show up," June said smugly. "Lloyd and I will be there."

CHAPTER
18

The weather on the day of the River Princess party was unseasonably cool and dry, like a crisp fall day up north. White, puffy clouds drifted across the bright blue sky, and there was a fresh, sweet-smelling breeze blowing off the ocean. For the first time in months, I drove with the car windows open.

At about four o'clock on that fateful Tuesday afternoon, I went home from the office to change clothes, figuring I'd make it over to the River Princess by five. When I walked in the door, Pete bounded over to me, welcoming me with sloppy wet kisses. It was nice to be wanted, and I returned his affection with a few sloppy wet kisses of my own.

It was a funny thing about my relationship with Pete. When he first showed up at my door, we had zero chemistry between us. I felt awkward and uncomfortable around him, like a spinster aunt who's suddenly been handed a baby to raise. Now, only a few weeks later, I couldn't imagine a time when he wasn't in my life. He was there when I woke up and there when I went to sleep, a constant presence during a turbulent period. No matter how bizarre his actions often seemed to me, I had a sense that he was on my side, protecting me, supporting me, shielding me from the fact that, in addition to being a darksider, I was a soon-to-be-divorcée, a woman without a man to care for her.

Of course, I would have been a fool to think that Pete's mysterious arrival at 666 Seacrest Way on the morning after my transformation was merely a coincidence; that it wasn't related to my becoming a darksider in some way; that Pete, like David Bettinger, had not been *placed* in my path. But part of me didn't want to know about any of that. Part of me rejected the idea that our bond was engineered by some supernatural force—a force that could take Pete away from me just as abruptly as it had delivered him to me. Once I'd gotten past the inconvenience of having a dog around— the mess, the smells, the barking—I had come to depend on Pete and vice versa. What I'm trying to say is, he loved me and I, who had never really loved anything or anyone, loved him, too.

"What do you think of this dress?" I asked him as the two of us stood together in my bedroom. I wanted to look my best for the party and so, while Pete looked on, I modeled various outfits for him, all of which had been altered to accommodate my new figure. Mitchell had never been much help in the Which-outfit-should-I-wear? department. I'd ask for his opinion about this blouse or that skirt and he'd say, "Never mind what *I* think of it. What do *you* think of it? Take a stand on something, Barbara. Stop being so damn passive!" But Pete was another story. He included himself in almost every phase of my life and was delighted to offer his opinion, even on something as mundane as my clothing.

Usually, if he liked what I was wearing, he barked. If he didn't, he whined. His response to the red dress I had on was a whine.

"Okay," I said, pulling it over my head and tossing it onto the bed. "Let's try another one."

I put on a hot pink number with a slit up the side. It elicited another whine from Pete.

Next came a more conservative garment, a high-necked white dress with gold buttons. That one got not one bark but two!

"So you like me in white," I said, reaching out to pet him. Mitchell used to say that white washed me out. He even said it on our wedding day. There I was, walking down the aisle in my virginal white bridal gown, and when I got to the altar, Mitchell leaned over and whispered, "White isn't your color, Barbara. It washes you out."

I ran a comb through my hair, put on some lipstick, and said good-bye to Pete. I could tell he didn't want me to go because he was blocking the front door.

"Come on, boy. Shove over," I said, trying to push him aside, first with my foot, then with my body. For a dog who was so finicky about his food, he was a heavy load when he wanted to be. I couldn't budge him.

"Pete, please," I said firmly. "This party is important to my career. Now move out of the way." Pete's devotion was heartwarming but I was in a hurry. "Come on, boy. Let's go, huh?"

Still, he refused to step aside.

On an impulse, I decided to use my darksider power on him. I looked him in the eye, folded my arms across my chest and said out loud, "Pete, I wish you'd get so tired that you'd crawl over to the sofa and fall sound asleep."

I waited, knowing it usually took a second or two for the power to kick in. But nothing kicked in. Pete didn't move a muscle. He stood his ground by that front door and wouldn't budge.

I repeated the wish. He remained by the door.

That's funny, I thought. Either I've lost my power or Pete is immune to it.

I tried one more time. Again, Pete didn't seem the least bit susceptible.

"Never mind," I said. "I'll go out through the back door."

Apparently, I had said the magic words because Pete suddenly abandoned his post by the door. He trotted over to the hall closet, wriggled his way through its partially open door until it was open all the way, and gripped the collapsible Totes umbrella that was resting on the floor of the closet between his teeth. Then he carried the umbrella over to me and dropped it at my feet.

"Is that what all this is about?" I asked, amazed yet again by Pete's actions.

He barked.

"Pete, look outside," I said, pointing out the window. "It's a gorgeous afternoon."

He nudged the umbrella with his nose and rolled it toward me.

"I don't need an umbrella, believe me," I said.

He barked a couple more times. Then, as if to emphasize his point, he repeated the routine, picking the umbrella up in his mouth and dropping it at my feet again.

"All right. Be a Jewish mother if you want to," I laughed, stooping over to pick up the umbrella. "If I take the damn thing, will you let me go to the party?"

He opened his mouth very wide and yawned. I took that as a "yes."

The umbrella tucked under my arm, I blew Pete a kiss and rushed out of the house, totally unaware that I was hurrying toward disaster.

The smell was the first thing I noticed when I stepped onto the patio of the River Princess. Not the smell of the hors d'oeuvres, which were sumptuously arrayed on silver platters. Not the smell of the brilliantly colored tropical flowers that made pretty centerpieces on the round, umbrellaed tables. Not the smell of the stylishly dressed guests, who, collectively, were wearing enough cologne to choke an elephant. And not the smell of my own brussels sprouts breath, which I had been successfully camouflaging with BreathAssure. No, the smell that assaulted me as I made my way through the crowd wasn't a smell at all. It was a stench. A stink. A rancidness. It was hard not to gag.

Moving to the beat of a steel drum ("Curtis the Jamaican" was the only musician we could get on such short notice), I found Suzanne standing with Deirdre, Althea, and Frances. She was busily surveying the guests, in search of eligible bachelors, I suspected.

"What in the world is that smell?" I whispered to her.

She shrugged. "We're all trying to pretend it's not there, but it's overpowering, isn't it?"

I nodded and held my nose. "Do you think the construction guys left their Dumpsters around? Maybe the wind is blowing the scent our way."

"Nope. No Dumpsters. Someone is checking on the sewage system, but nobody really thinks that's the problem."

"Then what is? Unless our customers have allergies and can't smell anything, they're not exactly going to be thrilled with the River Princess and this whole shindig will be for nothing."

"I know. Frances is tearing her hair out."

I glanced over at Frances, who was deep in conversation with one of the developers. Neither of them looked happy.

I peered out over the crowd of nearly two hundred guests and tried to locate other people I knew.

I spotted Charlotte Reed chatting animatedly with Anabel Littleton, the chairwoman of the Banyan Beach chapter of the Junior League.

I spotted June Bellsey hanging onto her husband Lloyd, who, in turn, was hanging onto Gary Kineally, the mayor of Banyan Beach, who, in turn, was hanging onto Roberta Smith, the perky television reporter for Channel Eight, who, in turn, was hanging onto former football great and South Florida resident Joe Namath, the only bona fide celebrity to show up at the party.

I spotted several of my customers sampling canapés and sipping champagne: Richard and Arlene Volk, the yuppy stockbrokers; Nancy Henken, the interior decorator; Dee Dee Holliman, the recipient of a large trust fund and a chronic purchaser of real estate. They had all expressed interest in buying in the River Princess. I hoped the rank odor that was filling the otherwise clear, dry air wouldn't change their minds.

I spotted David Bettinger standing all alone. He was holding a champagne glass in his right hand and gazing out at the river. Although he wore a pained expression, he was improbably handsome in his crisp khaki-colored slacks, blue-and-white-striped shirt and navy blue blazer, his golden hair gleaming like a halo in the late afternoon sun. What a waste, I thought sadly, as I continued to watch him. Sure, he was a gorgeous creature. But "creature" was the operative word here. He was a manufactured man, a man whose physical beauty couldn't begin to make up for the loneliness I know he felt, the loneliness of being a darksider whose only chance at happiness was to inseminate me and hold up his end of a despicable, diabolical plan.

What's he thinking? I asked myself as I stared at him. What must be going on inside his head? Is he wondering if I've confronted Jeremy yet? If I've gotten the devil to release me from the bargain? Or does he already know that I haven't succeeded? Does David Bettinger always know more than he admits to? Was that why he'd made me pull it out of him that Jeremy was Satan's cover in Banyan Beach?

And speaking of Jeremy, I spotted him and his father walking up to the bar. I was more than a little surprised.

What's *he* doing here? I thought, as I watched the white uniformed waiter hand him a glass of champagne. He looked incredibly out of place in his blue jeans and sneakers, his wavy red hair clashing horribly with his purple T-shirt. He couldn't have been on the guest list, seeing as he wasn't exactly a mover or shaker, nor was he a Home Sweet Home customer or even a potential condo buyer. He must have gotten an invitation from one of the retailers in town, I decided, remembering that we'd distributed a hundred invitations to local businesses for their customers. The question was, *why* would he want to attend the grand opening of the River Princess, given the way he felt about the building?

Maybe the devil made him come, I guessed. A regular party animal, that's what Satan was.

Of course, I still wasn't convinced that Jeremy *was* the devil's cover and his presence at the party made me uncomfortable. He had called me a couple of times since my visit to his house the week before, "to see if you're feeling better," he'd said on the messages he'd left on my machine. But I hadn't returned his calls. I couldn't. I didn't know what to say to him. After talking to my brother and hearing about his selfless fishing trips with those kids, I didn't know what to believe about him. Besides, he had asked if I was feeling better and how could I answer that question? I wouldn't feel better until the devil was out of Banyan Beach.

My eyes drifted away from Jeremy and Mike Cook and landed on another intrepid twosome: good old Mitchell Chessner and Chrissy Hemplewhite. Had we really put my asshole husband on the guest list? Or was Chrissy the one who'd been invited and Mitchell only there as her escort? And what about the Six O'Clock News? How could Chrissy give her nightly weather report if she was at a party instead of in the studio?

It wasn't until I noticed the Channel Five cameraman trailing behind her that I figured out what was going on—and it was all June's fault. In her zeal to arrange for media coverage of the River Princess's opening, she, or maybe it was Lloyd, must have talked Chrissy into doing the weather live, on remote, from the party. As a result, Miss Doppler Radar was evidently going to stand in our midst, point to the blue sky overhead, and tell her adoring television audience that it was going to be a beautiful evening. And people say real talent is hard to find.

She looked thoroughly ridiculous with that long blond mop she called hair piled on top of her head in tight little curls.

And Mitchell. Please. He was as twitchy and obsequious as ever, bowing and scraping and pumping the arms of people he barely knew.

"Why didn't you ever give me the same respect that you give perfect strangers?" I muttered. "I'd like to see you grovel at *my* feet."

Suddenly, I saw Mitchell spin around, look meaningfully in my direction, and then walk briskly toward me.

Chrissy called out in her high-pitched, helium balloon voice, "Hey, Mitchell honey? Where are you going? Mitchell? Come back here."

He ignored her and kept walking. I swallowed hard as he made a beeline for me. He was moving quickly, purposefully. For a second, I felt that old paralysis set in, that old panic that I would say or do something that would displease him, that he would criticize me for it, that I would hate myself for allowing it. And then, the panic vanished and when Mitchell parted his lips to speak, I felt strong, courageous, nasty.

"Barbara? Is that really you?" he asked, assessing my "new look."

"No, it's Vanna White," I replied. I had never dared mouth off to Mitchell. Not in person anyway. But he was facing me now, standing only inches away. It was our first meeting since the night he left.

He didn't say anything for a second, and then he laughed much too loud and too long. The line wasn't that funny. He was overdoing it.

"Vanna White," he chuckled. "I never realized what a terrific sense of humor you have."

"It's not that terrific."

"Oh, but it is. I just never noticed it."

"You never noticed much of anything about me. Anything positive, that is."

He smiled. "Well, I'm noticing something now. You look fabulous, Barbara. Whatever you've done to yourself has only made you more beautiful."

"More beautiful than what?"

He ignored my question. "The truth is, you're the most beautiful woman at this party."

"Really? What about Chrissy?"

"Chrissy who?"

Boy, this darksider power sure is amazing, I thought. "How's business? The restaurants doing okay?"

"Fine. Great. Why don't you have dinner at one of them some night this week. I'll have the chef prepare something special for you."

Something special for me. I was enjoying this.

"You know, there's no reason why we can't be friends," he said. "I really admire you."

"Since when?"

"Since . . . I'm not sure." He stopped, appearing confused, then began again. "I have a lot of respect for you, Barbara. I think I only realized it a few minutes ago. Isn't that strange?"

"Very." I could have listened to Mitchell suck up to me all night, but we were interrupted by the voice of Mayor Kineally, who was standing at the microphone and saying, "Testing 1-2-3. Testing." The crowd applauded and the TV cameras—there were four; it must have been a slow news day—were poised to record every moment.

"You'd better run along, Mitchell," I said. "The ribbon-cutting ceremony is about to start."

"Is there anything I can get for you before I go?" he asked, bowing as if I were one of his customers at Risotto!. "An hors d'oeuvre? Champagne? Anything?"

"Yes," I said sweetly. "You can get lost."

I left Mitchell in his servile crouch and went to join David, with whom I had more in common.

"Hi," I said, tapping David on the back.

He was glad to see me, but we couldn't really talk because the mayor was bellowing into the microphone. He was saying something about our embarking on a new chapter in the history of Banyan Beach, about the River Princess representing the beginning of the town's Golden Age. Blah blah blah. I looked around for Jeremy and his father, to try to catch their reaction, but couldn't find them in the crowd.

When the mayor had finished his speech, Ronald Dubin, one of the developers of the River Princess, stepped up to the microphone and said how proud he was that *his* building would offer the residents of Banyan Beach the ultimate in luxury. He assured us that no expense was spared in the construction and design of the condominiums, no detail overlooked.

"No detail overlooked? They obviously forgot to take out the garbage," I whispered to David, referring to the stench that was still permeating the air.

The ribbon-cutting ceremony followed. Then Mr. Dubin introduced DeWitt Charney, the sculptor responsible for the three mermaids that were about to be unveiled in their sparkling fountain habitats.

"Before we take the tarpaulins off the fountains and show you Mr. Carney's magnificent mermaids," said Dubin, "I want to invite you all to tour the River Princess during the evening. The model units will be open until nine o'clock tonight, as will the card room, the gym, and the cabanas. There are brochures describing the various features and amenities of the building on the tables in the lobby. Feel free to pick one up on your way out. Any questions, speak to Frances Lutz or any of the other realtors at Home Sweet Home, all of whom are here tonight. And now, without further ado . . ." He paused, looked toward Curtis the Jamaican and requested—and got—a drumroll. A steel drum roll.

"Are we ready?" Dubin asked the workmen who were stationed at each of the three fountains, poised and waiting for the signal to remove the tarpaulins.

"O-kay," Dubin beamed, nodding at the men. "We have lift-off!"

At the word "off," the men removed the three tarpaulins with a dramatic flourish, like waiters lifting silver domes off dinner plates. Flashbulbs went off as the power in the fountains went on, sending the flow of water up through the mouths of the fabled mermaids.

Suddenly, DeWitt Charney, who was still standing beside Ronald Dubin at the microphone, poised and ready to admire his creations, cried out in anguish.

"My God! No!" he screamed, his voice echoing out over the patio.

There was a collective gasp as many of the partygoers saw what DeWitt Charney saw.

And then all hell broke loose. And I don't mean hell as in "pandemonium." I mean hell as in "the devil was not amused."

CHAPTER

19

Someone had polluted the fountains.

At the unveiling of the mermaids, we discovered that the culprit had apparently gotten into the building in advance of the party and, knowing the fountains would be covered until the festivities began, dumped rotting slime into all three of them. One was filled with dead fish, the second with thick, black oil, and the third with raw sewage. No wonder the place stank.

The developers were apoplectic. Ronald Dubin's face was so purple with rage that I thought he might have an aneurysm. When he wasn't shouting obscenities, he was trying frantically to herd the partygoers into the lobby of the building, away from the offending sights and smells. But nobody budged. I think we sensed that there was more to come.

Mayor Kineally looked more humiliated than enraged, as if by appearing beside fountains that were polluted, he, too, had been polluted.

And then there was poor DeWitt Charney, the mermaids' creator. He was distraught that his works of art had been defiled and quickly left the party in tears. He was lucky. He escaped before things really got ugly.

Charlotte didn't seem the least bit fazed by the polluting of the fountains and acted as if it were merely a childish prank, a case of bad manners. "Boys will be boys," I actually heard her say. But the other Home Sweet Home agents were far more concerned that the incident might put a stain on the River Princess's chichi image. Who would buy a condo in a building with such lax security, a building that was such an easy target for vandals? Or worse, who would buy a condo in a building that smelled rotten? That was the obvious message of the vandalism, as far as I was concerned; that something about the River Princess was rotten. To the core.

"Who could have done this?" Frances asked after she had stopped to talk with David and me. Her voluminous caftan was flapping in the breeze and her mind was undoubtedly calculating all the commission checks that would be lost.

Who could have done it?

Before I could ponder the matter further, I saw that Jeremy was making his way through the crowd, striding toward the microphone, his father looking on anxiously. Everything happened very quickly after that, but I'll try to report the events as best I can.

"Ladies and gentlemen," Jeremy said, as everyone quieted down, "I hate to spoil your party but I've got a little speech I wanna make."

I glanced at Mike Cook, who was drawing nervously on his cigarette.

"The River Princess and high-rise buildings like it are killin' our rivers," he announced. "Thanks to their developers, black ooze has taken the place of the sea grass beds where fish used to look for food, and algae have taken the place of the fish we all used to catch. The fact is, we don't have sea life anymore. Oh, we've got condo buildings with enough gates and guards to keep an army out. But our rivers don't have any gates and guards to keep the polluters out. Now, instead of sea life, our rivers have dead fish, black ooze, and raw sewage—samples of which are sittin' right here in these fancy fountains, ladies and gentlemen. I thought y'all might like to experience firsthand what a polluted river looks and smells like."

So Jeremy was responsible!

He was met with a torrent of boos as he stepped away from the microphone, but I felt an odd sort of respect for him. It all made sense to me now . . . his warning that within a few days the condos in the River Princess wouldn't be worth much . . . his statement about giving the money he made from The Fire Ants gigs to the Save the River Initiative . . . his comment about putting his money where his mouth was and standing up for what he believed in. Ben was right about him, I realized. Jeremy Cook had principles—and guts. He was an activist who was willing to take on the movers and shakers of Banyan Beach—in order to save the river that had meant so much to him since he was a child. But he hadn't used violence or damaged property. Not really. Not anything that couldn't be remedied with a good scrubbing. He had simply sent everybody a message. A symbolic message.

As I watched two of the River Princess's security guards each take one of Jeremy's arms and walk him inside the building, with the next stop the police station, I guessed, I envied him suddenly. Unlike Jeremy Cook, *I* had never stood up for something that mattered to me. Come to think of it, nothing ever had mattered to me. Until now. Now, what mattered to me was getting the devil out of town.

But, as I was to learn within seconds, Satan wasn't going anywhere.

"Barbara?" asked David, who was still standing next to me. "What is it?"

I was about to confront him, to tell him that he had to have been mistaken about Jeremy's being the devil's cover in Banyan Beach, when the blue sky overhead literally turned black. I mean *black*. Like the oil Jeremy had dumped into one of the fountains. One minute, we were bathed in sunshine. The next, we were in total darkness. It was as if someone had flicked a light switch to the "off" position.

The suddenness was so terrifying that some people screamed. I was one of them. The last time I'd witnessed such an abrupt change in the atmosphere was the night of my transformation. Which could only mean one thing.

"My God!" I cried, grabbing hold of David's arm. "It's the devil, isn't it?"

David looked as terrified as everybody else. "It must be," he said. "Brace yourself. He's not happy."

"Why?" I asked as we huddled together, two darksiders in a sea of civilians. "What did we do?"

"*We* didn't do anything. Your friend Jeremy did," David said bitterly. "The River Princess was one of the devil's pet projects in Banyan Beach. Jeremy shouldn't have interfered."

I ripped my arm out of his grasp. I was furious at him, fed up with his little games. "How do you know all this?" I demanded. "And why did you tell me that Satan was hiding in Jeremy's body? It's not true, and it never was, right, David? Right?"

He didn't get a chance to answer me. The devil answered for him. A monstrous bolt of lightning ignited the sky, a charge of electricity that was so powerful and so blinding that my eyesight hasn't been the same since. The thunder came next, followed by more lightning, gale-force winds and then rain. Well, "rain" doesn't begin to describe what Satan unleashed on us that afternoon. What came down from that black sky were pellets of moisture, hail-size raindrops that tore into our bare skin like knives.

Suddenly, umbrellas blew off tables, flowerpots smashed, champagne glasses crashed to the ground, and trays full of hors d'oeuvres landed in the once–crystal-clear swimming pool.

Two hundred people nearly stampeded each other to death as they tried to find shelter from the intensity of the storm. There was shrieking and sobbing and total panic, not exactly the mild irritation you experience when you're caught in a rain shower without an umbrella. But then what we were experiencing wasn't a simple rain shower. It was a storm of Biblical proportions, a display of demonic wrath.

Of course, I *had* brought an umbrella. Pete had insisted that I bring it. How had he known it would rain? And why hadn't I listened to him instead of leaving the damn thing in the car?

"Why is the devil doing this and why did you lie to me about Jeremy?" I wailed at David, who had removed his navy blue blazer and was holding it over my head, in a chivalrous but ultimately fruitless attempt to shield me from the soaking rains.

"Tell me, David!" I yelled again.

He didn't answer. The blazer had just blown out of his hands and flown clear across the patio, into the fronds of a nearby palm tree.

"Let's make a run for it," he said as he grabbed my elbow and hustled me away from the others, in the direction of the River Princess's underground parking garage.

We started to run, but the marbled patio was incredibly slick, treacherous. I slipped and fell. David helped me up. He slipped and fell. I helped him up. The devil wasn't making things easy for us.

We were dashing toward the garage, the wind and rain lashing at our faces, when, out of the corner of my eye, I saw Mike Cook lying on the ground. He was surrounded by three or four people, one of whom seemed to be performing CPR on him.

"Wait!" I shouted as I came to a sudden stop. "That's Jeremy's father. I've got to go back and help him."

David glanced at Mike Cook but tightened his grip on my arm.

I tried to wrest my arm out of David's grasp, so I could go back and help, but he held me tighter.

"Come on, Barbara," he said, forcibly pulling me away from the scene. "I don't like the look of all this lightning. If we stay here on the patio, we're putting ourselves in danger."

"I know, but I—"

He grabbed my hand and drew me along with him. We ran until we finally made it to the garage. David tried the heavy metal door. It was locked. From the inside.

"Now what?" I said as we stood there, soaked and scared, the rain beating down on us with ungodly force.

"Let's duck under here," David said, gesturing toward the pink-and-white awning that curled out over yet another of the River Princess's maze of doors, all of which were locked.

The awning wasn't much in the way of shelter, but it was better than nothing—certainly better than walking all the way around to the front of the building and risking being struck by lightning.

"Okay, as long as we're stuck here together, you can tell me the truth about Jeremy," I said, breathless from all the running. "He's *not* Satan's cover in Banyan Beach, right?"

"No, he isn't."

"So you lied to me!" I was so angry I wanted to choke David.

"I didn't want you to find the devil," he said sheepishly. "I *had* to throw you off his trail."

"But why?"

"I want you to remain a darksider, that's why."

"But you said you cared about me. People don't lie to people they care about."

"I had to. You and I are supposed to pair up. If you convince the devil to let you out of your bargain with him, I won't be able to fulfill mine. Our bargains are linked, you see."

"How do you know all this stuff? Maybe *you're* the one whose body the devil is hiding in."

David shook his head. "I've just been a darksider longer than you have, and, unlike you, I haven't resisted. If you don't resist, you're given more and more information. So I happen to know that if I lose the female darksider I'm supposed to pair up with, the devil could turn me back into the man I was before my transformation and essentially nullify the deal."

"What's wrong with that? Why hold on to an identity that isn't even yours? Is having money and power and movie-star looks so important to you?"

"Yes. I was miserable before my transformation, Barbara."

"So was I, but at least the misery was of my own making. It wasn't engineered by some 'force of darkness.' *I* chose to marry Mitchell Chessner, knowing full well that he wasn't the man of my dreams. *I* didn't work as hard as I could have at my real estate career. And *I* was the one who stuffed my face with Pepperidge Farm Sausalito cookies night after night. I was responsible for my *own* unhappiness, David. I know that now. I don't need the devil to make me thin, successful or happily married. If I want those things, I can get them for myself."

Just then, a giant bolt of lightning set the sky ablaze and literally seared the patch of grass right in front of us as it hit the ground!

"Are you all right?" David asked, touching my arm.

I nodded. "You?"

He nodded.

It seemed to me that the storm was following us. Or, at least, the lightning was.

"Listen, David," I said. "You're not an evil person. You don't really want all the bad things that have been going on around here to continue, do you?"

"No."

"Well then, tell me the name of the person the devil is using as a cover. The truth, this time."

"I want to, Barbara. Really I do."

"Then do it," I urged. "Help me get Satan out of Banyan Beach. You'll be a big hero. People here will love you."

His eyes widened. "They will?"

"Yes."

I had a feeling that all David Bettinger really wanted was to be loved. He didn't especially care how.

"If I tell you, Satan will see it as a betrayal," he said.

"Betrayal implies loyalty and Satan has none," I reminded him. "Not to you, not to anyone. So, please. Tell me, David. Tell me what I need to know."

He sighed. "All right," he said. "It's—"

Before he could finish the sentence, another bolt of lightning struck. And this time, the devil's aim was perfect. The lightning tore through the awning and hit David dead-on. In an instant, he was gone—his entire body enveloped by an enormous cloud of blood red smoke!

I screamed and, just as I did, the storm ended as abruptly as it had begun. The rain stopped, the wind died, and the thunder and lightning ceased. The sky was now as blue as it had been earlier in the afternoon, and the air was clear, clean, fragrant.

Thoroughly overcome with fear and fatigue and disbelief, I sank to the wet ground, buried my face in my hands, and cried.

"Poor, poor David," I said tearfully. "He was only trying to help me. He was about to spill the beans and the devil electrocuted him for it! It's all *my* fault!"

I sat there with my head in my hands, sobbing, moaning, berating myself.

And then a voice said, "What's your fault?"

The voice wasn't as deep and velvety as David's, but it was a male voice.

"David!" I cried, thinking perhaps he wasn't dead after all.

I flung my hands away from my eyes and stood up.

The cloud of red smoke had disappeared and in its place was a man, but he wasn't David. Or was he? He was in his forties and he was standing on the very spot where David had stood. He was wearing the identical clothes that David had been wearing, but he didn't look anything like David. He was short, chubby, and balding, his eyes were a muddy, nondescript brown, and his complexion was pitted with acne scars. I blinked to make sure I wasn't seeing things. I wasn't.

"This is some storm, huh?" he said.

I just stared at him, my mouth hanging open, my mind trying frantically to comprehend what was happening.

"Is it really you?" I asked tentatively.

He laughed good naturedly. "I'll try not to be insulted that you don't remember me, Barbara. You sold me the Nowak house on Pelican Circle. Now, do you remember?"

My God! So this nebbish *was* David! David Bettinger! The devil's lightning hadn't killed him—it had turned him back into the man he was before he became a darksider! To shut him up!

"You remember me now?" David asked.

"Of course," I said, realizing suddenly that it was David who didn't remember.

"You're not a darksider anymore, are you?" I asked.

He looked puzzled. "Not a *what* anymore?"

"A darksider," I tried again. "You know, a person who's been taken over by the force of darkness."

He chuckled, which made his double chin shimmy. "Lord, no," he said, holding his fat stomach. "You real estate agents may be into all that New Age stuff, but not me."

Well, that answered that.

I felt my heart sink as I realized that I was now without my only source of information about the devil; that David Bettinger, my single hope for getting my old life back, was no longer of any use to me.

"Hey, Barbara!"

I turned and saw Suzanne waving and running toward David and me. Her dark hair was matted to her head and her clothes were soaked and askew, but she was smiling.

When she reached us, she hugged me and kissed me and told me how she and Althea had waited out the storm in a broom closet. After a minute or two, David, feeling neglected, I guess, cleared his throat.

"Oh. Excuse me," Suzanne said to him. "I should have introduced myself. I'm Suzanne Munson."

"And I'm Danny Bettinstein," he said.

Danny Bettinstein? Even his *name* had been bogus?

"Are you new in town?" Suzanne asked him, slipping into her singles bar mode.

"Yes," he said. "I'm an orthodontist. I'm opening a practice here."

"That's great," said Suzanne, checking his left hand for a wedding ring.

Yeah, great, I thought. Just what Banyan Beach needs: another man with a selective memory.

Suzanne and David—er, Suzanne and *Danny*—began to chat like two kids on a date, while I plunged into a major depression. At some point, I announced that I was going home and getting into some dry clothes.

"Need a lift?" Danny asked.

I looked at him. He was so homely, poor devil.

Sorry. Bad choice of words.

He was . . . Well, let's just say he wouldn't be making the cover of *GQ* anytime soon. What was worse, he wouldn't be helping me out of my unfortunate predicament anytime soon, either.

"No, I don't need a lift," I said glumly. "Not the kind you mean."

PART
THREE

CHAPTER
20

Charlotte's Monday morning gathering was more of a post mortem than a business meeting. Everyone had war stories—about the party, the storm, the customers who no longer wanted to buy a condominium in the now-notorious River Princess.

"My buyers want to back out of their contract," Althea said, her scowl even more pronounced than usual. "They're those politically correct types that won't use toilet paper if it's made from dead trees. When they heard what Jeremy Cook did to the fountains and why, they said they wouldn't live in a building that killed fish. Of course, they told me this over a meal of grilled snapper."

"What about my customers from New York?" said Frances, who was on her third croissant and had smothered it with butter and Polaner All Fruit. "They were thinking of buying in the building because of its supposedly great security. Now, they're not interested."

"Neither is Joe Namath," June sniffed. "He doesn't want to live in a place that's gotten so much media attention. He likes to keep a low profile."

"It's the profile of those mermaids that caused my customer's hissy fit," said Deirdre. "The minute she saw naked mermaids standing in the middle of the fountains, she said she refused to live in a building that exploited women."

"Sounds like your friend Jeremy hasn't had a very positive effect on our condo sales," Suzanne said to me later over coffee. "Has your brother spoken to him?"

"Yes. Ben said he spent a night in jail on a charge of reckless mischief or something like that. Basically, he paid a fine and promised never to do it again. Of course, Dubin and Company have threatened him with a lawsuit, saying he's responsible for damaging the building *and* their reputation as developers."

"How about his father? Somebody said he had a heart attack during the storm."

"He did, but Ben says he's doing okay. He's in the hospital but stable."

I felt awful knowing the truth about Mike Cook; that the devil had caused his heart attack, just to punish Jeremy. I also felt burdened by the knowledge that the River Princess had been Satan's "pet project." Not that I fully understood what that meant. Only David would be able to explain it to me and David wasn't David anymore. He was Danny Bettinstein, the orthodontist who didn't remember being a darksider.

"Hey, tell me about this Danny Bettinstein," Suzanne said suddenly. "The guy we were talking to after the storm."

"What do you want to know?" I asked, feeling guilty that I would have to lie to her about him.

"For starters, I thought you said the name of the person who was buying the Nowak house was David Bettinger."

"Oh, that." How was I going to explain? "I think Danny uses the name David Bettinger for business. You know, like actors have stage names and writers have pseudonyms." Well, why not?

"You mean, Danny Bettinstein and David Bettinger are the same person?"

"That's right."

"Then Danny's the guy you went out with. The one you said had a dark side."

"In hindsight, it wasn't that dark," I said. I didn't want to ruin Danny for Suzanne. She seemed to like him and now that he was tailless, why not encourage a friendship between them? She was single, he was single. She liked to eat, he liked to cook. She wanted a man with a profession, he straightened teeth for a living. They were perfect for each other, I thought, and I told Suzanne so.

"But he's bald," she whined.

"So? At least he won't shed."

* * *

Speaking of shedders, Pete had a new hairdo. When I'd come home after the party at the River Princess, damp and depressed, I'd walked in the door, reached down to pet my loyal and trusty canine, and discovered that the white patch on his chest—the lone albino fur amid all that satiny black—had grown, expanded, spread! Now, the patch, once the size of my fist, covered almost the entire width of his chest. He looked as if he'd just had a lobster dinner and forgotten to take off his bib.

Is this normal? I wondered. Are dogs more like humans than I thought? Does their hair get whiter as they get older, just like ours does?

I considered my own hair and that of the members of my family. We'd all turned gray practically overnight, and while we didn't jump for joy about it, we didn't consider it especially bizarre.

But Pete was something else again. His chest had grown whiter in a matter of hours. While I was at a party. While my back was turned. And then there were all the other things about him that I didn't understand. I couldn't help wondering: was he somehow part of the devil's plan for me? Had Satan placed him on my doorstep to deceive me in some way? To distract me? If so, why? From what?

There was only one way to find out: by getting the devil out of town and waiting to see if Pete went with him.

How would I find Satan without any help from David or Danny or whatever the hell his name was?

I had an idea—and I planned to follow it up the very next evening.

Constance Terry lived alone in a small, Victorian-style house well outside of town, about ten miles from Benjamin's cabin. It was the type of house I expected a psychic to live in—isolated, slightly run-down, brimming with character. It gave me the creeps and so did the mourning doves who greeted me with their haunting "Hoooo hoooo hoooo" as I walked up to the front door. I looked for a bell or buzzer to press. There was none. Just wind chimes, which announced my arrival without my having to.

"I remember you now," Constance said, motioning for me to

enter the house. "You were the one who interrupted the séance and disturbed the energy in the room."

"Yes," I said. "I didn't know Ben had company."

She nodded and led me into the dusty, windowless, claustrophobically small den, which, she explained, was where she conducted her readings. She gestured toward the ottoman. I sat down on it.

"You'll want to take off that jacket," she said, referring to the beige linen blazer I'd worn over my short-sleeved dress.

"Why? Will that help me get in touch with the spirits?" I asked.

"No, it will help you stay cool. The house isn't air-conditioned."

I nodded and removed the blazer.

"I don't believe in air-conditioning," she went on, settling into a slipcovered wing chair. "It chases entities out, all that cooling and churning and stirring up. They're not comfortable in a space unless the air is still, calm."

"I see," I said, seeing only that the woman sitting in the room with me was alarmingly pale, her skin tone nearly the same color as her long white hair, both of which were in stark contrast to her all-black dress—the same dress she'd worn the night of the séance at Ben's. Her black-and-whiteness reminded me of Pete.

"Shall we get started?" she said.

It wasn't a question. She placed her hands on her lap, tilted her head up toward the ceiling and closed her eyes.

Obviously, she was dispensing with the chitchat and getting right down to business. I liked that. When I had telephoned her and said I wanted to book an hour of her time, she'd explained that she charged eighty-five dollars. The figure had sounded a little steep, but she'd assured me that the time would be well spent. I certainly hoped so.

"Should I close my eyes, too?" I asked.

"Shhhh," she whispered. "I'm dialing into the vibrations."

I wondered if she was an AT&T customer.

"MCI," she said, her eyes still closed.

So much for my doubts about Constance's ability to read minds.

"I feel a dark entity in the room with us," she said. "A foul, rotten odor."

"Oh, that's probably me," I said, a little embarrassed. I reached into my purse for the BreathAssure.

"No." Constance shook her head. "It's someone hovering around you, someone who wants you to do something you don't want to do."

"Yes!" I said excitedly, thinking of the devil and his refusal to let me out of our bargain. I felt optimistic for the first time since this nightmare started. "That's why I'm here, Constance. So you can tell me *who* that person is. I happen to know that there's a very negative entity here in Banyan Beach, the most negative of all entities, the darkest of forces. Can you see him? Can you see whose body he's hiding in?"

She held her hands out in front of her, palms up, a supplicant. And then her eyelids began to flutter.

"I feel a . . ."

"Yes, Constance?" I urged. "What do you feel?"

"I . . . I feel that it's an older man who wants you to do this thing you don't want to do. Yes, an older man. In his seventies, possibly."

"An older man in his seventies," I said.

"Yes, with a foreign accent. A German accent."

"A German accent." The devil was hiding inside the body of a seventy-year-old man with a German accent?

"Yes. I'm getting a name."

"Really?" God, this was going to be easier than I thought.

"I'm getting the initial 'G.' "

"For the first or last name?"

" 'G,' " she repeated, ignoring me. "Greg. Glenn. Garth. George."

"Those names don't ring a bell," I said, trying not to get discouraged.

"Gerald. Gilbert. Gordon. Gus," she went on.

"Gus!" I said. "I know a seventy-year-old man with a German accent named Gus. Gus Liederman. The guy who owns the bagel place on Center Street. I stop there practically every morning on my way to work."

Constance nodded. "Yes, this is the man who wants you to do something you don't want to do."

"Gus?"

I frowned and was glad Constance's eyes were closed so she couldn't see the disappointment on my face. Gus Liederman wasn't the devil's cover in Banyan Beach. He was a nice Jewish baker who was always reinventing the bagel. Actually, Constance was right about him. He *did* want me to do something I didn't want to do: he wanted me to try his latest creation—the pepperoni bagel. I kept telling him that poppy seed bagels were about as out-there as I wanted my bagels to get and that he should stop badgering me or I'd start going to Dunkin' Donuts.

"I don't think Gus Liederman is the dark force I'm looking for," I told Constance. "Perhaps you could pick up someone else's vibration."

"Shhhhh," she quieted me. "I *am* picking up someone else's vibration."

"You are?" I said eagerly.

"Yes. I'm seeing her clearly now."

"Her?" I waited. Constance's eyelids were fluttering again.

"She's coming to me as a gray-haired woman," said Constance. "An older woman."

It's probably Gus Liederman's wife, I guessed. She worked in the bagel place with him.

"Does this woman work on Center Street?" I asked.

"No. She's coming to me from the other side."

"The other side? You mean she's dead?"

"She's in the spirit world. I'm a medium. I connect with those who've passed on."

"I remember," I said, hoping this gray-haired woman Constance had connected with wasn't Denise and Janice's grandmother. I liked meat loaf as much as the next person, but I had more important business here.

"She's calling your name," said Constance. " 'Barbara. Barbara. Barbara,' she's saying."

"Is she saying anything else?" I asked. We could be talking about my mother, my Aunt Sadie, my Grandma Natalie, anyone. I had a lot of dead female relatives with gray hair.

"Yes," said Constance. "She's saying, 'Barbara. Barbara. Barbara. What have you done to yourself? You look like a cadaver.' "

The scary thing was that Constance had not only connected with my mother, she had spoken in her exact voice. It was as if Estelle Greenberg were right there in the room with me.

"Do you know this woman?" Constance asked me.

"Yes. She's my mother. I haven't spoken to her in years and the first words out of her mouth are, 'You look like a cadaver.' She should talk, huh?"

"Would you like to speak to her?"

I considered the question. When my mother was alive, I tried to avoid speaking to her. But now, what did I have to lose? She was just a spirit, a dead person. Besides, I knew how to stand up for myself now. Maybe even to her.

"Yes, I would like to speak to her."

"What is her name?"

"Estelle."

Constance held her hands out once again, palms up, eyes closed tightly.

"Estelle," she called out. "Your daughter would like to communicate with you."

After a few moments of silence, Constance opened her eyes and nodded at me.

"She's waiting," she said.

I swallowed hard. "Mom?"

Constance nodded again, encouraging me to continue.

"I . . . I'm sorry you think I look too thin," I said, then stopped myself. "No, cancel that. I'm not sorry. This is how I look now that I've lost weight. I don't give a shit if you don't like it."

The lights flickered in Constance's little room.

"Your mother says, 'Watch your mouth,' " Constance reported.

"Tell her to watch hers," I said. "She's the one who can't control herself. All she does is criticize. Once a nag, always a nag, I guess."

The lights flickered again.

Constance translated. "Your mother says, 'I only want what's best for my daughter.' "

"Tell her what's best for her daughter is a mother who supports her; who builds her up instead of tears her down; who accepts her for who she is; who tells her she loves her."

The lights flickered, then went out altogether.

I looked over at Constance. "Don't tell me she's at a loss for words."

The lights came back on.

"Well?" I asked my medium.

"Your mother is crying," said Constance. "She's attempting to communicate something but I can't understand her."

"Maybe she's speaking in tongues," I said.

Constance shook her head. "Wait. I'm tuning into her now. She's saying, 'Tell Barbara I love her. More than I ever showed her.' "

"My mother said that?"

"Yes."

I didn't have a clue whether Constance's communications with the dead were on the level or a terrific con, but I let my mother's supposed expression of love hang in the air for a few minutes. It never feels bad to hear an "I love you." Even when you hear it secondhand.

Eventually, I was able to steer Constance back to the reason I had come to see her. I asked her to get in touch with her vibrations or energies or whatever they were and tell me who in Banyan Beach was harboring the force of evil. She tried, but couldn't come up with anybody. Which is not to say she didn't make any psychic predictions. She predicted that I would receive a wedding invitation in the mail from a college friend named Diane (my roommate's name was Diana, which was close enough, I thought); that Mitchell would call to tell me he and Chrissy wanted the house on Seacrest Way (he already had); and that I would feel anger toward a tall dark-haired woman with a run in her pantyhose (it happened later that night, at the supermarket, where a woman fitting that description cut in front of me in the checkout line).

As my hour with Constance drew to a close, I began to feel disheartened, defeated, frustrated by her inability to tell me what I needed to know, and I didn't have any idea what my next move should be.

And then Constance said something that pointed me in the right direction. As I was fumbling in my purse for my credit cards (she had informed me that she took Visa or MasterCard, but not American Express), she said, "Who's the fisherman in your life?"

I looked at her. "What did you say?"

"I said, 'Who's the fisherman?' I'm picking up a man with red hair and a red beard who likes to fish."

"That must be Jeremy," I said. "Jeremy Cook. He's a friend of my brother's."

Constance shook her head. "He's a friend of *yours*," she said. "Make no mistake about that. He's going to help you."

"With what?" I asked.

"With the evil that's come into your life," she said. "He's going to help you get rid of it."

I found this little tidbit quite interesting, obviously.

"But he must be persuaded to help you," she continued. "You must use your *power* to persuade him. Do you understand?"

"I . . . I think so. It's just that Jeremy and I don't get along that well, and I can't imagine that he would—"

"Does he sing?" Constance cut me off.

"Yes," I said.

"He will sing a song for you," she said. "Especially for you."

And on that note, she told me our time was up.

CHAPTER
21

Who's the fisherman? He's going to help you. With the evil that's come into your life. He's going to help you get rid of it.

Constance's words haunted me all night long. She'd been amazingly accurate in so many of her predictions, but was she right about Jeremy? About his helping me get the devil out of town? Should I tell him about the bargain I'd made with Satan? Would he believe me? Of all the people I knew, he was the most likely to take a risk. But risking a night in jail to protest pollution and risking his soul to cast out the devil were two different things, weren't they?

I debated these questions throughout the night and by 4:00 A.M. I finally came to a conclusion: I would tell Jeremy everything and ask for his help. What else could I do? I wasn't exactly full of options.

So I didn't go to the office the next morning. I left the house early and drove down to Eddie's Marina, hoping to catch Jeremy before he went out on the *Devil-May-Care*. Fortunately, I not only found him at "C" dock, slip 14—I found him alone. He was standing next to the Hatteras but not doing much of anything, as far as I could tell. He was just hanging out, drinking coffee, and surveying the scene, looking every bit the Irish seaman in his blue jeans, Kelly green T-shirt, and rusty red hair and beard.

I stopped short of the slip, remained slightly out of his view, and watched him for a minute or two. He had such an easy way about him, a thoroughly unmannered body language that suggested that he didn't concern himself with what people thought of him, with whether or not they liked him. For the second time in a week, I envied him.

"Hey, look who's back at Eddie's Marina. I must be dreamin'," he called out when he caught a glimpse of me. He smiled and raised his Styrofoam cup in a gesture of greeting.

Jeremy smiled a lot, I realized, unlike Mitchell, who wore a perpetually harried expression, as if he were always being sued. In this case, it was Jeremy who was being sued, by the River Princess's developers, but you'd never know it. He looked as happy and carefree as I wished I felt.

"You're not dreaming," I said as I approached him. "I came here to talk to you."

He groaned. "If this 'talk' is gonna be anything like the last one, I think I'll pass, BS."

"I want to apologize for that," I said. "I was totally out of line that day."

"Hey, forget it," said Jeremy. "Ben said you've been havin' a rough time lately."

"Ben doesn't know the half of it."

"Why? You in some kind of trouble?"

I nodded, then leaned closer to him and whispered, "Actually, we all are."

"What's that supposed to mean?"

I glanced to my left, then to my right, to make sure no one could overhear our conversation. I had made the decision to tell Jeremy about the devil, but I wasn't about to broadcast the story to the entire marina.

"I really do have to talk to you. Are you busy?" I asked.

"Now?"

"Yes."

He checked his watch. "I've got about a half an hour before my charter people are supposed to show up. At least, I think they're supposed to show up in a half an hour. With my dad in the hospital, the bookings are kind of screwed up."

"Oh, that's right," I said, embarrassed that I hadn't asked how Mike Cook was doing the minute I saw Jeremy. "Is he going to be okay?"

"The doctors say he had a 'mild heart attack,' which sounds like double-talk to me. Either he had one or he didn't, ya know?"

I nodded.

"Anyway, they're givin' him medication and keepin' an eye on him, and if everything goes all right, they'll let him come home in a week or so. But I'm not sure he's gonna be ready to come back to work."

"Why not? Booking your charter groups doesn't sound very strenuous."

"Not strenuous but stressful. Especially for a guy whose health isn't all that great. You gotta deal with the hotels where I've got the concessions. You gotta deal with the individual clients who want to charter the boat—some of 'em nutcases. You gotta deal with the advertising and promotion people. You gotta juggle the cash flow. Just because Cook's Charters is a Mom-and-Pop kind of business doesn't mean it isn't a bitch to keep afloat."

"I didn't think of all that," I said. "How is business anyway? Did the fallout from your little stunt at the River Princess cause any cancellations?"

Jeremy laughed. "Are you kiddin'? The phone's been ringin' off the hook. I'm famous now, BS. Before, people knew me 'cause I sing in a band. Now, they know me 'cause I dumped sewage in a fountain. I'm a big hero around here, and everybody wants to hang out with me all of a sudden."

"I know a way you can be an even bigger hero," I said.

"That's okay. I'm not really in the hero business," he said. "I just don't like seein' my river polluted."

"What would you say if I told you I knew who was behind the pollution of the river and all the other things that have been going on in this town—the murders, the corruption, all of it?"

He regarded me, a look of skepticism on his ruddy face. "I'd say you should stick to real estate and leave the criminals to the cops."

"I'm serious, Jeremy. But we can't talk here. Not in front of everybody."

"Aw, come on. These guys are all busy with their boats. They're not payin' any attention to us." He waved at a couple of men who were working nearby.

"Please, Jeremy. What I have to tell you is very confidential, very secret. We'd have some privacy on your boat, wouldn't we?"

He checked his watch again. "My charter group is comin' in twenty minutes."

"So give me twenty minutes. I promise I'll leave the minute they get here."

The *Devil-May-Care* wasn't a new boat, but it looked it. It was well maintained—clean, neat, shipshape. Jeremy explained that Hatterases are expensive, but that he had sold his old boat and bought this one used and that it had more than paid for itself in charters. He offered to give me a complete tour, but I declined. I only had twenty minutes to tell him my tale of woe and I didn't want to waste a second of it.

I began by explaining how badly things had been going for me in my marriage and at work; how I'd started drinking too much; how Mitchell had come home one night and announced that he was in love with Chrissy; how I'd gotten drunk and stumbled outside in that thunderstorm; how I'd said I would do anything if I could sell a house and find true love (I blushed when I said that); and how I'd woken up the next morning with blond hair, big boobs, and a flat stomach but didn't know how I got that way.

Jeremy found the whole thing hysterically funny.

"I've heard that women lie about havin' plastic surgery, but this is ridiculous," he smirked.

When he finally managed to stop laughing, I went on with the story. I told him about finding Pete on my doorstep; about selling the most overpriced house in town to David Bettinger; about discovering that David and I were so irresistibly drawn to one another that it was scary.

"You actually slept with that guy?" Jeremy asked, looking surprised, as if it were inconceivable that I might have a sex life, never mind that someone like David would find me attractive.

"What if I did?" I said hotly. "Would it be so hard for you to picture a devastatingly handsome man like David Bettinger wanting to sleep with me?"

Jeremy didn't answer right away. I figured he was comparing

me to those nineteen-year-old bimbos he was always slobbering over and thinking I didn't measure up. Instead, he said, "Sure, I can picture a guy wantin' to sleep with you. Even if you *are* Ben's kid sister and even if you *do* have an overactive imagination. Besides, David what's-his-name isn't all that handsome."

I squelched a smile. Was Jeremy jealous? "Fine. He's not so handsome," I said, thinking he should see David now. "But I don't have an overactive imagination. Everything I'm telling you is the truth."

"Okay, then tell me some more truth: did you sleep with Mr. Palm Beach or not?"

"Almost," I said, and took a deep breath. I had a feeling that the minute I brought up the issue of David's tail, Jeremy would either laugh me off the boat or ship me off to a psycho ward. But I had to tell him what happened between David and me that night, as humiliating an experience as it was. It was central to the story.

"He had a *what?*" he shouted when I had finished describing my encounter with David's unusual appendage. Well, I hadn't expected him to buy it on the first try.

"It's true," I said and went on to explain about the devil making me and David darksiders in exchange for our producing darksider babies. I also gave Jeremy the little bulletin about the devil living right in Banyan Beach, hiding in the body of someone I knew.

"At first, I thought that 'someone' was you," I told him.

That did it, apparently, because Jeremy jumped up from his seat and began to back away from me.

"You're crazier than I thought," he said.

"I'm not crazy, Jeremy. I'm telling you the truth," I said.

"Then prove it!" he challenged.

"All right, I will!"

I thought for a minute. "You can call David and ask him," I said. "He'll confirm everything."

And then I remembered that David wouldn't be able to confirm anything, because David was now Danny and Danny didn't even know he'd been a darksider.

"I think I will call him," said Jeremy. "Just to see what kind of bullshit story the guy gives me."

"No, don't," I said and told him why. I recounted the whole

scene at the River Princess party—about how David was just about to tell me the name of the person who was Satan's cover in Banyan Beach when he was punished and turned back into his old, predarksider self.

"So you can't prove one word of all this," said Jeremy.

I had the sense that he wanted to believe me; or, more accurately, that he didn't want to believe I was crazy. But the story was too fantastic, too implausible. I wouldn't have believed me either.

Still, I couldn't give up. I needed Jeremy's help and, according to Constance, I was going to get it.

"Jeremy, please listen to me," I said, trying not to let desperation creep into my voice. "You love this town as much as I do. You grew up here. It's your home. You care what happens to the place."

"So?"

"So Banyan Beach is going to hell. Literally. Unless we stop it. Unless we stop *him.*"

"Stop who?"

"I already told you: the devil. He's living here in town—in the body of someone I know."

"Oh, brother. Not that again."

"It's true." I sighed. I was getting nowhere and my twenty minutes with Jeremy were running out.

"I gotta go," he said. "My people will be here any minute."

He started toward the cabin door.

"If you won't help the town, then help me," I said, making one last effort. "I don't want to be a darksider for the rest of my life. I don't want blond hair. I don't want big boobs. I don't want to look like a 'Star Search' spokesmodel. And I don't want bad breath."

"Bad breath?"

"Here. Smell."

I breathed on him. He recoiled.

"See? I never used to smell like that. Not until I became a darksider. So please, Jeremy. Help me find the devil and talk him into letting me out of the bargain. *Please.*"

He gave me a long, searching look, then shook his head and climbed off the boat, onto the dock. I followed him. I was about to continue my harangue when I saw four men off in the distance, walking toward us. I guessed they were Jeremy's charter group, because they didn't look like your scruffy, Eddie's Marina types. Even from several feet away, I could tell that those weren't tattoos covering their arms and necks. Those were gold chains. Shiny gold chains that sparkled in the sunlight.

"Sorry, BS. Gotta go," said Jeremy.

Quick! I told myself. You've still got a few seconds to convince Jeremy you're telling the truth. Think of something that will make him believe you. Hurry!

He must be persuaded to help you. You must use your power to persuade him.

My power!

I suddenly remembered Constance's words. I must use my *power* to persuade Jeremy. And then he *would* help me.

Quick! I urged myself on. Do something!

As the four men continued to advance toward us, I said to Jeremy, "Remember how I told you about my darksider power? Well, now I'm going to show it to you. And then you'll know I've been telling the truth."

"You need help, pal," he said, shaking his head. "You really do."

"You see those men coming toward us?" I asked, ignoring his remark.

"Yeah. They're the ones I'm takin' out today. Looks like they're wearin' enough jewelry to sink the boat."

"You don't care for their gold chains?"

"You don't see any on me, do ya?"

"Fine. Watch this." I took a deep breath and then said, "I want those gold chains to disappear."

In an instant, the four men, who were still several feet away, were suddenly stripped of their jewelry! In front of our eyes, they had gone completely chainless! It was as if four muggers had crept up behind them and, in perfect sync, ripped them off and then fled. Now *that* was power.

"Don't worry. They can buy new ones," I smiled as Jeremy looked appropriately shocked—so shocked he had to grab on to one of the dock lines and steady himself.

"You did that?" he asked.

"I did."

"But how . . . I mean, what made their . . . I don't see—"

"Now do you believe me?"

Before he could answer, his charter group was upon us. The men didn't appear to notice that their jewelry had vanished, even though each of them was probably a couple of pounds lighter without it.

"Are you Jeremy Cook?" one of them asked.

Jeremy was too startled to answer. So I answered for him.

"Yes, he's Jeremy Cook," I said. "He'll be your captain today. Won't you, Jeremy?"

I nudged him, hoping to snap him out of it, but he was still speechless.

"He's a little shy," I said, apologizing for Jeremy, who was anything but. "He'll loosen up as you guys get to know each other better."

At least, I hoped he would. I didn't want to be responsible for his losing a day's charter business. Fortunately, his two crew members, the boys I'd seen on the *Devil-May-Care* the first time I came to the marina, showed up and helped the four men aboard.

When Jeremy and I were alone, I asked him if he was all right.

"Never mind me. It's you who's got this . . . this . . . power to make things happen to people." He looked as if he were afraid of me, afraid to be anywhere near me.

"Yes, but I don't bite," I reassured him. "Honest. Biting is for vampires and werewolves, not darksiders."

I was trying to make light of the situation. I certainly didn't want to scare the man off.

"Does Ben know about this?" he asked.

"No," I said. "I didn't think he could handle it."

"And you thought I could?"

"Evidently. Was I wrong?"

He shrugged. "I don't know what to say. I can't believe this. I just can't believe that someone like you would turn into—Jesus, I've known you since you were the pain-in-the-ass kid sister of my best friend."

"I'm still the pain-in-the-ass kid sister of your best friend. But now, I'm in big trouble, and I need your help. Will you help me, Jeremy?"

He hesitated, but just for a split second.

"Only if you promise me something," he said.

"What?"

"That you won't use that power of yours on me, like you did on those guys."

"You don't wear gold jewelry."

"No, but I wear clothes. I don't want to be walkin' down the street and find myself buck naked, just because you don't like the way I dress."

"I promise. Who wants to see you buck naked anyway?"

He allowed himself a small smile.

"I gotta go," he said.

"I know," I said.

"What happens now?" he asked.

"Dinner tonight? At my house?"

"You eat?"

"What do you mean?"

"I mean, do you eat? Now that you're a 'darksider' or whatever you call yourself."

I laughed. "Yes, I eat. But I don't cook. So we'll order a pizza or something, okay?"

He nodded and turned to go. Then he glanced at me one more time, as if to make sure I hadn't sprouted horns.

I parted my hair, first on the left side, then on the right. "Look, Ma. No horns," I said.

He smiled and climbed aboard the *Devil-May-Care*.

CHAPTER
22

It hadn't rained in over a week, not since the devil unleashed that horrific storm at the River Princess party. And it hadn't rained for weeks before that. Normally, August is Banyan Beach's rainiest month, but then nothing about Banyan Beach was normal that summer. We were having a drought instead of a flood, and, as a result, we weren't allowed to water our lawns, fill our swimming pools, or wash our cars. The River Princess even had to shut off its fabled fountains.

The situation was made worse on the afternoon of my dinner with Jeremy. At about three o'clock, there was a watermain break at a construction site off Route 1, and the entire town was without water for several hours. Everyone went rushing off to buy bottled water, only to discover that the supermarkets were sold out of it.

The devil is doing this, I thought as I peered out the window at my brown lawn while I waited for Jeremy to show up. He's playing with us, having a little fun at our expense. I wondered what was next on his agenda. Did he intend to scorch us the way he was scorching our grass? Dry us out until we burned? Turn our lush, tropical paradise into a living hell?

Pete seemed to sense that I was having company that night. He was even friskier than usual, bouncing from room to room like a speed freak. By the time Jeremy arrived and I opened the front door to greet him, Pete was so keyed up that he leapt onto Jeremy, nearly knocking him over.

"Hey, down, boy," Jeremy laughed. "You're messin' my dress-up clothes."

Actually, Jeremy *was* dressed up—for him. He was wearing his customary blue jeans and sneakers, but instead of a T-shirt he had put on a crisp white button-down shirt, sleeves rolled up, collar open. His hair and beard were still scruffy and his gut stuck out the way it always did, but at least the shirt was tucked in over the gut, which made him look neater, better groomed, more handsome somehow.

More handsome? I took another look at him. Yes, he did look handsome, I realized. And he smelled good. It was a clean, citrusy scent. A brand of cologne.

Cologne? Jeremy wasn't exactly the Calvin Klein Obsession type. And it wasn't as if he and I were on some kind of date. Hardly.

Maybe he thinks the cologne will ward off the evil spirits waiting for him inside my house, I thought as I noticed how reluctant he seemed to enter.

"Why don't you come in?" I said to him after sending Pete into the bedroom.

But Jeremy didn't come in. He hung back, remaining by the front door.

"Okay," I said impatiently. "What's the problem?"

"Is it safe to go in there?" he said, peeking inside. "I mean, nobody's gonna stab me with a pitchfork or anything, right?"

I grabbed his hand and pulled him into the foyer, walked him into the living room, to the sofa, and gave him a gentle shove onto the middle cushion. Then I sat down next to him. "There. Comfy?"

"Sure, for a guy who's sittin' on the same couch with a she-devil."

"Would you stop? I'm not a she-devil. I'm me. The person you've always known and loathed."

"I haven't always known you, BS," said Jeremy, not commenting on the loathing part. "Not since high school, and even then I didn't really know you. Nobody really knew anybody in high school."

"So I'm discovering." Back then, Mitchell was my idea of a good catch.

"For example, I never knew why you backed out of goin' to the prom with me. Why did you?"

"What is this? A trip down Memory Lane? I thought we were going to talk about—"

"Humor me, BS. I was thinkin' about it on my way over here."

"But that was such a long time ago," I protested, not really wanting to discuss the past. "I think we should move on to more important issues."

"This *is* important. Not life and death stuff. Just important. Why *did* you cancel out that night?"

God, he wasn't going to let up. "Two reasons, I guess."

"What's the first?"

"I knew that Ben *made* you ask me to the prom, because he felt sorry for me. Back in high school I was pretty pitiful, remember?"

Jeremy didn't say anything. I took that to mean that he remembered all too well.

"What's the second reason?" he asked.

I felt myself blush at this one.

"Come on, BS. Tell me."

"All right. The second reason is that I was afraid of you."

He laughed. "That's pretty funny, considerin' that now I'm the one who's afraid of you, sweetheart." He laughed again. "Why were you afraid of me?"

"You were a wild man, that's why. You hung around with all the degenerates. Just the other day, your father told me you were madly in love with Bobbi Delafield, that slut."

"My father doesn't have a clue who I was in love with in high school."

I arched an eyebrow. "So there *was* someone? Who was it? Or don't you want to tell?"

"I don't want to tell. It's personal. Between me and her."

"Aw, you're not ashamed of the girl, are you?"

"Ashamed? No."

"Then what are you?"

"I'm still in love with her."

"Oh."

I felt a twinge of something—disappointment?—that Jeremy was emotionally involved with someone. God knows why. I suppose it was because I'd never pictured him as the sort of man who would carry a torch for twenty minutes, let alone twenty years. And if he was still in love with someone from high school, why didn't they live together? Settle down? Get married?

"She and I have had our ups and downs," he said by way of explanation. "And to tell you the truth, I don't know how things are gonna play out between us. Waitin' for a woman to make up her mind is kinda like catchin' a fish—you never know how long it's gonna take."

I rolled my eyes. "Yeah, and life is like a box of chocolates—you never know whatcha gonna get. Please, no more Gumpisms," I groaned.

He smiled. "No Gumpisms. Just Cookisms. What I was tryin' to say was that love and fishing are not that different. Both of 'em take patience and persistence, and timing is everything. Sometimes, you gotta just sit there and let things be for a while. You can't hurry feelings and you can't hurry fish. They'll come when they come. You know what I'm talkin' about, BS?"

I had always thought of love in more immediate terms—i.e. that it would strike quickly, like the proverbial Cupid's arrow to the heart, and the trick was to grab it while you could. But maybe Jeremy's concept was more realistic, more mature. After all, what did I know about love or patience? I had married the first man who had shown the slightest interest in me.

"Okay. Enough of the philosophical bullshit. What do you say we get to work on this devil stuff," Jeremy suggested when I didn't respond to his little speech.

"I really think we should," I said. "Can I get you a drink first? Or do you just want to order some pizza and talk over dinner?"

"No booze for me," he said. "I think I'm gonna need a clear head tonight. But the pizza sounds good. Are you gonna call Domino's or just beam the pie over here with that darksider power of yours?"

"Very funny. I'm going to use the telephone," I said, and ordered us a large sausage and mushroom pizza.

When it arrived twenty minutes later, we sat at my dining room table and ate it. Or, to be more accurate, *I* ate the pizza. Jeremy *inhaled* it. I swear, the man was a human vacuum cleaner. He shoved each slice into his mouth and swallowed it whole. Pete had better table manners.

And speaking of Pete, he was being remarkably well behaved

while Jeremy and I ate dinner. Never once did he jump up on the table or stick his head between our legs or bark obnoxiously. He sat in front of the television set, which I had turned on to CNN news as I always did at seven o'clock, and stayed quiet.

"So, you want me to help you find out where the devil's hidin', right?" asked Jeremy.

"Right," I said.

"What if we do find the person he's hidin' in? Then what?"

"Then we find a way to get him out of the person's body and out of Banyan Beach. Otherwise, I'm stuck with being a darksider forever."

The second the words left my mouth, I produced one of those attractive growls that the devil had endowed me with. I thought Jeremy was going to have a heart attack.

He jumped up off his chair and moved several feet away from me, a look of terror on his face.

"Where the hell did that come from?" he shouted.

I smiled weakly and patted my chest. "It's a darksider thing," I said. "Apparently, the devil makes me growl. Supposedly, it pisses Satan off when I start talking about getting him out of town."

Jeremy was only moderately pacified.

"Please. Sit down," I urged. "There's nothing to be scared of. I promise. But now you can see why I'm so desperate to stop being a darksider. It's downright embarrassing at times."

Jeremy nodded and sat back down at the table. "You have any idea who this person could be? The one that's hidin' the devil?"

"All I know is that, according to David, the person is someone I know. Someone I know *well*. Since I don't exactly have a wide circle of friends, I've sort of narrowed it down to the women I work with at Home Sweet Home. Of course, it could also be Mitchell. Or Chrissy. Or even Ben."

"Ben? Give me a break. He's your brother, for Christ's sake."

"I know he's my brother. But that doesn't mean he's not possessed by the devil. He raises emus for a living. He must be possessed by something."

"Ben isn't the one we're lookin' for. I'd know it if the devil had taken over his body, believe me."

"You didn't know that the devil had taken over *my* body, did you?"

Jeremy appraised my body for what seemed like an hour but was probably only a minute. He started at my face and let his eyes work their way down, slowly, languorously, without the slightest awareness that he was making me uncomfortable.

I cleared my throat. "As I said, the people I know best—or spend the most time with, anyway—are the women I work with at Home Sweet Home."

"Tell me about 'em, BS." His gaze was still drifting, still moving across my body. I wished he would cut it out. Well, sort of.

"There's Charlotte Reed, the owner of Home Sweet Home," I began, but was interrupted by Pete, who had picked that very moment to go on a barking jag.

"Woof! Woof! Woof!"

"Pete, shut up!" I yelled at him. "Watch the news while Jeremy and I talk!"

Pete shut up.

"That's pretty impressive the way the dog listens to you," said Jeremy. "You said he's got this mind-blowin' intelligence. I guess he understands English too, huh?"

I shrugged. "It's hard to say what he understands. All I know is that he made me take an umbrella to the River Princess party. All the weather forecasters—including Chrissy Hemplewhite—said there was absolutely no chance of rain that night. So how did Pete know the devil was going to make it pour—unless, of course, Pete is one of the devil's operatives the way David was? Maybe there's such a thing as a darksider dog and Pete is one."

"Or maybe Pete's the one who's hidin' the devil," Jeremy suggested.

That comment provoked more barking. Loud, insistent barking.

"No. He's much too loving," I said. "He protects me, Jeremy. He's my companion, my best friend. Besides, David spoke of a *person* who was hiding the devil. He never said anything about a dog."

Pete continued to bark. He was standing in front of the television set but was clearly not interested in CNN's report on the O.J. Simpson trial.

I got up from the table and went over to see what was the matter. I bent down and scratched the ever-growing white patch on his chest. "It's okay, Pete," I said in a low, soothing voice. "We know you're not in cahoots with the devil."

He quieted down immediately and began to rub up against me. I patted his head, then cradled it in my arms and kissed it.

When I returned to the table, I said, "He does understand English, I swear he does."

Jeremy shook his head in disbelief. "So I'm sittin' here with a woman who growls and a dog that understands English," he said. "The next thing I know, you're gonna tell me he *speaks* English too."

"I think Pete has his own way of communicating," I said. "Like when he started flipping through my MLS book that day and left it open to the page with the listing of the Nowak house."

"And the time he went into your bathroom to weigh himself," Jeremy offered.

"Yes, but what do these things mean? What's he trying to tell me?"

Jeremy shrugged. "Let's leave Pete for a while and get back to your friends at Home Sweet Home. You were tellin' me about Charlotte."

"Charlotte Reed," I said.

I gave Jeremy a thumbnail sketch of each of the women I worked with: Charlotte, Althea, Deirdre, Frances, June, and Suzanne.

"Suzanne's the one I met, right?" he asked. "At the Hellhole that night?"

"Yes, you did meet Suzanne. I had forgotten about that."

"I doubt the devil's inside *her*. Judgin' by the way she was lustin' after every guy in the place, I'd say nobody's been inside her in years."

"God, must you talk like an animal?"

"At least I don't growl like one. Maybe we should forget your friends and move on to Mitchell. If anyone is possessed by the devil, it's that guy."

"You and he never did have much chemistry, did you?"

"No, and neither did you two. Why did you marry him, BS? You coulda done so much better."

"That's the nicest thing you've ever said to me, Jeremy."

"I'm serious. Even Freddie Reese would have been a better deal than Mitchell Chessner."

Freddie Reese was the president of the audiovisual club in high school and was also its only member. Out of all the kids in our class, he was the most universally disliked. But, hey, maybe he grew up to be a real charmer. You never know how the people you went to high school with are going to turn out. Look at Jeremy and Mitchell. Back then, I had figured Jeremy for the flake and Mitchell for the solid citizen. But Jeremy turned out to be the solid citizen and Mitchell turned out to be the flake. As for how I turned out, well, the verdict wasn't in yet.

"I married Mitchell because I thought I loved him," I said. "Obviously, I acted precipitously."

"That's because nobody ever explained to you that bein' in love is kinda like fishing," Jeremy smiled.

I returned his smile. "No, nobody ever did."

Jeremy's eyes held mine for a moment, only for a moment, but it was long enough to make my stomach do a cartwheel. Why, I couldn't fathom.

"Getting back to Mitchell," he said, "has he been actin' stranger than usual? Not that you could tell with that guy."

"Well, he gave up accounting for the restaurant business. He had an affair with a TV weatherperson. And he left me so he could marry her. But that doesn't smack of the devil. It smacks of a mid-life crisis."

Jeremy nodded. "How about this Chrissy he's hung up on? Could she be the one we're lookin' for?"

I shrugged. "I don't know her, other than what I see of her on TV."

"Well then, tell me something: how are we supposed to find the devil if we don't know where to look?"

I heaved a sigh of frustration. "I've been asking myself that for weeks. I'm starting to think that we'll never find him. Not without divine intervention. Unless we're given some sort of clue or direction, I'll be under the devil's influence forever and so will Banyan Beach."

I felt the tears welling, and out of the corner of my eye, I saw Jeremy's hand move across the table and reach for mine, presumably to comfort me. But then I saw him change his mind and sur-reptitiously pull it back.

We sat there in silence for a few minutes, discouraged, defeated, depressed. Suddenly, the mood was broken by the sound emanating from the television set, which had been broadcasting the news on CNN but was now blaring with the theme music from "Jeopardy."

I looked at my watch. "It's seven-thirty," I said.

"So? Do darksiders turn into pumpkins at seven-thirty?"

"No, but CNN has 'Moneyline' at seven-thirty, not 'Jeopardy.' "

I got up and walked toward the television, in search of the remote control so I could flip it back to CNN, but I didn't see it in its usual place on top of the TV.

I looked down at Pete, who was sprawled out in front of the set. The remote control was resting between his front paws.

"Oh, there it is," I said, taking the remote away from him. "He must have been playing with it and changed the channel by accident."

"I don't think so," Jeremy called out to me. "Nothing that dog does is an accident."

Jeremy had a point. Was the changing of the channels another of Pete's "communications"? And if so, what was he trying to say?

I put CNN back on and returned the remote to Pete's paws. And then I watched. And waited. Seconds after I'd handed the remote back to him, Pete placed his right front paw on the button for Channel Eight—the channel that broadcast "Jeopardy" at seven-thirty every night! Yes, there was Alex Trebek, the host of the show, welcoming the three contestants and explaining the rules of the game!

"Did you see that, Jeremy?" I said, motioning for him to join me. "Did you see what Pete just did?"

Jeremy hurried over. "See if he'll do it again," he suggested.

I bent down and took the remote away from Pete, changed the channel to CNN and returned it to him. Once again, he placed his right front paw on it and punched in Channel Eight! On came "Jeopardy"!

"I'll be damned," Jeremy said. "The dog channel surfs."

"But he's not channel surfing," I said. "He only wants one channel and one show."

I knelt down beside Pete and took his face in my hands.

"What does it mean?" I asked the dog.

"Maybe he's tryin' to tell you that you're in *jeopardy* from the devil," Jeremy said.

"I already know that," I snapped. "It's gotta be something else."

"Okay, smart-ass. Then what is it?"

I lowered my head and went nose to nose with Pete. "What is it, huh, boy?" I asked. "Tell me why you keep switching the television to that dopey game show."

Suddenly, Pete bounded out of my arms, nearly breaking my nose in the process. He began to bark and jump and run around in circles. I'd seen him act hyper, but this was ridiculous.

"What did I do?" I shouted, trying to be heard over Pete's barking. "I obviously provoked him in some way, Jeremy."

"Repeat what you said," he suggested. "Just before Pete went berserk."

"I said, 'Tell me why you keep switching the television to that dopey game show.'"

In response, Pete leapt into my arms, licking my face with such ferocity I had to ask Jeremy to pull him off me.

"Let's see what happens if *you* say it," I told him.

"Say what?"

"The thing that seems to provoke him."

Jeremy grabbed Pete by the collar and said, "Tell me why you keep switchin' the television to that dopey game show."

Pete licked Jeremy's face with equal gusto.

"I think we've established that he gets excited when he hears that sentence," I said. "The question is: why?"

"Let's rewind the tape, so to speak," said Jeremy. "What were we talkin' about right before that sentence?"

"We weren't talking. We were pouting. We were discouraged that we couldn't figure out where the devil was hiding."

"Right. And then you said something about needin' a clue."

"Yes, a clue."

Jeremy and I looked at each other.

"If Pete understands English, then he heard what you said," Jeremy theorized. "The 'Jeopardy' thing might be some kind of clue."

"It's possible, I guess. Maybe the clue has something to do with

Alex Trebek," I said. "But he doesn't live in Banyan Beach, so the devil can't be hiding in *his* body."

"How do you know he doesn't live in Banyan Beach? He might have a winter house here. A lot of celebrities do."

"Trust me, June Bellsey would have told me."

"Then maybe it's something else about the show. Maybe it's the fact that 'Jeopardy' starts with a 'J.' Maybe Pete's tryin' to tell us that June is the one we want."

I shook my head. "If the initial 'J' were so important, why didn't Pete press Channel Eleven on the remote control instead of Channel Eight? Channel Eleven shows reruns of 'The *Jeffersons*' at seven-thirty."

"What do you do, sit home and watch TV every night? You're a walkin' *TV Guide*, BS."

"We can't all lead the thrill-a-minute life you do. Now help me figure this out, would you?"

"Hey, if you don't like the job I'm doin', get somebody else."

"Sorry. This whole thing is driving me crazy. First, Pete pulls that stunt with the MLS book. Then he gets on my scale and weighs himself. Now he insists on watching a game show."

"Do the three things have anything in common?"

"Not that I . . . Well, wait a minute. Let me think."

I thought—and then the answer finally dawned on me.

"What?" Jeremy asked. "Tell me!"

"It's Frances Lutz!" I cried, grabbing Jeremy by the shoulders and hugging him to me.

"How do you know?" he said.

"Because it all fits together now. Every time I tried to figure out who the person was, Pete would give me another clue, only I was too stupid to get it. First, he opened my MLS book to the Nowak house, and the Nowak house is Frances's listing. Then he jumped on the scale to weigh himself, and Frances weighs 300 pounds. Tonight he switched the television to a game show, and Frances is a game show addict. Oh, Jeremy. I asked for divine intervention and instead I got *canine* intervention! This is incredible!"

"It's incredible, all right," said Jeremy, his hot breath on my cheek.

In my zeal, I had completely forgotten that I was still holding on to him, that I was still in his embrace. I lingered there for just another instant and then felt the muscles in his arms stiffen.

"Oh. Sorry," I said and pulled away.

We quickly let go of each other, as if we each had a contagious disease.

"No problem," he said.

There was an awkward silence. And then Pete began to bark. Jeremy and I turned to look at him.

"We're still only guessin' about these clues Pete's given us," he said. "Why don't you ask the dog straight out if it's Frances? See what happens."

"Good idea."

I knelt down in front of Pete and brought my face close to his once more.

"Pete," I said, gazing into his soulful hazel eyes. "Is the devil camping out in Frances Lutz's body?"

Pete's response was astonishing and miraculous, even more so than all his previous displays.

He lifted his right front paw, like a maestro about to conduct an orchestra, and set it back down on the ground. Then he began to move it along the carpet in such a way that his paw marks created a little design, a pattern of some sort.

"Look," I said to Jeremy and pointed to the carpet.

The two of us watched, openmouthed, as Pete completed his task. What he had drawn wasn't a design or a pattern, we discovered, but a word:

Yes.

The next morning, I called Frances at home and asked her if she would be coming into the office.

"No," she said. "I'm working out of the River Princess sales office today. Why?"

Because I want to free you from the devil, I was tempted to say. But why bother? According to David, Frances had no idea she was possessed.

"Because I want to talk to you about the Nowak house," I lied. "And a couple of other things."

"Oh. Well, we could talk later. Would you like to come for dinner?" she asked. "I made lasagna last night and I've got plenty of leftovers."

"Enough for me and a friend?" I said. Jeremy and I had come up with a plan. We were going to find a way to get Frances alone, ply her with liquor, and then perform an exorcism on her. Jeremy had gone to Blockbuster Video and rented *The Exorcist,* and we'd spent half the night watching it, taking notes. The movie gave us ideas and now we were going to put them into action, along with a few of our own.

"A friend? Who?" asked Frances.

"You're not going to like this," I said. "It's Jeremy Cook."

"Barbara! You call that man a friend?" she said. "He's cost us thousands of dollars in commissions. I haven't sold one condo in the River Princess since he destroyed those fountains."

"He didn't destroy them, Frances. He only dirtied them a little. Besides, he'd like to apologize to you, since you're the listing agent on the building. He feels guilty about what he did. He wants to make amends."

"I bet."

"It's true. Look, he's my brother's best friend and I've known him since we were kids. He would never do anything to hurt anybody. Anybody who didn't deserve it, that is. So what do you say? Can I bring him tonight?"

She hesitated, then said, "Does he like lasagna?"

"I'm sure he does, but his table manners aren't the greatest," I said. "I seem to remember that you've got white carpet in your dining room, Frances. If I were you, I'd put plastic down before we get there."

The devil was not happy about the dinner date with Frances. I could tell because he made me growl six times while I was waiting for Jeremy to pick me up. But there were other, much more serious, manifestations of his displeasure. Two people in Banyan Beach had been shot to death overnight. Four others were injured in car accidents. What's more, it still hadn't rained, and several brushfires had broken out across town. Everything had a parched, brittle look about it—the lawns, the trees, the people. We needed relief. And it was up to Jeremy and me to provide it.

He came for me at six-thirty. I met him at the front door, armed with a shopping bag full of the items we had agreed that I would bring to Frances's house—items that were supposed to drive the devil out of a person's body.

"Did you have any trouble getting the things on your list?" I asked, peeking inside the bag he was carrying.

"Yeah, I struck out on the holy water," he said. "I went to four different churches, but nobody would sell me any."

"Never mind," I said. "I'll bring a couple of bottles of Evian. We can say a prayer over them on the way over."

I was about to run off to the kitchen when Jeremy tapped me on the shoulder.

"What?" I asked.

"How about a hello?" he said.

"Hello," I said.

He smiled. "Remember when we were in Mr. Garvey's math class together?"

"Mr. Garvey's math class? Why on earth would you think of that at a time like this?"

"Because you just reminded me of the way you were back then. You'd come into that classroom, sit down next to me, and stick your head in a book, and I'd have to tap you on the shoulder and say, 'How about a hello?' Just like I did now."

"I told you last night. I was scared of you when we were in high school."

"What about now? Still scared?"

I met his eyes and felt my stomach do another one of those stupid flips.

"No," I said, my mouth a little dry. "There's only one person I'm scared of, and if we don't get moving, we'll never get him out of town."

"Fine. Go get the designer water."

I nodded and went off to the kitchen. When I came back a minute later, Pete was sniffing around Jeremy's bag of goodies.

"Something in there appeals to him," I said.

"It must be the Perdue Oven-Stuffer Roaster," said Jeremy. "Dogs love raw meat."

"Raw meat? You've got an uncooked chicken in there?"

He nodded.

"But Frances made lasagna," I said. "What's she going to do with a chicken?"

"She's not gonna do anything with it," said Jeremy. "*We* are. I've got a fishing buddy named Roland. He's Haitian. He told me, 'If you wanna get rid of the devil, lay a dead chicken at his feet.' Well, I didn't have time to go out and shoot a chicken, so I bought one at the supermarket."

"Brilliant," I smiled.

"Thanks," he said, then checked his watch. "Better get goin', huh?"

"Right."

We took Jeremy's pickup truck. About halfway over to Frances's house, he pulled the truck over to the side of the road.

"What'd you do that for?" I said, knowing we were already late.

"I smell something," he said. "Something really foul."

"It's just me," I said. "I forgot my BreathAssure."

"No, it smells like something's burnin'." He leaned over the steering wheel and peered at the dashboard. "The temperature gauge is lit up. We must've overheated."

Great, I thought. The devil's not even going to let us *near* Frances.

"Can't you fix it?" I asked impatiently.

"No, Your Highness. I can't fix it," said Jeremy. "But you can."

"Oh, right. I know as much about trucks as I do about exorcisms."

"What about that power of yours? If there ever was a time to use it, it's now."

"Sorry. My power only works when I want to do something mean and nasty to someone," I said.

"How do you know? Just try it. Say, 'I want the water temperature in this truck to cool down to 170 degrees.'"

I shrugged. "I suppose there's nothing to lose." I cleared my throat. "I want the water temperature in this truck to cool down to 170 degrees," I announced.

We waited. Nothing happened.

"I told you," I said. "The devil doesn't give darksiders the power so we can fix things. He gives it to us so we can cause pain and suffering."

"Then we'll have to find another way to get to Frances's house," said Jeremy.

I reached into my purse for my cell phone. I called a towing company for the truck and a taxicab for us. Shopping bags in hand, we finally made it to Frances's by seven-thirty, just in time for "Jeopardy."

"You both must need a drink," she said when we told her of our travails. From the way she was wobbling, it looked as if she'd given herself a head start in the drink department. Her lipstick was smudged, too. Otherwise, she seemed completely normal. She was wearing one of her caftans—a lemon yellow one—and matching yellow sandals. People often say about fat women, "But she has such a pretty face," and in Frances's case it was true. She *was* pretty in a boyish sort of way. From her pudgy, baby-soft skin to her short, close-cropped haircut, she was youthful looking in spite of her heft. Still, youthful or not, I couldn't help feel sorry for her as I watched her waddle around her living room, cheering the "Jeopardy" contestants on. She had no idea what was going on inside her own body, no clue that she was being used as a receptacle, a vessel, a temporary shelter for the force of darkness.

Dinner was uneventful. Jeremy made nice to Frances, apologizing profusely for his gesture of protest against the River Princess. I knew he didn't mean a single word of it, that he was just sucking it up and taking one for the team, and I shot him a look of gratitude when Frances wasn't looking. He responded by blowing me a kiss.

Getting Frances drunk proved to be a no-brainer, given that she was halfway there before we arrived. Every time she got up to go to kitchen for another helping of lasagna (the woman's idea of "leftovers" was my idea of a Roman orgy), Jeremy poured more wine into her glass and she returned to the table and drank it. By nine-thirty, she had passed out in her chair.

"Oh, great," I said. "How are we going to move her? She weighs more than my car."

"We're not," said Jeremy. "We're gonna have to do the exorcism right here."

"In her dining room?"

"Why not?"

"I don't know. I kind of pictured us doing it in her bedroom. With her lying on the bed. The way Linda Blair was lying on the bed in the movie."

"That was just a movie, BS. This is real life and we can do whatever we want."

"I suppose."

"Let's go outside and get the bags."

Jeremy and I tiptoed out of the house to retrieve the bags of props, which we had hidden behind some shrubs. When we came back inside, we dumped the contents of the bags onto the dining room table and took a quick inventory.

"Gee, I don't know about this," I said, suddenly coming down with a bad case of second thoughts. "We *are* doing the right thing, aren't we?"

" 'Course we are. We're savin' you from bein' a darksider for the rest of your life and the town from bein' the devil's playground."

"True. It's just that I've never been involved in an exorcism." I shuddered. "What if something goes wrong?"

"Like what?"

"I don't know. Frances is an innocent victim here. It wasn't her fault that the devil chose her for possession. What if we chant the wrong thing over her body and accidentally turn her into a rabbit?"

"She'll be no worse off than she is now, believe me."

"Maybe not, but what about us? What if we start doing the exorcism and the devil goes berserk and turns *us* into rabbits?"

He grinned lasciviously. "You know what they say about rabbits."

I sighed again. "I guess we'd better get started. What should we do first?"

Jeremy thought for a minute. "Let's kick things off with the holy water."

"Why not."

I handed him a one-liter bottle of Evian and watched him unscrew the cap. He was about to pour it over Frances's head when I stopped him. "Wait!" I hissed. "You saw the movie. You're supposed to *sprinkle* it over her, not dump it on her! She'll wake up in two seconds if you throw cold water in her face."

"All right, all right."

He poured some of the water into Frances's empty wineglass, stuck his fingers into it, and then flicked the Evian across her body, repeating the process several times.

"Much better," I complimented him. "Now what?"

"The religious symbols," he said.

"Yes, Father." I reached for the shiny gold objects on the dining room table: a cross and a Jewish star. "I bet this is the world's first multidenominational exorcism," I said and placed both the cross and the star on Frances's ample bosom.

"Now, let's go with the cayenne pepper," said Jeremy.

I scanned the table for the cayenne pepper but couldn't find it.

"The cayenne pepper was on *your* list," I scolded Jeremy. "You forgot to bring it."

"No, I didn't. The supermarket was out of it so I got paprika instead. Same color."

Men. They can be so dense sometimes, especially when it comes to telling one spice from another.

I shook the tin of paprika over Frances's body, careful not to get any up her nose. God forbid she should sneeze.

"Next?" I said.

"How about lighting the candles?" Jeremy suggested.

"Good idea." I gathered the four white votive candles I'd brought, formed them into a little circle on the table, in front of Frances's chair, and lit them. Then I said, "I might as well go ahead and light the incense while I'm at it, don't you think?"

"Yeah, go for it."

I put the match to the incense and the room began to smell like my college dorm.

"Nicely done," said Jeremy. "Now, do you know if she's got a tape deck?"

"I'll go look."

I left the dining room and went in search of some stereo equipment.

Frances's house (a ranch, of course) was a three-bedroom/two-and-a-half-bath home, vintage 1970s—a rather undistinguished era in home decorating, when brown was considered a hot color. Consequently, everything about Frances's house was brown—from its chocolate-colored exterior to its clunky maple furniture. The only bright spot was the dining room carpet, which used to be white but was now white with red dots, thanks to Jeremy's inability to successfully maneuver even one forkful of lasagna into his mouth.

It was in Frances's brown living room that I found a stereo system. Well, it was actually a boom box, one of those portable tape decks that kids take to the beach. I lifted its handle and carried it into the dining room, setting it down on the table.

"You think the music might wake her up?" I asked Jeremy, who was deeply involved in trying to free the Perdue Oven-Stuffer Roaster from its thick plastic wrapping.

"Our talking hasn't woken her up. Why should the soundtrack from 'The Exorcist?' "

I guessed Jeremy was right and popped the audiotape into the tape player. Seconds later, "Tubular Bells" filled the room.

"Okay, here's the chicken," said Jeremy, who was dangling the roaster by its legs.

"Aren't you going to cut it up?" I asked.

He shook his head. "Roland didn't say anything about chicken *parts*. He just said a chicken. A *dead* chicken."

"Fine. So we'll use it whole, giblets and all. It's not as if we're going to eat it afterward."

Jeremy nodded and placed the chicken on the floor, near Frances.

"I wish I had a camera," I said as I looked at her. She was quite a sight, let me tell you. Picture a three-hundred-pound woman, passed out cold in a chair, mouth open, hair damp with Evian water, skin and clothes dusted with paprika, a dead bird at her feet. And let's not forget the cross and the star.

"I wish I had the garlic clove," said Jeremy.

"You mean you didn't bring it?" I said. Garlic had been on the list. *His* list.

"Nope."

"Don't tell me the supermarket didn't have that either."

"They might have. I just forgot it."

"Well, don't worry. Now that I think about it, garlic is supposed to keep vampires away. I don't think it works on the devil."

"Then we're almost ready. All except the travel brochures."

"Oh. They're in my purse."

I dug into my handbag for the brochures I'd swiped from the travel agency next door to Home Sweet Home. There was one on Mexico, one on Costa Rica, and one on the island of Grenada. I had nothing against those countries, you understand, but the idea was to coax the devil into relocating and I knew he preferred places with warm climates.

"What should I do with them?" I asked.

"Fan 'em out on her lap," Jeremy suggested.

I laid them gently across Frances's lap, careful not to wake her, although how she could still have been out, given all the noise we were making, was beyond me.

"I guess that's it," I said. "I think we're ready for the important stuff."

Jeremy handed me one of the two Bibles we'd brought and kept the other for himself. We arranged our chairs so that we were flanking Frances but could also see each other.

"I'm not exactly a Biblical scholar," I said, leaning over her body to talk to Jeremy. "What page should we turn to?"

"Beats me," he said. "I can sing you the lyrics of any rock 'n' roll song written since 1950, but I don't know the words of the Good Book."

"Maybe there's an index and all we have to do is look under 'Exorcism,' " I said, flipping to the back of the Bible.

"It's not a Goddamn encyclopedia, BS," Jeremy said.

"All right. Then maybe everything's alphabetical and we should check under 'E.' "

"It's not a dictionary either."

"Well, then what do *you* suggest we do?"

"For starters, I think we ought calm down," said Jeremy. He smiled. "We're in this together, ya know?"

I took a deep breath. "I'm sorry," I said. "Maybe we should just pick a page at random and start reading to her. Maybe we can cast the devil out of her body just by saying a couple of thee's and thou's."

"Sounds good to me."

"You do it. You're the performer."

Jeremy opened his Bible and began reading from some psalm or other. He had a surprisingly commanding speaking voice, much like his singing voice, I realized, and I found myself sitting back in my chair and listening attentively to what he was saying. The gist of the passage seemed to be that love not only conquers all, it conquers evil; that the only way to defeat Satan is to treat one's fellow human beings with affection, respect, generosity, tolerance; that when we show our love for ourselves and others, we strip Satan of his power and cast him out of our lives.

"Jeremy," I interrupted him. "Did you hear what you just said?"
He nodded.

We both looked over at Frances, who was still sleeping soundly. If the devil was listening, he wasn't letting on.

"Keep reading," I suggested. "Something's bound to happen sooner or later."

"I hope it's sooner," he said. "The incense is killin' my sinuses."

"Yeah, well the chicken is making me nauseous. I think it's starting to turn."

"Could be. It was sittin' in my truck all afternoon. In the sun."

I gagged. "Just read for another few minutes and let's see if anything happens."

"And if it doesn't?"

"I'll call us a cab and we'll call it a night."

Jeremy opened the Bible and was about to read another passage when Frances stirred.

Oh God! It's the devil! I thought, the lasagna backing up in my throat. He's going to speak to us! Through Frances!

I tried not to panic, but all I could think about was that damn movie, where the devil makes Linda Blair growl and swear and throw up all over those poor priests.

I wanted to scream, but Jeremy placed his forefinger over his lips, indicating that I should keep quiet.

So I kept quiet. And then Frances moved again, and this time she opened her eyes. Wide! She stared at us but didn't seem to know who we were, her gaze glassy, trancelike, as if she were under a spell. And then she spoke, only the voice wasn't hers.

"Aghhhhhhh," she said, sounding not at all human, much the way I sounded when the devil made me growl.

I jumped off my chair and scurried over to Jeremy's, then plunked myself down in his lap and threw my arms around his neck.

"Aghhhhhhh," Frances said again. "Aghhhhhhh!"

I closed my eyes and clung to Jeremy, fear gripping me so tightly I could scarcely breathe.

"It's gonna be okay," Jeremy whispered. "I'll make it okay."

He pushed me off his lap and then moved his chair closer to Frances.

"Can you hear me?" he said. To her. To Satan.

Frances looked at him, but seemed not to register his presence.

"It's time you showed yourself," Jeremy went on. "Time you got your ass out of this town."

I braced myself for the devil's response. And yet when it came, I was totally unprepared.

"Look!" Jeremy pointed in the air.

The Perdue Oven-Stuffer Roaster was levitating! The bird had risen up off that white carpet and was floating two feet from the ceiling!

I couldn't contain myself. I screamed.

Frances, or should I say Satan, began to laugh. A high-pitched cackle that made my skin crawl.

"Oh, shit. Now look what he's doin,' " said Jeremy.

I followed Jeremy's gaze to the dining room table and saw that the boom box that had been playing our *Exorcist* theme music was melting! Like the wicked witch in *The Wizard of Oz!* What's more, the cross and star that had supposedly been protecting Frances's body were flying across the room like 747s and didn't stop until they landed in the powder room around the corner—in the toilet. Another cackle came out of Frances, just as we heard the toilet flush!

"Let's get outta here!" Jeremy shouted, taking my arm and leading me toward Frances's front door.

"But we've got to talk to him," I said, desperate to leave but determined not to. I had been waiting a long time to confront Satan. As terrified as I was, I had to seize my opportunity. "How else can we convince him to let me out of the bargain?"

"Does he seem like he's in a bargaining mood?" Jeremy asked.

"No, but maybe if we read him some more of the Bible he'll chill out a little," I said. "Or we could sprinkle another bottle of Evian on him. We can't give up, Jeremy, just because he made a chicken levitate."

"If we hang around here, he could do something worse. Much worse."

Just then, Frances emitted another "Aghhhhhh," followed by that hideous cackle. I went back into the dining room, put my hands on my hips and confronted the devil.

"Why don't you stop playing games," I said.

"Aghhhhhhh," he growled.

"Oh, cut the growling," I snapped. "If you're so powerful, Satan, let's see if you can speak."

Another cackle, then, out of Frances's slackened, lipstick-smudged mouth came: "I have a message for your boyfriend."

The voice was deep, menacing, as low as the cackle was high. And it was monotone, mechanical, like those computer-generated voices you get when you call someone's voice mail.

"You have a message for my *boyfriend?*" I said. Jeremy was hardly my boyfriend, but I reminded myself that this was not the time or the place to discuss the status of our relationship.

"Yes, the fisherman," intoned the voice. "The singing fisherman."

"I'm right here," said Jeremy, who stepped up in front of Frances and tried to look brave. "What's the message?"

"It's about your fa-ther," said the devil, drawing out the word and making it sound like a taunt, a mocking. "I gave the old geezer another heart attack. Only this time I gave him a major leaguer."

Another heart attack? But only the day before, Mike Cook was in such good health that the doctors were going to send him home!

Jeremy ran into the living room, picked up the phone on the end table, and quickly called the hospital to check on his father's condition. When he hung up, he said nothing. Instead, he grabbed my hand and pulled me out of Frances's house so fast that I left my purse there. We ran and ran and ran—four or five blocks or so—and it wasn't until we hit Route 1 that we finally stopped to catch our breaths.

"What did the hospital say?" I asked between gasps of air, my chest heaving, my heart racing.

"They said my father took a sudden turn for the worse," he panted, "and they don't expect him to make it through the night."

CHAPTER
24

We took a taxi straight to the hospital, where we were told that Mike Cook was in the Intensive Care Unit. Since only members of a patient's immediate family were permitted on that floor, I waited in the hospital lounge while Jeremy checked on his father's condition.

"He had a massive heart attack. They're callin' him 'critical,' " he explained when he appeared in the lounge just before midnight and sat on the couch next to me. He looked exhausted, his customary swagger gone. "The doctors didn't see it comin' at all. They don't understand what happened."

"Of course, they don't," I said. "Who's going to suspect that it was the devil that caused this heart attack? But *we* know that he did it to punish us. Just the way he caused the first heart attack. To punish you for spoiling the River Princess's opening."

Jeremy put his head in his hands. "What are we gonna do, BS?" he murmured.

I almost reached out to stroke his back but didn't know if he would welcome the contact.

"We're going to pray that your father pulls out of this," I said. "And we're going to get the devil out of town before he does any more damage."

"Oh, yeah. Sure we are."

"Come on, Jeremy. We're not defeated yet. We made real progress tonight. We got the devil to talk to us. Now we just have to get him to *listen* to us. Do you remember the exact moment when he began to reveal himself through Frances?"

Jeremy shook his head.

"Well, *I* do. You had just finished reading the passage in the Bible that talked about the power of love. It was those words, Jeremy, that ultimately smoked him out of Frances's body. He got scared when he heard all that."

"How could you possibly know that?"

I shrugged. "I just do," I said. "Maybe because I'm a darksider. Maybe that gives me a special intuition where the devil is concerned. I don't know for sure. I only know that we've got Satan where we want him now."

"Tell that to my father."

"I will. As soon as he's feeling better. And he *will* feel better, Jeremy. Because the devil's days in Banyan Beach are numbered. All we've got to do is—"

"Is *nothing,*" he cut me off. "I sure as hell am not goin' back to Frances's house with a Bible and a dead chicken. Not in this lifetime."

"But we can't give up now. We just can't."

" 'We?' Listen, BS. You gotta count me out from now on," said Jeremy. "I'd like to help you out of this mess, but not if it means sacrificin' my father's life. I can't afford to piss the devil off if he's gonna take it out on my dad."

"Oh, and I *can* afford to piss him off? He could just as easily give my brother a heart attack as he gave your father one."

"Yeah, but he hasn't. Ben's not lyin' in a hospital bed with tubes comin' out of him."

"Not yet, but who knows what will happen next? I need your help, Jeremy. You said last night that we were in this together."

"That was last night," he said. "Obviously, things have changed. Now, I gotta lie low for a while, BS. You're gonna have to handle this stuff without me. I'm sorry."

"So am I," I said, feeling even more abandoned than when Mitchell told me he was walking out on me.

Oh, I understood full well that it was unfair to make Jeremy choose between me and his father. After all, he had no obligation to me. I wasn't a member of his family. I wasn't even one of his friends. I was just Ben's kid sister, an old high school classmate who had avoided him for years and then suddenly walked up to him and asked him to save her life! Still, I had come to count on him in the brief period since I had trusted him with my story. It had been such a relief to tell him I was a darksider, to be able to talk to him about the devil, to be able to . . . to . . . what else?

I thought for a minute, trying to determine exactly what I was feeling. It had been more than a relief to spend time with Jeremy, I realized. It had been fun. Yes, despite the traumatic and terrifying moments, I had actually enjoyed sparring with him, trading insults with him, being with him. And now, he wanted out? No more exorcisms? No more pizza dinners? None of it?

I stood up from the couch.

"Your father seems like a nice man. I really hope he makes it," I said, aware of the catch in my voice.

Jeremy looked at me but remained seated. "Me too, BS. Me too."

When I got home, I ran to my answering machine, hoping that Jeremy had called from the hospital to tell me he had changed his mind about helping me. But he hadn't called. Ben had called. He left a message saying that someone had poisoned every single one of his emus and that they were dead—and so was his emu business.

The devil was striking back at *my* family, too, I thought with a shudder, thanking God that, if Satan had to destroy something of Ben's, it was his livelihood, not his life.

Since it was too late to call Ben back, I flopped onto my bed, thoroughly spent from the evening's activities, and lunged for the remote control on the night table. I hoped a little late-night TV would distract me. Pete jumped onto the bed and curled up next to me, giving my toes an occasional lick as I flipped from one channel to the next. The last thing I remember as I drifted off to sleep was some blow-dried anchorman on CNN talking about a new cure for snoring.

I couldn't have been asleep for more than five or ten minutes when Pete began to bark.

"What is it?" I asked as I tried to rouse myself, rubbing my eyes until I could focus. It took a few seconds before I realized that Pete was no longer sprawled out across the bed and CNN's blow-dried anchorman was no longer on the screen. Pete was now standing next to the television set and the person on screen was none other than Chrissy Hemplewhite!

"What on earth is she doing on TV at this hour?" I said. I didn't even bother to ask how the television had gotten switched from CNN to our local NBC affiliate. Pete, I assumed, had gone channel surfing again.

He responded to my question with more barking.

Remembering the "Jeopardy" experience and how significant it had turned out to be, I sat up in bed and paid close attention.

". . . This special bulletin is coming to you from the Channel Five Storm Center. It has been nearly three years to the day that Hurricane Andrew devastated the Miami area," Chrissy was saying. "Andrew came ashore as a Category 4 hurricane, which means that its winds were in the 131 to 155 miles-per-hour range. Our exclusive Channel Five weather technology projects winds of similar or greater force for Hurricane Frances, although Frances isn't behaving like any storm we've ever seen."

Hurricane *Frances?*

I got out of bed, ran to the television, and turned up the volume.

". . . Normally, we can track a hurricane from the moment it forms as a tropical wave or disturbance in Africa and then gathers strength in the Caribbean," Chrissy went on. "But this hurricane literally popped up out of nowhere on our radar screen—just within the past few hours—and, according to the coordinates, it appears headed straight for Banyan Beach. We're projecting landfall sometime within the next twelve hours."

A major hurricane? Hitting Banyan Beach within the next twelve hours? After we'd had weeks of a drought?

I couldn't believe it! Floridians still hadn't gotten over Andrew and now the devil was socking us with another, potentially more devastating storm? Yes, it was August, and yes, it was the height of the hurricane season, but I'd lived in Banyan Beach long enough to know that hurricanes didn't form overnight. They took days to show up. Weeks, even. There was always plenty of time to prepare—stock up on canned food and bottled water, install hurricane shutters or board up windows with plywood, hop in the car and get as far away from the center of the storm as I-95 would take you. But this time there was no warning whatsoever. We were as vulnerable and helpless as we could be, which was just the way the devil wanted us, I supposed. His sitting ducks. Or, more to the point, his *dead* ducks.

". . . Once again, we want to alert our viewing audience that the National Weather Service has issued a Hurricane Warning—that means a strike is expected within twenty-four hours—for the entire Denton County, with a special warning for the residents of Banyan Beach," Chrissy said. "We urge those residents to evacuate their homes, particularly if they live in low-lying areas within one mile of the town's waterways. A list of shelters will immediately follow this news bulletin. Meanwhile, we encourage everybody to remain calm, exercise extreme caution, and stay tuned to Channel Five for further updates."

I tried to think what to do next. Sleep was out of the question, obviously. If the storm was going to hit around noon the next day, I only had a few hours to prepare for disaster.

By nine o'clock the next morning, I was ready for the devil *and* his hurricane. Having lived in Florida for so many years, I knew the drill. I also knew that keeping busy helped to relieve the terrible anxiety that came with the anticipation of a major storm. I put the hurricane shutters in place over the windows, moved all my deck furniture into the garage, shopped for canned goods, bottled water, and extra batteries, filled my bathtub with water in case the bottled water ran out, and packed a suitcase. Since my house was on the ocean and was, therefore, likely to be among the hardest hit, I assumed I would have to evacuate the area and spend the foreseeable future in a shelter. But shelters didn't allow pets, I reminded myself, and I wasn't going anywhere without Pete. I called Ben and asked if Pete and I could wait out the storm at his cabin. I also told him how sorry I was about the emus, but didn't mention that if it weren't for me, they would still be alive.

Throughout the morning, I listened to the weather reports on television, which kept predicting that Banyan Beach would feel the brunt of the storm between noon and one o'clock. By nine, the sky had darkened, a light rain had begun to fall, and the wind had picked up slightly, but there was still plenty of time to get out, plenty of time to evacuate the house.

My plan was to pack Pete and my belongings into the car and drive over to Ben's at nine-thirty.

But then Mitchell called. No, he wasn't worried about me. He was worried about the house. *His* house, as he didn't hesitate to remind me.

"Don't forget, I've got an investment in that place," he had the nerve to say. "Chrissy and I will be moving in as soon as the divorce is final."

"I won't forget," I said. "I've done everything to prepare *your* house for the storm."

At about nine-forty-five, Suzanne called to ask if I'd spoken to Frances since my dinner at her house the night before.

"No, why?" I'd asked.

"Nobody knows where she is," said Suzanne. "Charlotte asked me to call everybody in the office to see if they had a place to stay during the storm, but I haven't been able to reach Frances, and I've been trying her since eight o'clock this morning."

My God, I thought, was Frances still passed out in her dining room chair, oblivious to the deadly storm that was about to hit Banyan Beach?

"I'll let you know if I hear from her," I told Suzanne. "Where are you going to be during the storm?"

"I'm going to—"

I didn't hear the rest of the sentence. The line went dead. At the same instant, the power in the house went off. I was now standing in the kitchen in total darkness. The lights were out and the windows were boarded up and the air-conditioning was off and I felt as if I were in a coffin.

I foraged in the kitchen drawer for the flashlight and let it guide me out of the room.

"Okay, Pete. We're outta here," I said, realizing that I didn't have as much time to evacuate as I thought I did, and that there was no way to predict what this hurricane would do.

Pete bounded over to me, wagging his tail excitedly.

"I know. I know. We'll take an umbrella," I said, reaching down to pet him.

I was about to pick up my suitcase and head for the door when I suddenly heard the surge. The surge of the ocean. I couldn't see out the windows or the sliding glass doors, but I couldn't help hearing the roar of the sea as the waves began to slam against the shore, just underneath the house. From the sound of it, which reminded me of a Mack truck going eighty miles an hour, the ocean had swelled to monstrous proportions. I knew what that meant. I'd seen surges that had struck houses and high-rise buildings with the force of a battering ram. I'd even seen surges that swallowed buildings whole. I knew there was a chance that I'd never see my house again, and the thought made it difficult to breathe.

"Come on, Pete. We've got to get out," I said tightly, moving once again toward the door, my flashlight leading the way.

And then I stopped.

The rain suddenly began to pound so hard against the roof that I thought it might collapse—if the wind, which was now thrashing against the house, didn't blow it off first.

"What's going on?" I said out loud. "We're not supposed to feel the brunt of the storm for hours yet."

I opened the front door just a crack and saw, to my horror, that Seacrest Way was totally flooded, impassable, a veritable river of water. There wasn't a car in sight.

My throat closed. In that split second, I knew I was trapped . . . that Pete and I would have to stay in the house for better or worse. There was no way to evacuate now.

And then came the first crash.

Something had slammed into the house. A roof tile? A tree limb? What?

Before I could investigate, there was another loud noise. A bang. Something had broken or been ripped off the side of the house. But there was no way I could tell what it was.

I ran to the phone to call Ben, to tell him I couldn't get there. And then I would call the police, to ask them to come and help me. But I couldn't, I realized, when I didn't hear a dial tone. My phone was dead.

Use the cell phone, I told myself, and reached into my handbag for it. I punched in Ben's number and then listened for a ring or a busy signal or some sign of life. But there wasn't any. Obviously, Ben's phone was dead too.

I called the police, thinking they could send a boat for me and I could sail out of Seacrest Way to safety, but the 911 operator said they were swamped with calls and that I should try to stay calm and sit tight.

Maybe that's the ticket, I thought. *I'll have a few belts and get tight.*

"What do you say, Pete old boy? Wanna get drunk?" I asked him.

He answered by wrapping himself around my legs.

Dog by my side and flashlight in hand, I made my way back into the kitchen and poured myself a glass of wine, then downed it in one long swallow. Feeling a little more fortified, I flipped on the small transistor radio I'd bought in the hardware store that morning and listened to our local station babble on about the storm. But I didn't need them to tell me about it. I could hear it. The wind and rain were growing even stronger, more violent, and the ocean was whipping the shit out of my deck. Hurricane Frances was not going to be a pussycat, that I knew, but I had done all I could to protect myself and my house. I would just have to follow the 911 operator's advice when she'd said: try to stay calm and sit tight.

The question was: *where* to sit tight?

From past experience I knew that it was wise to pick an interior room in the house, away from windows and doors and flying debris. I decided on the master bathroom. It was windowless, the Jacuzzi was full of water in case I got thirsty, and the acoustics were great in case a good song came on the radio and I felt like singing along.

I gathered everything I would need over the long haul—radio, flashlight, canned food, can opener, utensils, already-opened bottle of Merlot and a wineglass—and arranged them carefully in a gallon-sized plastic garbage bag. Then, fully provisioned, Pete and I went off to the bathroom.

Pete hunkered down next to the bidet. I staked out the rim of the tub as my territory.

"Well, buddy. It's just you and me now," I told the dog, trying to sound chipper. The truth was, I was terrified. Being the object of the devil's wrath wasn't my idea of a day at the beach.

I was about to close the bathroom door to seal Pete and me off from the rest of the house, when there was a loud banging by the front door. Pete jumped up and started barking.

"Quiet!" I said. "It sounds like a tree fell on the house!"

I crept out of the bathroom, through the bedroom, into the hallway, and listened, Pete at my heels.

There was another bang! Three bangs, in fact!

It's someone knocking, I realized, panic-stricken, as Pete barked and jumped and ran around in circles.

I froze as I pictured Frances standing at my door, the devil in her eyes, evil seeping from every pore. Yes, Satan was out there knocking, waiting for me to let him in, waiting to punish me as he had punished David, Mike Cook, and the emus. It had to be Satan. Who else could it be? No normal person would be out in a hurricane.

There was more knocking—pounding was more like it—and then a voice that was barely audible over the roar of the storm and Pete's barking.

"Hey! Open up! Don't make me stand here soakin' wet. Give a guy a break, huh, BS?"

It was Jeremy! But how—

I grabbed the flashlight, ran to the front door, and pulled it open, which wasn't easy, given the force of the wind.

"Trick or treat," he said and winked at me.

Pete calmed down while I shined the flashlight on our unexpected guest. He *was* soaking wet, every inch of him, and, judging by the assorted leaves and twigs that had nested in his thick red hair, he'd been tossed around by the wind, too.

"What on earth are you doing here?" I asked, and closed the door behind him.

"How about a hello?" he said, stepping out of his fishing boots and foul weather gear and laying them on the floor of the foyer.

"Sorry. Hello," I said sheepishly. "It's just that I wasn't expecting . . . Now will you tell me what you're doing here?"

"Ben said you didn't make it over to his house and didn't call to say you were okay," Jeremy explained as he marched past me into the house, shaking his wet head the way Pete did after a bath. "He was worried about you."

"What about you?" I asked, arching an eyebrow.

"What *about* me?"

"Were *you* worried about me?"

"Yeah, sure. Why do you think I waded through three feet of water?"

"You walked here?"

"I walked part of the way here. I drove until I got to Seacrest Way. When I saw how bad the street was flooded out, I parked the truck on higher ground and did the rest on foot. What's a little standing water to a fisherman, ya know?"

I shook my head. The man may not have been normal but he wasn't timid, I had to give him that.

" 'Course, I just had the damn pickup fixed. Put in a new thermostat after it overheated last night. Now the engine will probably be flooded."

"Jeremy, you really didn't have to come here and check on me. What about your father? He's the one who needs you."

"He's got the doctors and nurses to take care of him. The hospital's probably *The* place to be right now."

"But just a few hours ago, you said you didn't want to risk his life by helping me," I pointed out. "You said you couldn't afford to piss the devil off."

"I can't," he said, not elaborating.

I didn't press him. I was just glad he had come. And flattered. I wasn't used to having men take risks on my behalf.

"Has there been any improvement in your father's condition?" I asked.

"Nope. But he's hangin' on. That's about the best I can say about it."

"What about your boat? And your house?"

"I went down to the marina first thing this morning. Tied up the Hatteras as best as I could. The house? Well, who knows? It's up a little higher than yours. Maybe that'll make a difference and maybe it won't."

"You must be as exhausted as I—"

I was interrupted by a loud bang, this time from the back of the house. It sounded as if a section of the deck had broken off.

"Jeremy!" I cried. "The house is falling apart!"

He shook his head. "Nothin' you can do until the storm's over. Now, where were you plannin' to sit this thing out?"

"In there," I said, nodding in the direction of the master bathroom.

"Well, what are we waitin' for?"

CHAPTER
25

"Now this is cozy, isn't it," said Jeremy as he hoisted himself up onto the vanity and sat next to the sink, his legs dangling against the vanity doors.

"A little *too* cozy," I said. "I've never been the communal type, unlike Ben, who'd think it was normal for two people and a dog to spend hours in a bathroom together."

"Aw, cheer up, BS. It could be a lot worse. You could be standin' out there in the storm, gettin' blown to Cuba. Instead, you're sittin' in a fancy bathroom that's bigger than most people's living rooms."

"I know. It's just that I'm worried about the house. The place is falling apart. Listen."

We listened. There was no mistaking the sounds of destruction, even from our cocoonlike shelter in the bathroom, and it was hard to focus on anything else. There was constant banging and crashing and creaking. I guessed that the wind had now reached over a hundred miles an hour and that the surge from the ocean was threatening to demolish the deck. That could only mean one thing: 666 Seacrest Way was in danger of going under—and so were we.

"I'm scared," I announced.

Pete barked.

"You too, Pete?" I said.

He yawned.

"I guess not."

"Look, BS. It's stupid to sit here worryin'," said Jeremy. "I say we have some of that good-lookin' wine you've got there." He pointed at the Merlot. "A couple of glasses of that and we won't care about anything."

"I only have one glass," I said. "I wasn't expecting company."

"You keep the glass. I'll drink out of the bottle."

I smiled as I pictured the red wine dribbling down Jeremy's chin, onto his white Cook's Charters T-shirt. The man probably spent a fortune on Spray 'n Wash.

He filled my glass and then took a couple of swigs out of the bottle.

"Hmmm," he said. "Kinda makes you feel warm all over. Taste it."

I sipped the wine.

Then I heard a thunderous crash.

"What was that?" I said, jumping up off the rim of the bathtub.

"Shh," Jeremy quieted me. "Drink the wine."

"But—"

"Sit down. It doesn't matter."

He was right, of course. It didn't matter what was going on outside our little fort. The house was falling down around us, but, for now, there wasn't a thing we could do about it.

I sat back down and drank more wine and forced myself to listen to Jeremy tell stories. There was the one about the time he and his father went tarpon fishing in the Keys . . . the one about the time his mother caught her first fish . . . the one about the time he sang for an executive from a record company and was so nervous he couldn't hit a note. They were charming stories and Jeremy told them well and I found myself beginning to relax, to make up my mind to let the devil do whatever he was going to do to us. The next time I heard a crash, I flinched but didn't jump off the tub. And the time after that, I didn't even flinch. Was it the alcohol I was surrendering to? Or was it Jeremy?

"What do you say we change radio stations?" he asked during a lull in his storytelling. The transistor had been set to the local news station, which was broadcasting nothing but updates on Hurricane Frances.

"You think we'll find another station with decent reception and decent music? In *this* storm?" I said.

"Only one way to find out."

He took another swig from the wine bottle, draining it down to the last drop, reached for the radio, and fiddled with the dial. At first, all he got was static. And then, as if by magic, he lit on a song.

"Hey, remember this one?" he asked me, his expression heavy with nostalgia.

I nodded. It was Neil Young's "Heart of Gold." Jeremy and I were sophomores in high school when it came out and it was sort of an anthem then—a slow, lazy, poignant song about the hope of finding love before it was too late. Back in high school, who *wasn't* searching for a heart of gold? We were all looking for that one person who would accept and love us as we were. Some of us were *still* looking.

"How about a dance, BS?" Jeremy asked.

"A dance? In here?" I said. My bathroom *was* bigger than most people's living rooms, but it wasn't exactly Roseland.

"Sure. Why not?" He hopped off the vanity and turned the volume up on the radio. Then he stood in front of me, his arms outstretched.

"But I . . . Well, it's kind of a strange—"

I glanced over at Pete, as if to ask his permission, as if he were our chaperone, but the dog stayed right where he was, sprawled out next to the bidet looking totally unconcerned.

Jeremy turned the volume up even louder. The music reverberated across the bathroom tiles and I felt as if I were in an echo chamber.

"You won't hear the storm now," he said, his arms still waiting to encircle me.

I gulped suddenly, unsure of precisely what I was afraid of. Was it the hurricane? The devil's wrath? The thought of losing my home? Or was it touching Jeremy that had me trembling? The anticipation of intimate physical contact with a man I'd known virtually all my life but never known at all? The possibility that *I* would enjoy being held by him, while *he* would be thinking of the woman who still claimed his heart, the one whose identity he wouldn't divulge?

"Barbara?" he asked, holding out his hand to me.

He had never called me by my name—well, not in years—and the sound of it on his lips made my cheeks flush.

It's the wine, I told myself, and the threat of danger from the storm.

"If you don't hurry up and dance with me, the song'll be over," he said. "It only lasts about three minutes."

"I know," I said. "I remember."

I slid off the edge of the bathtub and stepped into Jeremy's arms. His body was warm against mine, soft, but not unpleasantly so. There was something oddly sexual about his stockiness, particularly after Mitchell's wiriness. I even found his protruding, middle-aged gut appealing and suddenly wondered why everybody was so obsessed with toning and firming and pumping up. I liked the way we fit together, liked how it felt.

Since the dance floor, such as it was, was small, our movements were compact. We didn't so much dance as take tiny steps in time with the music. Jeremy held me closely, tightly, pressing his bearded cheek against mine. When he began to hum along with Neil Young, I hummed along with both of them.

Funny, I thought as we moved. Funny how I would never have dreamed that I'd be dancing with Jeremy Cook and enjoying it. Funny how it sometimes took a life-threatening situation to bring people together, to create unlikely partners out of near-strangers.

We danced right through till the end of the song and then danced through two or three more. We danced through the wind and the rain and the surge of the ocean. We danced through the crashes and the bangs and the violence of the storm. We were dancing to the sound of the Beatles' "Something in the Way She Moves" when Jeremy pulled away, but only slightly, his strong hands still on my back, our bodies continuing to sway to the music.

"Hey," he said, so softly I barely heard him.

"Did you say something?" I asked.

"Uh, yeah. I did," he said awkwardly.

"What?" I said.

He cleared his throat. "I wanna tell you about—" He stopped.

"About?" I said.

"About the girl from high school. The one you asked me about the other day. The one I'm still in love with."

I didn't say anything. I didn't want to hear about the woman Jeremy loved. Not now. Not when *I* was the one in his arms.

But part of me—just a tiny part—wondered if the woman might be *me*.

I held my breath as I waited for him to continue.

"Remember I told you that love is kinda like catchin' a fish?" he said.

I smiled. "Your Cookism," I said.

"My Cookism," he acknowledged. "I told you that they both take plenty of patience and persistence and a sense of timing. In other words, you can't rush either of 'em."

"I remember," I said, eager to know where all this was leading.

"Well, ya see, BS—Barbara—I think the time is right now," he said, seeming to be urging himself on. "The wine is probably helpin' me out here, but what I'm tryin' to say is we're stuck in this bathroom together and we don't know what's goin' on outside and we might not have homes when this storm is all over. Hell, if a tornado hits the way they predict, we might not make it outta here at all. And then there's the devil thing. Who knows where all that's headed? Ya know what I mean?"

I nodded tentatively.

"So there's nothin' to lose now," he said. "No reason for me not to just let it rip. Ya see what I'm sayin'?"

I nodded again. I got the distinct feeling that Jeremy was waiting for me to guess what he wanted to tell me.

"So anyway," he pressed on when I didn't, "before I say any more, I want you to know that this has nothing to do with the hair and the boobs."

"Excuse me?" I said.

"Well, I mean, I was in love with you before all that. Since tenth grade, if you really wanna know."

I pulled away from Jeremy so I could get a better look at him. I wanted to see his face, make sure he wasn't smirking or jeering or mocking me as he often did. But his expression was as earnest and solemn as a choirboy's.

"Say something, would ya, BS?" he pleaded. "I know this bathroom isn't the kind of romantic setting you women dream about, but it's the best I could do in a hurricane."

I didn't know what to say. I was flooded with a jumble of emotions—confusion, gratitude, excitement, even a little melancholy. The very idea that Jeremy Cook had loved me all those years and never told me made me sad. Sad for him, sad for me. But he was right about love: you couldn't hurry it, couldn't force it, couldn't even recognize it until the time was right. And the time wouldn't have been right either twenty years ago or twenty days ago. I didn't see Jeremy as anything other than Ben's redneck buddy, the type of man I'd been raised to disdain. I was too busy ministering to my husband, Mr. Armani suit.

"You think I'm a lunatic, right?" he said.

"Of course not," I said. "It's just that this comes as kind of a shock to me. I had no idea how you felt. Not really."

He reached out to stroke my cheek. The gesture was so exquisitely tender, so contrary to my old image of him.

"You don't have to love me back, ya know," he said. "Or even tell me how you feel about me. I know I'm not your idea of Mr. Right. I'm not a fancy dresser and I don't talk like a college professor and I'm never gonna make a million dollars. I don't expect you to jump up and down with excitement about my little speech. But I love you anyway. Always have, always will. Gray hair, blond hair, it doesn't matter to me. I'll admit, the darksider business threw me. I mean, it's not every day that the girl you love tells you she's been taken over by the devil. But hey, love is love. Nobody's perfect, huh?"

"No, nobody is," I smiled.

"The main thing was to get it off my chest. In case anything happens to us. I wanted you to know before it was too late."

Tears filled my eyes and Jeremy wiped them away. I tried to talk but the lump in my throat wouldn't let me.

"Nothin' to cry about, BS," he said. "Hopefully the storm won't do as much damage as they're sayin'."

"It's not the storm that's making me cry," I said. "It's you."

"Gee, thanks," he laughed.

"No, I mean, it's what you said about loving me no matter what. About accepting me no matter what. No one has ever said anything like that to me."

"No one?"

I shook my head. "Until now."

The tears continued to fall, despite my attempts to stop them. I was incredibly moved by Jeremy's declaration, and yet I couldn't tell him I loved him back. I didn't know how I felt. It was too soon, too sudden.

He must have sensed my ambivalence because he took me in his arms and said, "Just know that I love you." He gave me a squeeze to emphasize the point.

"Jeremy, I—"

"I told you. You don't have to say anything back."

He drew his face close to mine. My heart thumped wildly in my chest as I closed my eyes in anticipation of our first kiss.

And then came a thump of another sort—a thunderous, ear-splitting crash that neither of us, no matter how amorous we were feeling, could ignore. Even Pete, who had slept through the whole romantic scene, sprang up from the floor next to the bidet and began to bark.

"What do you think happened?" I asked Jeremy, who quickly reached out to turn off the transistor radio.

Before he could reply, there was another crash as the door to the bathroom was suddenly forced open by an onslaught of water! I screamed as it poured into the small space where we had taken cover, carrying with it various household items that were now bobbing like buoys in the ocean.

"Jesus," Jeremy said. "A wave must've smashed clear through the sliders in the living room."

"What do we do?" I said, trying unsuccessfully not to panic. "The whole house is filling up with water!"

"Here. Give me your hand," Jeremy commanded. "You're gonna climb up on this vanity and stay there until the water recedes. We all are."

Good thing Mitchell insisted on putting in a double vanity, I thought, as Jeremy helped me up onto it.

"Now it's Pete's turn," he said. "Come on, boy." He slapped his thigh as he called for Pete to come to him.

"You want him on the vanity too?" I said. "A dog his size will never stay put. The minute you get him up here he'll jump right down."

"Pete's not your average dog," Jeremy reminded me. "He may not feel like campin' out in your sink, but he knows it's better than sittin' in water up to his ears."

Jeremy picked Pete up in his arms and deposited him on top of the vanity. The dog not only stayed there but licked Jeremy's face in a gesture of thanks.

His two charges taken care of, Jeremy joined us on the vanity. The three of us watched in horror as the water continued to rush into the bathroom, spreading across the floor and flooding the small space. I didn't have to wonder what the rest of the house looked like. I knew that the carpet, the furniture, the electrical wiring, everything would be ruined.

"I don't think I can just sit here and watch this," I said. "I've got to do something."

"How about listenin' to some more of my bad stories while we wait this out?" Jeremy suggested, feigning a cheerfulness I was sure he didn't feel. He was just as scared as I was, I knew, and just as helpless. "I've got enough of 'em to outlast a dozen storms."

"I'm sure you do," I smiled.

He took my hand.

"Okay, now I'm gonna tell you about the time I took Teddy Kennedy dolphin fishing . . ." Jeremy began.

I can't recall what he said, only that I tried to stay focused on the sound of his voice, not on the sight of the rising water.

Just think about the fact that he loves you, I told myself as Jeremy talked. Focus on how that feels.

The water continued to rise, reaching at least two feet up the vanity, but Jeremy never stopped trying to distract me. Midway through his umpteenth tale, I noticed that the water had not only stopped rising but appeared to be receding. The wind, too, seemed to have died down.

"Jeremy," I interrupted. "Look."

I pointed to the water as it was moving back out of the the bathroom, almost as if something were sucking it out.

"There must've been a shift in the wind," he said. "The water's goin' back out the way it came. That happens when there's a wind shift. The ocean surge recedes and the water seeks its own level. It looks like the devil's givin' us a break for some reason."

"But why would he do that?" I said. "He could just as easily have let us drown."

Jeremy grinned. "Remember all that stuff you were givin' me in the hospital last night? About love bein' the key to gettin' Satan out of town and out of our hair?"

I nodded.

"Well, there was a lot of love in this room today. Maybe he got an earful and couldn't take it anymore."

Pete barked in what was clearly a response to Jeremy's theory. And then he lifted his right front paw, just as he had done in my living room the night he told us about Frances.

"Look!" I pointed when I realized that the dog was scratching little markings into the Formica top of the vanity.

"Sweet Jesus. He's doin' it again," said Jeremy as the two of us hovered around Pete, our eyes wide with amazement.

"He's writing something," I whispered. "He's actually carving a message to us on the countertop! With his nails!"

Pete barked again and kept writing. When he was finished, he jumped off the vanity, into the slowly receding water, to give us room to read what he had written. His penmanship wasn't the greatest, and his tone was pretty lofty for a dog, and I would certainly have to replace the scratched Formica at some point (or, rather, Mitchell would), but here is what he wrote:

"Satan is powerless in the face of love."

CHAPTER
26

I was one of the lucky ones. My house was still standing after Hurricane Frances. Most of the deck had broken off and been swept into the ocean; the sliders had been shattered, leaving shards of glass all over the furniture; and the salt water that had poured into the house with each surge of the sea had destroyed much of the electrical wiring, but it was all fixable. And, given the fact that Mitchell owned the house and was planning to install himself and his mistress there after our divorce, the thousands of dollars in repairs were *his* responsibility, not mine.

Jeremy's house, too, had been rendered temporarily unlivable. But there were people in town who would never live in their houses again, because their houses were no longer there. They had either been demolished by the storm, literally flattened into a heap of debris, or had gone up in flames as a result of a gas explosion.

The real estate market, too, was devastated by the hurricane. Never mind that there were no longer a variety of houses in good enough shape to show to customers. There weren't any customers, period. Local buyers were too busy cleaning up after the storm to go house shopping. And out-of-state customers were having second thoughts about buying in hurricane-riddled South Florida, where insurance companies had all but stopped writing policies, especially for properties on the water.

The good news was that Jeremy's boat survived the storm with very little damage, which meant that he had a place to stay while his house was being repaired. And Ben's cabin, which was several miles west of the storm's eye, was virtually untouched, which meant that Pete and I had a place to stay, too.

Of course, Ben's cabin *looked* as if it had been hit by a hurricane. Never the neatest person on the planet, Ben was now aided and abetted in his sloppiness by his housemates, Janice and Denise, whose idea of "cleaning up" was winning at poker, which the three of them played nearly every night. When I suggested to Ben that he should spend his nights trying to figure out how he was going to earn a living now that his emu business was kaput, he said I should mind my own business. So I did. I left Ben to his women and his poker and spent my evenings with Jeremy.

We visited his father in the hospital, where Mike Cook continued to hover between life and death. The doctors were puzzled by his condition, which, they said, wasn't typical for someone who had suffered a heart attack. Jeremy and I did not tell them that it was Satan who was manipulating Mike's health and that modern medicine would be of no use whatsoever.

In fact, we didn't tell anyone what we knew about the devil. Not Ben, not the police, not any of my fellow agents at Home Sweet Home—all of whom were still wondering where Frances was. She had not come into the office or even called in since the night of our fateful dinner at her house. Charlotte suggested that she might have left town just before the storm hit and neglected to tell anyone, but Jeremy and I knew the truth. We knew that the devil was behind her disappearance. What we didn't know was where and how he would strike next.

"I've got an idea," said Jeremy one night, about two weeks after the hurricane. We were sitting next to each other on the front steps of Ben's cabin. The air was dense and damp, a thunderstorm imminent.

"About what?" I asked.

"About how to chase Satan out of town," he said.

"Tell me," I said eagerly, hooking my arm through his. I was touching Jeremy with increasing regularity now, ever since our dance in the bathroom, but I had yet to kiss him. We'd come close a few times, but one of us always pulled back. I supposed that Jeremy didn't want to appear as if he were rushing me, given his

Cookism about love and fishing. For my part, I was just plain scared to kiss him. I was growing to like him, very much in fact, but a kiss? Well, a kiss—a long, slow, groin-stirring kiss—would take things to another level, and I wasn't sure I was ready for that. Not with memories of Mitchell's treachery and David's tail still dancing in my head.

"If Pete's right," said Jeremy, "and the devil loses his power when he comes face-to-face with love—"

"*If* Pete's right," I interrupted. "Have you given any thought to how a dog would know what makes the devil lose his power?"

Jeremy shrugged. "I just figure he's a magic dog or something. *You've* got that darksider power, don't you? *You* know stuff no normal person would know. It's the same with Pete, I guess."

"But where did he come from? And why was he sent to my door?"

"Look, I don't have a clue. Now do you wanna hear my idea or don't you?"

"I do," I smiled.

"Okay. Banyan Beach is in bad shape now, right?"

"Right."

"Some of our neighbors are homeless. Some have lost their homes temporarily. Some have lost their businesses—all thanks to the hurricane. So we're gonna do something. We're gonna pull this town back together, lift the morale, help the people who need help, promote a spirit of community," he announced.

"That's a lovely idea, Jeremy, but how do you propose to do it?"

"By puttin' on a townwide Fire Ants concert. Right smack in the middle of Main Street," he said, becoming more and more animated. "Ya know, like those shows they put on to benefit the farmers or the rain forest or whatever. The difference is, we're not gonna ask anybody to pay to get in. We don't want people's money. We want their show of support. We want them to agree to pitch in and help their neighbors, whether that means offerin' homeless people a place to stay while their houses are bein' rebuilt or rollin' up their sleeves and doin' some manual labor, cleanin' up debris and stuff like that. If people turn out for this, BS, and show their goodwill, it'll not only bring the town together and lift the morale here—it'll send Satan packin' once and for all."

"How do we know he won't try to disrupt the concert?" I said. "Don't forget what he did at the River Princess party."

"That was different," said Jeremy. "Greed was the motivatin' force that day. Love will be the motivatin' force on the day of the concert. And love is exactly what's gonna drive the devil out of here."

I considered Jeremy's argument. "It might just work," I said. "If Satan sees that the people of Banyan Beach are good, decent, loving people who offer their help to those in need, maybe his power will be diminished and he'll be foiled. He'll be forced to leave town and I'll be restored to my old self! Oh, Jeremy, it's a possibility, isn't it?"

"We've got nothin' to lose," he said. "That exorcism on Frances didn't get him out of town. So now we're gonna show him that the town doesn't want him."

"Yes," I said, my excitement growing. "When do you think we could start organizing the concert?"

Jeremy stood up and held out his hand.

"Right now," he said and led me inside the cabin.

The concert proved remarkably easy to arrange. Once Jeremy contacted the other members of The Fire Ants and got their okay, we spoke to Mayor Kineally, to the head of Banyan Beach's Recreation Department, to the news directors at the local television stations, and to the publisher of the *Banyan Beach Gazette,* who agreed to advertise the event gratis. Before long, everybody in town—young and old, newcomers and longtime residents—was talking about the concert, planning for it, looking forward to it. It became a sort of beacon of hope for people, a respite from their troubles and their chores, a couple of hours of rock 'n' roll to lift their spirits.

Ben was in charge of the volunteer program we were organizing to coincide with the concert. People were being asked to pitch in and help their neighbors in any way they could: by donating food and clothing and even room and board to those stranded by the storm; by offering tools and manpower to rebuild homes and businesses; by providing comfort and companionship to the elderly victims of the storm; by contributing whatever money they could to the establishment of a special Hurricane Relief Fund.

"You're doing a great job," I told my brother when he reported that one of the local developers he'd spoken to had pledged $10,000 to the relief fund.

"This is more rewarding than raising emus," he said with a straight face.

The weather on the day of the concert was overcast, gloomy. The forecasters (including Chrissy) had predicted rain, and a slight mist had been falling throughout the morning, but the gray skies didn't deter the more than six thousand people who showed up at the village green, just off Main Street, and spread their blankets and beach chairs across the lawn. There was a carnival atmosphere as Banyan Beachers greeted their neighbors, introduced themselves to people they didn't know, and acted as if they were just glad to be alive.

Mayor Kineally, never one to miss a photo op, stepped up to the microphone and thanked everybody for coming, then went on and on about the hardships we'd all suffered, how resilient we were, how it would take more than a hurricane to keep us down, blah blah blah. He was in the middle of a sentence when the crowd began to clap in a not-very-subtle attempt to get him off the stage.

"Okay. Okay. I can take a hint," he laughed, waving his arms in surrender. He introduced The Fire Ants, to thunderous applause, and made way for the members of the band.

My heart did a little flip as Jeremy came into view. I was standing to the right of the stage, next to Suzanne, close enough to see him wink at me.

"Hey, what's all this?" Suzanne nudged me when she noticed the wink—and the fact that I responded by blushing. "I thought you said you hated the guy."

"I've had a change of heart," I said. "He and I are friends now."

"Friends?" she said skeptically.

"All right. We're . . ." I didn't know what to call us.

"Dating?" she suggested.

"Yes, we're *dating,*" I said, thinking that the word sounded incredibly high schoolish but, in this case, very appropriate. Jeremy was courting me the way he'd never been able to in high school. And I was allowing myself to be courted.

Suzanne smiled at me. "And you're happy about this," she said. "I can tell."

"Can you?" I asked.

"You should see how you look at him," she said.

"How do I look at him?" I asked.

"Well, let's just say you never looked at Mitchell that way," she said.

"I never looked at Mitchell, period. Not if I could help it."

"I'm serious, Barbara. I know you've been going through something. Something you haven't felt comfortable talking to me about. Whatever it is, I hope you know I'm here for you. Especially after what you've done for me."

"That's nice, but what have I done for you?"

"Are you kidding? You introduced me to Danny, for God's sake. At the River Princess party, remember?"

"Don't tell me you two are seeing each other?"

"We're *dating,*" she smiled, mimicking the self-conscious way I had said the word. "He's a little on the needy side—his wife left him for another woman, poor thing—but I've never met a man who was as desperate to settle down as I am. We're very compatible."

I was about to ask Suzanne why Danny hadn't come to the concert when Jeremy took hold of the microphone and welcomed the crowd.

"Let's hear it for Banyan Beach!" he exhorted the audience, who clapped and shouted and whistled their approval. "Let's hear it for all you folks who turned out here today." More applause. "Let's hear it for all you folks who signed up at our booth across the street and volunteered to help your neighbor." Still more applause. "To say thanks and to show you how fantastic we think you are and how proud we are to call ourselves Banyan Beachers, we're gonna play some good old-fashioned rock 'n' roll for y'all. So sit back, forget your troubles, put your arm around the person next to you, and thank the good Lord that you're alive."

Six thousand pairs of hands clapped in response. Jeremy nodded at his band and they launched into what would be an entire set of songs extolling the virtues of love—romantic love, spiritual love, love for friends, love for family. We had planned it that way. We had decided that we would bombard Satan with love songs which, even if they didn't put a dent in his evil power, would up- lift the crowd. The Fire Ants opened the set with James Taylor's "Shower the People." Then came the Doobie Brothers' "Real Love" . . . Eric Clapton's "See What Love Can Do" . . . Steve Winwood's "Higher Love" . . . and Carole King's "You've Got a Friend." The audience loved it, clapping and swaying and singing along with every tune.

"I can't believe this," Suzanne said. "It almost feels as if we're in church. There's a sense of—I don't know—*goodness* floating around. It gives me a funny feeling in the pit of my stomach."

"It's probably perimenopause," I teased, and hugged her. I felt it, too, of course. It was as if we were all huddled together in a bubble of goodness, as if the dark forces that had gripped the town had been quashed, as if the dark forces that had gripped *me* had been quashed. Oh, I was still a darksider and the devil was still skulking around in the body of Frances Lutz, as far as I knew, but for the moment, we had warded off his evil. If only for that after- noon, we had won.

"And now, I'm gonna sing y'all a very special song," Jeremy was speaking into the microphone. "A song I wrote just for this occa- sion. For my lady."

"His *lady?*" Suzanne elbowed me. "This is unbelievable. I don't talk to you for a few days and it turns out some guy you went to high school with is writing you love songs? Obviously, there's a lot more going on between you two than dating."

"All I know, Suzanne, is that Jeremy has never written a song in his life—not that he's finished anyway. I'm totally amazed that he did this. For *me.*"

"What if it's terrible?" Suzanne said.

"It couldn't be," I said. "Just the fact that Jeremy took the time to compose something—anything—for me boggles my mind."

"Shhh," said Suzanne. "He's starting to sing."

We listened intently to Jeremy's song, the song his love for me had inspired. It was a slow, bittersweet ballad, backed only by the band's acoustic guitarist, and its melody and lyrics were simple, honest—just like Jeremy himself. It was called "As Long as It Takes," and it chronicled all the years we'd known each other; all the years that Jeremy had wanted me and I had wanted some impossible dream. It conveyed all his yearning, his patience, his willingness to wait for me to return his love. The chorus, a poignant refrain which ran throughout the song, went like this:

> I'll wait. Wait. Wait.
> Say I'll wait as long as it takes.
> 'Cause when love's so strong
> It can't be wrong
> To wait as long as it takes.

When the song was over, the crowd applauded wildly as Jeremy took a bow. I could only stand there motionless, silent, staring at the man who had just proclaimed his love for me in front of six thousand people; the man who was waiting for me to tell him I loved him. And I *would* tell him. I knew that now. I would tell him because there was no reason to wait, no reason to hold back. Life was too short, too unpredictable, too fraught with demons—real or imagined—to hold back. And I did love Jeremy, maybe even for as long as he had loved me. Maybe the hostility I'd felt toward him all those years had been my cover, my armor, my shield against loving a man my parents never approved of. Maybe it was time to start living *my* life, to let Jeremy know how much I wanted him, how much I probably always wanted him. What did I care that his table manners were the pits, that he talked like a hick, that he'd probably come home at night smelling of fish guts. So I'd deal with it. There were worse things to deal with, right?

"Barbara? You okay?" asked Suzanne after I hadn't said anything for several minutes.

"I'm fine," I said. "I'll be even better tonight."

"Why? What's happening tonight?"

"My brother and his friends are going out for dinner," I said. "That means Jeremy and I will have the cabin all to ourselves."

"Oh, so you're going to thank him for writing the song, is that it?" Suzanne asked.

I smiled. "For starters."

27

I couldn't wait until Jeremy and I were alone. During the entire ride back from the concert, I sat in the passenger's seat of his pickup truck, silently rehearsing what I would say to him, how I would thank him for the song, how I would admit that I'd been wrong about him, how I thought he was sweet, honest, brave. Yes, brave. I mean, how many men would hang around once you told them you were an agent of the devil? None, that's how many. These days, all you've got to do is tell a guy you have a widowed mother and he's out the door. But not Jeremy. I'd told him every last detail of my bargain with Satan and he not only stuck with me, he told me he loved me—brussels sprouts breath and all.

We parked the truck in the driveway and held hands as we walked toward Ben's front door. My brother never locked the house, so there was no need to fumble for a key. We just opened the door and stepped inside, expecting Pete to bound over to us the way he always did, jumping and barking and making us feel wanted. But he didn't come to the door to greet us or even bark.

"Pete?" I called out. "We're home!"

Still no Pete.

"Maybe he's around back," Jeremy suggested, knowing the dog often liked to prowl around in the woods behind Ben's cabin.

"Ben wouldn't have put him outside and then left the house for the evening," I said. "Pete ran away the last time my dear brother did that."

We went further inside the house, into the living room and listened.

"Pete? Come here, boy!" I tried again, clapping my hands.

There was still no answer. And then a thought—a chilling, paralyzing thought—overtook me.

"What if the devil did something to him?" I said to Jeremy, my heart sinking. "He's already used your father and my brother to punish us."

I felt my eyes tear up at the very notion of something happening to Pete.

"Well, we wondered when or if Satan would strike again," said Jeremy. "He didn't bust up the concert, so I figured our little love fest had shut him up for good. I hoped so anyway."

"Me too," I said. "Look, maybe we're just jumping to conclusions and Pete is here somewhere. Safe and sound."

"Why don't you check around the house and I'll check out back," Jeremy offered.

We went in separate directions, Jeremy outside into the backyard, me into the kitchen. In the corner of the kitchen, over by the garbage pail, I found Pete.

"So there you are, quiet as a mouse," I said, so glad to see that he was all right. Or was he? On closer inspection, I realized that he didn't look or act like himself at all.

For one thing, the white patch on his chest had grown even larger, covering nearly half of his body—and it had only happened while I was away at the concert! For another, he barely looked up when I came into the room. He was hanging around the garbage pail, picking up various objects from the floor, gripping them between his teeth, stepping on the little metal pedal that made the garbage pail's lid go up and then dropping the objects into the trash. I didn't say anything. I was too dumbfounded. Pete had done many unusual things over the past few months, but this was the first time he'd played sanitation worker.

I watched in amazement as he continued to dispose of the items he had apparently gathered from closets and drawers throughout the house—items that I had purchased especially for him when he'd first come to live with me and had recently brought over to Ben's.

There was his food, his favorite tennis ball, his flea and tick shampoo, his hairbrush, everything that was *his*. It was as if he were discarding anything remotely related to his own existence.

I finally went to him, kneeled down beside him, and kissed his face.

"What is it, Petey?" I said softly, my throat closing as he licked me. It suddenly occurred to me that he might be preparing to leave me, to disappear as magically and improbably as he had appeared, and I couldn't bear it.

"You're not going anywhere, are you, Pete?" I managed.

He didn't answer, didn't bark or whine or make scratch marks on Ben's kitchen floor. He just looked at me with his penetrating hazel eyes, eyes that were so kind, so wise and knowing. I wondered if I would ever be given the real reason he had come into my life and if I would understand it if I were.

"Hey, you found him!" said Jeremy, just back from his backyard search for the dog. "What's he doin'?"

I stood up and went to Jeremy. "He's throwing his things out," I moaned. "Like a kid cleaning out his dorm the day he graduates from college."

"What should we do?" Jeremy asked. "Let him keep goin'?"

Just then, there was a knock at the front door. Jeremy and I both jumped when we heard it. Pete, on the other hand, didn't even budge, nor did he bark. The dog was definitely not himself.

"Who could that be?" I asked, disappointed by the interruption. This was to have been my night alone with Jeremy, the night I was going to pour out my heart to him, but I had a feeling there were bigger, less romantic things in store for us. Just how big I could never have predicted.

"I'll get it," said Jeremy.

"No, I will," I said.

"Tell ya what. We'll both go," he laughed, curling his arm around my waist and pulling me to him.

Whoever was at the door knocked again. Harder this time.

I started for the door but Jeremy pulled me back.

"What's the matter?" I asked.

"Let the guy wait," he smiled. "There's something I gotta do and

I gotta do it right now. It's been a long time comin' and I don't feel like waitin' anymore, never mind what my song said. I want to kiss you, BS, and nothin' and no one's gonna stop me."

He placed both of his hands on my face, one on each cheek, and brought his mouth gently down on mine. His lips were soft, meaty, in delicious contrast with his coarse, steel wool–like beard, and I surrendered to them, let them caress mine, caressed them back with everything in me. I would happily have remained locked in our long-awaited first kiss forever, but the person who'd been knocking on Ben's front door knocked again, this time even more insistently.

Using every vestige of willpower I possessed, I pulled my mouth from Jeremy's.

"We should get that," I said.

"We will, but first: I love you."

"I love you too," I said.

"You do love me?" He appeared stunned and happy and relieved all at once, as if the burden of twenty years of waiting were finally lifted off his shoulders.

"I do," I murmured, and ran my hands across his chest.

"No matter what comes?" he prompted, his eyes serious. There was still the devil to contend with, of course. Neither of us knew what his next move would be, how he would punish us for our insurrection.

"No matter what comes," I said.

I left Jeremy standing in the kitchen with Pete while I went to answer the door. It was a heavy door, made of solid Florida pine, and it took all my strength to pull it open. But it took even greater strength to greet the person who now stood on Ben's threshold.

"Frances!" I screamed.

Believe me, you would have screamed too if you'd gotten a look at her.

I hadn't seen her since the night of the aborted exorcism—neither had anyone else at Home Sweet Home—but then this was a Frances none of us had ever seen before, not even at Charlotte's annual Halloween party. She was wearing a new caftan—a blinding, lobster red one—and the color matched her eyes, which looked like a couple of glowing hot coals. Her skin tone was no longer its usual creamy white but a sickly olive green, and her teeth were like olives too—*black* olives. And then there was the nauseatingly foul odor that emanated from her every pore. I'm telling you, the woman wasn't just a character from a horror movie, she was a walking sewer.

"May I come in?" she said, but not in her own voice. The voice was low, exaggerated, like a record played on slow speed.

I didn't answer. Instead, I yelled for Jeremy, who was at my side in an instant.

"Holy Jesus," he said when he saw her. Saw *it.*

"Jesus can't help you, stud muffin," Frances/Satan said derisively, punctuating the remark with a high-pitched cackle. "You're mine now. Both of you."

"You've got that all wrong," said Jeremy, standing up to the devil. I was so proud of him. "*I'm* not yours and *Barbara* isn't yours. But I sure am glad you're here. Now you can let her out of that bargain she didn't even know she made and put her back to the way she used to be."

The devil laughed uproariously. "Oh, don't be naive," he said, returning to the deep, low voice. "Barbara doesn't really want to be fat and dumpy and down on her luck. She wants to be thin and beautiful and successful."

"Excuse me, Satan," I interjected, "but I've learned something in the past few months—that I don't have to make a bargain with you to get what I want. I have the power to lose weight or change my hair color or work harder at my job, if that's what's important to me. I can do these things for myself."

"Well, bully for you," the devil said sarcastically. "And I suppose you can find a man to love you, too?"

"She already has found a man to love her. *I* love her, no matter how she looks or how many houses she sells. No matter *what*," said Jeremy, echoing the pledge we'd made to each other.

"Oh, spare me," said Frances/Satan, rolling his eyes in disgust. "I find all this lovey-dovey stuff repulsive."

"Well, it's true," said Jeremy. "I love Barbara. LOVE HER! Get it?"

"Not only do I 'get it.' I'm going to fix it so you'll be able to love her even more," he said.

"What are you talking about?" said Jeremy.

"When I'm finished with you, you'll be able to produce children with her," said the devil. *"My* children."

"What?" I shouted. "You're not thinking of turning Jeremy into—"

"I'm not just *thinking* of turning your boyfriend into a darksider, Barbara. I'm going to *do* it. In a matter of minutes."

"But why?" I wailed. "Jeremy didn't make a deal with you. *I* did."

"Yes, but he must be punished," said Frances/Satan. "First, there was that silly, silly stunt at the River Princess party—*my* River Princess party. Then there was that bungled exorcism the other night. And now he organizes a concert intended to bring the town together in a spirit of goodness and love. Yech! The whole thing makes my stomach turn. Your boyfriend's gotta go, babe. Right now."

"No! Please don't transform him," I begged. "He only got involved in all this to help me. If you have to pair me with a male darksider, pick someone else. Someone who'd probably get a big thrill out of working for a celebrity like you. Lloyd Bellsey, for instance. He and his wife are the biggest star fuckers in Banyan Beach."

Frances/Satan smiled. "Lloyd's been a darksider for years, dear," he chuckled. "How do you think he wins all those high-profile murder cases?"

I was stunned. "Lloyd Bellsey is a darksider?" I said. "He's got a tail?"

Frances/Satan nodded.

"But that means that June is—"

He nodded again.

I couldn't believe it. The Bellseys were darksiders and I didn't know it? I wondered how many other people in town were agents of the devil, how many tails were being stuffed into Calvin Klein briefs.

"Many others," said Frances/Satan, reading my mind. "You'd be surprised."

"Is Mitchell a darksider?" I asked. We hadn't had sex in the last six months we were together. The jerk could have sprouted two tails and I wouldn't have noticed.

Frances/Satan winced, as if he'd just caught a whiff of his own foul odor, then shook his head vehemently.

"Your husband is not a darksider," he said. "Even *I* have my standards."

Normally, I would have laughed at any put-down of Mitchell, but not this time. Not when the devil was threatening to turn *Jeremy* into a darksider and then force us to produce devil babies.

Where the hell was Pete? I wondered as I stood between the force of darkness and the man I loved, desperate to stop the inevitable from happening. Why hasn't the dog charged in here and mauled our intruder? Why hasn't he rushed to our rescue?

"Now, may I come inside?" said Frances/Satan. "I don't think you want Mr. Cook's transformation to occur in front of your neighbors, do you?"

He barreled right past us, Frances's girth no match for our flimsy barricade, and waddled into the living room. Then he wheeled around, looked angrily at Jeremy, and pointed Frances's fat, stubby finger at him.

I closed my eyes, held my breath and braced myself—for a bolt of lightning, a silvery face in the sky, some indication that my Jeremy, the love I'd finally found, had been turned into the same sort of creature I was.

Please, God, I prayed silently, tears streaming down my face. Please don't let this happen. Please grant us a miracle.

I heard something then—a movement, a pitter-patter of feet, a swish of a tail.

A tail! Oh, no! The devil had done it! He had turned Jeremy into a darksider!

I didn't want to open my eyes, didn't want to see what Jeremy had become, didn't want to see the result of the transformation. But then I heard a bark.

A bark?

I opened my eyes and saw that Jeremy was still Jeremy—and that Pete had come bounding into the room just in the nick of time!

But the dog didn't jump up on the devil and maul him. He didn't even growl at him. Instead, he stopped a few feet away from him, stopped dead in his tracks in fact, and stared him down. Just stared him down!

And Frances/Satan stared right back at Pete. Their eyes remained locked on each other, glowering, daring, threatening, like a pair of gunfighters about to do battle.

Jeremy took hold of my hand and then walked me ever so slowly and silently away from them, toward the corner of the living room, where we could watch the strange interaction from a distance. We had no idea that what would happen next would contradict everything we'd ever been taught about Good and Evil; no idea that when I had asked God for a miracle, He would deliver one—in person.

CHAPTER
28

Pete was the first one to break the stare and he did it by turning to Jeremy and me and barking. Just once. And then, right before our eyes, right there in my brother's most ordinary of living rooms, the most extraordinary thing took place. Pete's body, which had been turning whiter and whiter in the past several days, suddenly went completely white! I mean, the dog, in a single instant, became an albino! And just when we were trying to get over the shock of *that,* Pete not only changed color, he changed shape and texture and substance and was no longer a dog at all! In fact, he no longer had *any* shape, but was, instead, a totally amorphous being. Yes, while Jeremy and I huddled together in our little corner, as awed and terrified as two people could be, he actually metamorphosed into a huge, white, formless entity—sort of a cross between a big, puffy cloud and an enormous mass of spilled milk! And then, guess what: the white blob began to speak! *Speak!* Even though it had no mouth!

"Come out of there, Satan. It's time for us to have a little chat," said the white thing in a voice that was part Walter Cronkite, part Paul Harvey.

Our heads turned to look at Frances/Satan, who, in response to the white thing, suddenly underwent a transformation of his own. As we looked on in utter amazement, the red caftan billowed up, as if blown by a strong gust of wind, and grew and spread and expanded until it literally enveloped Frances's body and she disappeared altogether. In her place was a giant red blob, an entity just as shapeless and formless as the white one—except that *it* had a tail!

"All right, I'm out of her body. Satisfied?" said the red thing to the white thing. "Just don't think I jump every time you say so, Mr. G."

"Let's not bicker," said the white entity.

"Give me a break," said the red-tailed blob. "Bickering is what you and I do. Throughout eternity. We're like a couple of old, punch-drunk prize fighters."

"I thought golf was your sport," said the white thing.

"Not anymore. My handicap is way up there and I don't have a clue what to do about it."

"Are you dipping your left shoulder under your chin on your backswing?" asked the white thing.

"No."

"Then try it," said Mr. G. "I shot an eighty the last time I played."

"There you go again. Always lording it over me how much better you are. It makes me sick," said Satan.

"And you *have* been sick lately, haven't you, old man?" said Mr. G. "You've been feeling sluggish, weak, much less powerful. Isn't that right?"

"Yeah, thanks to those troublemakers." The red blob didn't have hands, so he couldn't point to us, but we knew who he meant. "They started poking in places where they didn't belong, reading the Bible at me, throwing dead chickens at my feet, making everybody in this town band together against me. If it weren't for them, I probably could have lasted another five years here. Maybe even ten. Who knows?"

"*I* know. The people of Banyan Beach wouldn't have put up with you for much longer. With or without my help, they would have sent you away. Because love wins. Goodness wins. Always. Always."

"All right already. Enough with the sermon," Satan snapped. "It was the concert this afternoon that really put a hurt on me. All those people clapping and singing and hugging their neighbors. Having to listen to that sappy Carole King song was almost as bad as having to listen to you."

"Then you know why I'm here, don't you, Satan?"

"Sure, sure. You're here to tell me my time is up. But I'm not ready to leave Banyan Beach. Not just yet."

"Now, now, Satan. You know the rules. I'm casting you out of Banyan Beach. Now. Tonight."

"I had big plans for tonight. A couple of murders, a bank robbery, a carjacking."

"It's over," said the white entity. "All you've got to do is admit defeat."

Satan remained silent, his red tail still.

"I'm waiting," said Mr. G.

"All right already. So I admit defeat. Tomorrow's another day and we'll start this little rivalry of ours all over again somewhere else."

"Exactly. But first: you must release those whose bodies you took over. Including poor Ms. Lutz."

The red blob snorted. "Sure, sure. I know the drill. Barbara, let's get this show over with. I want to blow this popsicle stand."

I looked at Jeremy and gulped.

"Go on, BS. This is what we've been waitin' for," he urged, the color coming back into his cheeks. "Satan's finally gonna let you out of the deal. You'll be your old self again. Say good-bye to the hair and the boobs."

I nodded and started to walk toward the red entity, then hesitated.

"You sure you'll still want me?" I asked Jeremy. "It wasn't just because—"

"Go," he said. "Before we wake up and find out this was all a dream."

I nodded again and walked toward the devil. I wasn't afraid, oddly enough. Not with the white entity so close by.

"Ready, Barbara?" said Satan as I stood before him, my long blond hair shimmering in the moonlight, my perfect figure the stuff of exercise videos.

"Yes, I'm ready," I said without a trace of regret.

According to Jeremy, who told me this later, Satan struck me with a bolt of lightning. I was enveloped by a cloud of red smoke, just as David Bettinger was on the day of the River Princess party, and when the smoke cleared, I was Barbara Chessner again—frizzy hair, flat chest, and all.

"Is it really me?" I cried, running my hands along my body, feeling for my old lumps and bumps and flaws, ecstatic when I found them.

Jeremy ran toward me, hugging me so tightly I thought I'd break in two.

"It's really you, BS," he said adoringly. "Just like before."

"I've got to see for myself." I ran to get my purse, which I'd left on the table by the front door, and reached inside for my compact. I pulled it out, flipped open the cover, and studied my reflection in the mirror.

It was the old me, all right. The gray hair, the double chin, the potbelly. But I wasn't grossed out by my appearance, not anymore. Sure, I could stand to lose a few pounds. So I'd join a gym, big deal. The main thing was that it was *my* body again. I had reclaimed it. I could do whatever I wanted with it. Of course, I didn't have a clue how I would explain my latest transformation to Ben and Suzanne and the people I worked with. I supposed I would just say that I fell off the wagon and scarfed down an entire case of Pringles Potato Chips in one night.

The image suddenly made me think of Frances.

"Hey, you promised to restore her too," I reminded Satan, no longer afraid to speak my mind. To my delight, I had not reverted to my old self when it came to my personality. I had the old looks, yes, but not the old fear of offending people. Had Satan forgotten to void that part of the deal? Did the white entity have something to do with it? Or was it simply that I had learned a new way of being and incorporated it into my life? I like to think so.

"Frances is a done deal," Satan said.

"Oh, you and your deals," I said disgustedly.

"No, really," he said. "She's at home as we speak, tucked under the covers, fast asleep. When she wakes up in the morning, she won't remember any of this."

"None of it?" Jeremy asked.

"That's what I said, sport. Now, anything else before I split?"

"Yeah," said Jeremy. "You can make my father well."

"Oh, that. Fine. Presto. He's well. The doctors will congratulate themselves and think they're geniuses because he was on his deathbed one day and cured the next, and then they'll send him home. And speaking of home, I've got to find a new one. Any ideas, anybody?"

The white entity spoke up. "Your choice, Satan. Wherever you go, I'll go."

"Don't I know it. Always hovering, like a nervous wife. Well, I guess that's it, folks. Don't say it hasn't been fun."

With that, the red entity was struck by an electrifying lightning bolt of his own, then reduced to a cloud of red smoke. When it cleared several seconds later, only the caftan remained, now just a heap of cloth on the floor of Ben's living room.

"My God, it's over," I said as I stared at the red material. "He's really gone."

"For now," said the white entity.

"You mean, he could come back to Banyan Beach?" Jeremy asked.

"Why don't we sit and discuss this quietly, just the three of us," said Mr. G.

"I wouldn't think you'd be able to sit," I observed. "Given your rather unconventional body type."

He laughed. "I can do whatever I need to do," he said.

As proof, the white blob drifted over to Ben's beat-up old couch, like a soap bubble floating through the air, and molded himself perfectly into a sitting position.

"Why don't you two sit on either side of me," he suggested. "I'd like that."

Jeremy and I looked at each other and shrugged. At this point, nothing fazed us. We sat next to the entity, who, when we got close to him, radiated a sort of cozy warmth.

"You must have questions," He said, His voice kindly, fatherly. "Lots of questions."

"Well, yes," I said. "Satan referred to you as 'Mr. G.' I assume that means you're—"

"It means that you can refer to me as anything that gives you comfort," He said. " 'God' is a little intimidating to some people. So if you prefer 'The Higher Power' or 'The Man Upstairs' or something of that nature, it's fine with me."

"So you really are Him?" I said, full of awe.

"He," He corrected my grammar. "I really am He."

"Sorry," I said. "But maybe you could explain how you used to be a dog. My dog."

"I'd be glad to, Barbara. You see, I follow Satan everywhere he goes, to keep an eye on him, to keep his evil power in check. He and I are like two old warhorses, battling over this, arguing over that, wrestling over the collective soul of mankind. He settled in Banyan Beach. I settled in Banyan Beach. But when I come to a new town, I can't very well show up on people's doorsteps, looking as I do now. So I take a different form each time, much as Satan does. This time I chose to be a dog, a black Lab named Pete. He was named for Saint Peter, one of my closest associates. He was a rather nice dog, too, if I say so myself."

"Was?" I said, feeling tears prick at my eyes. "Pete's gone? For good? I'll never see him again?"

"I'm afraid not, Barbara," said God. "Remember, he wasn't a dog. Not really."

"Not a dog?" I said, not wanting to show any disrespect by questioning Him, yet intent on sticking up for my Pete. "Of course he was a dog. He was *my* dog, the only dog I ever had. He was real to me and I want him back. Please, your Lordship. Sir. If you don't mind."

"I can't bring him back, Barbara. He was just my temporary cover. I arrived on your doorstep in the guise of a dog the morning after your transformation so that I could protect you from the devil, to help you help yourself."

"Helpin' her? You're talkin' about those clues you gave us?" Jeremy asked.

"Exactly," said God. "I was doing what I came here to do, which was to foil Satan."

"But if you had the power to foil him, why did you wait so long to use it?" Jeremy demanded. "Why did you sit back and let Satan destroy Banyan Beach, ruin lives, demolish houses, commit murder? Why didn't you confront him sooner? Why did you wait until tonight to cast him out?"

"I will not save a town or its people until they prove that they are *worthy* of being saved," God explained. "The people of Banyan Beach weren't very worthy when I first arrived here. They had *invited* Satan into their town without knowing it. He felt there was a market for his kind of evil here. All he did was seize on it and enable it to grow."

"Then what changed?" Jeremy asked. "What made you intervene?"

"First, it was Barbara," he said. "She could have knuckled under to the devil, but she fought back. She decided to save her soul and her town. That's when I—Pete—started to help her. And then *you* entered the picture, Jeremy. You and your big love for Barbara and for Banyan Beach. The two of you went up against Satan and deflated him."

"Not enough. He came back at us with a major hurricane," Jeremy pointed out.

"That was Satan's last gasp," said God. "When you organized that concert this afternoon and got the town to pull together in a spirit of love and goodwill, you defeated the devil. I only came along and mopped up."

"And now you're finished here, aren't you," I said.

"Yes, right away," said God, who drifted up out of the couch and hung in the air in front of us, a huge white cotton ball.

"Please, don't go," I said, suddenly overwhelmed by unbearable sadness, by the realization that if God was leaving, there was no chance that I'd ever get Pete back, my sweet, sweet dog, who was there when I came home at night, there when I woke up in the morning, there whenever I needed comfort. I couldn't imagine my life with him. I didn't want to.

I buried my head in Jeremy's lap and began to sob, heaving, uncontrollable sobs. I missed Pete already.

"He knew he was leaving," I cried. "That's why he was throwing his things away. He knew he was never coming back. And the worst of it is, I didn't even get to say good-bye."

That brought more tears. I was crying so hard I had trouble breathing. When Pete had first shown up at my door, I couldn't wait to dump him. Oh, how I wished I had him back. I'd never let him go, never give him up.

"Pete will always be with you, Barbara," said God, trying to console me. "In spirit. Whenever you need him. Look."

I looked at the floor in front of the couch where we were sitting, and there, suddenly, was Pete's leather collar! I reached down to pick it up and held it close to my face.

"He'll always be with you," God repeated. "In your heart."

"Thank you," I whispered, emotion choking me. "Thank you for this. For everything."

Jeremy turned to God. "There's just more one thing," he said.

"What's that?" God asked.

"You said Satan left town. *For now.* Does that mean he might come back? That this whole nightmare could start all over again? That Barbara could become a darksider a second time?"

"It's possible," said God, "but if he were to revisit Banyan Beach, you'd have all the tools to cast him out," God explained. "You've had them all along, both of you. You've had *love* all along. You just didn't know it."

Jeremy and I looked at each other and smiled.

"Now," said God, "it really is time for me to say good-bye. Take good care of yourselves. Take good care of Banyan Beach."

I was about to say, "Thanks," but I was too late. All I did was blink and when I opened my eyes, the white entity was gone.

Jeremy and I sat there on that couch for what must have been two or three hours. Neither of us said a word. We were still in shock, I guess, still letting the events of the evening sink in, letting our feelings take hold. After all, it's not every day that you get to watch God and Satan debate. It's a lot more life-altering than, say, watching Michael Kinsley and John Sununu go at it on "Crossfire."

"BS?" Jeremy said, finally breaking the silence.

"Yeah?"

"Let's make sure you're really over this darksider thing."

"What are you talking about? Of course, I'm over it. Look at me."

"Yeah, but what about the power? Maybe you've still got it. Maybe you can still make people do things they don't want to do."

"Don't be silly," I said. "The devil took away all that. I'm a normal person now. Relatively speaking."

"Come on, BS. Humor me. Try to make me do something I don't want to do."

"Like what?"

"Well, let's see if you can keep me from askin' you to marry me."

I smiled. "That's a no-brainer. You'd never propose to a woman you only kissed once."

"Go on, try it."

"Seriously, Jeremy. We've only been seeing each other for a couple of—"

"Try it," he urged. "See if you've got the power to shut me up about this marriage thing."

I sighed. "All right." I closed my eyes and tried to recreate the feeling I used to get whenever I tapped into my darksider power. And then I opened my eyes and said, "I wish that your jaw would lock and that you would not be able to ask me to marry you."

But his jaw didn't lock.

"Marry me, Barbara," he said, no longer joking. "After you and Mitchell have figured things out."

"That might take a while," I cautioned. "We haven't even started negotiating the divorce settlement."

"I've waited this long. I can wait a little longer," he said. "Love's a lot like fishing, remember?"

"I remember." I smiled and knew that when it was time to catch the fish, we would.

E P I L O G U E

The seas were calm—two feet or less—and the skies were dark, overcast, threatening, on that Monday morning in June, nearly two years since the night I was liberated from darksiderdom.

"Perfect fishing conditions, BS," pronounced my husband, the charter captain, after waking me at six-fifteen by throwing open the bedroom curtains.

"Perfect *sleeping* conditions," I grumbled, and rolled over in bed, pulling the covers up over my head.

Jeremy promptly pulled them off of me, then kissed my cheek.

"Up up up," he said. "You and I've got a date with some dolphin. If we're lucky."

Since Mondays were a slow day for Cook's Charters, we often took the *Devil-May-Care* fishing on that day of the week.

Not that I was much of a fisherperson, mind you, even after two years of intense coaching. Oh, I could tell a bonito from a barracuda, and I knew that when Jeremy spoke of dolphin, he wasn't talking about Flipper, everybody's favorite mammal. I guess you could say I was a fisherperson in that I loved being out on the boat, loved being able to feel the wind in my hair and the salt water on my skin and all that Jack London stuff, loved the thrill of catching a fish and then bringing it home and cooking it for dinner, knowing it was as fresh as it gets.

Mostly, I just loved being with Jeremy. We'd gotten married six months after my divorce was final and had barely spent any time

292 / Jane Heller

apart. We were happy together, happier than I'd imagined two people could be. I absolutely adored the man, adored him so much that I let him wake me up on this dark and dreary Monday morning, the type of Monday morning that I ached to sleep through, particularly now that I no longer had to get up for Charlotte's Monday morning meetings.

I had given up real estate when I'd realized that I no longer gave a shit whether Mr. and Mrs. So-and-So bought the house with the coral fireplace in the master bathroom or the one with the twelve-burner range in the center island kitchen. And since Jeremy's father, who was in good health now but more interested in hanging around the sixty-five-year-old widow who'd moved in next door than he was in hanging around Eddie's Marina, I took over the booking of the charters and became Jeremy's business partner as well as his wife.

We lived in Jeremy's beach house, which had been restored to its former, prehurricane glory. My old house on 666 Seacrest Way was currently vacant and for sale, as Mitchell and Chrissy had decided not to live there after all. Mitchell had opened yet another eatery—a Thai restaurant and bar called Thai One On. Like Risotto! and Moo!, Thai One On was very successful—so successful that Mitchell and Chrissy saw themselves in grander quarters than 666 Seacrest Way. The last time I saw Althea Dicks, their real estate broker, she told me they were looking at the former Kennedy mansion.

Other than the occasional mugging, life in Banyan Beach was remarkably crime-free once again. People were leaving their doors unlocked, trusting their neighbors, even trusting the police, who were no longer more corrupt than the citizens they were paid to protect. Other than the never-ending development and the steady influx of Northerners, it was almost as if the devil had never come to town at all. Except that he *had* come, and lives were changed inexorably. Some for the better.

Take Ben. Yes, the devil had killed his emus, leaving him without a business. Uncertain of the direction he should go in next, Ben contacted Constance, the psychic, who predicted that the telephone would play an important role in his life. By the end of the reading, he and Constance had decided to go into business together: Ben would operate a 900 telephone number on which Constance would dispense psychic advice.

Suzanne, too, actually benefited from the devil's stay in Banyan Beach. If it weren't for the storm he'd brought down on us on the afternoon of the River Princess party, she might never have met Danny Bettinstein. He had a thriving orthodontic practice in town, was living in the newly refurbished Nowak house and looking forward to marrying Suzanne in August.

Frances didn't exactly benefit from the devil's visit to town, but she didn't seem to have any lasting scars from it either. She didn't remember anything about having been possessed—or exorcised—although she did remark that she had developed a sudden aversion to chicken.

Charlotte, too, was thriving. She handled my defection like a lady, wishing me the best of luck with the fish market I planned to open and promising to stop in and buy some salmon.

Althea was still griping, but not about her customers. It was her husband, the undertaker, who was the latest object of her wrath. His offense: he talked in his sleep. I did not ask about what.

As for Lloyd and June Bellsey, they weren't doing very well at all since the devil took off and left them without their darksider powers. Lloyd lost court case after court case, and, before he knew it, he and June were dropped from the A-list, and the only celebrities they got to brush up against were Mitchell and Chrissy, who were hardly Hollywood royalty.

Of course, I'm leaving someone out—saving the best for last, actually. You see, Jeremy and I don't live alone. We have a little one at home: a black Labrador retriever puppy whom we call PJ—for Pete Junior. I'm hopelessly impartial, but he's the cutest dog I've ever seen, not including his namesake. PJ doesn't stand on my scale and weigh himself or change the channels on the television remote control or write pithy messages in the carpet. Still, he's a little trickster, I'm telling you. He hides the Brillo under our bed and swipes the newspaper right out of the delivery boy's hands and chews on Jeremy's favorite sneakers. But he saves his best stunts for the boat, for when we take him fishing with us on Mondays.

The minute he's on board the *Devil-May-Care,* he thinks he's Esther Williams and dives into the ocean without the slightest provocation. Another dog on a passing boat is an excuse for a swim . . . or a jet-skier whizzing by . . . or a seagull flying close to the boat. Our PJ is fearless when it comes to the water, but a total wimp when it comes to fish! Whenever Jeremy or I reel one in, PJ takes one look at it flopping around on the floor of the cockpit and buries his head in my legs! Obviously, the dog has personality, just as his predecessor did.

On that Monday morning in June, when Jeremy woke me to cloudy, gray skies, the three of us climbed aboard the Hatteras and made it out of the Inlet, into the ocean, by eight-fifteen. When the depth sounder indicated that we were in about sixty feet of water, Jeremy took the frozen ballyhoo out of the ice chest and rigged the four trolling rods, attaching two to the outriggers. We began trolling at four knots, heading north into the Atlantic, looking for dolphin, which tend to travel in schools and like to hide under weed lines or logs or anything that's floating in the deep water.

We trolled and we trolled and we trolled. There was no action whatsoever—if you don't count the pelican that did his business all over the boat's spiffy teak decks. Jeremy kept reeling in the lines to see if the fish had taken the bait, but the ballyhoo were intact, so we trolled some more. PJ was so bored he went below to the cabin and fell asleep on one of the berths. I was so bored I went below to the galley to fix lunch. I made roast beef sandwiches for Jeremy and me, a bowl of Iams for PJ. I ate my sandwich in the cockpit and brought Jeremy's up to him in the tuna tower. No, we weren't fishing for tuna and a tuna tower is virtually unnecessary for the sort of fishing we were doing, but the Hatteras had one and sitting up in it made Jeremy feel like a king on his throne, so I kept my mouth shut. I watched as he ate the sandwich, watched as the Russian dressing I'd spread on it leaked out from between the slices of bread and squirted onto his white T-shirt, watched as the Bud Lite I'd given him sprayed the crotch of his shorts. So what else was new.

I'd made my sandwich with mustard instead of Russian dressing and drank Evian water instead of beer because I was dieting. Jeremy loved my hair gray and wild, so I'd left it alone, but we agreed that it wouldn't be a total loss if I lost the double chin.

I did the dishes and came back up to the cockpit, then concentrated once again on the business of fishing. I searched the waters for dolphin. And waited. And searched. And waited. I knew that fishing, like love, required patience, but mine was wearing thin. It was nearly two-thirty in the afternoon and we'd been out in the ocean all day. I was getting restless. I wanted to go home. I wanted to give up. Hell, I figured we could go to the store and *buy* the damn dolphin faster than we were going to catch one.

I pulled my chair closer to the edge of the cockpit and sighed in exasperation. Then I looked up into the cloudy, gray sky and, totally without thinking, said out loud, "I'll do anything to catch a dolphin. Anything."

The minute the words were out of my mouth, I wanted to take them back. I didn't mean what I said, I told myself. I was just venting my frustration. I didn't care if I ever caught another fish. Really, I didn't. Please. No devil this time. Not again.

Seconds later, a bolt of lightning flashed across the darkening sky. And then, one of the fishing rods jerked forward. Something was pulling on it. Something big.

"Hey, BS! Looks like you've got a live one down there," Jeremy called to me from the tuna tower.

I pretended I didn't hear him. I pretended I didn't see the fish on my line or the lightning in the sky. I pretended I hadn't said what I'd said.

"Hey!" he yelled. "Start reelin' him in, would ya?"

I ignored him. Maybe it was just a coincidence that I'd made my "I'll-do-anything" speech and then the fish had grabbed on to the line and the sky had lit up. Maybe the devil hadn't come back to Banyan Beach, back into our lives. Maybe he wasn't trying to get me to make another deal with him. Maybe the nightmare wasn't beginning all over again.

Well, I wasn't taking any chances. While Jeremy barked orders at me, I left the line—and the nice, meaty dolphin at the end of it—alone, hoping it would eat the ballyhoo and take off.

Which is exactly what happened.

Jeremy was positively baffled by my seeming indifference that the fish had gotten away.

"I can't believe it!" he said. "You just sat and watched the dolphin take the bait!"

"Better he than I," I said, and let it go at that.